CRITICS ARE RAVING ABOUT LEIGH GREENWOOD'S *THE COWBOYS* SERIES!

POSSIBLY NAKED

Ellen heard the soft sound of clothes dropping to the floor and had to try very hard not to picture Matt standing naked in the dark. Just the thought of it caused her to swallow hard.

She felt the bed sag under Matt's weight, and her breath caught. Had he had time to take off his long underwear and put on a nightshirt? The possibility that he had gotten into bed naked was too nerve-wracking to consider.

"Anything you want to tell me about today?" he asked.

"Like what?" She didn't know where to begin. She was married. She'd promised to help him adopt Orin and protect Toby. She'd committed herself to sleep next to him. She didn't know if she could survive that. Next to sharing his bed, everything else seemed easy.

"I know you didn't want to marry me," Matt said. "I want to make being here easier."

The sincerity in his voice touched her. She knew he had to be as uncomfortable as she was.

"We'll get along all right. It'll just take a little time to adjust," she answered.

She heard him turn, felt the mattress move as he shifted position. He must have put his back to her. She wanted to reach out and be sure but didn't dare. If she touched him, he'd probably think she wanted a whole lot more. Still, she had to know. She couldn't go to sleep if he was facing her, maybe staring at her while she slept. It was hard enough knowing he lay just a few inches away, *possibly naked*.

The Cowboys

LEIGH GREENWOOD

MATT

LEISURE BOOKS NEW YORK CITY

*To every child who has suffered abuse
and had nowhere to turn.*

A LEISURE BOOK®

June 2001

Published by

Dorchester Publishing Co., Inc.
276 Fifth Avenue
New York, NY 10001

Cover art by John Ennis
www.ennisart.com

ISBN 0-8439-4877-9

Printed in the United States of America.

Visit us on the web at www.dorchesterpub.com.

The Cowboys

MATT

THE FAMILY OF
JAKE MAXWELL AND ISABELLE DAVENPORT
(m. 1866):

Eden Maxwell b. 1868
Ward Dillon m. Marina Scott 1861
      Tanner b. 1862
      Mason b. 1869
      Lee b. 1872
      Conway b. 1874
      Webb b. 1875
Buck Hobson (Maxwell) m. Hannah Grossek 1872
      Wesley b. 1874
      Elsa b. 1877
Drew Townsend m. Cole Benton 1874
      Celeste b. 1879
      Christine b. 1881
      Clair b. 1884
Sean O'Ryan m. Pearl Belladonna (Agnes Satterwaite) 1876
      Elise b. 1866 (Pearl's daughter by previous marriage)
      Kevin b. 1877
      Flint b. 1878
      Jason b. 1880
Chet Attmore (Maxwell) m. Melody Jordan 1880
      Jake Maxwell II (Max) b. 1882
      Nick b. 1884
Matt Haskins m. Ellen Donovan 1883
      Toby b. 1858 (adopted)
      Orin b. 1872 (adopted)
      Noah b. 1878 (adopted)
      Tess b. 1881 (adopted)
Pete Jernigan m. Anne Thompson 1886
Luke Attmore m. Valencia Badenburg 1887
Bret Nolan
Will Attmore
Night Hawk
Zeke

Chapter One

Texas Hill Country, 1883

"You've got to get married," Isabelle Maxwell told Matt Haskins. "If you don't, they'll take these boys from you."

They were seated in Matt's ranch house kitchen. A household of men didn't need a parlor. A wide hall separated the kitchen from two bedrooms. He had no curtains at the windows, no fancy tablecloths, no upholstered chairs. Everything was plain, every surface as clear as possible. He and the boys had to keep the house clean. They didn't want anything to make the job more difficult.

"You can't get married," Toby nearly shouted. "Every woman in that town hates me." The vehemence of his answer, coupled with the anger in his face, told

9

Matt that Toby feared an outsider even more than he disliked the idea of a woman in their all-male household.

"They don't hate you," Isabelle said. "They're just afraid your handsome face will turn their young daughters' heads."

"I can't help it if they like me better than the white boys."

Toby was only sixteen, but he was already six feet tall, dark, and so handsome young girls fluttered like a covey of doves when he rode into town. His arrival had prompted more than one mother to remember a "pot left on the stove" that required that she and her daughter rush home to tend. The town mothers objected to Toby's Mexican blood, his lack of prospects, and that his mother had given birth to him without the benefit of marriage.

"I haven't seen you trying to keep your distance," Isabelle observed, an edge to her voice.

"You can't expect me to spend all my time with horses and cows."

"As much as they don't like him hanging around their daughters, it's Orin they're determined to take," Isabelle said to Matt, referring to the slight blond boy sitting silently next to Matt.

"They were happy enough for me to take him a year ago," Matt said.

"His grandfather hadn't left him a small fortune then," Isabelle pointed out.

"So money makes him worth the trouble?"

"Don't be a fool. You know there's nobody but you interested in these boys for their own sakes."

Matt had been in the little town of Bandera two years ago when the sheriff was about to put Toby in jail.

Instead, Matt hired him to work on his new ranch. Not everybody was happy with that arrangement, but they were glad to get Toby out of town.

Orin was another matter.

Several families had volunteered to take the orphaned nine-year-old after his parents' tragic death. But when the money from the sale of his parents' property ran out, the family that had taken him in discovered they really didn't have room for a boy who was constantly in trouble. Traumatized by the death of his parents, thrust into an unsympathetic foster home, then kicked out, Orin had been volatile and uncooperative when he arrived at the ranch. It had taken Matt close to a year to break through the barriers of his anger and hurt. The past three months had been good. Toby and Orin had begun to treat each other as friends and the ranch as their home.

When Orin's grandfather died and left the boy a large inheritance, the family that had turned him out started agitating for his return. It was unlikely anyone would have listened if the Reverend Wilbur Sears hadn't announced that Matt was an unsuitable guardian because he wasn't married. He claimed that a young boy needed the warm, humanizing care of a mother figure.

"They can have my money," Orin said. "I just want to stay here."

Matt put his hand on Orin's shoulder. The boy's thin body worried him. An eleven-year-old child should weigh more, but in the last month Orin hadn't eaten more than a few mouthfuls before he pushed his plate away.

"I'll run away," Orin said.

"That's stupid," Toby said. "Where would you go?"

"He's not going anywhere," Matt said, "and nobody's taking him away."

"Then you'll have to get married," Isabelle said. "That damned preacher has stirred up everybody from here to San Antonio. Have you thought of anybody you could ask?"

Isabelle had reached her fortieth birthday, but she still looked vibrant and beautiful. It was no wonder Jake still acted like a newlywed after all these years. Maybe her own wedded bliss was the reason she thought marriage was the answer to practically everything. Matt had discarded the possibility of marriage without serious consideration. No woman would marry him once they knew his secret. And he'd have to tell. It wasn't something he could keep from a wife. "There's got to be another way."

"Maybe," Isabelle said, "but I can't think of one that will settle the issue for good. This is no time for half measures, Matt. You're facing pure greed on one side and self-righteous indignation on the other, not to mention a little fear that some of them might end up with a dark-skinned grandbaby."

"If I have to, I'll take the boys and leave," Matt said.

"That's not what Jake and I want."

"You'll lose all the money you put into his place," Toby pointed out.

"Money's not a problem," Isabelle said. "Jake and I can—"

"I'm not taking your money."

"Then what are you going to do?"

Matt didn't have an answer yet. "Do you want me to get married?" he asked the boys.

"This isn't a group decision," Isabelle said. "We're talking about your wife."

"And their surrogate mother. I can't make a decision like that without knowing how they feel."

Isabelle rolled her eyes. "Sometimes I don't know why I keep trying. Where's your common sense?"

Matt smiled. "You're always complaining that Will hasn't a lick of sense. Why should his brother have any?"

Isabelle's harrumph indicated that she would have a great deal to say on that subject if she had the time. "You have brains enough if you'd use them, but there's no use talking to you when it comes to these boys."

"Would it have been any use talking to you about us?"

"Don't change the subject."

Seventeen years earlier she'd talked Jake into adopting eleven orphans she'd pulled from the teeth of indifference and abuse. There was no one she wouldn't have taken on to protect her boys, and they all knew it.

"Do you want Matt to get married?" Isabelle asked Toby.

"No. Women cause trouble."

"How about you?" she asked Orin.

"Will it mean I can stay here?"

"Yes."

"Then I guess it's okay."

"Marriage would be good for you as well as the boys," Isabelle said to Matt. "You spend too much time alone."

"I have the boys."

"If you want to put an end to this business once and for all, get married and adopt them."

"Nobody's adopting me," Toby said.

"You can adopt me," Orin said.

"Okay, we've settled that," Isabelle said.

"The vote is split."

"You cast the deciding vote. What is it going to be?"

Matt had never seriously considered marriage. No, that wasn't entirely true. He thought of it often and dismissed it. He liked women, but he was uncomfortable around them. He never knew what to say. But that wasn't the real reason he couldn't get married.

His parents had died when he was nine, and he and his younger brother, Will, had gone to live with their uncle. For three years their uncle had sexually abused Matt. Nearly any physical contact brought up some memory of the pain and humiliation, the feeling of being sordid and foul. It would be cruel to marry any woman knowing he couldn't perform as a husband. He counted himself lucky to be able to provide for two boys who needed a home and a friend. He was as close to having a family and being happy as he expected to be.

Now that damned preacher was determined to take it away.

The only way he could imagine marriage working for him would be as a business arrangement. There would be no pretense of emotional involvement, no physical relationship. They would look on each other as business partners.

That way no one would be hurt when the breakup came.

Matt didn't know any woman who would accept such an arrangement. Women saw marriage as a lifetime commitment. They expected love and devotion. Matt could provide that, but it was the passion, the unblemished character, and a past that wouldn't threaten their safety that he couldn't provide. "I guess I have to consider it."

14

Isabelle sighed. "You're finally being sensible. Is there anybody you'd like to marry?"

Matt didn't know why he should suddenly feel flushed. But if things had been different . . . Well, they weren't, and there was no use thinking about it.

"Matt don't like women," Toby said. "He won't even speak to them."

"Doesn't like women," Isabelle corrected. "And there's somebody he'd like to speak to," she said, a slow smile spreading across her face as she watched Matt with eagle-eyed intensity. "He blushed."

"I didn't see it," Toby said.

"Me neither," added Orin.

"Who is she?" Isabelle asked.

"It better not be that schoolteacher," Toby said. "I'll leave the minute she sets foot on this place."

"It's not the schoolteacher," Isabelle said, watching Matt carefully. "What about Eugenia Applegate?"

Bandera was a small town, the county sparsely settled. There weren't more than a dozen single women of marriageable age. It didn't take Isabelle long to reach the end of her list.

"That just leaves those two women who work at the saloon," Toby said.

"Is that right?" Isabelle asked.

Matt didn't answer.

"Which one is it?" Toby asked.

"It shouldn't be either one of them," Isabelle said. "If you think you're in hot water now . . . It *is* one of those women. Don't bother denying it. I can see it in your face."

"I don't see nothing," Orin said.

"It's got to be Ellen!" Toby exclaimed as his face split with a wide grin. "She's got a body like—"

15

"You will not speak of any woman's appearance as though you were describing a horse," Isabelle said, turning a quelling look on Toby. "Is the boy correct?" she asked Matt. "Are you interested in Ellen?"

"I'm not interested in any woman," Matt said. "But I'd have to be blind not to think Ellen attractive."

"You know what people say about her?"

"Everybody knows," Toby said, grinning like any sixteen-year-old boy over a salacious story. "She—"

"She didn't do it," Isabelle declared. "I worked for a man like Patrick Lowell. When he tried his tricks on me, I scratched his face and called for his wife. Ellen is a respectable woman forced into a dubious profession because of a man's brutish nature and a woman's jealousy. She'll make a good wife and companion, as well as help you bring up these boys."

"I don't need no bringing up," Toby said.

"You especially," Isabelle said. "And it's *any* bringing up. Matt, did you hear me?"

He'd heard her. He'd thought of Ellen from time to time. Outside of the fact that she was beautiful—what man could forget those pouty lips just begging to be kissed, her glossy black hair and haughty stance—she'd been caught in the same kind of web as Matt. Only her shame was public.

"She's got those two kids of that young woman who died a few months ago," Isabelle said. "With your penchant for taking in strays—"

"I ain't no stray!" Toby announced.

"—she's exactly the right person, especially if she knows anything about grammar."

Matt had enjoyed thinking about Ellen now and then. It was a daydream he could indulge in when his physical needs pressed him hard, but marriage would put an end to that. All the guiltless pleasures, the secret fantasies, would be replaced by cold reality. She would be around all the time, wanting and demanding. She would probably expect him to make love to her. Just the thought of being touched brought back the nausea that had overcome him every time his uncle touched him. But if marriage would protect the boys, he'd do it. He'd figure out how to handle the physical part later.

One thing worried him. Everyone agreed Ellen was beautiful. They also agreed she was hard as stone. She would flash a brittle smile, but her eyes warned men to keep their distance. The boys needed warmth, love, understanding, and support. He didn't know if Ellen could provide that, but there was only one way to find out. "Okay. I'll talk to her."

Ellen Donovan slammed the glass down on the bar so hard it broke. The sound of shattering glass caused the men in the saloon to fall silent. They all looked her way. "That's nothing but children getting up to harmless mischief," she said, glaring at the sheriff. She tried to ignore the anger churning inside her, to speak in a level voice rather than shout. "They just scattered the chickens. They didn't kill them."

"They've got into trouble before," the sheriff reminded her, easing onto the stool right across from her.

"Nothing any different from half the kids in this town."

She wished he hadn't come to the saloon to make this complaint. It would be all over town before supper. Even though it was a slow afternoon, the few regulars would quickly spread the word. Ellen's gaze took in the large room packed with tables for men to drink and gamble, and the bar stacked with plenty of glasses to fill up during the long evenings when she served her customers and tried to avoid their wandering hands. She couldn't do anything about their eyes . . . or their thoughts.

"Those other kids have mothers at home to watch after them," the sheriff said, "and fathers to tan their backsides when they need it."

Ellen didn't need the sheriff's long-suffering look to tell her that she couldn't work in the saloon and fulfill the roles of mother and father to two rambunctious children. Her landlady, Mrs. Ogden, tried to help, but she had her hands full taking care of her boarders and dishing up three meals a day.

"It's got nothing to do with chickens or chasing pigs into the street," Tulip Owens said. "It's got to do with them being fatherless brats of a dead saloon girl. If they was the banker's kids, everybody'd be saying they was cute and high-spirited."

Ellen wasn't especially fond of her co-worker, but she had to admit Tulip cut to the heart of the problem.

"That may be, but they're not the banker's kids," the sheriff said, "though it's his chickens they chased and his pigs they let out."

"It's all because of his wife," Ellen said. "Mabel Jackson can't pass Noah and Tess in the street without commenting on how it's a shame children like that are allowed to run free all over town like wild dogs."

"I admit Mrs. Jackson may overstate the case now and again—"

"It's that preacher's fault," Tulip said, hands on hips, a frown on her heavily made-up face. "She didn't act so holier-than-thou until he arrived."

"I wouldn't be talking bad about the Reverend Sears if I was you," the sheriff warned Tulip.

"Nobody complained about Noah and Tess until he got here," Ellen said.

"That's not the point."

"Then what is?"

"They're not your kids, not legally."

"Their mother left them to me."

"Where's the will?"

"You know April didn't leave no will," Tulip said. "I'm not sure she could write that good."

"April told everybody in town she wanted me to have her children," Ellen said.

"She told people," the sheriff said, "but she didn't get anybody to write it down. Things might have been all right if there hadn't been any trouble—I'm saying *might*, mind you—but there is trouble. According to the law, those kids are orphans, and it's the state's responsibility to put them into good homes."

"There's nobody around here going to open up their good homes to the fatherless children of a saloon dancer."

"Those kids didn't do nothing to be ashamed of," Tulip said.

"You don't have to *do* anything," Ellen snapped. "I did everything I could to stay away from Patrick Lowell and his lecherous son, but there's nobody in this town who believes me."

"I believe you," Tulip said.

"You don't count," Ellen said. "You work in a saloon."

"Look, Ellen, I'm not here to argue with you," the sheriff said. "I'm just here to tell you them kids are causing trouble again. Mrs. Jackson and the preacher have made up their minds they ought to be sent to an orphanage."

"They can't do that," Ellen said.

"The state can. You know no judge will consider a single woman who works in a saloon fit to bring up two little kids."

"What am I supposed to do?"

"Get married. The state's not anxious to take on more orphans. They'll be happy to have them adopted by a respectable married couple."

Ellen's laugh was bitter. "What respectable man is going to marry me? Everybody believes I tried to seduce my employer's son and husband in her own bed."

The sheriff smiled. "Old Patrick Lowell wouldn't be the first man to attempt to take advantage of a woman, even in his wife's bed."

"Are you saying you believe me?"

"It doesn't matter what I believe. What's important is what happens to those kids. As near as I can figure, you've got about two weeks. That's when the judge swings by here on his circuit. Mabel is all ready to hand him a list of things the kids have done."

"I'll kill Mabel Jackson!" Ellen didn't mean it literally, though she rather fancied the idea. Noah and Tess were the two best things that had ever happened to her. She loved and wanted to care for them, and Mabel was determined to ruin it.

Ellen had no desire to get married. She didn't like men. She didn't trust them.

When she was fourteen, an enraged tenant had killed her parents. To this day she could still see the rage in his eyes, hear the menace in his voice, when she'd identified him. He'd sworn he'd make her wish she'd died. They'd hanged him, but she couldn't get the picture of his face out of her mind.

Ellen had gone to live with a cousin. The situation

might have been bearable if her cousin's husband hadn't ogled Ellen and made sly suggestions. Unable to retaliate against her husband, the cousin had taken her anger out on Ellen by using her as a drudge and loudly begrudging every bit of food Ellen put in her mouth. Ellen had been relieved when she got a job as a nurse-governess in the household of Patrick and Nancy Lowell. Until Nancy caught her son, Eddie, trying to force his attentions on Ellen. To protect his son, Mr. Lowell had accused Ellen of trying to seduce Eddie. He claimed Ellen had approached him as well. Mrs. Lowell had found it easier to accept her husband's allegation than accept the fact her son was a bully and a lecher.

"Nobody will marry me," she said.

"Reverend Sears said he'd offered."

"Wilbur doesn't want Noah and Tess." He only wanted to save her soul. She'd rather work in a saloon, dodging drunks and evading wandering hands, than have to be grateful to Wilbur Sears for the rest of her life.

Two kids came tearing into the saloon, oblivious of the men eating, drinking, and gambling. "Ellen, guess what?" Noah, the older of the two, shouted. "We—"

He skidded to a halt when he saw the sheriff. His sister bumped into him, then took refuge behind Ellen's skirts.

"I think I know what," Ellen said. "It was chickens, wasn't it?"

"Oh, that," Noah said. "I'd forgotten all about that."

"Mrs. Jackson hasn't. Haven't I told you to stay away from her place?"

"Yes, but—"

"There's no 'but,' Noah. If you don't stop aggravating her, she's going to have you put in an orphanage."

Noah's smile grew absolutely brilliant. "She can't never do nothing to us again."

"Why?" Ellen asked.

"Orin says Mr. Haskins has come to ask you to marry him. He's going to adopt everybody."

Ellen walked so fast, Noah and Tess had to run to keep up.

"You are going to marry him, aren't you?" Noah asked again.

Ellen remembered Matt Haskins. No woman could forget a man that good-looking. Still, she'd never imagined such a shy man would want to marry her. He rarely came into Bandera, didn't talk unless he had to, and didn't hang around once he'd finished his business. Some people whispered there was something peculiar about Matt, that maybe he'd hit his head on a rock when he got bucked off a horse. He was one of that batch of orphans Isabelle and Jake Maxwell had adopted some fifteen years ago. Whatever people might think, they didn't say anything out loud. Nobody wanted to get on the wrong side of one of the most powerful families in this part of Texas.

"What are you going to tell him?" Noah asked.

"I don't want to go to a ranch," Tess said. "Orin says you have to ride a horse if you live on a ranch."

"I don't know what I'm going to say. You don't have to ride a horse if you don't want to."

She wished she had left them at the saloon with Tulip. She needed to think, and she couldn't with them bombarding her with questions. She'd vowed never to marry even before Eddie Lowell tried to climb into her bed, but she'd assumed if she ever did marry, she'd love the man and he'd love her. The idea that a virtual stranger would ask her to marry him without a minute's notice would have made her laugh . . . or swear, depending on her mood. Only now she was being forced to consider such a marriage. That it had been thrust on her in front of Tulip, the sheriff, and the kids made her furious.

Yet Ellen also felt fluttery and confused, a totally unfamiliar condition for her. She was a very direct woman; too direct, Tulip said. After the scandal with the Lowells, she'd faced criticism from those who believed she might be telling the truth and ostracism from those who didn't. She'd also had to fight off men who wanted to believe she was all too ready to jump into any available bed. She'd had to be tough to protect herself. But the men liked looking at Ellen, even if she gave them the rough side of her tongue.

"I don't like Toby," Noah said. "He's mean."

"Who's Toby?" Tess asked.

"Can I have my own horse?"

"Can I have my own room?"

"Stop! I expect Orin got confused. I'm sure Mr. Haskins wouldn't—"

"No, he didn't," Noah insisted. "He said they talked about it for a long time. He said Matt was dead set against marrying anybody. He said Miz Maxwell said you were the best of the lot, that if Matt didn't marry you before somebody else snapped you up he was a great fool."

That was too much for Ellen's temper. She'd been certain Noah or Orin had somehow managed to mistake Matt's intention. But to learn he'd talked it over with two boys and only decided on her because his adopted mother had told him to—well, no woman could tolerate that.

When she rounded the corner and saw three horses in front of her landlady's house, she knew exactly what she intended to do. "Noah, you and Tess stay here on the front porch."

"But I want to—"

"If you even put your hand on that doorknob before I come out, I'll take the skin off your backside. Understand?"

"Yes," Noah said as he flopped down in a white rocking chair. "But I think you're mean."

"You have no idea how mean I can get," Ellen said over her shoulder as she entered the house. "But Matt Haskins is about to find out," she muttered.

She met Mrs. Ogden in the hallway, clearly agog with curiosity. "Where are they?" she asked.

"In the parlor."

"Thank you. And don't listen at the keyhole." She marched into the parlor and announced in clear, unmistakable tones, "I don't know why you're here, Mr. Haskins, but if it's to ask me to marry you, you've made a great mistake."

Chapter Two

Matt didn't know how a person could feel relieved, disappointed, angry, and worried all at the same time, but that was how he felt. Relieved he didn't have to get married, disappointed—he wasn't sure about that one—angry she'd made up her mind before he'd had a chance to state his reasons for such an unusual request, and worried how to keep Orin.

He had gotten to his feet when Ellen stormed into Mrs. Ogden's parlor. It was a small room with flowered wallpaper, chintz-covered chairs, and crocheted doilies on every surface. The breeze coming in the open window swayed the tassels on a red lamp shade.

"It wouldn't be my first mistake," he said, smiling. A man would never have any trouble knowing her mood. She wore her emotions like a ship wore its flag.

"But you're so handsome I'm expected to fall all over

25

myself to accept your flattering proposal."

Something had got her back up good and proper. He'd have a hard time getting her to listen to him.

"I haven't made any proposal," Matt said. "And all you seem in a rush to do is empty the slop bucket over me."

"But you're going to make one," Ellen said.

"Not if you keep looking like you want to notch my ears."

Apparently having followed Ellen, the sheriff entered the parlor. "Sit down, Ellen," he said without preamble. "Listen to what the man has to say. It's in the best interests of both of you."

Ellen seemed to waver, but she seated herself on a small love seat. Her ramrod-straight back didn't touch the couch; her restless hands smoothed and re-smoothed her dress.

"I'm about to do something I've never done before," Matt said. "I hope you'll listen to me kindly in case I make a fool of myself."

Ellen's gaze narrowed, like she suspected him of making fun of her. "I'm listening."

Matt looked from Ellen to the sheriff, who'd settled himself into an armchair.

"I'm not very good with words," he began.

"Some people say they've never heard you utter one," Ellen said.

"I don't believe in talking unless I've got something to say."

"But you've got something to say now."

He did, but how did a man ask a woman to marry him when everybody knew he didn't want to be married? "I'm thirty years old. I own a ranch, a thousand cows, and a couple hundred head of horses."

"Is the ranch paid for?"

That question irked him, but he guessed she had a right to know the answer. "You might say the bank owns the ranch, but they've been kind enough to let me work it while I make payments on it."

"Any other debts?"

"No."

"What kind of help do you have?"

"It's just me and the boys."

"Tell me about the boys. I've seen them, but I don't really know anything about them."

He decided to take that as a positive sign. Everybody else in town knew more than they wanted to know. "Toby is sixteen. He's never had a father, and his mother's dead. He's a good worker and great with horses."

"I hear he does pretty well with young girls, too."

"You can't expect a boy his age to back off when a pretty girl shows an interest in him."

"Would you have backed off?"

"What I would have done has nothing to do with Toby," Matt said. "He's high-spirited and resents the way adults treat him. He's not happy about my getting married." He might as well get everything out up front.

"What about the other boy?"

"Orin is eleven and completely different. He hasn't gotten over the shock of his parents' death or the way the town turned its back on him when his money ran out. He'll welcome you to the ranch, but it'll be a while before he's comfortable around you."

"What about you? Will you welcome me to the ranch?"

Matt knew what she meant. He also knew he couldn't answer that question the way she wanted. "Of course. I think your children will like living on the ranch."

"They're not my children. They're—"

"They're orphans. We're all orphans. It seems natural we should stick together."

"Mabel Jackson says Noah's a menace."

"He's a high-spirited boy who needs an outlet for his energy. If I give him a horse to ride and care for, he'll have something more to think about than letting chickens out. If he doesn't, no harm's done as long as he gets them back before the coyotes eat them."

"You really wouldn't mind having two more kids around?"

"I can use a couple of extra hands."

"They're children," Ellen snapped, "not cowhands."

"Even children do chores. It makes them feel useful and keeps them out of mischief."

"What about me? Will cooking, cleaning, and washing make me feel useful and keep me out of mischief?"

He couldn't help but smile at the anger that flared in her eyes. "I started cooking, cleaning, and washing when I was nine. I think we can work something out."

Her skeptical expression said she thought he might just be looking for a housekeeper.

"Toby and Orin do their share."

"It doesn't sound like you need a wife."

He didn't. He didn't even want one. "Look, Miss Donovan, there's no point in tiptoeing around the cat-amount. I need a wife if I'm going to keep Orin. You need a husband if you're going to keep your kids."

"Noah and Tess. They have names."

"I'll remember that, but there's no point in pretending things we don't feel."

"Do you know what people say about me?"

"I don't listen to gossip."

"A lot of people believe I'm a strumpet. Some think I'm a lot worse."

"People say a lot of things they don't mean. They just like something to gossip about."

"You believe me?"

"Why shouldn't I?"

"Because the Lowells say I'm guilty."

"They would, wouldn't they?"

Ellen looked at him like he had just grown an extra head. "You're either the most generous man in Texas or the biggest fool."

"I imagine I fall somewhere in between. Now, about this marriage . . ."

"I haven't said I'm going to marry you."

"You haven't said you aren't."

"You haven't asked me."

He was a fool. Just because she knew why he'd come to town didn't mean she didn't want him to act like this was something more than a business arrangement.

"Miss Donovan, would you do me the kindness of becoming my wife?"

She glared at him. "Why should I?"

She knew why. She knew *he knew* she knew why. Isabelle would say she was trying to salvage her pride. Well, he'd let her. He had no pride to preserve. "We need you, the boys and me. A woman has a civilizing effect on men. I'm sure you'd be able to turn us into respectable human beings in no time."

He thought he saw her lips twitch.

"I never heard such nonsense."

"Isabelle says a man without a woman to make something of him isn't worth the bullet it'd take to shoot him." He didn't think Isabelle meant it, but she'd said it often enough.

"I'm not interested in turning you into something worth more than a couple of bullets."

"Stop being hard to get along with," the sheriff said. "You got no choice. You marry Matt or you lose your kids."

Matt wished the sheriff had kept his mouth shut. Nobody liked being backed into a corner, especially a woman when it came to marrying.

"Nobody's going to make you a drudge," Matt said. "We'd consider it an honor to have a woman about the place."

"How can I know I'm going to be safe stuck out on that ranch with you and those boys?"

"He's gonna be your husband," the sheriff said. "It'll be his job to see no harm comes to you."

"I know all about men," Ellen said. "They've only got one thing on their minds."

"He'll be your husband," the sheriff said. "He's supposed to have it on his mind."

"If you don't mind, Sheriff, I'd like to do my own talking," Matt said.

"Then don't be so dad-blasted slow."

"This is one of those times when it's better to take it slow. We're talking about getting married. There's no going back once the preacher's had his say."

"I'm not going to be pawed or grabbed," Ellen said. "I've had enough of that in the saloon."

"I will never paw or grab you," Matt said. "Isabelle taught all of us to respect women."

"I'd like to meet her."

"You will. Despite teaching us how to do everything

for ourselves, she doesn't think we can get along without her."

The dangerous light had gone from Ellen's eyes. Matt had heard she once broke a whiskey bottle over the head of a man who didn't heed her warning to keep his hands to himself. Matt didn't blame her. He couldn't stand to be touched.

"Since I'll be giving up working in the saloon, I'll need to do something to support myself."

"That's Matt's job," the sheriff said.

"I refuse to depend on any man," Ellen said. "I make hats to sell to rich ladies. Don't either of you breathe a word," she said, looking from Matt to the sheriff. "If Mabel Jackson knew I made the hats she likes so much, she'd never buy another one."

"Neither of us will say anything," Matt said. The sheriff shook his head.

"I need time to make them. I refuse to spend all my time as a slave for you and your boys."

"You can have all the time you want."

"I keep everything I earn."

"That's fine with me."

"Are you two going to get married, or are you going to jabber all day?" the sheriff asked, fidgeting in his chair.

"We've got a lot to discuss," Matt said.

"Well, you'd better discuss it in a hurry. Reverend Sears is getting back tonight. You know he's dead set against you keeping Orin. If he finds out what you mean to do before you're hitched, he'll start preaching so much hellfire and damnation the justice of the peace won't be able to hold his hand steady enough to sign the marriage certificate."

"I want separate bedrooms," Ellen said.

31

"You can't have that," the sheriff declared.

"Why not?" Ellen asked, immediately suspicious.

"Because Reverend Sears is going to be as mad as hell when he finds out what you've done. He'll look for any reason he can find to prove this is a put-up job, and separate bedrooms will be all he'll need. He'll create such a hullabaloo you'll never be able to adopt those kids."

"What you mean is, lots of people will try to keep Matt from getting his hands on Orin's money," Ellen said.

"I don't want Orin's money," Matt said. "Let someone else keep it."

"They'll steal every cent and produce records to prove it was all spent on the boy," Ellen said.

"Forget about the money," the sheriff said. "Get all this nonsense worked out between you and get over to the courthouse."

"I'll agree to sleep in the same bed with you," Ellen said, "but I'm warning you right now I'm taking a gun to bed."

"Holy hell, woman!" the sheriff exclaimed. "You're liable to roll over on it and shoot yourself."

"You won't need a gun," Matt said. "You have my word I won't touch you."

"Why the hell would you agree to that?" the sheriff asked.

"Because Ellen asked me to."

"But she'll be your wife. A husband has a right to expect—"

"This is different," Matt said.

"If you two can sleep in the same bed and not touch each other, it sure as hell will be different."

"I think we ought to finish this discussion alone," Matt said.

"I'm not letting you agree to anything stupid," the sheriff said. "If anything goes wrong, Sears will come gunning for me." He heaved his bulk from the chair. "You've got five minutes."

"I think it'll be better if we stop trying to act like this is more than it is," Matt said as soon as the door closed behind the sheriff. "We each want something real bad and have to marry each other to get it."

"What are you saying?"

"I'm saying we ought to look at this like a business arrangement. I'll do my part and you'll do your part so we can adopt the children."

"After that?"

"We can figure that out later."

"I think we ought to figure that out now. I want you to help me open my own hat shop in San Antonio."

"Will you take the children with you?"

"Naturally."

"It might be better if they stayed on the ranch."

"I promised April I'd take care of those kids. I mean to keep my word."

He didn't press the point. A year from now she might not feel the same. If her hat business didn't work out, she might have to go back to working in a saloon.

"What do you want?" Ellen asked.

"To keep the boys."

"Nothing else? Not a wife? Kids of your own?"

He let his gaze fall as he shook his head. He didn't want her to know that was exactly what he wanted.

"I'll sleep in the same bed with you because I have no choice," Ellen said, "but you're not going to . . . You can't expect me to . . . No touching."

"No touching," Matt said, hoping she didn't suspect he was more relieved than she.

"Good. Because the first time you do, I'm leaving. I've been through that with the Lowells."

"I'm not like that. I told you—"

"All men are like that," Ellen said, interrupting him.

"You've had an unfortunate experience."

"Not just me. It's how men see women. Remember, if you want your kids, stay away from me."

Ellen couldn't believe she'd actually agreed to marry Matt, and that she was on her way to the courthouse to make it official. They walked down the street in a loose group, the sheriff, Matt, and the boys ahead, and Tulip, Tess, and herself following. Despite the warmth of the spring sunshine, she felt chilled through. She had to be crazy. She didn't even know the man. He could be a lunatic for all she knew. People said he had to be strange to want to stay on that ranch by himself all the time. Ellen didn't pay attention to malicious whispers, but there was a lot of whispering.

Nearly all of it by women.

No woman could catch as much as a glimpse of Matt without being affected to her core by his looks. Not every woman liked blondes—most seemed to prefer men with dark hair—but that preference went out the window when it came to masculine, rugged Matt Haskins. No clothes could hide the swell of muscle in his thighs and arms. Or his easy grace.

The haunted look in his eyes seemed to touch the heart of every woman who met him. She'd heard women say he was a man in pain, a man in need of a good woman's love. But Ellen had her doubts. In her experience, handsome men expected to get what they wanted for no other reason than that women wanted to give it to them. They acted like rules applied to everybody except them, promises were made to be broken, and their looks would earn them forgiveness regardless of what they did.

Matt had been quick to agree to all her conditions. In fact, he seemed ready to accept just about any requirement she cared to lay down. Why?

Because he didn't intend to abide by anything he said, so it didn't matter what he promised?

The thought made her uneasy. After her cousin's husband's efforts to catch her alone, Eddie Lowell's assault, and fighting off the men in the saloon, she didn't feel safe around any man. She'd vowed never to put herself at the mercy of a man, especially not by marrying him. Now she was about to do exactly that. She'd be alone with Matt on his ranch, miles from town, beyond the reach of her friends. Her friends! That was a joke. Tulip was the only person who might care what happened to her, and Tulip thought a woman should do just about anything to catch a man like Matt.

"You'll be the envy of every woman in Bandera," Tulip said to Ellen.

"Why?" Ellen asked, drawn out of her abstraction.

"Look at him." Matt walked ahead with the sheriff and the boys. "You'll be getting into bed with him every night." She made a shuddering sound. "It gives me the shivers just thinking about it."

Ellen tried to ignore the tightness that had developed in her belly from watching Matt's jeans cling tightly to his backside and thighs.

"He's agreed to keep his distance," she told Tulip.

"Maybe he can, but I lay odds you can't."

Ellen opened her mouth to deny it.

"Don't waste your time telling me different," Tulip said, forestalling her. "Just because you been burned by pepper don't mean you lost your taste for it."

Ellen wasn't going to say she didn't find Matt attractive, but she'd make sure he knew exactly what he could and couldn't do before she closed her eyes. Some women might say they liked sex, but for her it had meant fear, loss of self-esteem, loss of standing in the community. It had helped turn her into a belligerent, aggressive woman. She could see no reason why sleeping with Matt would make her feel any different.

Noah dropped back to walk with her. "Matt says I can have my own horse," he said, his face wreathed in smiles. "He says I can take care of it and everything."

"I don't want a horse," Tess said. She tightened her grip on Ellen's hand and pushed against her thigh so hard, Ellen nearly stumbled. "Do I have to have one?"

"You don't have to have anything you don't want," Ellen assured her.

"Having a horse is fun, stupid," her brother said. "You'll be left home while we ride all over."

"Will you be riding all over?" Tess asked Ellen.

"I'll stay with you," Ellen said. "You can help me make hats."

And cook meals, wash clothes, and clean up after four men. Ellen had no faith in Matt's claiming he and the boys would take care of themselves. She'd never known a man who didn't live like a pig when left on his own. She dreaded what their house would look like. Well, she wasn't about to bed down in a pigsty. She'd come right back to town until it was cleaned up.

She felt anger churn in her belly. They had no right to force her to marry Matt. Or any other man. They had no right to threaten to take Noah and Tess from her.

They had no right to believe she was a fallen woman just because Patrick Lowell said so. There was no justice for women in Texas. At least not a woman alone, without money, husband, or family connections.

Well, she wouldn't be alone anymore. She would have a husband and three children, four if you counted Toby. She'd soon be part of the Maxwell family. She would have a position in the community, respect, safety from people like Mabel Jackson and Preacher Sears. She had been forced into something she could never have achieved on her own: marriage to a respectable man.

It still left a bitter taste in her mouth. It was a marriage of convenience, a business arrangement. He needed her as much as she needed him. She'd been bought and sold as surely as if she'd been a sack of coffee beans.

Despite the weight of her anger and bitterness, the desire to punish everybody who'd had a part in forcing this marriage on her, Ellen felt depressed. If she had to be married, she'd like her husband to care for her at least a little.

She gave herself a mental shake. There was no point in making trouble for herself. She would keep her children, start her own business, and have the protection of the Maxwell family, all of which had been beyond her reach just a few hours earlier. She needed to stay focused on her goals, freedom and safety.

The courthouse loomed just ahead, and she felt a sudden urge to cry off, to protest she couldn't marry any man who looked upon their marriage as a bitter necessity.

"Can I pick out my own horse?" Noah called as he left Ellen and ran to catch up with Matt. "Can I have a black one? I always wanted a black horse."

She felt Tess's grip on her hand tighten.

Ellen took a deep breath and resolutely swallowed her anger. Noah and Tess were not the children of her womb, but she loved them as if they were. She had meant it when she promised April she'd do whatever was necessary to keep the children safe. She wouldn't go back on her promise now, not even though she feared she was about to make the biggest mistake of her life.

"Put a smile on your face and a dance in your step," Tulip said. "That's old lady Jackson coming down the street. Let her know you mean to beat her at her own game and have fun doing it."

But Ellen had an uncomfortable feeling the game had only just begun. She had an equally uneasy feeling she didn't know the rules.

Matt offered to take her hand as they entered the courthouse. She couldn't say what she saw in his eyes. It was there less than an instant. It was important for her to win this game, but Matt's look made her think maybe it was even more important for him.

Chapter Three

"I'm sorry it's not bigger," Matt said when the ranch house came into view.

"I'm sure we'll manage." Ellen still couldn't believe she was married or that the sum total of her life could be crammed into the two boxes and large suitcase that rested in the back of Matt's buggy.

The ranch buildings backed up against a stone wall that rose almost vertically two hundred feet or more above the floor of the long, narrow valley that formed the heart of Matt's ranch. Tall grass undulating in the breeze covered the entire flat landscape. A narrow ribbon of maple, willow, and cottonwood trees bordered a stream that meandered along the far side of the valley. Beyond it a rock-strewn cleft rose to high ridges. Cows grazed among the outcrops of gray, mossy-looking boulders.

"How many bedrooms does it have?" Ellen asked.

"Two downstairs and a loft."

"I guess that means Orin and I get the loft," Toby said. He didn't sound happy about it. He'd done little but scowl at Ellen and the kids since they left the courthouse.

"I want to sleep in the loft, too," Noah announced.

"You're too little," Toby said. "You got to sleep with your sister."

"I'm not little," Noah said. "And I won't sleep with a girl."

"There's no use arguing," Matt said. "We'll take a look at how things are, then decide."

"I want to sleep in the loft," Noah repeated.

"I'm not looking after no kid," Toby said.

"If Isabelle were here, she'd correct your grammar, then make you sleep outside for arguing," Matt said, his temper still unruffled.

"You going to make me sleep outside?"

"I will if you intend to spend half the night arguing."

Ellen had expected Matt to side with Toby. But what really surprised her was Toby's reaction to Matt's softly worded reprimand. He looked angry and sullen, but he didn't contradict Noah again. She wondered what hold Matt had over the boy to cause him to bite his tongue.

"Do you snore, kid?" Toby asked Noah.

"No," Noah said, clearly offended. "And don't call me kid. My name's Noah."

"It's a silly name."

Noah's anger evaporated. "I know. I hate it."

"What would you like to be called?" Matt asked.

"What do you mean?"

"Pick a name you like. If your mother agrees, that's what we'll call you."

"Ellen's not my ma."

"She will be when we adopt you. You might as well get used to calling her that now."

"I'd rather they call me Ellen."

"You sure?"

"Yes." She didn't want the kids to forget their real mother. She certainly didn't want them to think she was trying to take her place.

"Come on, Orin," Toby called out. "I'll race you to the house."

They galloped toward the small building, eight steel-shod hooves throwing up dirt clods behind them. Ellen was pleased to see Orin stayed even with Toby. She'd expected him to be lost in Toby's dust. The child hadn't said a word all day.

"If I had a horse, I would beat them both," Noah announced.

"It'll probably be best if you learn to ride first," Matt said.

"I know how to ride," Noah announced.

Ellen was about to contradict him, but Matt said, "Good. Then we'll have to pick out a really good horse for you."

"Will it be just as good as Toby's horse?"

"Yes. We'll go see Drew. She's got hundreds of horses."

Noah's eyes lit up. "You kidding me?"

"Do I look like I'm kidding?"

"No. You look sober as a preacher. You're not like Reverend Sears, are you? 'Cause if you are, I ain't staying here."

"I don't think I'm that bad, but if I start sounding like him, you tell me right away."

"I will. I don't like Reverend Sears."

41

"I'm not too fond of him myself."

"When can we start looking for my horse?"

Ellen decided she knew even less about Matt than she thought. He calmly discussed horses with Noah like he thought the boy actually knew something about them. It took only a few minutes before she realized Matt was teaching Noah. The boy became more and more excited as he learned what to look for and what to avoid.

"I can pick out a horse for you," he said to Ellen. "I'll make sure you don't get one with a spavin."

"Thank you," Ellen said. "I never would have known to look for a spavin."

"He could never be as fast as my horse if he had one." Noah peppered Matt with more questions.

Ellen decided to shed all her preconceived notions about Matt. She knew only one thing for sure: He was extremely handsome. She wondered if he thought she was attractive. He had barely glanced at her during the trip, even though she sat next to him. She didn't feel ignored, but she didn't feel special.

She reminded herself that they had married out of necessity rather than inclination. She told herself she was glad they weren't in love, that emotion would only complicate things; but that didn't make her feel better. She knew her independence was more important to her than any man—even one as handsome as Matt. But even that thought didn't cheer her.

Matt pulled to a stop before the house. Noah jumped down immediately. "Can I go look at the horses?"

"You need to carry your things into the house."

Toby and Orin got up from the steps where they'd been waiting. Without being asked, they started unloading the wagon.

"Where do you want this stuff?" Toby asked.

"In the hallway," Matt said. "We'll decide where it goes later."

Ellen was pleased with the look and size of the frame house. She'd expected a log or adobe structure. Even in the Hill Country, where trees were plentiful, it was expensive to build with sawed lumber. Usually only rich people lived in wooden houses.

"Sorry the house isn't bigger, but I could only borrow so much money. I choose to put most of it into livestock."

"Why didn't your parents give this ranch to you?"

She saw a flash of emotion in his normally expressionless face. "Jake and Isabelle adopted me. That didn't mean they owed me a ranch."

"But they're rich." Ellen hadn't meant to say that. The words just popped out.

"They gave me a home when no one would have me. I could stay as long as I wanted, come back as often as I wanted. That was more valuable than anything else."

Ellen felt embarrassed and a little angry that her question made her appear crass. "Everybody thinks they did."

"Not Tom Jackson. He expects my payment at the bank as regular as clockwork."

Matt had mentioned the bank loan earlier, but Ellen hadn't realized that meant Matt had borrowed money from Mabel's husband. She hoped Tom Jackson kept his business well separated from his home life. If not, Matt could be in for trouble.

"Go on inside and look around. The boys and I will get everything unloaded."

Ellen hadn't expected the house to be decorated at all. She was pleasantly surprised to find pictures hung on the walls, two covered settees set between doorways, wing chairs, piecrust tables and lamps adorning the other available space, and a rush mat on the floor.

"That's Isabelle's doing," Matt said when he came inside to get down a box. "I returned things at first, but they just reappeared the next day. Jake said I'd have to burn the house down if I wanted to get rid of them."

"Will I get to meet Isabelle?"

"Probably before you want to," Matt said as he headed out the door.

"You don't have much stuff," Toby said as he set down a suitcase that contained half the clothing Ellen owned.

"You don't need much when you live in a rooming house and work in a saloon."

"My ma lived in a rooming house and worked in a saloon. She had lots of stuff." Toby went back outside without waiting for her response.

Ellen had been too preoccupied with her own troubles to think about Toby's parents. She'd have to ask Matt to tell her more about both boys. She didn't intend to get involved in their lives, but she didn't want to say anything that might hurt them.

"Check out the rest of the house," Matt said when he came back. "The kitchen is over here."

She didn't want to look at the kitchen but headed in that direction. She could just imagine the mess three unattended males would have made. She stepped into the room and came to a dead stop.

It was immaculate.

There wasn't a dirty dish or pot in sight. The countertops had been wiped clean and everything put away. The chairs were under the table and folded napkins lay on the spotless tabletop. Obviously Isabelle sent someone to clean up after them. Good! They could clean up after her, too. Living in a rooming house had gotten her out of the habit of cooking and cleaning.

But she didn't like the idea of Isabelle coming behind her, probably complaining about the mess she and the children made.

"Show me where you want to put things," Matt said from the kitchen door.

"How often do the servants come in?" She hadn't meant to sound sarcastic, but she felt like a fool for feeling sorry for Matt and the boys being on their own.

"What servants?" Matt asked, a slightly perplexed look lining his normally expressionless brow.

Ellen gestured to the kitchen. "Somebody obviously came today so you could impress me."

"What are you talking about?"

"This kitchen."

"I don't have a servant. I do the cooking and the boys clean up."

Ellen couldn't believe he was serious. No men kept a house this clean. "What about the napkins?"

"That's Isabelle's doing. She was raised by a rich aunt in Savannah, Georgia. She can't get it through her head we don't need napkins in Texas."

Noah pushed his way though the doorway. "Can I sleep in the loft, Ellen? Please. There's lots of room. I promise I won't cause any trouble."

"We'll see," Ellen said, too shaken to think clearly. If Matt and the boys really did do their own housework, she was in trouble. She doubted she could do half as well. Matt stepped back to let her enter the hallway.

"This is our bedroom," he said, opening a door on the other side of the hall.

Ellen could tell from his expression that he didn't like

having to share his room and his bed, but he had already put her luggage inside.

"You can move any of my stuff you want," he said. "I don't need much space."

"Neither do I. Toby just commented on how little I have."

"If you decide you want to make changes, go ahead. But let me know if you need more furniture or anything like that. Whatever you do, don't tell Isabelle. She'll have it over here within the hour."

Ellen couldn't help but laugh. "And you object to that?"

"Isabelle and Jake have given me more than enough. I don't intend to be a burden."

"I don't know Isabelle, but if she adopted you, I doubt she considers you a burden."

Ellen was thankful she'd taken the trouble over the last several years to study men closely. The changes in Matt's expression were so subtle, came and went so quickly, they were almost impossible to notice, but they were there. And if she interpreted this fleeting look correctly, it said there was something more involved here than the desire of a man to be independent of his mother.

"Just tell me if you need anything." He looked like he thought she might not.

"I will. Now, where is Tess going to sleep?"

Matt led her to a second bedroom, as neat as the first, but furnished with two of everything—beds, chairs, tables, wardrobes.

"This is Toby and Orin's bedroom, isn't it?"

"They won't mind sleeping in the loft. It'll be something of an adventure."

"For a week. After that they'll resent it."

"Then we have a week to figure out what to do."

"Do you ever get upset?" she asked.

His face seemed to freeze. "Why do you ask that?"

"You've been forced to marry a woman you don't know, bring her to your house, install her in your bedroom, and have your boys moved into the loft. Toby resents us, and Noah wants a horse he doesn't know how to ride. You'll have that damned preacher and Mabel Jackson down on your head any day now, and as far as I can tell you're playing a game of hide-and-seek with your mother. You keep this house neat as a pin, yet you've brought three people into it who're guaranteed to interrupt your routine, destroy your serenity, and get everything out of place. All that, and you have yet to raise your voice or appear to be the slightest bit put out."

His frown transformed into a smile that made her feel weak in the knees.

"Getting upset won't change anything."

"Maybe not, but I'd want to scream and throw things."

"That wouldn't set a very good example for the boys."

"Are those boys that important to you?"

"I know what it's like to be alone and unwanted. I can't take in every boy who needs help, but I don't mean to fail these two."

Ellen couldn't pinpoint what changed about Matt as he said these words; it was as if she glimpsed a determination that had been there all along, a depth of emotion he was very careful to keep hidden. It was almost frightening in its intensity.

Then his expression shifted, and he looked as calm and unflappable as always.

"That's how I feel about Noah and Tess."

"Then we should rub along together without too much trouble. The boys and I have work to do before supper. I know Noah would like to go, but I can't take him with us until I'm sure he knows how to ride."

It had never occurred to Ellen that Matt would expect Noah to work alongside him and the older boys. She'd assumed they'd have chores like feeding the chickens and pigs or milking the cow—she didn't even know yet if he had any of these animals—but nothing as dangerous as working with cows that were practically wild. "He's too young."

"I agree, but he's not going to see it that way. I'll think of something by tomorrow."

"You don't have to worry about Noah and Tess. They're my responsibility."

Matt's surprise was unmistakable. "We're going to adopt them. They'll be as much my responsibility as yours."

Ellen didn't want Matt involved with the kids. It was okay for him to give Noah a horse, provide food and shelter, but she wanted the emotional side of their lives to be neatly separated.

"You don't know anything about little girls." She had to make it clear there was no real joining here, no sense of becoming a family.

"I had a sister orphan, Drew, and I watched Eden grow up."

"Why do you keep calling yourself an orphan? Jake and Isabelle adopted you. They're your mother and father. Drew is your sister. I know you love Isabelle—it shows in your face every time you mention her name—but you talk about your family like you're separate from them."

Ellen would have given all she possessed to have been a loved and valued member of a family rather than an unwanted burden endured because of family ties. But she could tell she'd strayed into forbidden territory. Shutters came down in the back of Matt's eyes, closing off any trace of emotion.

"Jake and Isabelle were wonderful to me, but I'm an adult now. There's no need to keep pretending."

"Do you plan to sever the relationship with Toby and Orin when they're old enough to be on their own?"

She'd assumed Noah and Tess would always be part of her life. If Matt hadn't been able to feel like a real part of Jake and Isabelle's family, if he didn't expect Toby and Orin to remain part of his life, maybe she couldn't expect Noah and Tess to think of her as their family. That frightened her. She couldn't escape the feeling that somehow Matt's failure threatened her.

"If that's how you feel, why did you buy a ranch close to Jake and Isabelle? Why do you let her keep bringing things for your house?"

"The boys are waiting for me. We'll be back in time for supper."

"What about supper?"

"I'll cook. We can talk about any changes you want to make after you begin to feel comfortable."

"I'll cook for myself and the children."

"We have to act like a family, remember? That means we all eat together. Don't worry. I won't be late."

Ellen followed him to the door, watched him walk from the house to the corrals. She felt all over again the physical attraction she experienced when around him. He was a fine specimen of a man. She wondered why he didn't consider himself a member of the Maxwell family. If Isabelle was advising him on marriage, helping him furnish his house, it was obvious she did. He was willing to take on the whole community, even marry a stranger, in order to keep Toby and Orin with him, but he didn't think they would remain close to him after they grew up. It was as though he was pushing people away before they had a chance to leave.

Tess tugged at her skirts. "What is it?" She felt guilty for having practically forgotten the child for the last several minutes.

"I want to go home."

Ellen looked down at the adorable three-year-old. She didn't know who had fathered Tess—April had never named the father of either of her children—but she clearly took after her mother. She had the same soft brown hair and eyes, the same sweet expression that could melt anybody's heart.

"This is our new home," Ellen said.

"I don't like it. I want Mrs. Ogden."

"We can't live with Mrs. Ogden anymore."

"Why?"

Ellen had never told Tess that she and her brother might be taken away and put into an orphanage. She hadn't wanted to scare the little girl.

"I married Matt," Ellen explained. "I'm his wife, and when a woman becomes a man's wife, she has to live in his house."

"Can't he live with us at Mrs. Ogden's house?"

"No. This is his house, his ranch. He's got horses and cows to look after and all kinds of work to do. I'll bet he has a milk cow." Tess liked Mrs. Ogden's brown and white cow. The placid animal allowed Tess to help Mrs. Ogden milk her.

"I don't like Toby. He makes faces at me."

"It's just because you're going to sleep in his bed."

"I want to sleep with you."

Tess looked ready to burst into tears. Ellen felt sorry for the child. She'd had too much turmoil in her short life.

"Matt said I had to help you," Noah said as he burst into the house, out of breath. "I don't want to. I want to go with Matt."

Noah didn't look at all like his sister. Ellen kept his nearly black hair cut short because it stuck out in all directions even when Noah stood still long enough for her to comb it. He had deep blue eyes and a thin, gangly body that promised considerable height when he reached maturity. His slightly pinched face was as animated and full of cheerful mischief as his sister's was quiet and biddable. It was Noah who thought of and initiated all the trouble. Tess followed him out of pure adoration.

"We have to unpack before supper."

"I can get unpacked in a minute," Noah said, heading for the bedroom. "I'll show you. I'll—"

"You can't go with Matt."

He turned, lower lip out, eyes angry. "Why?"

Noah usually did what she asked without arguing, but once in a while he dug in his heels and wouldn't budge until she gave him an answer he could understand.

"You don't have a horse."

"I can ride one of Matt's."

"You don't know how to ride well enough yet."

"Matt said I knew a lot. He said he could have me riding in no time."

"We have a lot of work to do getting settled in the house."

"But—"

"We've got to be very careful not to get in Matt's way."

"I won't. I—"

"We're in his way just by being here," Ellen said. "You and Tess are taking Toby and Orin's bedroom, sleeping in their beds. Our being here will be a lot more work. We're going to have to learn to clean up after ourselves, wash dishes, help with the chores, milk the cow—"

"That's girl stuff!"

"Matt and the boys have been doing it. See how neat this house is? We'll have to do our share."

Ellen had tried to be a good parent, to give them chores and supervise them, but most of the supervision had fallen to Mrs. Ogden. That softhearted lady could never make the children give their chores more than a lick and a promise before they ran outside to play. She was sure Matt would make every effort to accommodate Tess and Noah, but she knew he wouldn't accept his house being in shambles, his well-ordered life turned topsy-turvy. He had given them a way to stay together. In return they would have to upset his life as little as possible.

"Do we have to be neat?" Noah asked.

"Yes. You don't want Matt to make us leave, do you?"

She could tell that was a possibility he hadn't considered.

"Would he make us leave?"

"I hope not."

"Will Reverend Sears get us?"

Tess clung more tightly to Ellen's hand. "I don't like him."

"We're safe as long as we're here," Ellen said.

"I'll try to be neat," Noah said. "But I'm going to ask Matt to find my horse right away."

"How long do we have to sleep in the loft?" Toby asked Matt as they neared the ranch.

"You've been after me to let you sleep up there for the better part of a year." Matt had put him off because he wanted him to share a room with Orin. He had hoped that would make Orin feel more a part of their family.

But Matt understood why Toby resented having to sleep in the loft now. After his mother died, nobody wanted him. He never felt like he belonged anywhere until Matt hired him to work on the ranch. Matt had done everything he could to make Toby feel he had a home, not just a job, that Matt cared about him, not just whether he did his work. He'd enlisted Toby's help in doing the same for Orin. Now they were being pushed out of their beds and their room. Understanding the necessity for the marriage only made things worse. They knew their place in the family, as well as their refuge on the ranch, was threatened.

"Nothing's going to be the same with them here," Toby said.

"I don't imagine it's easy for them, either," Matt said. "They've had to leave their home, and Ellen had to give up her job."

"Can you sleep in the loft with us?" Orin asked.

Matt leaned far enough out of the saddle to give the boy's shoulder a squeeze. "The sheriff told us we had to make everybody believe this is a real marriage. In a real marriage a husband and wife sleep in the same bed. If we don't, they won't let us adopt you."

"I don't want to be adopted," Toby said.

"You don't have to be, but that's the only way they'll let Orin stay here."

"I don't mind being adopted," Orin said.

"Is she going to cook?" Toby asked.

"Are you hoping she's a better cook than I am?"

Toby looked slightly startled. "She eats at the saloon. I bet she can't even make coffee."

"We'll keep everything as it is for the time being. Once they get settled, we'll see about making changes."

"Those kids are too little to help," Toby said. "They'll just cause trouble."

"I need you both to help look after them, act like big brothers."

Orin seemed to be considering the idea, but Toby looked incensed.

"I already said I wasn't looking after no brats."

"You have to act like family, too," Matt said. "In a real family, brothers and sisters look after each other."

"They're not my brother and sister," Toby declared. "I'm putting up with them because I have to."

"I don't mind," Orin said. "I always wanted brothers and sisters."

"I don't," Toby declared.

"Don't you want to be my brother?" Orin asked.

His question apparently shocked Toby. "We can't be brothers. Look at me. Every mama in Bandera can see the Mexican in me from way down the street. You're as white as chalk. You probably come from some of those people that talk funny, the ones Jake was telling us about at Christmas."

"He's not Polish," Matt said. "He's German."

"They talk funny, too."

"Would we be brothers if you adopted us?" Orin asked Matt.

"Yes, in the eyes of the law."

"Then the law is stupid," Toby said.

"Isabelle said all her boys were brothers," Orin said. "One of them is a black man and another is an Indian."

"It don't make no difference," Toby said. "We ain't brothers."

"I wish we were," Orin said.

"I'll be your friend if you don't get stupid about it," Toby said, "but I ain't your brother."

Matt had never realized Orin wanted a brother so badly. Getting married to Ellen and having to adopt the children to keep them had uncovered a deep need in Orin to feel more connected. It had exposed Toby's fear of that same connection. Matt didn't know how he could teach Toby not to fear being close to others, to be open and accepting of their love. He'd never been able to do that himself.

Yet he must help Toby to trust others. He didn't want either Toby or Orin to suffer from the feeling of isolation that was his lot in life.

"Who's that at the house?" Toby asked.

"I'll bet it's Isabelle," Orin said, a smile banishing the solemnity from his expression. "She said she was coming over to welcome the bride."

They rounded a grove of live oak to gain an uninterrupted view of all the ranch buildings. A buggy had been drawn up to the hitching post under a large oak. Matt felt the smile of welcome that had begun to curve his lips slip away. That wasn't Isabelle's buggy. Unless he was badly mistaken—and he hoped he was—that buggy belonged to the Reverend Wilbur Sears.

Chapter Four

"I never would have guessed you'd do anything so foolish," the Reverend Wilbur Sears said to Ellen. "I wouldn't have allowed it if I hadn't been in Medina helping those good folks drive the Devil from their midst."

Ellen had been a little nervous when she heard a buggy approach the house. She and the children had finished moving their few belongings into their rooms, but she was feeling far too unsettled to face Isabelle Maxwell. Ellen had nearly swallowed her tongue when she realized it was the Reverend Sears and Mabel Jackson. She would rather have faced a dozen Isabelles.

"I can't believe you could have developed any deep feeling for Mr. Haskins on such a brief acquaintance," Mrs. Jackson said.

Sanctimonious old bat. She knew why Ellen had been forced to marry Matt.

"I've known Mr. Haskins for quite some time," Ellen said. "I've always admired him." Nobody had to know her admiration had been solely for his body.

"He's just the kind of man to turn a foolish woman's head," Wilbur Sears said, his disapproval no less severe, "but I expected more from you."

Wilbur Sears was a handsome man. He had black hair and eyes, clear skin, and a tall, solid build. In any other town his looks would have been remarkable, but next to Matt he looked ordinary. Ellen wondered if simple jealousy was the source of Wilbur's dislike of Matt.

"Why?" Ellen asked, her patience growing short. "Nobody has ever expected anything of me except that I would jump into bed with the first man who offered."

Mabel Jackson looked appalled. Wilbur Sears looked pained.

"You know I don't believe that story," Wilbur said. "My offer of marriage should be sufficient proof of that."

"More than sufficient proof of your goodness and charity," Mrs. Jackson intoned.

Nothing had ever surprised Ellen nearly as much as the reverend's startling offer of marriage. Though Wilbur Sears said he admired her, there was a look lurking far back in his eyes that said the reverend's holy exterior hid a lustful interior. She had no desire to be saved by Wilbur Sears. She had even less desire to be the object of his lust.

"I have no wish to go through life as the poor fallen female you sacrificed yourself to save."

"Who dared say such a thing?" Wilbur was getting

wound up perilously close to his blood-and-thunder voice.

"No Christian woman, I'm sure," Mrs. Jackson said.

"No one put it into words," Ellen said, though she knew Mrs. Jackson and her friends would have been the first to whisper it about, "but that's what they would think. Besides, you know I couldn't give up Noah and Tess." Wilbur thought the children should be put into an orphanage.

"I travel too much to adopt any kids. A boy needs a man home at all times." The tone of his voice indicated hurt at her undervaluing his sacrifice.

"Noble man," Mrs. Jackson murmured.

"We're put on this earth to help our fellow man any way we can, Mabel," Wilbur said, patting Mrs. Jackson's hand.

"Well, that's all meaningless now. I'm already married," Ellen said.

She hoped Wilbur would give up and go away. He frightened the children. Tess had practically burrowed into Ellen's side, and Noah had withdrawn to a corner. "Matt and I mean to adopt the children," Ellen said.

Wilbur clearly didn't like that. "That's the first I've heard of this."

"We haven't had time to do anything about it yet."

"I don't have time to discuss that right now," Wilbur said. "I've come so Mrs. Jackson can assure Mr. Haskins that Orin will be well taken care of when he leaves here."

"We mean to adopt him, too," Ellen said.

"What!" Wilbur and Mrs. Jackson exclaimed at the same time, though Wilbur's well-modulated thunder out-gunned Mrs. Jackson's startled squeak.

"I thought my wife spoke very plainly."

Matt

Ellen nearly sagged with relief when she heard Matt's voice. She didn't know how he'd managed to enter the house without her hearing him. She didn't care. To her surprise, he put his hand on her shoulder.

"We plan to adopt all four children," Matt said.

"You can't," Mrs. Jackson began. "You—"

"I will not have it!" Wilbur Sears, who had risen to his feet, brought his tightly balled fist down into the palm of his other hand with a loud smack. "You are not a fit parent for this boy."

"I disagree with you," Matt said. His voice was calm, but Ellen could feel the tension flow through his hand into her body. "I'm a respectable married man with a wife to help care for him and give him moral guidance. We have three other children to give Orin love and companionship."

"None of these children love each other," Wilbur argued. "They're nothing but a collection of strangers living under one roof."

"I love Orin," Toby said, coming to stand next to Matt. "On the way in just now he asked me if I'd be his brother. It touched my heart the way he said it."

Ellen didn't know what had happened on the ride in, but she was certain Toby's heart being touched hadn't been part of it.

"It's true," Orin said. "Matt said he wanted to adopt all of us, and I did ask Toby if he'd be my brother."

"You're lying," Wilbur thundered.

"Nobody calls one of my boys a liar," Matt said, "especially not in his own home." His quiet voice had an edge of steel.

"Are you threatening me?" Wilbur asked.

"Yes. I'll beat the hell out of you before I let you turn Orin over to people who want him for his money."

"Did you hear him, Wilbur?" Mrs. Jackson asked. "He cursed in front of these children."

"I only curse when sanctimonious busybodies push their way into my house trying to justify a mean-spirited plan by calling it God's will. Orin will stay here as long as he wants."

Ellen had never heard Matt speak so forcefully. Nor had she ever seen anyone stand up to Wilbur Sears.

"Do you want to stay here, son?" Wilbur asked Orin. He tried to make his voice sound comforting, but his anger could be heard in its timbre, seen in his hard eyes.

"Yes," Orin answered. "Nobody wants me. They only want my grandpa's money."

"This boy's soul is in danger of falling into the clutches of the Devil," Wilbur proclaimed. "You've poisoned his mind against God and His work as done through the God-fearing people of our community."

"Nobody poisoned me," Orin declared, "and the Devil won't get me. Matt won't let him. He won't let anybody get me."

Orin pushed hard up against Matt, who rested his hand on the boy's shoulder.

"Anybody coming after Orin will have to answer to me," Toby declared.

"You alone are reason enough this child should be removed from this place," Wilbur said, pointing an accusing finger at Toby. "You are a fount of evil, a wellspring of dishonesty—"

"That's enough," Matt said.

"No words are enough if they fail to protect this poor, innocent child from the influence of evil," Wilbur said, warming to his subject. "This young man is ruled by unbridled passion. He's a menace to every innocent girl in Bandera. He's wicked, lecherous—"

Matt stepped forward, his fist shot out, and the Reverend Wilbur Sears hit the floor with a thud.

"You dared strike a man of God!" Mabel Jackson shrieked.

"He can count himself lucky I didn't break his neck," Matt said, his tightly controlled voice vibrating with anger.

"You'll be struck down," Mabel said.

"Not unless your preacherman's words pack a bigger punch than his fists."

Ellen thought she heard Toby snicker. She didn't know what the boy found funny. Matt had just assaulted the preacher who virtually ruled over the souls and consciences of everybody within fifty miles of Bandera. Wilbur wouldn't forget this outrage. His vengeance would be personal, but he would wrap it up in the will of God so the people of Bandera would be forced to stand behind him.

Now she'd never be able to adopt the children.

"You've invited God's wrath," Wilbur mumbled from between lips that were beginning to swell. He sat up.

Toby started to speak, but Matt stopped him. The makeshift family, joined together only hours before by Matt and Ellen's marriage, stood motionless and silent, while Wilbur cleared his head and Mrs. Jackson helped him to his feet. Tess clung to Ellen's side, her tiny hands clutching Ellen's fingers with all her might. Noah had crept from his corner to stand at her other side, his grip on her arm painfully tight. Matt continued to stand next to her, one hand on her shoulder, the other across Orin's shoulder reaching over to Toby.

They were all connected, held together and supported by the energy that flowed from Matt into each of them.

61

"Hellfire will be your reward for this day's work," Wilbur said. "God will destroy you and burn your house to the ground."

"You will never get Orin," Matt said quietly.

"I will see that Orin is placed in a home with loving, God-fearing parents who will bring him up in the paths of righteousness and truth," Wilbur threatened. "I will see that *you*"—he jabbed an accusing finger at Toby—"are put in jail where you belong. As for those two—" He whirled about to glare angrily at Noah and Tess. "They will go to an orphanage. There'll be no more running loose through the streets destroying the peace of mind of good, law-abiding citizens."

"You're scaring the children," Matt said when Wilbur seemed about to wind up for another speech. "If you don't leave, I'll knock you down and dump you in your buggy."

"When you assault me, you assault God's messenger."

"I don't believe God talks to you any more often than he does to the rest of us," Matt said. "Now my patience is gone. It's time for supper."

Ellen closed her ears to Wilbur's threats and promises, one of each uttered for nearly every step he took. Matt and Toby followed him to make sure he left. Orin remained inside with her and the children.

"Will he put us in an orphanage?" Noah asked, visibly frightened.

"Matt won't let him," Orin said. "He won't let him do anything to us."

But Ellen could hear the fear behind the boy's brave words. "I'm sure he will do his best, but Wilbur is a powerful man."

"Matt said if I wanted to stay here, I didn't ever have to leave," Orin said.

"Why do you want to stay?"

"Matt's the only one who likes me," Orin said. "He never said I was trouble. He never threatened to give me away if I didn't do what he wanted. He told Toby and me that no matter what we did, we was to come to him and he'd see nobody did anything to us."

Five minutes ago Ellen would have asked why Orin thought Matt could protect him. She remembered the hand on her shoulder, the reassurance that came from his touch, the way he stood up to Wilbur and Mabel. Now she had no doubt he'd attack anybody who threatened his boys.

He didn't shout. He didn't even raise his voice, but she'd felt anger vibrate through him. Deep anger, hot enough to turn to violence if he didn't keep it under tight control. She had wanted to look up into his eyes, to try to understand why Matt seemed willing to take on any battle in defense of those he considered under his protection.

Did he consider Noah and Tess under his protection? Did that protection include her? Ellen had never known security or safety. She had never known anybody who would fight for her.

"Did you see his lip?" Toby asked as he and Matt returned to the kitchen. "Everybody in Bandera will know you knocked him down."

Ellen had no doubt Wilbur would use it to inflame public sentiment against Matt. What could be more damaging to a man's reputation, especially a man who wanted to adopt a fatherless boy, than attacking a minister?

"We'd better see about getting supper ready," Matt said.

Without waiting to be told, Orin got up, went to the

cabinet, and began taking out plates, cups, knives, and forks—everything necessary to set the table. Toby started grinding coffee beans. Matt took a ham from the pantry and started cutting slices from it.

"Don't forget we have six people tonight," Matt said.

"What can I do to help?" Ellen asked.

"You can help the children wash up," Matt said. "We'll have dinner ready soon."

Ellen didn't exactly feel shoved aside, but she felt the protective cloak Matt had thrown over her dissolve. This wasn't a household where Matt simply protected the boys from outside threats. They were a unit. Everything each person did was braided into the lives of the others. As she watched Matt and the boys move quickly through their well-established routine, listened to the comfortable talk among them, even an occasional joke making light of something that had happened during the day, she began to feel separated from Matt.

She didn't like the feeling.

"I feel useless just sitting here. The children can help, too."

"They'll just get in the way," Toby said.

Ellen was finding it difficult to like Toby. He resented their presence and clearly intended to make no effort to like them.

"We'll take care of everything tonight," Matt said. "We can work out something tomorrow."

"I don't want her cooking," Toby said. "How do we know she can fix anything fit to eat?"

"You don't," Ellen snapped. "You won't find out until you eat something I cook."

"I think Matt should do all the cooking," Toby said.

"What do you think I ought to do?" Ellen asked.

"You can do the washing and the cleaning," Toby

said. "The kids can bring in the firewood and feed the chickens."

"I ain't feeding no chickens," Noah announced.

" 'I'm not feeding any chickens'," Matt said quietly. "And no one is allowed to refuse to do an assigned chore, no matter how menial."

Noah opened his mouth to argue, but Ellen clamped her hand over it. "I think we should discuss the assignment of chores," she said.

"We will," Matt said. "But we rotate chores. Sooner or later everybody has to feed the chickens."

He had cut the ground out from under her. She couldn't be angry when he was so fair and sensible. Her cousin had made Ellen do more than her share of the work, constantly reminding her that she lived on their charity. Matt had brought her into his house, moved everybody around to accommodate her and the children, defended them at what would certainly be a great cost to himself. Now he wouldn't let them help in the preparations for supper. She felt like a guest in his home, and she hated it.

When she left her cousin's house, she'd sworn she'd never again live on somebody else's charity. She didn't like working in the saloon, but she had the consolation of knowing she wasn't beholden to anybody for anything. She would let him fix supper tonight, but starting tomorrow morning she would insist on doing her share of the work. "Let's wash up," she said to the children.

They went outside to a pump on the back porch. "I never saw a man cook," Noah said.

"Can I set the table?" Tess asked.

"I'm sure you can," she said to Tess. "A man has to cook when there are no women around," she said to Noah.

"Are you going to make me cook?"

"You'll have to help."

"Doing what?"

"I want to collect eggs," Tess said. "I like chickens."

"You can collect them when it comes my turn," Noah said. "Feed them, too."

Ellen suspected Matt wouldn't approve of trading chores, but right now she had her hands full trying to get Noah to let her wash his face and ears. She'd rarely had the leisure to make sure the children washed thoroughly. Mrs. Ogden usually had fed them and put them to bed long before she got home from the saloon.

"Hold still," she said when Noah tried to pull away from her. "You've got enough dirt in your ears to grow carrots."

"That's what Mrs. Ogden says."

"I can see why. Now wash your hands while I help Tess."

Tess was as cooperative as Noah was ornery. Noah's fingerprints on the towel told her he had a lot to learn about washing thoroughly.

"I want you both to be on your best behavior at the table," Ellen said as they went inside.

"Why? Aren't we going to live here?" Noah asked.

"Of course."

"You want us to be on our best behavior all the time?"

"Well, maybe not all the time," Ellen said, smiling at Noah's obvious alarm, "but I want you to make a good impression tonight. Matt got himself in trouble with Mr. Sears because of us. This is a good way to thank him."

"Can't we just say thanks?" Noah asked.

"Sometimes words aren't enough. This is one of those times."

She could tell Noah didn't understand, but she didn't feel she could explain it just yet. Maybe in twenty years.

Dinner had been delicious. Matt was an excellent cook, but he had made her and the children sit at the table while he and the boys wrapped up the leftover food, and washed and put away the dishes. Afterward they had waited in the hall, like uncomfortable guests perched on the good sofa, while Toby and Orin moved their belongings to the loft.

"There's no reason for them to move all their clothes," Ellen said. "They can dress in their old room."

"I ain't dressing in front of no girl," Toby said.

"She's a child," Ellen snapped.

"We'll wake her up," Toby said. "Orin's noisy."

"I'm not," Orin said. "You're the one who's grouchy before breakfast."

"It'll be better if they move everything to the loft," Matt said. "We have to be out of the house at dawn."

"Then that's when we'll get up," Ellen said.

"What for?" Toby asked.

Ellen was angry at herself for letting Toby's needling goad her into speaking before she thought. It would be easier if Matt and the boys left before she and the children got up. Yet even though it was a sensible solution, Ellen wanted Noah and Tess to feel the same sense of belonging the boys did. They couldn't as long as they kept being pushed to the side.

"Naturally they'll get up when we do," Matt said.

Ellen decided she was a capricious female. As soon as Matt agreed, she wanted to argue.

"We got to act like a family," Orin reminded Toby. "Isabelle says that's the only way to stop that preacher from taking me away."

"You'll be safe after Ellen and I adopt you," Matt said.

"Nobody's adopting me," Toby said.

"Don't you want to be safe?" Noah asked.

"I'm too big to be adopted," Toby growled, rounding on Noah.

"Isabelle and Jake adopted Buck and Zeke when they were older than you," Matt said.

"And I don't want any little brothers," Toby said, looking straight at Noah.

"Orin's your brother."

"Nobody will be my brother if I'm not adopted," Toby said. "I don't need no mother and father. Come on, Orin. We gotta go to bed."

"I want to sleep in the loft," Noah said.

"I'm depending on you to stay with your sister," Matt said to Noah. "This is her first night in a new house. She'll probably be too frightened to sleep unless her big brother is there to protect her."

Noah still wanted to sleep in the loft, but Ellen could see he liked the idea of being thought big enough to protect Tess.

"Can I sleep in the loft if she's not afraid?" he asked.

"You don't have a bedroll," Toby said.

Noah turned to Ellen. "Can I have a bedroll?"

"I think you'd better concentrate on getting a horse first," Ellen said.

That proved to be a fortunate thought. Noah immediately forgot about sleeping in the loft.

"Can we look for my horse tomorrow?" he asked Matt.

"Matt has a ranch to run," Ellen said. "You have to wait until he finishes his work."

"I can help," Noah said.

"You'll be feeding the chickens," Toby said.

"That's enough," Matt said. "You and Orin get to bed. We have a rough day ahead of us."

The two boys scrambled up the stairs to the loft. Noah's gaze followed them.

"You'd better get to bed, too," Matt said. "Five o'clock comes awfully early."

"Get into your nightclothes," Ellen said. "I'll be in to tell you good night in a little bit." As the two children scampered into their bedroom, she turned to Matt. "Do we really have to get up that early?" She had flinched when he said five o'clock.

"We're breaking and branding some new horses tomorrow. Jake said they'd be here at daybreak."

"What do you want me to fix for breakfast?"

"I'll cook."

"Let's get one thing straight right now: I'm not trying to take over. I'm not trying to change anything. But the children and I are going to do our share of the work around here, and I mean to start at breakfast."

Matt's unblinking stare made her uneasy.

"You were the one who said we had to be a family. We can't if I sit back and let you do all the work."

"You can help me cook," Matt said. "Noah can help Orin set the table."

"What can Tess do?"

"I don't know. What can she do?"

"I'll think of something. She'll feel left out if I don't."

"Fine. You'd better get to bed, too. I'll be in as soon as I check the livestock."

Ellen nodded her head absentmindedly as she moved toward the children's bedroom.

After she had tucked Noah and Tess in for the night, she moved back into the hallway and sank down onto one of the settees. The hurried marriage, the interview with Wilbur and Mabel Jackson, and moving into Matt's house had left her emotionally and physically drained. She couldn't fool herself into thinking she was done with Wilbur Sears. She was certain he intended to put Noah and Tess into an orphanage.

Ellen was equally certain he meant to take Orin. She had no doubt Matt would refuse to give up the boy.

She didn't know what to do about Matt's intention to mold them into a family. She'd assumed Matt, too, would want to keep their lives separate.

What if he wanted the marriage to be real?

She was certain he didn't. He couldn't fall in love with a woman who had been publicly accused of trying to seduce the son and husband of her employer. But maybe Matt didn't believe the Lowells. Earlier he hadn't seemed to put much faith in their words against her. She couldn't be sure. He had a reputation for being a stiff-necked prude. She was practically a soiled dove. Anger at the unfairness of the accusation, at her inability to disprove it, rose up in Ellen's throat, nearly choking her.

The front door opened and Matt entered the hall. He paused when he saw Ellen. She saw a look of annoyance cross his face.

"Why are you still up?" he asked. "It's time to be in bed."

Chapter Five

Matt had hoped Ellen would be in bed when he returned to the house. He'd never undressed in front of a woman, and he didn't want to start now. It would have been a great deal easier in the dark. He had been certain Ellen would take advantage of his making his nightly rounds to be in bed when he returned. "Is something wrong?" he asked.

The look she gave him was far from the aggressive, I-don't-need-anybody look she generally used. Now she looked vulnerable.

"I keep thinking I'll wake up and find this whole day was a dream."

"I expect it'll take a little time for all of us to adjust."

"I'm not talking about adjusting. I'm talking about believing. When Noah told me you wanted to marry me, I was sure he'd heard wrong. When I realized you did mean to ask me to marry you, I intended to refuse. It seemed too far-fetched to consider. Now I'm married, living in your house, and have agreed to adopt a boy I know nothing about. I keep telling myself I'm not crazy."

"Is that so hard to believe?"

"Yes. Things like this are supposed to happen to other people, not me." She got to her feet. "I feel more worn out than after a day in the saloon."

He wondered if she missed the excitement, the attention of so many men. His looks always attracted interest, but everything else about him was dull and boring. Women wanted someone like Luke, so feared as a hired gun that no man would dare touch any woman Luke considered his own.

The sound of muffled crying caught his ear.

"That's Tess." Ellen said.

They went immediately to the children's bedroom.

"Make her stop crying," a tired Noah said. "I can't go to sleep."

The dim light from the lamp in the hallway barely illuminated the little girl who lay on her stomach, her face buried in her pillow. She had kicked the covers aside, and her small feet showed below the hem of her nightgown. Brown ringlets, damp with tears, stuck to her pink cheeks as she looked up. Matt didn't have much experience with little girls, but he moved toward the bed. "Are you afraid of the dark?"

Tess turned her face toward him, tear-filled eyes glistening. She looked to Ellen, then back to Matt before nodding her head.

"There's nothing to be afraid of," Ellen said. She knelt down next to the bed. "Noah's right next to you, and I'll be in the next room. Nothing will happen to you."

Tess stared at Ellen a moment before looking back to Matt. It was obvious she wanted him to do something, but he stood back and waited for Ellen.

"Do you want me to stay with you until you go to sleep?" Ellen asked.

Tess looked at Matt when she nodded.

"Do you want Matt to stay with you?" Ellen asked, surprise in her voice.

Tess shook her head more vigorously. Ellen didn't like this. Matt saw it in the way her body stiffened, but right now Tess's fearfulness was more important. He squatted down next to the bed. "Would you like me to tell you a story?"

Tess nodded her head slowly.

"How would you know bedtime stories?" Ellen asked.

"I used to make them up when Will couldn't sleep," Matt said.

"Do you know any about Indians?" Noah asked.

"We want her to go to sleep, not stay awake shaking with fright." Ellen turned to Noah and tucked the sheets around him. "You'd better get to sleep. We have to wake up early."

"I can't sleep if Matt's telling stories."

"Would you like to hear a story about a little girl's birthday party?" Matt asked Tess.

The child's eyes brightened and she nodded.

"Ugh!" Noah said in disgust. "I don't want to hear some dumb girl story about a birthday party."

"I'll talk very quietly," Matt said, "so just Tess can hear." Matt sat down on the bed, which sagged under his weight. "The little girl's name was Jessica," he began, "and she lived on a ranch far away from anybody."

"Jessica is a sissy name," Noah said, "even for a girl."

"She had long blond hair, but it didn't curl as prettily as yours does," Matt continued, ignoring Noah. "She had blue eyes, but they weren't clear and shiny like your eyes."

"How old was she?" Tess asked.

"She was going to be four on her birthday."

"I'll be four on my birthday," Tess said.

"I wouldn't want a story about birthdays," Noah said. "I'd want one about Indians killing—"

Ellen put her hand over his mouth.

"Jessica's daddy had gone all the way to town to buy her a pretty new dress for her birthday," Matt continued. "But that made her very sad."

"Why?" Tess asked.

"Because what Jessica really wanted was a birthday party so all her friends could come and have a wonderful time."

"Did she have a party?" Tess asked.

"You'll have to wait to find out," Matt said. "Jessica thanked her daddy for the dress. She loved him and didn't want to hurt his feelings."

Ellen pinched herself to keep from falling asleep. Sitting in the dark listening to the soothing sound of Matt's voice made it hard not to give in to the fatigue that weighed down her whole body. Noah had already gone to sleep, curled up in a ball next to her, his head in her lap. Tess, sleep gradually overtaking her, lay next to Matt, two of his fingers held tightly in the grasp of her small hand.

What kind of man had she married? What about him had caused Tess to turn to him, a man she'd never met

74

until today, rather than Ellen, the woman who'd practically been her mother for the last year? Matt was a cowboy, a man who broke wild horses, a loner who preferred the company of cows to people. Yet Tess had gone to him like a baby rabbit to its nest. What sort of magic enabled him to enchant Tess and command the allegiance of a boy like Toby?

Ellen lifted Noah's head from her lap and settled him on his pillow. Matt eased off Tess's bed. They covered both the children and tiptoed from the room. Thankfully the door closed without squeaking.

"How did you know a story would put her right to sleep?" Ellen asked.

"It always worked with Will."

"Did you tell him stories about birthday parties?"

"No, but I didn't tell him about Indians, either."

"I'd like to meet him."

"You will get your chance tomorrow."

An awkward silence settled between them.

"We'd better get to bed," Matt said.

He opened the door to the bedroom. She picked up the lamp, stepped inside, and immediately all feeling of lethargy left her body. Tension snapped like sparks along her nerve endings. Even though Matt stood several feet from her, she was achingly aware of his physical presence.

She went to the wardrobe, paused while she tried to remember where she'd put her nightgowns, then took out a blue flannel. It would probably be a little too warm for late spring, but the thick material made her feel safer. She didn't understand herself. This morning Matt's telling Tess a "dumb girl story" would have disgusted her. Now it increased his attractiveness even though it wasn't a talent that would make him a more successful rancher or help him outwit Wilbur Sears.

She pulled herself together. She had to find a way to get ready for bed without having to undress in front of Matt. "Aren't you thirsty?"

"I'm glad you thought of it. A long drink of water is exactly what I need. I'll be outside. Let me know when you're in bed."

Ellen didn't know how long he meant to wait, but he remained outside while she changed and washed her face and hands. She knocked on the door, then practically jumped into the bed.

"Tess is sleeping soundly," Matt said when he entered the room. "Noah is still curled up in a tight ball."

She was surprised he had thought to check on the children.

"How about Toby and Orin?" She was ashamed to admit she hadn't remembered either boy until then.

"Toby is fast asleep, but Orin's still awake. It'll take him a while to settle down. Change upsets him."

Matt turned down the wick in the lamp until it went out. Ellen heard him open and close a drawer in the wardrobe. "I'm sorry we had to move him out of his room," she said.

"It was Wilbur Sears who upset him. He likes having Noah and Tess here. It would be good if you could give him a little attention, even a hug once in a while. He pretends he's grown up like Toby, but he's still young enough to miss his parents."

She heard the soft sound of clothes dropping to the floor and had to try very hard not to picture Matt standing naked in the dark. Just the thought of it caused her to swallow hard.

"I'm not very good with boys," she said. "I have more experience with men." Not that she was very good with them, either. She had no idea what to do with a boy yearning for a woman's touch ... or a man who seemed not to need or want it.

"There must be some similarities."

"I hope not, at least to the men I know."

She felt the bed sag under Matt's weight, and her breath caught. Had he had time to take off his long underwear and put on a nightshirt? The possibility that he had gotten into bed naked was too nerve-racking to consider.

"Why were you so uncomfortable when Tess took hold of your hand?" Now was a good time to ask him about that, anything to take her mind off his lying next to her.

"I'm not used to touching," he said. "Boys don't do it much."

Something about the tightness in his voice hinted that there was more than unfamiliarity at work. She wondered what.

"You were right about Orin needing a hug once in a while. Children need touching to feel secure, especially girls." But not grown women. The thought of him touching her practically scared her to death.

"Anything you want to tell me about today?" he asked.

"Like what?" She didn't know where to begin. She was married. She'd promised to help him adopt Orin and protect Toby. She'd committed herself to sleep next to him. She didn't know if she could survive that. Next to sharing his bed, everything else seemed easy.

"I know you didn't want to marry me," Matt said. "I want to make being here easier. Like I said before, if you have anything you want to change, let me know. I discuss everything with the boys, but we want you and the children to be happy."

The sincerity in his voice touched her. She knew he had to be as uncomfortable as she was.

"We'll get along all right. It'll just take a little time to adjust."

A silence ensued.

"You sure there's nothing bothering you?" he asked.

"Yes, I'm sure."

"Then good night."

"Good night."

She heard him turn, felt the mattress move as he shifted positions. He must have put his back to her. She wanted to reach out and be sure but didn't dare. If she touched him, he'd probably think she wanted a whole lot more. Still, she had to know.

"Did you turn your back to me?"

"Yes. Why?"

"Nothing. I just wanted to know."

She rolled onto her side, her back toward Matt. She couldn't go to sleep if he was facing her, maybe staring at her while she slept. It was hard enough knowing he lay just a few inches away, *possibly naked*.

But she found as she relaxed, as fear melted away to be replaced by the heaviness of fatigue, her awareness of his being so near became more intense. She tried hard to think about what she had to do tomorrow, how to make the children happy living on a ranch, how to get to know Orin better, even how to overcome her dislike of Toby.

But it didn't work.

Nothing made her forget Matt lying within arm's length. How could any woman calmly drop off to sleep knowing that? She thought of what Tulip said and turned warm all over. She had to forget Tulip's comments. She needed sleep. She had to face her in-laws tomorrow.

Matt woke out of a dead sleep. Someone had hit him.

"You said you wouldn't touch me," Ellen said. She punched him in the chest. "You're just like every other man. You'll promise anything to get your hands on a woman."

"What are you talking about?" he asked, struggling to understand what was going on.

She punched him once more before rolling out of bed. "I'm talking about you grabbing me the minute we fell sleep."

He couldn't see her expression in the dim light filtering through the window, but he saw her outline in the shadows, her hand clutched to her bosom, a blanket pulled around her to shield her body from his gaze.

"I didn't touch you." He couldn't have. He didn't even touch people in his adopted family unless he had to.

"You most certainly did. I knew I shouldn't have let the sheriff talk me into sharing a bed with you. And he thinks you're shy. You're just as brazen as any other man."

"I must have rolled over in my sleep."

"Don't think I'm going to believe *that* story. You can march right up to the loft and sleep with the boys."

Matt didn't know how to convince Ellen any touching had been innocent and accidental, but he did know their scheme would be ruined if they started sleeping in separate rooms. "We have to talk."

"We'll talk tomorrow when it's light and I can watch your hands. Tonight you sleep in the loft."

"I can't."

"Then I'll sleep with Tess."

"You can't."

"What are you going to do, pull me back into bed?" She backed closer to the door. "If you try, I'll scream loud enough to be heard in Bandera."

"Light the lamp."

"I'm not staying in here with you."

"If you leave this room, all four children will know something is wrong. One of them is bound to say something that will get back to Wilbur. If you really want to adopt Noah and Tess, you'll listen to me."

She remained motionless for several moments.

"I know you don't trust me," he said, "but I'm going to keep Toby and Orin if I have to tie you to this bed."

"You wouldn't dare."

"Don't try me. Believe me when I say nothing is more important to me than those two boys."

She struck a match and lit the lamp. She settled warily on the end of the bed, obviously ready to jump up at the slightest provocation. She kept the blanket pulled tightly around her. "I didn't have to get married to get a woman into my bed. I got married so I could keep these boys. I'm not stupid enough to jeopardize that for a few seconds of juvenile fun."

"You grabbed me."

"Weren't you asleep when it happened?"

"Yes, but—"

"So you don't know exactly what I did. Look, I don't deny I might have touched you, but I didn't do it intentionally. I expect you'll touch me before long."

"I won't."

"Maybe not, but if you do, I promise not to jump to conclusions. Is it too much to ask you to do the same?"

He couldn't tell if she was considering his proposal or preparing to walk out. Her shadowy silhouette remained motionless. "I don't know what your experience has been, but not all men make a grab for the first female within reach."

"I've seen you in the saloon," she shot back. "You know that's exactly what happens every night."

"Have I ever made a grab for you?"

"No."

"Or anyone else you know about?"

"No, but that doesn't mean—"

"Do you know any Maxwell man who grabs at women in saloons?"

A pause. "No."

"Do you know one of us who lies?"

"No." The admission sounded reluctant.

"Everybody, even my family, says all I care about is my ranch and these boys. If that's true, do you think I'm going to risk it all for a bit of a romp in bed?"

"No." An even more reluctant admission.

"You don't have to like me, but you can trust me."

"It isn't that I don't like you."

"You're afraid I think what Eddie Lowell said is true."

Silence.

"I believe you."

"Why should you?"

"Because I know what it's like when people tell lies about you."

More silence.

"Look, we both want the same thing and have gone to unusual lengths to get it. Neither of us is willing to risk it foolishly. If I touch you, wake me up and I'll move away. If I keep doing it, I'll sleep on the floor.

81

But you can't leave this room. It would jeopardize what we both want."

More silence. "Don't you trust anybody?" he asked.

"No."

"Could you learn to trust me?"

More silence. And people said he didn't talk. "Okay, I'll sleep on the floor."

"You don't have to."

"Yes, I do. Give me that blanket. It gets cold before morning."

"You don't have to sleep on the floor. I trust you."

"Are you sure?"

"Yes." She didn't sound sure.

"You promise to wake me right away if I touch you?"

"I never met a man like you."

"You're a beautiful woman. I'm sure hundreds of men want you. I just want something else more." He'd probably made her angry, but at least she lay down.

"I don't understand you," she said.

"You don't have to. Just remember I'll do what I must to keep those boys and you won't go wrong."

That wasn't quite the whole truth, but he had to make her believe it was.

Matt lay in bed, all desire for sleep gone. He ought to get up, feed the livestock, and start breakfast, but he didn't move. He lay in bed with his wife. While she was his wife in name only, he found comfort in her presence. Her warmth reached his body. The soft sound of her breathing soothed him. Her presence banished some of the loneliness that had been his constant companion for so many years.

But that wasn't his only unexpected discovery. His body had responded to Ellen's presence. Even more important, he hadn't experienced any revulsion when he touched her.

He'd never had any trouble imagining a physical relationship with a woman. There had been times when he thought he would explode from the pressure inside him, but any physical contact conjured up memories of terror, pain, and humiliation, and all physical desire vanished. Yet he'd spent half the night in a state of arousal, inflamed by Ellen's presence rather than terrified by it. He'd wanted to touch her. He still wanted to touch her. He could imagine the softness of her skin, the warmth of her caress.

But he kept his distance. If he didn't, she would leave, and his chances of adopting Orin would sink out of sight. The boys were more important than his physical needs. He was probably having an atypical reaction, because he'd never been this close to a woman for such a long period of time. Probably the moment he touched her when she was awake, the old revulsion would come down on him with the force of a rockslide. Better to think he had overcome his inhibitions than to prove conclusively that he hadn't.

Besides, it wouldn't do any good. Ellen didn't want him to touch her. She'd clung to the far side of the bed with the tenacity of someone clinging to a cliff. He felt shunned, and he resented it because he didn't deserve to feel that way. He'd upheld his part of the bargain. He'd kept his distance.

But he didn't want to. He wanted to—

Matt sat up. There was no point in staying in bed. He would either do something he shouldn't or be miserable because he didn't. It was not yet dawn, but he eased himself out of the bed, stood, and pulled the nightshirt over his head. Despite his frustration, he couldn't help but grin as he realized that for the few seconds it took him to discard his nightshirt and step into his long underwear, he stood naked in the bedroom with his wife. That was something he wouldn't have thought possible just a couple of days ago.

As he buttoned up, he thought of Ellen standing naked as she discarded her nightgown and reached for her chemise. It had the result of making his arousal more painful than ever. No other woman had had this effect on him. He didn't understand why Ellen should.

Matt dressed quickly and left the bedroom. He knew his weakness now. By tonight he would have himself under control.

He'd better. He couldn't go months without sleep.

Ellen decided if every morning was going to be like this, she'd have to take the kids and run for it. Breakfast was becoming a nightmare, and it was everybody's fault except Matt's. He never lost his temper, though considering she had lost hers several times, she was in no mood to consider that a virtue.

"This biscuit is hard enough to knock a horse senseless," Toby complained as he ladled peach jam on a biscuit he'd practically torn to pieces. He knew Ellen had made the biscuits.

"If you don't like it, don't eat it," Matt said.

"I can't be expected to wrestle wild horses without a decent breakfast."

"Wake up," Matt said to Orin, who stared absently before him. "The horses will be here soon."

"He didn't get much sleep," Toby said. "That floor is too hard."

"I'll get some more blankets," Matt said.

"Toby took all the jam," Noah said. "I wanted more jam."

"There's more in the pantry," Matt said.

"I'll get it," Toby said, getting up with a great show of self-sacrifice. "The brat would probably knock one of the jars off the shelf. It would be a shame if he got hit in the head."

"I'm sure Noah has excellent coordination," Matt said.

"He wouldn't if he'd spent half the night trying to get comfortable enough to sleep."

Tess started to whimper. She always did when people around her were angry or upset.

"That's enough," Ellen snapped, her patience finally at an end. "You can have your bedroom back. Noah and Tess will sleep in the loft."

"Pay no attention," Matt said. "Toby's always out of temper in the morning, and Orin always stares into space. Noah and Tess are too small to sleep in the loft."

"I'm not too small," Noah protested. "I want to sleep in the loft."

"You'll have beds soon," Matt said.

"A bed won't make any difference," Toby declared. "I—"

"It's time you and Orin made sure everything is ready for the horses."

They jumped to their feet, put their dishes in the sink, and practically raced out of the kitchen. Matt got up more slowly and took his plate to the sink. "I'll have a talk with them. I want everybody to be happy."

Ellen doubted anything could make this family happy. Though she felt sorry for Toby, she was glad he didn't want to be adopted.

"I know it's hard to be orphaned and unwanted, but

I won't let Toby attack the children," Ellen said. "They're too small to defend themselves. Besides, they didn't create this situation."

"Neither did Toby and Orin," Matt said. "When they start feeling threatened, they forget they're not the only ones. They'll adjust. Are you sure you don't mind cleaning up? The boys and I will help."

"No. You do the horses. I'll do the dishes."

Matt's smile was almost enough to banish the dark mood of the morning. "You'd better be careful. I might get used to it."

"I'll cook and wash up after every meal as long as I don't have to come near a horse or a cow."

"You sound like Isabelle."

"She must be a sensible woman."

"I've got to go," Matt said. "You want to come with me?" he asked Noah.

"Yeah," Noah said, jumping up so quickly that he knocked his plate onto the floor.

"Noah's staying with me," Ellen said. "You'll be too busy to watch him."

"I want to go with Matt." Noah puckered up, ready to cry.

"Tell you what," Matt said. "If you help Ellen clean up, I'll have my brother Will take you with him. Then Ellen won't have to worry about you."

Noah looked like he was trying to decide whether to throw a tantrum or accept Matt's offer.

"If you throw a fit, you'll stay inside all day," Ellen said.

Noah's shoulders sagged. "Okay, but I don't like you, Ellen."

Ellen turned toward Matt.

"I'm not sure—"

"He's got to learn sometime," Matt said. "You can't keep him inside forever."

"But he's so young."

"I'm almost six," Noah said.

"I'll send Orin to tell you when the horses are close to the house," Matt said to Noah. "After I break the horses, we'll see if there's one good enough for you. Watch them very carefully when they go by to see if there's one you like."

Ellen had to bite her tongue to keep from saying something just to irritate Matt. It annoyed her that he remained so calm when she was about to explode. It was like being married to a shadow. You could see him, but you couldn't get your hands on him. "What do you want me to fix for dinner?"

"Isabelle will be here soon. You can decide together."

"Why can't I go?" Noah wailed as soon as the door closed behind Matt.

"You're too young, and you don't know anything about being around wild horses."

"I'm not afraid of no horses."

"Wild horses are dangerous. They don't like being put in a corral. They try to get away. Sometimes even big men like Matt get hurt."

"Orin's helping."

"Orin's been living here for over a year. When you've been here that long, you can help, too." But they wouldn't be here a year from now. The adoption would have come through, and she'd have her hat shop in San Antonio.

"I think you're mean."

"Let's get breakfast cleared away."

"Matt would let me help," Noah said. "I like Matt."

Ellen didn't respond. She gave Matt credit for trying

to include Noah in everything, but he had to remember Noah was a child.

"I like Matt, too," Tess said. "He told me a story."

Tess had been so frightened by the flaring tempers, she hadn't said a word all morning.

"Matt's very nice," Ellen said, feeling more out of charity with him than ever.

"Matt likes stories," Tess said.

"No, he doesn't," Noah said. "He just told you one because you're a scaredycat." He puffed out his chest. "Men aren't afraid of the dark."

Ellen didn't know if she could stand much more of Matt's being idolized. He was just a quiet, unflappable man who acted like she didn't exist. She didn't want him fawning over her, but she didn't like being ignored. Men had admired her for so long, she'd taken it for granted. Now she wasn't getting any attention at all, and that worried her.

The kitchen door burst open. "They're here!" Orin shouted. "Jake must have brought at least twenty horses."

Orin's head disappeared immediately. Noah jumped to his feet and raced to the door.

"Stay on the porch," Ellen called. "I don't want you trampled."

She doubted Noah heard her. Only Tess seemed immune to the magic of wild horses.

"Do I have to go outside?" Tess asked. She'd been content to sit in her own chair during breakfast, but she'd jumped down and clutched onto Ellen the minute Matt and the boys left.

"I have to welcome Mrs. Maxwell. She'll think it's rude if I don't go outside."

"Why?"

"It's polite to meet visitors at the door. We can come back inside after that."

Tess seemed relieved enough to stay with Ellen when she opened the door and stepped out into pandemonium. What seemed a herd of at least a hundred horses filled the space in front of the house. They milled about, neighing, throwing their heads in excitement, striking out with their hooves at anything that came within reach. Ellen pulled Noah out of the way of a piebald mare who appeared ready to take her anger out on him.

"Stay on the porch or go inside," Ellen ordered.

"I've got to see them," Noah said, trying to pull away. "Matt said I could have one if it was good enough."

"Then let Matt decide," Ellen said, keeping her hold on the squirming boy.

She saw Toby and Orin astride their mounts, moving in and out of the herd. She held her breath, but they kept the horses moving toward the corrals beyond the barns. In a few minutes the animals had moved past, and quiet was restored.

"Can I go now?" Noah asked.

"Not until Matt gets the horses in the corral," Ellen said. "I don't trust you to keep your distance from their hooves."

"Ellen!" he wailed.

"You've got to be careful of danger if you expect me to let you out of the house. This isn't Bandera, and those aren't chickens or pigs."

"He's just like every boy I ever knew. He can't wait to put himself in the path of danger."

Ellen had been so worried about Noah that she hadn't noticed a woman had ridden up to the porch. Isabelle Maxwell.

"He doesn't understand about wild horses," Ellen

said, frantically trying to collect her thoughts.

"Boys never do," Isabelle said as she threw her leg over the saddle horn and slid to the ground. She advanced toward the porch with a grace at variance with the wilderness setting. "I'm Isabelle Maxwell, Matt's mama." She took off her riding gloves, pulled a startled Ellen to her, and gave her a kiss on the cheek. "And this must be Noah."

Noah's attention had been distracted from the horses long enough to realize he was facing a strange woman. He took a step backward.

"I'm your grandmama," Isabelle said.

Noah nodded and accepted a kiss with what Ellen thought was surprising presence of mind for a five-year-old.

"And this beautiful little girl must be Tess," Isabelle said. She knelt down and held out her hands. "Come here and let me give you a big kiss. I'm especially fond of little girls."

Ellen expected Tess to bury her face in her skirts, but she walked into Isabelle's embrace without hesitation.

"I brought something for each of you," Isabelle said.

She reached into a large bag and took out a bandana, which she handed to Noah. "You'll have to wear this when you help Matt with the horses. They stir up a lot of dust."

"Tie it on me," Noah said excitedly, turning to Ellen. "Can I go show Matt?"

"The horses are in the corral," Isabelle said. "Jake will look out for him."

Noah practically danced with impatience until Ellen tied the handkerchief around his neck, then he was off like a shot.

"Remember to stay away from the horses," Ellen called.

"This is for you," Isabelle said to Tess as she reached inside her bag once more and brought out a doll wearing a bright red dress with lace at the collar and sleeves. She had red bows in her hair and black buckled shoes. Her white cotton drawers showed beneath the hem of her dress. Isabelle held it out to Tess.

Tess stared at the doll, afraid to touch it.

"Go ahead," Isabelle coaxed. "It's yours."

Tess took the doll, held it away from her for a moment, then hugged it almost fiercely.

Isabelle reached into the bag and brought out another package. "Here are some extra clothes," she said to Tess. "No woman can survive with only one dress.

"Now, my dear," she said, standing and turning to Ellen, "you can take me inside and give me a cup of coffee. My throat is parched. I understand horses are necessary creatures, but it would be so much better if they had fewer feet to stir up the dust."

Momentarily nonplussed, Ellen led her mother-in-law into the kitchen. Tess stayed on the porch, happily playing with her new doll. "I'm afraid we don't have anything very fancy."

"Don't apologize," Isabelle said. "Matt has defied my best efforts to make the place tolerable. I'm depending on you to turn it into a home I won't be ashamed of."

"I can't do that," Ellen said. "It's his house."

"It's your house, too, unless you've some peculiar notion of taking up quarters in the barn."

"No, but I don't think Matt would take kindly to my changing everything."

"Has he told you that?" Isabelle asked as she sat down at the table.

"No. He told me I may change things. I only have to tell him."

"But you've been strictly forbidden to say anything to me."

Ellen could tell from Isabelle's gaze that she knew Matt far too well for Ellen to try to pretend. "He says you've done more than enough for him, that you and Jake have your own children."

"We only have one child, but it wouldn't matter if we had a dozen. I don't consider Matt any less my son for not having been born of my body."

"I believe he—"

"You don't have to tell me what he thinks. I've heard it often enough. I've tried to talk sense into him, but you know how men are. They think they know everything when half the time they're stumbling in the dark. I'm depending on you to talk some sense into him."

"I don't think Matt will listen to me."

"Of course he will. You're his wife."

Ellen didn't know what to say. She didn't know how much Isabelle knew.

"You don't have to stand there tongue-tied. I know all about this silly business arrangement. That's a lot of nonsense. Matt is my most difficult son. I worried I'd never find the right woman for him. He needs someone strong to bring him out of himself, and you're the perfect woman to do that."

"I'm not. I couldn't."

"Nonsense. You not only survived that Lowell family lying about you, you grew stronger because of it. That's the kind of woman I wanted for Matt. I want you to be a real wife to him. It'll be the best thing for both of you."

Chapter Six

Surprise held Ellen speechless. It had never occurred to her that Isabelle would see her as Matt's savior.

"But we're strangers. We don't know anything about each other."

"I can tell you all you need to know about Matt."

"What do you want in your coffee?" Ellen asked, hoping for time to gather her scattered wits so she could convince Isabelle that she and Matt would never be truly husband and wife.

"I like it black, but if you make it the way Matt likes it, put cream in it. I've been married to Jake Maxwell for seventeen years and I still can't force myself to drink coffee the way he and the boys like it. I gave up trying to get them to drink tea."

The sudden image of what would happen if a cow-hand had ever entered the saloon and asked for tea nearly caused Ellen to burst out laughing. "I don't imagine that went down well."

"It's a very civilized drink, but I know when to stop wasting my time. Just like I knew when to stop bringing things over for this house. We've got five families besides you living in these hills—Chet, Ward, Buck, Sean, and Drew. There's a whole barn full of discarded furnishings back at our ranch. You can have anything you want."

"All we need right now are beds for Orin and Toby. Noah and Tess have taken their room."

She handed a cup of coffee to Isabelle, who looked askance at the pale brown liquid. "I see you drink it strong, too."

"I'm afraid so."

"I guess that means I couldn't talk you into switching to tea."

"I'm willing to try it," Ellen said, hoping she wouldn't be forced to honor her promise.

Isabelle took a sip of her coffee. "There's no point in fighting what can't be changed. You can have plenty of beds and wardrobes. You'll need one for Will, too. He and Matt are about as different as two boys can be, but they're real close. You'll have him underfoot more often than you like. Which will be a relief to me, though I admit I'll miss the brat. You're not to tell him that," Isabelle said in a severe tone. "He takes far too much advantage of me as it is."

Ellen couldn't imagine anybody taking advantage of Isabelle. Then she remembered the bandana and the doll. This woman might rule her men with an iron hand, but it was clear she did it out of love. Ellen had never met anybody quite like Isabelle. That made it all the harder for her to say what she had to say. "I'm sorry to disappoint you, but Matt and I can't have the kind of marriage you want."

"Why?" There was nothing belligerent or aggressive in her tone.

"Getting married was the only way we could keep these children. As for ourselves"—she felt the heat rise in the cheeks—"we agreed to keep to ourselves."

Isabelle took a sip of her coffee, frowned slightly and set down her cup. "I don't see why that should prevent you from staying married."

"Matt isn't interested in a wife," Ellen said, feeling a bit like a cornered animal. "And I'm not interested in a husband, just in making sure April's children don't end up in an orphanage."

"Why?"

"I know what it's like to be unwanted. I'm determined it'll never happen to them."

"Good. I knew Matt had had the good fortune to stumble onto the perfect woman for him. He deserves some luck for a change."

Every word out of Isabelle's mouth pushed Ellen farther into a corner.

"Matt has promised to help me open a hat shop in San Antonio."

"Do you know anything about hats?" Isabelle took another sip, frowned, and pushed her coffee away.

"Quite a lot, actually." Ellen hesitated, then decided she would have to trust her mother-in-law. "I make hats for Susan."

She was pleased to see that she'd succeeded in surprising Isabelle.

"I thought she made her own hats."

"She makes most of them, but she buys everything I

make." Ellen hesitated. "She says that Mabel Jackson won't wear anybody's hats but mine."

Amusement danced in Isabelle's eyes. "Does she know?"

"No, and you can't tell her. She'd never buy another one."

"I wouldn't think of telling her," Isabelle said, smiling broadly. "It will be too much fun watching her parade around, oblivious to the fact that she is wearing a hat made by you. You have quite a talent. I didn't buy any of my hats from Susan until a year ago. Is that when you started making hats for her?"

"Yes."

Isabelle looked more pleased than ever. Ellen didn't know what was going through her mind, but she had a feeling she wasn't going to like it.

"You don't like Toby, do you?"

The question jolted Ellen. She stared at Isabelle, unsure of how to answer.

"You don't have to look like you've been caught with your hand in the till. I'd be surprised if you did."

"He doesn't like me or the children very much."

"It's not a question of his liking you. He's afraid your being here will change things."

"I wouldn't have pushed him out of his room if the sheriff hadn't insisted Matt and I had to sleep in the same bed."

"When you've been unwanted all your life, it's hard to believe it will ever be any different. Toby didn't mind when Orin came. You're different."

"Nobody wants us, either."

"Matt does."

"He just needs somebody."

"True, but it was you he wanted."

"Only because he knew I was in the same situation."

"No. I mentioned several women, but I knew as soon as your name came up that Matt liked you."

Ellen decided Isabelle saw what she wanted to see.

"Matt is the most sensitive of all my boys," Isabelle said, "but certain things in his life caused him to repress his feelings. I never thought any woman could bring them out until I saw how he reacted when I mentioned your name."

"What did he do?"

"He blushed."

"Are you sure it wasn't shock?" She couldn't imagine him feeling any strong emotion for her.

"He wouldn't have married you if he hadn't liked you. He would have taken the boys and headed west. I couldn't stand that. I've already lost too many boys to that awful place."

Ellen hardly knew whether to believe Isabelle or not. She didn't seem like a woman given to fooling herself, nor one willing to lie. How could she believe Matt liked her?

"You like him a little, don't you?"

Ellen didn't know how such a simple question could make her feel so trapped. Isabelle sat quietly, her gaze steady. It was impossible to lie to this woman, to try to mislead her. She loved Matt and wanted the best for him. The fact that she was mistaken in thinking Ellen was best for him didn't negate her good intentions.

"It's hard not to like Matt. As you said, he's sweet, thoughtful, sensitive, and he'd do anything, including marrying me, to give those boys the kind of security they've never had. Since I'm trying to do the same thing for Noah and Tess, I've got to like him for that."

The humor was back in Isabelle's eyes. "And that's all you like about him, his humanity?"

Ellen felt herself blush. "You know better," she said, experiencing a tiny spurt of temper at being forced to admit what she didn't want anyone to know. "There's not a woman in this world who could look at Matt and not feel weak in the knees. He looks like every woman's Prince Charming come to rescue her from danger."

Isabelle laughed. "I can't wait to see his face when you tell him that."

"I never would. He's not that kind of man. Last night he hit Wilbur Sears when he came here, threatening the children. I was surprised, but Wilbur is about the only man in Bandera who wouldn't hit him back. Matt's not a . . ." Ellen didn't know what to say without belittling Matt to his own mother.

"He's not a man's man," Isabelle said for her. "He's not the kind of man to fight for what he wants, to stand up to a real bully. You believe if things ever really got tough, you'd have to defend him."

"Not that bad, but—"

"Of course it's that bad," Isabelle said, her own temper beginning to show. "You think that deep inside Matt's a coward. You disappoint me," Isabelle said, getting to her feet. "I thought that after your experience you'd be able to see what most women are too silly to see." Isabelle fixed her with an angry glare. "I hope you never have occasion to discover just how much courage Matt does have. No matter what the situation requires, Matt will do it. And without hesitation."

Ellen felt like she'd been slapped in the face. "I like Matt," she protested, "I really do. He's a kind and gentle man. He's probably a good rancher, too."

"Come with me," Isabelle said, heading to the door.

"I think you ought to see how Matt breaks a horse."

Ellen didn't want to see Matt break horses. "Tess is afraid of horses. I don't want to leave her alone."

"I'm not fond of horses either, but if she plans to stay in Texas, she's got to get used to them. I was twenty-three when Jake forced me to make my peace with horses. Believe me, it's a lot easier to do when you're young."

Ellen wanted to argue, but she had enough sense to know Tess couldn't avoid horses. She followed Isabelle outside and collected Tess from the porch. "I don't really think Matt's a coward," she said as she struggled to keep up with Isabelle's suddenly very unfeminine stride. "He's just not the kind of man to catch my fancy."

Isabelle's laugh was harsh. "Do you think I thought Jake was the kind of man to catch my fancy?" she asked, looking back at Ellen without slowing her stride one iota. "I thought he was a crude barbarian, and I told him so. It's no fun swallowing your words, even when you're crazy in love with the maddening, frustrating man who caused you to say them in the first place."

"But Matt said you loved Jake."

"I was raised by a wealthy aunt in Savannah, but the money vanished and I was sent to an orphanage. I got a job with an aristocratic family. My kind of people, I thought, until the husband tried to rape me. I ended up in Texas, trying to help some boys nobody else wanted. I couldn't think of enough words to express my disgust at everything I saw, including the men. I finally learned to look beneath the lack of manners and harsh attitudes to see inside Jake to the man he really was, not the one who'd built a hard shell to enable him to live in this world. Matt's like that, only worse. You've got to learn to see inside him, or you aren't fit to be his wife."

A second slap. Isabelle had more than lived up to Ellen's expectations, just not in the way she'd anticipated.

"If things had been different—"

"Things will never be different."

They would be different when she moved to San Antonio and opened her own shop. No one would know she had been accused of trying to seduce a boy, had worked in a saloon, had adopted the fatherless children of a saloon dancer.

"I do like Matt. I've been trying to figure out why ever since he asked me to marry him, but it wouldn't make any difference if I loved him. He's the one who suggested the business arrangement."

Isabelle stopped and turned to face Ellen, her face wreathed in smiles. "You do truly like him? I know he's so handsome he makes women act silly, but I'm not talking about that."

"Neither am I, but it doesn't make any difference."

"Yes it does," Isabelle said as she took Ellen's hand and pulled her toward the corrals. "It makes all the difference in the world."

"Matt doesn't want to be married," Ellen said as she rescued her imprisoned hand.

"Of course he does," Isabelle said. "Every man wants to get married. Matt doesn't think he's worthy."

"Why?"

"He'll have to tell you that. Now, let me introduce you to some of your new brothers-in-law."

Ellen knew every man gathered around the corral. You couldn't live in Bandera and not know the Maxwell clan.

"This is Sean O'Ryan," Isabelle said as she introduced Ellen to a mountain of a man with flaming red hair. "You two ought to get along like pigs in a blanket. His wife used to own a saloon."

"Best singer and dancer you ever saw," Sean said, as Ellen's hand disappeared into his massive paw. "And the most beautiful. I still don't know why she married me."

"Neither does anybody else," said Buck. "The worst part is, she keeps having sons who look just like him."

"Don't discourage the newest member of the family," Sean said. "She's still got to swallow Will. Will," he called, in a voice that matched his body, "come meet your new sister-in-law."

Ellen could never see Will without catching her breath. He was absolutely gorgeous.

"Will got the looks and Matt got the brains," Sean said.

"He's good-natured for all that," Isabelle said. "It's impossible to be gloomy for long with Will around."

"You'll just want to strangle him in five minutes," Buck said. "I think Isabelle's ulterior motive in having him help Matt is to get rid of him for a few days."

"I love him just as much as the rest of you," Isabelle insisted.

"I know," Buck said, giving her a kiss on the cheek. "We love you for it. We just don't understand it."

Noah burst into the group. "Ellen, you've got to come watch Matt. Jake says he's going to ride the meanest horses first."

Ellen grabbed Noah before he could run back to the corral fence. "I want you to meet your uncles."

"I've already met them," Noah said. "Come on." He pulled at Ellen's hand.

"Why don't you take your sister to watch?" Isabelle suggested.

Tess tried to hide in Ellen's skirts.

Buck knelt down. "You want to come with me? I'll make sure those horses don't come anywhere near you."

"It's okay," Ellen said when Tess hung back. "Noah will stay with you. I'll be over in a minute."

"Ellen!" Noah complained.

"You stay with Tess until I come. Otherwise you have to go back to the house."

Buck eyed Ellen. "You sound remarkably like Isabelle when she tricked Jake into marrying her and adopting all of us."

"I sure do pity Matt," Sean said, grinning, "and him thinking you so meek and biddable."

"He didn't think any such thing." Will had reached the group in time to hear Sean's last remark. "He probably wanted a workhorse to take care of all the wayward boys he plans to take in. Hi, I'm Will Haskins, Matt's brother. They'll tell you I'm an idiot, but they're just jealous because I'm prettier than they are. And I'm not so big I'd give a decent woman a fright," he said to Sean.

Ellen didn't know what to think when Will threw a punch at Sean, and Sean immediately caught him in a bear hug.

"Ignore them," Isabelle said. "Sean has to be a sober, married man most of the time. When he gets away from Pearl, he acts like the boy I foisted off on Jake."

Sean had Will down on the ground.

"Don't listen to a word she says," Will said as he struggled against the powerful muscles of his huge brother. "She's crazy about us."

"You wondering what kind of bizarre family you've wandered into?"

Ellen turned to find Jake watching the tangle of men on the ground.

"They'll get it out of their systems in a minute," he said.

"No they won't," Isabelle said, "because their father's just as bad."

"I'm not down there with them."

"But you'd like to be."

"Come watch your husband before she gives you a bad impression of me," Jake said to Ellen. Sean and Will stopped wrestling as quickly as they'd begun.

"I'm stronger than you are," Sean said.

"And I'm prettier," Will shot back as he dusted himself off.

The two men laughed and headed toward the corral. Ellen decided all Matt's family was crazy.

"Cole said Matt's getting ready to ride the meanest horse in the whole bunch," Noah announced when Ellen reached the corral. "He said he's got to hold him or he'll savage Matt. What does *savage* mean?"

"It means they'll try to kick or bite him," Isabelle said. "Wild horses don't like to carry men around on their backs."

Cole Benton was Drew's husband. Everybody knew his father was just about the richest man in Memphis. Nobody in his family could understand why he had married a tomboy like Drew Townsend and lived on a horse ranch in the Hill Country.

"Why is Matt riding that horse?" Tess asked. She was sitting on Buck's shoulder, apparently happy as long as he held on to her with both hands.

"Because there's not a horse in the world Matt can't

ride," Sean said. "Even Cole and Drew send for him when they get a real bad one."

Ellen hadn't really had a chance to see the horse Matt was about to ride. Now that she did, she wished she'd stayed inside. Someone had tied the horse's head so close to a post in the fence that the animal couldn't move. Cole and Matt stood on opposite sides of the horse, trying to keep the blanket and saddle on long enough to cinch the saddle. The horse, white with huge black spots, threw his hindquarters from side to side, trying to kick his tormentors. His eyes were wide and wild-looking.

"Isn't that horse dangerous?" Ellen asked.

"Very dangerous," Jake said.

Ellen felt some of the color drain out of her face.

"Don't worry," Will said. "Matt won't get off until the horse knows who's boss."

"Or until he's thrown off," Ellen said.

"Only one horse ever threw Matt," Will said.

"Sawtooth," Buck and Sean said in unison.

Ellen could tell Will was proud of his brother. In her opinion, he was just too bullheaded to know when he was in danger. She wanted to tell Matt that if he had to risk his own neck, to at least make Orin and Toby stay out of the way. A single blow from one of those hooves could kill.

Matt got the saddle cinched up. Ellen felt reluctant pride in his accomplishment but realized that brought him closer to getting on the horse's back. She knew that moment had arrived when Toby and Orin scrambled through the rails to safety outside the corral.

"He's going to ride him!" Noah called out in excitement.

"You can't see from down there," Will said to Noah. "You want to get up on my shoulders?"

He might as well have asked Noah if he wanted the moon. The child danced with excitement. Will stooped down, picked him up, and settled him on his shoulders. Will stood just in time for Noah to see Matt spring into the saddle. Cole pulled the slip knot that held the horse's head to the post and quickly backed out of the way.

The paint was loose, and he had every intention of getting rid of the man on his back. Ellen couldn't name all the jumps and twists, but Will was giving Noah a jump-by-jump account.

"That's a fishtail," he said. "It'll snap your back in half if you're not careful."

Ellen didn't think Noah heard a word of Will's description. He was screaming encouragement at Matt and having far more fun than if he'd been riding the horse himself. Ellen wasn't having any fun at all. Her heart was in her throat.

"Can you imagine any man wanting to do that?" Isabelle asked.

"You wouldn't see me doing it," Sean said.

"You wouldn't have to," Will said. "The poor horse would take one look at your huge body and faint."

Ellen wished the paint had felt that way about Matt. He drove himself into the corral fence trying to crush Matt's leg against the poles, but Matt raised his leg above the saddle, then lowered it the moment the horse tried to break into a gallop. Stymied, the paint went back to bucking, spinning, and trying to reach back and bite Matt's leg. Matt didn't look the least bit nervous. Ellen hoped she was wrong, but she thought she saw a smile on his lips. Only a crazy man could smile about being on the back of a horse that wanted to kill him.

Ellen didn't see how Matt could stay in the saddle much longer. Flung about like a rag doll, his head snapped back and forth until she wondered why he didn't get so dizzy he'd let go and fall off.

"The paint's getting tired," Will announced. "He won't last much longer."

Ellen couldn't see any slowing in the speed or violence of the efforts the paint made to dislodge Matt.

"Matt will be disappointed," Cole said. He'd come over to join them. "He was counting on this horse to give him some real fun."

"Fun!" Ellen exclaimed. "How can you call that fun?"

"Matt likes riding wild horses," Will said. "He doesn't get much chance any more. He says even the wild ones are half tame."

Ellen couldn't understand why anyone would want to ride a wild horse, but watching Matt hang on with all the serene confidence of an expert did give her a different feeling about him. Whatever his shortcomings as husband material, lack of courage wasn't one of them. She'd always thought a man had to be a little bit nuts to face another man in a gunfight. She added bronco busting to her list of foolish things men did.

"Matt's been busting Jake's horses since he was thirteen," Will said. "Ain't nobody better. Jump down," he said to Noah. "I got to catch the paint. He's about done for."

Will crawled through the rails to join Cole. They walked toward the exhausted animal. Matt dismounted, a wide smile on his face.

"He wasn't as tough as I hoped, but it was fun as long as he could keep it up."

Cole clapped him on the shoulder. "One of these days we're going to have to go to Utah. I want to see what you can do with some of those mustangs."

"I've never been to Utah," Toby said. "Can I go?" He and Orin had piled into the corral behind the men.

"Stop worrying about places you've never seen and help Cole catch another horse."

Toby ran off to help Cole. Orin held the bridle of the exhausted paint, and Will stripped off the saddle. Matt walked toward them.

"You got off easy on that one," Jake said.

"I know," Matt said, smiling. "But I've got dozens more. I figure I ought to find one or two with more spunk."

"Are you going to break all those horses by yourself?" Ellen asked.

It was a stupid question. Even a woman knew a Texas cowboy broke his own broncos. He didn't have the right to call himself a man if he didn't.

"Just be careful," Isabelle said. "You'll be tired. There are a lot more of them than there are of you."

It was clear to Ellen that Isabelle was proud of Matt's skill as well as worried about him.

"I'll be fine," Matt said, a softness in his voice Ellen had never heard. "You worry too much."

"No woman could be the mother of this bunch and not get gray hairs."

"There's not a gray hair in your head," Jake said, appearing to search seriously. "Are you sure you aren't dying it?"

"If there are any gray hairs, you put the first one there."

"Will gave her at least a dozen," Matt said.

"I don't have any gray hair," Isabelle declared. "And

if you don't want to be boxed on the ears, you'll stop saying so. Cole's caught you another horse. Ellen and I are going to start dinner. If you're not more respectful, you won't get anything to eat."

She turned her back on the men, linked her arm with Ellen's, and started toward the house. Almost immediately her stern look vanished, to be replaced by silent laughter. "What do you think of your husband now?" she asked.

Chapter Seven

Ellen didn't know what to think of Matt. The man she'd seen today bore little resemblance to the man she thought she married. He smiled, even laughed, and talked to everybody. He asked Sean and Buck about their families. He asked Cole if he could take Noah to see Drew's horses. And though he didn't indulge in outward gestures of affection, he obviously adored Jake and Isabelle.

Ellen decided something terrible must have happened to Matt to make him distrustful of everybody outside his family. She doubted he would ever tell her about it. He treated her with thoughtful kindness but didn't show any inclination to take her into his confidence.

From the moment Will hoisted Noah on his shoulders, he'd become perfect in Noah's sight. He dogged him like a shadow, asked more questions than one human could answer in a week, and sat next to him at dinner. Tess thought the sun rose and set on Matt. When she wasn't talking about him, she was talking about Isabelle and the doll she'd given her.

Ellen's whole life had been swallowed up in Matt's.

All of which served to make Ellen feel more left out than ever. Jake and Isabelle had gone home after dinner. Sean, Buck, and Cole had departed a few hours later, leaving Will and Matt to finish up with the horses. They hadn't completed their work until dark. It was only logical that she fix supper. Matt had offered to help, but supper would have been at least an hour later if she'd waited for him. Will's antics kept everybody in a good mood, even Toby.

"You should have seen old Sawtooth trying to get rid of Matt." Will was telling them about the first wild horse Matt had ridden. "It drove him crazy he couldn't snake around and bite a hunk out of him. It just made him more determined to jump on him until he was dead."

Tess wiggled a little closer to Ellen.

"Did he really try to kill Matt?" Noah asked, completely enthralled and drinking in every word.

"Sure did," Will said. "Threw Matt twice. Tried to kill him both times, but the boys got ropes on him until Matt could mount up again."

"I wouldn't have gotten on him again," Orin said.

"I would," Toby said.

"He'd have killed you."

"He didn't kill Matt, did he?"

"You can't ride as good as Matt, either."

"I'm sure Toby can ride just as well as I could when I was his age," Matt said, heading off an argument. "I'm just glad we don't have any horses like Sawtooth in this bunch."

"I was kinda hoping we would," Will said. "I was looking forward to seeing Matt fly through the air, his butt facing the sky."

Everybody except Tess and Ellen laughed, Orin protesting that would never happen to Matt, Noah wondering if he'd land on his head or his bottom.

Matt pushed back his chair and rose. "We ought to go see how the horses are settling in." Toby and Orin jumped to their feet. "But first we've got to clean up." Both boys stopped in their tracks, their disappointment easy to see. "Ellen and the kids fixed supper," he said. "It's only fair that we clean up. You know the rules."

Neither boy argued. They started immediately to clear the table.

"You stay right where you are," Will said when Ellen started to get up. "No point in offering to do work somebody else is willing to do for you."

"Are you offering?" Ellen asked.

"I'm a guest." Will handed his plate to Orin and directed a dazzling smile at Ellen.

"I would have thought you'd been here enough times to lose your guest status."

"More than enough," Matt said.

"I sacrificed my time and endangered my body to help you with those savage animals," Will said with a wink at Ellen. "It's only right that I take my ease while you clean up."

Ellen couldn't help but smile. She imagined Will's looks and unabashed manner had gotten him out of a great deal of work in his twenty-six years. "Surely you'd help Matt out of brotherly love."

"I didn't ask him to go into debt to buy this huge

ranch or saddle himself with two brats. If he had any sense, he'd still be at the Broken Circle letting Isabelle fuss over him. She likes him better than the rest of us, you know. He broods. Women are a soft touch for a brooding man."

"I'm not a brat," Toby said. "Matt says he couldn't run this place without me."

"If he didn't have this place, he wouldn't need you."

"It's worth the debt and the brats to get away from you," Matt said. "He talks like this all the time. Now you understand why no one can stand him for long."

"He's just jealous because I know how to talk to pretty women while he stands around tongue-tied."

"Matt doesn't waste his time with girls," Orin said. "He says they're not worth it."

Will nearly choked himself laughing.

"Thank you, Orin," Matt said, "but I'm perfectly capable of putting a noose around my neck all by myself."

"That's what you said when Eugenia Applegate came sidling up to you acting like she got something in her eye and you the only one who could get it out," Orin said, obviously unsure why his remark had caused Will to laugh.

"But he saw the error of his ways when he met the fair Ellen," Will said, barely recovered from his mirth.

"No he didn't," Toby said. "He—"

Matt stuffed a dishcloth into Toby's mouth. "As soon as we finish cleaning up, you boys go outside and start digging a hole behind the corral. I'm going to need a place to bury my brother after I murder him."

Will, eyes dancing with enjoyment, jumped up out of his chair and crouched down behind Tess and Noah. "Save me," he cried. "I'm too young to die."

"A slow and painful death is long overdue," Matt said

without turning around from the dishes he was washing.

"You'll take my part, won't you, beautiful lady?"

"I think Tess is a little young," Ellen said.

"I'm talking about you."

"I'm not beautiful."

"Not the fairest of flowers could dull your beauty, nor the brightest of suns. You're—"

"She's probably sickened by your drivel," Matt said.

"Not sickened," Ellen assured Will, "but finding it difficult to take seriously."

"Don't tell me no man has sung the praises of your beauty," Will said, disbelieving. "Surely the men who frequented your place of business were lavish in their praises."

"The men who frequented the saloon were often too drunk to know what they were saying."

"Intoxicated by your beauty," Will said. He acted as though Toby's hoot of derision caused him great pain. "I would be satisfied with a single smile."

"Then why haven't you been in the saloon to get one?"

He looked hurt. "I can't tell. It's too embarrassing."

"I can't imagine anything embarrassing you."

"Watch it, Will," Matt said. "I think she's got you figured out."

"It's a weakness," Will said mournfully. "I can't drink, not even beer. One drink and I'm an idiot."

"A short journey," Toby muttered.

"Out," Matt said to the boys. "We're done." Matt grabbed his brother by the shoulder. "You're coming with us. I'm sure Ellen's had about all she can take."

"Your brother's charming," Ellen said, then felt herself blush. "A woman likes compliments."

Leigh Greenwood

"Isabelle likes them, too," Matt said, "but even she can stand only so much of Will's palaver."

"Defend me," Will pleaded. "Tell him ladies prefer sweet talk to tongue-tied silence."

"They certainly do," Ellen said.

"You're still coming with me," Matt said. "I've got a temperamental mare about to foal. She gets savage when labor starts. Let's see if a little of your sweet talk works on her."

Ellen had to laugh as Matt pushed his protesting brother through the door ahead of him. "I'll make him sleep in the barn if you want," Matt said.

"It's okay. I'm sure having to share the loft with Toby will calm him."

"Toby's a good kid. You've just got to give him a chance."

The door closed behind Matt and on Ellen's smiling good humor. She hadn't meant it as a criticism of Toby though she guessed Matt couldn't take it any other way.

"Why can't I go?" Noah asked. "I've never seen a horse have a baby."

"I don't think she's having it tonight," Ellen said. "Anyway, it's time to go to bed. We got up very early this morning."

"I'm not tired," Toby said.

"Well, I am, and I can't go to bed until you do. Now run along and get dressed."

"It's not fair," Noah said as he left the kitchen. "When I get big, I'm never going to bed."

"I'll be in in a minute," Ellen said to Tess. "I just have to make sure everything's finished."

She said that before she remembered Matt kept house better than she did. She couldn't understand why that should upset her. She didn't want to spend all her time keeping house. She intended to use it making hats.

She smiled, remembering some of Will's silliness. He was charming, but she couldn't help thinking of him as a boy. Still, she wished Matt had some of his brother's buoyant personality, his charm, his ability to enjoy life. She sympathized with Isabelle's desire to find Matt a wife who could teach him to smile, but she didn't want the job. She might have considered it if things had been different. He was so handsome it made her head spin, and he surely did not lack courage. She admired the way he had taken in two unwanted boys and made them feel like they belonged, but a woman didn't marry a man because he was great with kids and willing to do his half of the household chores. She married him because he made her feel like the most desirable, most beautiful, most wonderful woman in the world.

As far as she could see, Matt barely knew she was alive. She was shocked to discover that she cared. She tried to deny it, but it was too late.

She cared.

"You sure this is just a marriage of convenience?" Will asked his brother.

"What did you think it was?"

"Exactly that. I've never seen you do anything a woman could interpret as admiration."

"Then why did you ask?"

"Isabelle has got it into her head Ellen's the one to save you from yourself. I told her she was wrong, but you know Isabelle. She never gives up hope."

Matt heard the disgust in his brother's voice. Will couldn't understand why Matt still clammed up around women. "I know what Isabelle thinks, but we made a business arrangement. Considering the fact that we hardly knew each other, I couldn't have asked her to consider it on any other basis."

"Okay, but there's no reason it has to stay that way. She likes kids, and you like kids."

"And that's about all we have in common."

"You're a great cook."

Matt swore. "That's not a recommendation for a husband, at least not in Texas."

"I think she likes you. She watches you all the time."

"That's fear. She wants to keep an eye on me to make sure I don't do anything strange."

"Like what?"

"I don't know. Her employer tried to rape her, her customers couldn't keep their hands off her, and now she's stuck by herself on a ranch with a man she doesn't know."

"Surely she doesn't think you'd try to rape her."

"She doesn't trust any man."

"Hell, if she doesn't know she can trust you, she doesn't have any sense at all."

"Once your faith has been destroyed, it's hard to rebuild it."

Will stopped and faced his brother. "Will you ever get over what he did to you?"

"I don't know."

"You thought Ellen might be able to help?"

"We got married because of the children," Matt said. "If I hoped for anything else, it was just a dream."

"You've got to admit she's a pretty woman."

"Prettier than I thought. I'd never seen her without makeup before."

"A woman's got to wear war paint if she expects to make enough money in a saloon to support two kids."

Matt wondered if Ellen missed all the male attention she had gotten at the saloon. He'd found himself jealous of the way she laughed at Will's foolishness, the way she enjoyed his company.

"She loves those kids," Will said.

"Yeah. She was willing to marry me and live with Toby to keep them. There's nothing fake about that."

"I wouldn't give up without trying a little harder."

He'd have plenty of time for that, but how did you start when all the cards were stacked against you? Was Ellen the right woman for him? He didn't really know anything about her except that she was willing to marry a man she barely knew to keep Noah and Tess. Though that was a big plus in her favor, she'd given no indication she wanted to be married. Instead, she wanted to have her own hat shop in San Antonio, live in a rooming house, and probably have someone like Mrs. Ogden take care of Noah and Tess. It didn't sound like a good life for the kids. They'd be better off staying with him after she left.

She'd only been there a night and a day, but already he found it hard to think of the ranch without Ellen. "She doesn't want to be a rancher's wife," Matt said. "She wants me to set her up in her own hat shop in San Antonio."

"Does Isabelle know that?"

"No."

"She won't like it."

"This is something not even Isabelle can fix. Let's talk about something else. You sure you don't mind staying for a while to help with the horses?"

"Naw. I can always hope one of them will send you flying."

"You'll have to sleep in the loft with Toby and Orin."

"I don't care."

"And be shadowed by Noah."

Will chuckled.

"And don't start telling him any of your stories," Matt warned. "He's young enough to believe them."

"You take all the fun out of it."

"Being responsible for these kids is serious business."

"There's fun in everything, Matt, even children. If you don't stop letting the past control your life, you'll die without ever having had a good belly laugh."

Matt thought of what lay ahead and couldn't find any reason to laugh.

"I'm not a baby," Noah protested. "I'm big enough to sleep in the loft with Will."

"It's ridiculous to sleep on a blanket in the straw when you have a perfectly good bed," Ellen said.

"They sleep in a bedroll," Noah informed Ellen.

"You can't leave Tess by herself," Ellen argued.

"You can sleep with her."

At the sound of the front door opening, Noah ran from the bedroom. "Can I sleep in the loft with Will?" she heard him asking. "Please. I promise I won't do anything bad."

"Have you asked Ellen?" she heard Matt say.

"She says I'm too little, but I'm not, am I, Will?"

"Certainly not," Will replied. "I'm depending on you to protect me from the bogeyman."

"There ain't no bogeyman," Noah said.

"There sure is," Will insisted. "I've seen him lots of times. Big old fella, ugly and mean. Drools a lot and has arms like a bull."

Ellen got to her feet. She had enjoyed most of Will's

foolishness, but she couldn't have him filling Noah's head with the bogeyman.

"Stop talking nonsense," she said as she came into the hallway.

"It's not nonsense," Will assured her, giving what she could only suppose was his version of how a bogeyman would stalk its victim. "Big old hairy thing. Gave me nightmares for weeks."

Noah looked like he was caught between believing and not believing. "Will says he wants me to sleep with him in the loft," he said to Matt. "Can I, please?"

"That's up to Ellen," Matt said.

Noah turned to her. "I am *not* too little."

"I also said you couldn't leave Tess in a room by herself."

"You don't mind, do you?" Noah asked his sister.

Tess shook her head, but Tess would say anything her brother wanted.

"If Ellen lets you sleep with us tonight, do you promise not to plague her about it tomorrow?" Will asked.

"I promise," Noah assured Ellen.

"What do you think?" she asked Matt.

"I don't think Tess wants to be left alone," he said, "but it won't hurt for him to do it one night. But you've got to remember, Noah, this is a treat. You've promised you won't plague Ellen to let you do it again. If you do, you'll have to do Tess's chores for the day."

Ellen wasn't sure Noah was old enough to understand the responsibility of sticking to a promise. He was a little boy who saw only what he wanted.

"Do you promise no fussing and complaining tomorrow?" Matt asked Noah again.

"I promise," Noah said, so excited Ellen knew he would have agreed to anything.

"Go with Will to get a bedroll," Matt said. "There's an extra one in the barn."

Noah grabbed hold of Will's hand and practically pulled him out the door.

"You know he'll forget all about his promise by tomorrow," she said, irritated that Matt had given in, and even more irritated at herself for asking his opinion.

"He needs to learn there are consequences to his actions," Matt said. "This is a better way than punishing him for letting chickens out of their pen."

"He's only five."

"That's old enough."

Ellen noticed Matt's gaze shift. She turned to see Tess still standing in the bedroom doorway, her doll clutched in her arms.

"Let's get you in bed." Ellen said as she moved toward the little girl.

"Will you tell me another story?" Tess asked Matt as Ellen led her into the bedroom.

"Sure," Matt said.

"About a birthday party."

"If that's what you want."

Tess made room for Matt to sit down beside her. "Mrs. Ogden wants to hear a story, too."

"You named your doll Mrs. Ogden?" Ellen asked, surprised.

Tess hugged her doll against her chest. "Mrs. Ogden said I didn't have to be afraid of the dark. She would let me sleep with her until you got home."

Ellen felt a rush of guilt that she hadn't been there to comfort Tess. She felt even more guilty that she hadn't known the child needed comforting.

"You won't be alone anymore," Matt said. "Ellen and I will be here."

"Always?"

"You won't want us to be here always," Matt said, settling down next to her. "One of these days, when you're a grown woman, you'll meet a nice man, get married, and want to start your own family."

"Like you and Ellen?"

"You can even adopt boys and girls if you like."

Ellen didn't know how he managed to reassure Tess without making promises he couldn't keep.

"I don't want to go away ever again." Tess threw her arms around Matt and hugged him.

If the light from the single lantern hadn't been so weak, Ellen would have sworn Matt looked terrified. He took Tess's arms from around him and placed them around the doll she'd dropped.

"Crawl down under the covers and I'll tell you a story."

Tess snuggled beneath the blankets. The sheer adoration in her eyes as she looked up at Matt was like a knife in Ellen's heart. Tess'd never forgive Ellen for taking her away from Matt.

Ellen settled on Noah's bed while she listened to Matt's story. Who would ever have expected a man who could break two dozen wild horses in one day to come up with a story that would enchant a three-year-old girl?

"Jessica lined up her old dolls. *We're going to have a party,* she said. *I have a new dolly named Mrs. Ogden.*"

"That's my dolly's name," Tess said.

"Jessica thought it was a very good name," Matt said.

Ellen didn't know what he'd done to earn Toby and Orin's devotion, but she was certain it wasn't bedtime stories. There had to be something more, something inside him that the children sensed. She remembered how upset Orin had been when Wilbur Sears threatened to take him away. All Matt did was put his hand on his shoulder and the boy calmed down. All Tess needed was a story. Or was it the sound of his voice?

But even though it was a nice voice—warm and resonant—there had to be more than that. Even Noah responded to him, and Noah never responded to anyone without threats of punishment. She heard Noah and Will come in the front door. They went straight to the stairs and climbed to the loft, Noah chattering excitedly the whole time. Enthralled by Matt's story, Tess didn't appear to have heard her brother.

"All the other dolls liked Mrs. Ogden," Matt was saying. "She promised to help Jessica take good care of all of them."

That's it! He made the children feel that no matter what happened, he would take care of them. They were safe. Nothing could hurt them as long as Matt was here. She knew that wasn't characteristic of a weak or indecisive man. He might be unlike any other Texas cowboy she'd ever met, but he had a strength that had deep roots, roots so strong and unmistakable that Tess felt it almost immediately.

"Jessica put all the dolls in their beds," Matt said, "but she let Mrs. Ogden sleep in her bed. *I'll never be afraid again as long as I have you,* Jessica said to Mrs. Ogden, and they went to sleep holding each other very tight."

Matt tucked the covers around Tess. Her big brown eyes followed his every move. Ellen stood, leaned over, and kissed Tess on the forehead.

"Sleep tight," she said. "I'll be in the next room. If you need anything, just call."

They hadn't gotten to the door when a small, quavering voice said, "I'm scared."

Not surprised, Ellen moved back toward Tess. Matt shouldn't have let Noah sleep in the loft. He should have known any three-year-old child would be afraid to sleep alone in a strange house.

"I guess I'll have to sleep in here with her," Ellen said, looking over her shoulder at Matt.

"I want Matt," Tess said.

"What?" Ellen asked, turning back to Tess.

"I want Matt to stay with me."

Chapter Eight

Matt didn't appear as surprised as Ellen felt. Tess was her child; she ought to want her to stay.

"Don't you want Ellen to stay with you?" Matt asked. "She's—"

"I want you."

There could be no doubt of Tess's decision. Ellen longed to ask why, but she didn't wish to upset the frightened child. "I'm not sure Matt knows how to take care of little girls."

"I don't mind," Tess said.

She looked at Ellen, but her gaze returned almost immediately to Matt.

"Then it's Matt you will have," Ellen said as cheerfully as she could. "Go change," she said to Matt. "I'll stay here."

After Matt had left the room Ellen sat down next to Tess. "You like Matt a lot, don't you?"

Tess nodded her head.

"He's a very nice man," Ellen said.

"Can we live here always?" Tess asked.

"We'll stay here a while," Ellen said. "But one day we'll go to San Antonio. It's a big city with lots of people. You'll soon have lots of friends to play with."

"I don't want to go to 'tonio," Tess said. "I want to stay here."

"Noah and I wouldn't want to leave you."

"You and Noah can stay here, too. Matt will let you."

"We'll have to talk to him about that," Ellen said, "but now it's time to go to sleep. I don't want you to keep Matt awake asking questions. He has a lot of work to do tomorrow, so he needs his sleep. You do, too. We have to take care of the chickens and milk the cow."

"I like cows," Tess said.

Ellen didn't particularly care for cows, but she actively disliked chickens. They were noisy, ungrateful creatures ready to peck you or fly away when you wanted to catch them.

Matt reentered the room wearing a nightshirt that came to his ankles.

Tess sat up in the bed, looked at Ellen, and pointed to Matt. "He's wearing a nightgown just like you."

"That's a nightshirt," Ellen said, trying to smother a smile. "It's what men wear when they go to bed. Noah wears one."

"I didn't know big men wore clothes like Noah," Tess said.

"Big men wear all kinds of funny clothes," Matt said,

coming around to Noah's bed. "You'll have to ask Will what he wears."

"Is it funny?" Tess asked.

"You'll have to wait until tomorrow to find out," Matt said as he got into Noah's bed. "Now let Ellen tuck you in."

Tess appeared disappointed there wasn't going to be any excitement about having Matt share her bedroom, that they would just go to sleep.

"Sleep tight," Ellen said again, "and don't be afraid. Matt is right next to you."

"I know."

Ellen kissed Tess's forehead again. It was time to take the lamp and go to bed. There was nothing else she could do, but she didn't want to leave. She'd failed where Matt had succeeded, and she didn't like that. "If you want me, I'll be right next door," Ellen said.

"I know," Tess said.

When she entered her bedroom a feeling of isolation descended upon her. She told herself not to be foolish. She didn't need to share a bed or a bedroom with anyone. She should be relieved to have a room to herself. She had wanted that from the beginning.

As she set the lamp down and began to undress, she realized she didn't feel that way any longer. She wanted to feel part of this unusual family. They were six people from different backgrounds and families, different ages and sexes, yet somehow a feeling of belonging had grown up among them in less than two days, something so strong not even Toby's bad humor could spoil it.

Tess and Noah have reached out, but you've held back.

She hadn't wanted the children to become part of Matt's family because it would hurt them more when they left. But it came as something of a shock when she realized she'd been happier since she married Matt. She didn't have to worry about her job. She had help in caring for the kids, in finding a solution that would protect them from Wilbur and Mabel. She'd come to depend on Matt and, unbeknownst to herself, to like doing it.

Which is why she didn't like feeling left out. It made her feel vulnerable again.

She hung her dress in the wardrobe, untied the knots on her chemise and let it pool around her feet. It had been a busy day. She felt pleasantly tired, but not drained as she usually felt after working in the saloon. She owed that to Matt. She owed Tess's calm to Matt. She owed Noah's not being in trouble to Matt. If she were perfectly honest with herself, she didn't want things to change. She liked him well enough. Given a little time she might even . . .

She reined in her wandering thoughts and put her clothes away. She wasn't being sensible. Matt didn't love her, and he wasn't looking for a real wife. What's more, she wasn't looking for a husband, even one like Matt. Instead of protecting her, all the men in her life had tried to take advantage of her. She wanted to be free of men, free to mold her life to fit what she wanted, her safety.

She unfolded her nightgown and pulled it over her head. She would feel safe once she was settled in San Antonio and had her business. Her hats would be successful. She would have her own house, hire someone like Mrs. Ogden to take care of the children, hire someone to help in the shop. She would have everything exactly as *she* wanted.

Ellen blew out the lamp and climbed into bed.

But the moment her head hit the pillow and she closed her eyes, they flew open again. Was Matt Haskins trying to win the children's affections, make them so dependent on him that they wouldn't want to leave the ranch?

She told herself not to be foolish. Matt had enough to worry about with Toby and Orin. He wouldn't want two small children. He'd probably be relieved when she left. But she couldn't ignore the small, disturbing kernel of doubt. Noah already turned to Matt for everything. Even Tess preferred Matt to her. What would she do if the children refused to leave the ranch with her?

Stay.

That single word kept her awake far into the night.

Matt couldn't sleep. He knew Tess's choosing him to stay with her had upset Ellen. He supposed he would have felt the same way if things had been reversed, but he was actually a little bit relieved. He didn't think Ellen should take the children to San Antonio when she opened her hat shop. She'd soon become so caught up in her business that she wouldn't have time for anything else. It wouldn't be that she didn't want to spend time with the children, simply that the business would have to come first. It couldn't be any other way. She couldn't support herself and the children if it didn't do well, and running any business took a lot of time, especially when you had to make the product you sold.

He didn't know how he would manage to take care of two small children, but he knew if Noah went to San Antonio, he'd soon be in more trouble than he'd been in Bandera. He needed space to run and something constructive to occupy his mind and absorb his energy. A horse was a good start. Matt might even consider letting him have a dog.

He wasn't sure about Tess, but the quickness with which she'd begun to look to him when she felt threatened made him think she'd want to stay, especially if Noah stayed. That would create a difficult situation that could best be avoided by Ellen staying as well.

Matt wasn't as sure how he felt about that. Setting aside his own interests for the moment—and that wasn't easy to do—he had mixed feelings. Ellen said she wasn't interested in getting married, having a large family, or living on a ranch. She also kept saying she didn't intend to take over running the house, but that's exactly what she'd done in the last two days. It was too soon to tell for sure, but Matt had a feeling Ellen was beginning to like where she found herself.

But where did that leave him?

More attracted to her than ever. He loved the thick, glossy hair that fell in dusky curls to her shoulders. He loved the almond color of her skin, the dark rouge that tinged her cheeks when she was angry . . . or embarrassed. He loved her dark eyes and thick brows. He had never cared much for his own fairness. It seemed weak and colorless to him. Ellen seemed vivid and vibrant. She had made certain her body was well covered since she'd been at the ranch, but no dress could conceal the mound of her breasts or the tempting swell of her hips.

Matt turned over in the bed. His body had begun to swell. If he didn't think of something else, he'd soon be miserable. Besides, he had no business letting himself think of Ellen or the possibility that she might want to stay at the ranch. All he had to offer her was lust— lust he wasn't even sure he could act upon. Regardless, though, lust wasn't the basis for the kind of marriage he wanted. He was certain she felt the same way.

But it wasn't that simple. Having allowed the idea to become planted in his mind, he couldn't get rid of it. Despite the problems he would face, he liked the idea of being married to Ellen. Maybe things wouldn't be so difficult if he—

He kept forgetting what he'd done so long ago. There was no way around that.

"I don't understand why we have to go to church," Toby complained to Matt. "We never did before."

"It's never too late to start," Matt said.

"We wouldn't have to go if it wasn't for *them!*"

Matt didn't have to look to know who Toby meant. All week long he'd blamed everything he didn't like on Ellen and the kids. "I'm sure it would have been a condition for my adopting Orin."

"You're not going to adopt me," Toby said. "Why do I have to go?"

"Because everybody has to believe we're a family before they'll let us adopt Orin and the kids," Matt said. "You know that. There's no point in going over it again."

"I don't want to go, either," Orin said.

Matt knew Orin's objection had nothing to do with church. He was certain Reverend Sears would somehow find a way to snatch him away from Matt.

"Going to church once in a while won't hurt you," Will said. "Though I can't say I'm anxious to hear that Sears fella. Jake says he's got the town by the tail. That isn't really what he said, ma'am," Will said, directing his last remark to Ellen, "but I thought what Jake really said might be a little strong for the children."

"Then why did you bring it up?" Matt asked.

"Just making conversation," Will said. "Besides, she ought to be prepared."

"I'm quite prepared for anything the Reverend Wilbur Sears can say," Ellen said. "I doubt he'll have time to get around to you, Orin. He'll be too busy concentrating on me."

Will, Orin, and Toby had ridden into town. Matt, Ellen, and the kids had taken the buggy over the loud objections of Noah, who, even though he didn't yet have a horse, had insisted he could ride anything with hair on it.

Ellen and Tess had said hardly a word, Tess because she couldn't get a word in edgewise, Ellen because . . . well, he wasn't sure why. She'd hurried through preparing food, eating, and cleaning up after breakfast, but she hadn't said a word. Matt had the uneasy feeling she felt uncomfortable about appearing in town as his wife. As long as they stayed on the ranch, she could pretend their marriage wasn't real.

"I don't like Mr. Sears," Noah said.

"Nobody likes Sears," Will said.

"Then why are we going to hear him?" Toby asked.

"Because this is one of the ways Ellen and I can convince everybody we'll bring you up properly," Matt said.

"There's nothing wrong with the way I've been brought up," Toby argued.

"There's not a mother in Bandera with an unmarried daughter who'll agree with that," Will said.

Toby grinned broadly. Will couldn't have said anything that would have pleased him more.

They reached the outskirts of Bandera without attracting attention, but Matt knew that would change. Isabelle said people had been talking about them since their surprise marriage. Matt feared very few people would be wishing them well.

"Remember to tie your horses under the trees behind the church," Matt said. "We'll be here for a long time."

"What are we going to do after church?" Toby asked.

"Have dinner at the hotel," Matt said.

"Can I go to the mercantile?" Toby asked. "If we're going to be going to church all the time, I'll need some new clothes."

"We can all go shopping," Matt said. "Together." He had no intention of letting Toby loose just yet.

"You don't have to take everybody to the hotel because of me," Ellen said. "The kids and I want to go see Mrs. Ogden."

"You can spend as much time as you want with her," Matt said, "but we need to eat together."

Matt didn't know whether Ellen wanted to get away from him or away from the stares of the people they passed.

"It looks like Wilbur has been busy," Ellen said.

"I expected he would be," Matt said. "Keep smiling, and I'll keep driving. I don't want anybody to suspect we're aware there's anything wrong."

"How can we not be?" Ellen demanded. "That was Mrs. Armstrong. She glared at me like I'd committed a crime by marrying you."

"People think what they want to think. There's not much we can do except go about our business."

"How can you just sit there like nothing's wrong?"

"Nothing is wrong with us. It's them."

He couldn't tell Ellen that he'd thought so little of himself all his life that nothing anybody else thought had the power to bother him.

"I think they're jealous," Will said. "You're a damned

fine-looking woman, Ellen. Even though he is my brother, I have to admit Matt's a corker. They're just jealous they aren't as young and good-looking."

"Or that you have such a handsome cowhand," Toby added.

"I think all four of you children are mighty handsome," Matt said.

"I'm no child," Toby insisted.

"Okay," Matt said, "all three of the children are mighty handsome."

"And . . ." Toby said.

"And what?"

"What about how handsome I am?" he demanded, exasperated.

"I guess you're handsome," Will said, "but we're not little girls. We can't tell for sure."

Matt was glad to see Ellen smile. She was letting the tension get to her. They had to look happy and relaxed or no one would believe they were a real family.

"I want to go home," Orin said.

"Nothing's going to happen," Matt said. They'd reached the church, passing by more people who showed their disapproval. They had a few moments of peace while they tethered the horses under the trees and tied on their nose bags, but it only took a few minutes to climb down from the buggy, smooth out wrinkles, and be ready to go into the church. "Remember to smile at everyone you see," Matt said. "No matter what they do or say"—Matt directed his gaze to Toby—"you're not to respond."

"I can't just let anybody insult me," Toby said. "I gotta—"

"Do nothing," Matt said. "We're counting on you to act like the mature young man you say you are."

Toby didn't find that easy to swallow, but Matt knew his only chance to keep Toby in line was to appeal to his pride. The boy had a volatile temper, but he would do just about anything if he thought it would make him look grown-up.

"Young girls aren't swayed by insults or slurs," Ellen said. "But they are influenced by how a man acts, especially under pressure. It lets them know whether he's a man or just pretending."

"I ain't pretending," Toby protested. "I'm more of a man than any of these fake cowboys around here."

Matt hadn't expected Ellen to support him. He smiled at her. "Are we ready?"

Tess held tightly to Ellen's hand. Noah sidled a little closer to Will, and Orin got as close to Matt as he could. Squaring his shoulders, Toby looked like the proud young peacock he was. Matt held out his hand to Ellen. "Let's go."

Ellen dreaded what lay ahead. She didn't imagine that her having married Matt would change the way the women felt about her. They might be glad she had married and moved out of town, but they wouldn't be pleased to find her in their midst pretending to be a respectable married woman like them. It would take years to convince most of them that she had put her saloon days behind her. Some of them would never let her forget her origins.

"Don't drag your feet, Tess. Your shoes will be covered with dust."

She wanted Tess to look perfect. Any fault, no matter how small, would be sought out, magnified, and remembered when it came time to adopt the kids.

"There's Isabelle," Will said. "She's bringing some of the family to give you moral support."

But before Isabelle could reach them, the woman who'd been Orin's foster mother came marching up, her face stormy. Her expression changed to sugary sweetness when she directed her gaze to Orin.

"My husband and I have been so worried about you," she said. "Our children have asked about you every day. They can't wait until you come back to us."

"I'm never going back to you!" Orin shouted. "You hate me. You said I was a worthless nuisance."

Ermajean McCutchen's sugary expression slipped for a moment but slid right back into place. "I'm sure if I ever said such a thing, it must have been about one of my boys. They do stretch my patience from time to time."

Orin looked poised to run, but Matt's hand on his shoulder steadied him.

"Orin won't be going anywhere," Matt said, his voice betraying none of the anger Ellen was certain he felt. "My wife and I are going to adopt him."

Ermajean's smile vanished in the blink of an eye. She turned on Ellen, her eyes snapping with anger. "Reverend Sears will have something to say about that. You're not fit to have charge of decent kids, even kids who ain't got a father."

"You'd better go sit in the shade, Ermajean," Isabelle said, coming up behind her. "You look like you're about to faint from the heat." She stepped neatly between Ellen and Ermajean. "I don't think you've met my daughter," she said to Ellen. "This is Eden. She's a nice child except for being spoiled to death by men falling all over themselves to give her anything she wants."

"Mother, will you stop trying to prejudice everybody against me?" Eden said, her laugh and smile both charming. "You'll have her thinking I'm terrible."

Ellen doubted anyone could think badly about this lovely teenager.

"The others will be along in a minute," Isabelle said. "Let's go in before all the seats are taken. I don't want us scattered all over the church."

They left Ermajean standing alone with her mouth hanging open.

With a skill Ellen imagined Isabelle had honed on her own brood of twelve, she shepherded them into the church. "I asked Ward and Marina to save us some pews.

"The others will have to fend for themselves," she said as sixteen people filled two pews to capacity.

"Who's coming?" Will asked.

"Everybody except Chet," Isabelle said. "He and Melody have gone to visit Melody's brothers to show off their little boy."

Ellen was thankful for Isabelle's support. It was nice to have Matt to lean on, but Isabelle understood what it was like to be a woman in a situation like this. Matt would have brazened it out alone. Isabelle had rallied the family for support.

"I'm Marina Dillon," the lovely woman in the pew in front of them said, introducing herself. "This is my husband, Ward, and these are our four boys. I'm glad to welcome you into the family."

Ellen was familiar with Dr. Dillon, but she hadn't known he was part of the Maxwell family. He and his wife looked as old as Jake and Isabelle.

"We found Ward and Drew together," Matt explained. "Drew's parents had been killed by Indians and Ward wounded. Jake and Isabelle sort of adopted him along with all the rest of us."

Ellen didn't have time to organize her thoughts before she was distracted by Sean entering the church, followed by three redheaded boys who were obviously his sons. A beautiful, stately blond woman walked at his side, followed by an attractive teenage girl who smiled brightly at Toby.

"That's Pearl with Sean," Matt whispered. "You'll meet her later."

They were followed almost immediately by a couple Ellen recognized as Buck Maxwell and his wife. "Drew won't be coming," Buck whispered to Isabelle. "Celeste has a bad cold, and Drew has the sniffles. Cole won't let either of them out of the house."

"I'm Hannah Maxwell," the blond woman at his side said with a welcoming smile. "I hope you'll bring the children over when you get more settled. Sean has a son Noah's age and Drew has a girl Tess's age." She laughed softly. "Among the five of us, we have a boy or girl of just about every age between one and twenty-one. Your children won't ever be short of cousins."

They moved away to find a pew three rows in front of where Matt and Ellen sat, but the warmth of Hannah's greeting remained. There could be no mistake about the cordon of protection the Maxwell family had thrown around her. For the first time in her life she felt completely safe. It was an intoxicating feeling, one she liked very much. It helped her remain calm when Mabel Jackson swept into the church followed by her husband and two children. Mabel entered a private pew at the front of the church. Before she sat down, Mabel turned around and surveyed the congregation with a jaundiced eye. It was clear she didn't like what she saw. The presence of so many Maxwells was not lost on her, nor the fact that most of the congregation seemed excited to have them present. Mabel took her seat with a decidedly sour look on her face.

Ellen faced Wilbur Sears coming into the church without the knots that usually developed in her stomach. The Maxwell family formed a barrier that helped to shield her from the frowns he threw her way, the frowns that grew increasingly dark. Her feeling of security lasted until he stood up to begin his sermon.

"I had intended to talk to you today on the Beatitudes. But I've changed my mind. I will speak about Mary Magdalene."

Chapter Nine

"That man had a lot of nerve preaching a sermon like that," Isabelle fumed as they headed toward the hotel. "Some people will think he was speaking of you," she said to Ellen.

"Everybody knows he was talking about me," Ellen said.

"It doesn't make any difference what he says," Matt said. "It's not true."

"Ignore the man," Jake said. "He's a fool."

Isabelle exchanged a look with Ellen that said men just didn't understand.

"Threaten their property or their family and they'll kill you," Isabelle said in a quiet voice to Ellen. "Slander their reputation and you can't get their attention."

"I'm hungry," Noah said. "Are we really going to eat at the hotel?"

"Jake reserved the four largest tables," Isabelle assured him. "If Drew's family had come, there'd have been thirty-four of us."

"Did you count the girls they adopted?" Matt asked.

"Of course. They're just as much a part of the family as their two girls."

Ellen decided if this family kept up its penchant for adoption, she'd soon be related to half the people in— she caught herself. She had to stop thinking of herself as part of this family. Her marriage was temporary.

Getting everybody into the hotel and seated required the effort of several generals. Fortunately the Maxwell women proved more than capable of handling the situation. Within short order the children were seated together so they could get to know each other, but with adults close enough to make sure they didn't get rowdy.

Ellen was delighted to see Sean's daughter, Elise, and Isabelle's daughter, Eden, take Tess under their wings. Along with Buck's daughter, Nita, they laughed and whispered as though they'd been friends forever, forming a tight female enclave against their more numerous male cousins. Ellen's eyes watered and her heart swelled with thankfulness. Tess was already holding hands with Nita, looking from Elise to Eden with pure adoration in her eyes.

The boys weren't quite so well behaved. Toby and Ward's older boy ogled any girls who came into the hotel. Noah and Sean's two older sons had their heads together giggling within minutes. Buck's son, Ward's three youngest boys, and Orin sat together in a group, too young to be interested in girls but too old to be giggling. Ellen imagined they were doing a little bragging about how fine a cowboy they'd be when they grew up. Ellen had never seen Noah look so happy. She couldn't understand why Wilbur would want to tear him away from such a family.

"We should have brought food for a picnic," Isabelle said. "This crowd is almost too much for the hotel."

Ellen was relieved to notice that the townspeople seemed to see her in a new light. The women who came into the dining room continued to whisper when they saw her, but their looks had changed from condemning to noncommittal, even friendly. The men, most of whom had always had a kind word for Ellen, appeared welcoming.

Mabel Jackson was the only person who expressed outright annoyance that Ellen was in the dining room. Some heated words and pointed glances seemed to imply that the Haskinses occupied a table she considered her own. She led her family to an area as far away from Matt and Ellen as possible.

"What are you going to order?" Matt asked Ellen.

"I'll have the special. What about the children?"

"We ordered the special for all the kids," Matt said. "I hope they have enough."

"My boys will eat anything that's put in front of them," Ward's wife said.

"Sean's eat all the time," Isabelle said. "They're trying to be as big as their father."

Ellen worried Noah would misbehave, but the only one to cause any real worry was Toby, who kept ogling Mabel Jackson's daughter. It was obvious Tammy Jackson was as interested in Toby as he was in her.

It was just as obvious Mabel was furious. She spoke to her daughter repeatedly, but the girl kept glancing over at Toby and smiling. Once she winked. Ellen doubted Mabel saw it, but she was certain Toby did. He positively beamed, which caused Mabel to have a heated discussion with her husband. Moments later he heaved himself out of his chair and headed toward Toby.

Matt was immediately on his feet.

"Mabel is a fool," Isabelle said. "If she'd just ignore this, the children would soon forget each other."

Ellen felt herself tense as Matt approached Tom Jackson.

"It's good to see you, Tom," Matt said. "I hope you and your family are well."

Tom Jackson looked uneasy, but he also looked determined. "We'd be a lot better if that cowhand of yours didn't keep leering at my daughter."

"If you don't want people staring at your daughter, you'd better keep her at home," Matt said, smiling and genial. "Boys will always stare at girls, especially when they're as pretty as Tammy."

Everyone knew Tammy Jackson was the apple of her father's eye. Praise his daughter and he was your friend for life. He looked uncomfortable now, caught between the desire to enjoy Matt's compliment and the need to avoid his wife's anger.

"I know it's a temptation, but he's got to stop. It's upsetting Mabel."

"Wouldn't she be more upset if boys didn't look at Tammy?"

"He's a fatherless cowhand," Jackson said. "He's got no business staring at Tammy."

"So you're going to tell all the cowhands within fifty miles they can't look at your daughter when they come to town? Jake and Sean would like to know how you manage that. They've had cowhands staring at their daughters for years."

Tammy Jackson was a very pretty girl, but not even

a besotted father could believe she was prettier than Elise. As far as Ellen was concerned, she wasn't as pretty as Eden, either.

Tom Jackson was looking very uncomfortable. Nearly everyone in the dining room was doing their best to hear what he said. He had to know it would be repeated over and over before this day was out. He also had to know that except for Matt, not a single male in the Maxwell clan had a smile on his face. To make a scene over something as trivial as this would not only be ill-advised, it would be stupid.

"Young girls are always attracted to boys they consider exciting and a little bit dangerous," Matt said. "It's even more exciting if their parents disapprove, but they grow out of it in a few years."

Matt had given him a way out. Ellen prayed he'd take it.

"We're thinking of sending Tammy to school in San Antonio," Tom said. "Her mother thinks it's time for her to meet more people."

It was well known that both Eden and Elise attended a fashionable girl's school in Denver.

"I think that's a good idea," Matt said. "I see your dinner has arrived. You'd better go eat before it gets cold."

Tom Jackson hesitated, but the glances directed at him from all corners of the room appeared to convince him to leave well enough alone. He might own the local bank, but he wouldn't endear himself to his clients by making a fool of himself.

"Good to see you," Tom said. "I hear your ranch is doing well."

"We just got a new herd, so we're really busy."

Tom went back to his table. Ellen forced herself to

look at Toby instead of Mabel. Matt spoke to him briefly before returning to the table.

"I thought you handled that very well," Isabelle told Matt.

"His wife made him come over here," Jake said. "Tom would never say anything like that on his own."

Ellen thought Matt had handled it brilliantly, but before she got a chance to tell him so, Wilbur Sears entered the dining room and paused to survey the diners. He smiled when he saw Mabel Jackson. That smile vanished when his gaze settled on Ellen.

"Don't respond to anything he says," Matt said softly to everyone at their table as Wilbur headed in their direction. "Let me handle this."

"That man would be smart to let things go," Jake said.

"He thinks God has sent him to Bandera to save us from ourselves," Isabelle said. "He can't let things go without abandoning his mission."

"You," Wilbur intoned loudly enough for everyone in the hotel dining room to hear, "have desecrated the sanctity of God's house."

"I made all the boys take baths before we came," Matt said. "If you noticed a bad smell, I can assure you it didn't come from us."

A snicker from close by sounded loud in the silence that followed.

"It is not the smell from unclean bodies that defiled God's house," Wilbur said. "It is your false marriage, the violation of a holy sacrament. You might as well have entered the church with your concubine."

Matt stood. Ellen's hand reached out to pull him back down. Shocked at her reaction, she clasped both hands tightly in her lap.

"It's a good thing you said *might,*" Matt enunciated clearly. "Otherwise I *might* feel compelled to knock the words back down your throat."

Wilbur puffed up bigger than ever, but he took a step back. "You cannot threaten a man of God!"

"According to the Bible, we're all men of God," Matt said, "obliged to follow his commandments, one of which is never to bear false witness. Another is 'Thou shalt not covet.' "

"Don't quote the Bible to me!" Wilbur thundered.

"I thought you might have missed that part."

Ellen couldn't understand what Matt was trying to do. He might get the better of Wilbur through the law, but attacking him on his own ground was crazy.

"You're the spawn of Satan!"

Matt actually smiled. "I don't think I'm that bad, but if I am, I've come to church to ask forgiveness."

"You'll never get that child! I'll see that he's ripped from your clutches and delivered into a Christian home."

"I think Matt's home is about as Christian as you're going to find around here," Jake said, obviously unable to remain quiet any longer. "What's more, you're in no position to judge."

"You're not done with me," Wilbur said to Matt.

"I was afraid you'd feel that way."

"I'll see that you don't keep Orin or those two fatherless children. I'll see that Toby is run out of Bandera."

"Go away, Wilbur," Matt said, sounding tired. "You're making a fool of yourself. Ellen and I are going to adopt these children and there's nothing you can do about it. Now, if you've come here to eat, sit down and do so. You're disturbing everybody's digestion."

"God will punish you! And I will be his instrument."

"You're taking on a lot of people," Jake pointed out.

Wilbur positively swelled with righteousness. "I have God behind me, and He's more powerful than anybody, even the Maxwells."

"What a blowhard," Jake said as Wilbur threaded his way out of the dining room.

"He hates not getting his way," Matt said.

"He's a fool," Isabelle said, "but he's a dangerous one. He's got a lot of people listening to him."

"Well, I'm not one of them," Matt said. "Here comes our dinner. Let's eat and forget Wilbur Sears."

Everybody else seemed to be happy to do just that, but Ellen couldn't. She'd seen the fury that burned in Wilbur's eyes. She knew he would do everything in his power to prevent her from adopting Noah and Tess. The only way she might stop him was to remain married to Matt. An option that seemed more acceptable with each passing day.

"Do the kids like living on a ranch?" Mrs. Ogden asked.

"Noah loves it," Ellen said. "He idolizes Matt and his brother. He'll do things for them he never did for me."

"Boys need a man around," Mrs. Ogden said. "They don't much like a woman telling them what to do, even when they're little."

Ellen had come to visit her old landlady while Matt and the children visited with their newfound relations. Isabelle had taken Tess. Ellen expected the child would come home with several new dresses. Noah had come right out and asked Matt for a saddle. Jake had said he could have any one he wanted. Ellen had promised to rejoin Matt and the kids when it was time to go back to the ranch.

"What about my little darling?" Mrs. Ogden asked.

"Tess worships Matt. He tells her bedtime stories every night."

"Does she like his stories?"

"She loves them." Ellen smiled at the memory. "I don't know where he gets them."

"Who would have thought a man could do something like that?"

"Not me. I'm afraid I misjudged my husband badly." The sound of her words shocked her. She'd never called Matt her husband. She wondered what could have changed.

"People here in Texas expect something different from a man," Mrs. Ogden said. "They want him to be big, loud, and forceful, a lot like that Wilbur Sears. My Mr. Ogden was a quiet man. He didn't like fuss. Many's the time he said to me, 'Martha, I don't think we ought to go to this place or do that. It'll just be a lot of fuss and bother.' He was a quiet man, but he was solid."

Unshed tears made Mrs. Ogden's eyes shine. Her husband, a Texas ranger, had been killed by Comanches. The awkward moment ended when Tulip burst into the room.

"I knew you was in town, but I wasn't going to show up in church." She let out a whoop of merriment. "Wouldn't that have given old Wilbur something to shout about?"

"You should have come to the hotel," Ellen said. "Matt treated us to a nice dinner."

"I didn't want to go bustin' in when you was with all your fancy relatives."

"They're very nice." Ellen was glad to see Tulip, even though they'd never really been friends. "They came to support me in my first appearance in town."

Without waiting for Mrs. Ogden to invite her, Tulip dropped down on the sofa next to Ellen. "Tell me everything about that gorgeous man you married. If he hasn't made your eyes cross with ecstasy, you're not trying hard enough."

Ellen could have kicked herself for blushing. She had nothing to be ashamed of, no confidence she needed to share with Tulip, yet she felt some answer was required.

"That is not a suitable question to ask a young bride," Mrs. Ogden said.

"It is when she's married to a man who looks like Matt Haskins."

"It's all right, Mrs. Ogden. Tulip knows our marriage is a business arrangement. She's just teasing me."

"Lord, girl, I can't believe you haven't let that man come nigh you after sharing his bed for more than a week."

"We still hardly know each other," Ellen said, exasperated. "You can't expect me to jump into bed with a virtual stranger."

"Maybe he could have evaded me for one night, but I'd have caught him by the second," Tulip said. "There ain't another man like Matt Haskins within a thousand miles. I can't believe you're wasting him."

"We're not in love with each other," Ellen said.

"I could fall in love just thinking about getting into bed with him."

"That's not love," Ellen said. "It's lust."

"Which is something, if what you're telling me is true, you could use a great big dose of."

"I don't have time for a husband and children."

"You leaving those kids with Matt?"

"No."

"Then it wouldn't be much more trouble to add a husband to the heap."

"If I added Matt, I'd have to add Toby and Orin."

Tulip grinned. "If you added Matt, I'd bet my best gown you'd be adding more than that right soon."

Ellen felt herself blushing again. "Your gown is safe," she told Tulip. "But until I can legally adopt Tess and Noah, I'll do my best to convince everybody in Bandera we're a happily married couple."

"If you haven't convinced him to stay married to you by then, you're not much of a woman," Tulip said.

Ellen and Tulip rarely saw eye to eye when it came to relationships between men and women. But Ellen couldn't remember when she had disagreed more with the other woman. "I've never judged myself by whether I can attract a man."

"Everybody knows you can attract them, honey," Tulip said. "It's throwing away a perfectly good one that's stupid."

Ellen had begun to think Matt was a mighty good man, but she couldn't let herself forget that he had offered a business arrangement. Her feelings about her husband and the marriage might be changing, but she hadn't seen any sign his had.

"I can't throw away what I never had," Ellen said. "You know why Matt married me."

"If all he wanted was a wife, he could have asked any number of women, including me."

"He asked me because we have the same problem."

"That doesn't have to be the only reason."

"She's right, dearie," Mrs. Ogden said.

"Then why hasn't he said anything?"

"Why haven't you?" Tulip shot back.

Ellen was beginning to wonder why she'd ever thought she liked Tulip at all.

"We've never been exactly what you'd call friends," Tulip said, "but I've worked with you for nearly a year, seen how you act when a man comes near you. Even after you started wearing makeup so you'd get bigger tips, there was always a look in your eye that said anyone who stepped over the line could get killed."

"I was never that hard."

"I heard one of the men say you was like a diamond, beautiful but hard as hell."

"If I am, it's men who made me that way."

"What I'm gettin' at," Tulip said, "is you'd never have married a man you didn't like and trust, not even so you could adopt those kids. Hell, I expected you to pack up and head west when the sheriff said you oughta marry Matt."

"I thought about it."

"But you didn't do it. Why?"

"Because it was more sensible to marry Matt."

"When did it start being sensible to marry a man you don't like and want to get shut of in a year? You're fooling yourself, girl. You just can't admit it yet."

"I admit I like Matt," Ellen said, feeling cornered and angry. "He's a nice man who's been wonderful for the kids."

"He's done more than that," Tulip said. "I can see it in your face. You like what's happening to you."

"Why shouldn't I? I don't have to work in the saloon. I'm a respectable married woman, and I can keep April's children."

"You like more than that," Tulip said, getting to her feet. "I'll be off now before Mrs. Ogden gets a bad name for entertaining saloon dancers." She turned back at the doorway. "Catch him if you can. Aside from his looks, you'll never find a better man."

Tulip left an uncomfortable silence behind her. Ellen had been prepared to argue against everything Tulip said, but no sooner was Tulip out of the room than Ellen realized she had put into words feelings Ellen hadn't allowed herself to admit.

"Is he a nice man?" Mrs. Ogden asked.

"Very nice," Ellen said, "which is all the more reason I shouldn't stay married to him for my own convenience."

"Maybe it would be for his convenience," Mrs. Ogden said. "He needs a wife for those boys."

Ellen laughed without humor. "They keep house better than most women I know. He's got Isabelle hovering around, practically begging to do things for him. I've just met his sisters-in-law, but I'm sure they'd be just as willing to help."

"There's some things family can't do for a man."

Ellen knew that, but so far Matt hadn't shown that he needed any of those things. More importantly, he hadn't shown he wanted them from her.

She wondered why he had saddled himself with so much worry. He was a handsome single man who could have been out enjoying life. Instead he had to keep track of one boy who got into trouble any time there was a girl around and another who was afraid someone would steal him. And now he'd taken on her and the kids. And he seemed happy to do it. She didn't understand. Didn't he want anything for himself?

Fortunately, before Ellen could become depressed, Noah burst into the room, followed by Tess and Matt.

"It's time to go home," Noah said. He took hold of Ellen's hand and tried to pull her to her feet. "Matt

151

bought me a saddle. He says he knows just the horse for me. He's going to let me break it."

"Say hello to Mrs. Ogden," Ellen said. "She's been anxious to see you."

Tess had already thrown herself into Mrs. Ogden's arms. Noah put his arms around both of them. "I love you," he said. "I wish you could live at the ranch with us." Then he dropped his arms and turned back to Ellen. "Can we go now?"

"No. Sit next to me and try to remember you have some manners. If you don't," she said when she saw him start to argue, "I'll ask Matt to keep your saddle in the barn until you learn."

"Matt wouldn't do that." Noah turned to Matt for confirmation.

"It's as important for a boy to know how to behave well as to know how to ride a horse."

Noah sat down on the couch.

Ellen smiled at Matt in thanks. Most men wouldn't care about manners as long as a boy behaved like a real boy.

"We have a cow," Tess told Mrs. Ogden, "but she doesn't have a name. I don't think she likes me very much."

"Then you ought to give her a name," Mrs. Ogden said. "Poor dear, she's probably unhappy at being called cow all the time."

Tess turned immediately to Matt.

"You can name her anything you like," he said.

"I'm going to name my horse Thunder," Noah announced.

"That sounds like a very violent name," Mrs. Ogden said.

"He's going to be the fastest horse in Texas," Noah said.

"Dear me, I hope you don't intend to ride him," she said to Tess.

"I don't like horses," Tess said, "but I like cows."

"Cows are for girls," Noah said.

"Tell me that after you've dropped your rope around the horns of a fifteen-hundred-pound steer who wants to go in the opposite direction you want him to go," Matt said.

"I'm sure Mrs. Ogden doesn't want to listen to you two dispute the merits of cows and horses," Ellen said, getting to her feet. "Please come see us," she said to Mrs. Ogden, "sometime when Noah won't talk your ear off about his horse."

"I don't get out much, dearie," Mrs. Ogden said. "Not as young as I used to be."

"Tell Mrs. Ogden good-bye and climb into the buggy, kids," Matt said. "It's time to head home."

Much to Ellen's surprise, that was exactly how she felt. They were going home.

Chapter Ten

Ellen felt worn out. It had been a long day, made more difficult by knowing her feelings for Matt and her marriage had changed. She was looking forward to putting the children to bed and having a little time to herself. She needed to think.

"As soon as I get my horse, I'm going to ride over to see Kevin and Flint," Noah said. He only stopped talking about Sean's sons to talk about his horse.

"Can I go see Eden and Elise?" Tess asked. "I like Nita, too, but I like Eden and Elise better."

That wasn't hard to understand. She'd been completely enthralled by the attention the older girls had showered on her.

"We'll visit all your cousins soon," Matt said, "but now it's time to go to bed."

"Do Toby and Orin have to go to bed?" Noah asked.

"Not yet."

"Why?"

"Because they're older. You can stay up later when you're older," Matt said, forestalling the question on Noah's lips. "I need to get something from the barn," he whispered to Ellen. "I'll be back in a minute."

"Don't take too long. You know Tess won't go to sleep until she gets her story."

He was up to something. Matt was the most controlled human she'd ever met, but he'd smiled more since coming back from Bandera than he had the whole time they'd been married. The word married hit her like a blow. Before their union had been merely a contrivance, a trick, a way to get what she wanted. Now it meant something entirely different to her.

"If you boys mean to stay in the kitchen, keep the noise down," she said to Toby and Orin.

"Don't worry. I don't want the brats bothering me," Toby said. "Besides, we're just talking about girls."

"Your preoccupation with girls nearly caused trouble today. Maybe you ought to try thinking less about them."

"She was looking at me as much as I was looking at her," Toby said.

Ellen couldn't argue that. Mrs. Jackson should pay attention to her daughter first and worry about Toby later.

"Anyhow, she's not the only girl who's got eyes for me."

"Nor are hers the only parents who're on the lookout for you," Ellen replied. "Think about the trouble you cause Matt."

"I don't see that it concerns you," Toby said.

"Anything that concerns this family concerns me."

"Then you ought to be concerned about Ermajean McCutchen. Orin's scared she's going to snatch him."

"She followed us around all day," Orin said.

"The judge will soon come for his visit," Ellen said. "After that, you'll be safe."

"Good. I'm tired of him jawing about that woman all the time."

Try as she might, Ellen couldn't like Toby. He reminded her too much of Eddie Lowell. And while Toby's wasn't the same kind of selfishness that made Eddie think she'd welcome his advances, it was too close for her comfort.

"Mrs. McCutchen won't get her hands on you again," she said to Orin. "Even if Matt weren't here, I wouldn't let her."

"What could you do?" Toby asked, a scornful look on his face.

"I'm not sure, but if I needed help, I'd ask Jake and Isabelle. Now I have to put the children to bed. I'll see you both in the morning."

The children were already in their nightclothes when she entered their bedroom.

"Where's Matt?" Tess asked.

"He'll be in shortly." Ellen had both children washed and tucked into bed before Matt returned.

"Close your eyes," he said to Tess. "I have a surprise for you."

"What?" Tess asked, her eyes wide open.

"Noah's getting a horse, so I thought you ought to have something, too."

"I don't want a horse," Tess said.

"It's not a horse. Now close your eyes."

"Is it a cow?" Tess asked.

"Close your eyes and you'll soon find out."

Tess obediently closed her eyes, and Matt placed a gray and white kitten on the bed.

Tess's eyes flew open and grew wide with wonder when she saw the kitten, who looked just as surprised as Tess.

"Now you won't be lonely at night," Matt said.

"Can I pet it?" she asked.

"You can pet it, feed it, cuddle it, and let it sleep in the bed next to you. But you have to promise me one thing."

"What?" Tess asked as she held out a tentative finger to the kitten.

"Whenever the kitten gets scared, you've got to tell it a story."

"Cats don't like stories," Noah said.

"Kittens do," Matt assured Tess. "Go ahead, you can pet her."

Tess stroked the kitten with one extended finger. The kitten appeared to like it and crawled closer for more.

"She likes me," Tess said, excitement making her eyes dance.

"Of course she likes you," Matt said. "You're going to be great friends."

Ellen thought she was going to embarrass herself by crying. It was so sweet of Matt to give Tess a kitten. She didn't know another man who would have realized a frightened little girl would love to have a kitten for whom she could be brave.

"What's her name?" Tess asked.

"She doesn't have a name. You'll have to give her one."

"Will you help me, Ellen?" she asked.

"Sure, but we'll have to wait until tomorrow. Now thank Matt and get back under the covers."

Tess gingerly picked up the kitten and placed it on the edge of the bed. Then she stood up and threw her arms around Matt. Once again Ellen saw Matt's look of uneasiness, the way he stiffened.

"Thank you for my kitty," Tess said. "I'm going to sleep with her every night and tell her stories. You and Ellen got to listen."

"Sure."

So the two of them sat on the foot of the bed while Tess uttered exactly seven sentences. "That was a lovely story," Ellen said as she bent over to kiss Tess good night. "Now give Matt a kiss and let me tuck you in."

She said that before thinking of Matt's discomfort with physical affection. Tess held up her arms to Matt. He hesitated a moment before bending over so Tess could kiss him. Instead she put her arms around his neck and hugged him.

"Thank you for my kitty," she said, then kissed Matt about half a dozen times. Ellen could see Matt struggle not to pull away.

"I don't want to kiss anybody," Noah said.

"I mean to kiss you," Ellen said, tickling him when he tried to hide under his blanket. She gave him a very loud kiss on the cheek.

"Ugh!" Noah said and made a show of rubbing it off.

"Be nice, or I'll ask Matt to kiss you, too."

Noah looked horrified. "Men don't kiss each other."

"Maybe not, but sometimes they kiss little boys good night."

Noah dived under the covers.

"You can come out," Matt said, wiggling Noah's foot through the bedclothes. "I won't kiss you."

Noah peeped out. "You're not going to forget about my horse, are you?"

"No. Now go to sleep."

"I'll send the boys to bed," Matt said when they stepped into the hallway.

"Why did Tess's kissing you make you so uncomfortable?" Ellen asked.

"I'm not used to kissing and hugging. Will is the toucher, not me."

"Why?"

"No good reason."

"You're not going to tell me, are you?"

"It wouldn't make any difference."

"Maybe not, but I wouldn't feel so much like you're pushing me away. I know we agreed this would be a business arrangement, but I'm confused about what you really want. Sometimes, especially when you talk to the children, I feel like you want this to be a real family. You do so many thoughtful things, it's like you believe Tess and Noah are your children. At other times you draw a ring around yourself so we can't come too close. That's how I think you feel about me, especially."

"You said you wanted a purely business agreement."

"I know I'm not explaining it well, but I sensed something today I haven't felt before. Maybe it was just your family, but I thought it came from you, too."

"What was it?" He wasn't backing away from her, nor was he looking uncomfortable. His interest seemed sincere, his concentration total, as if what she was saying, what she was feeling, were important to him. For the moment, at least, the barriers were down.

"I felt like I was part of your family. I've never had that feeling before, and I didn't know how wonderful it would be. I felt like I'd been accepted, that everybody in that room would have protected me and the kids regardless of the danger."

"They would."

"Why?"

"You're part of the family. Isabelle says being family has little to do with blood. It has to do with wanting to be together."

"I like that. I like it so much, I don't ever want it to stop."

"It won't."

"Not even if I move to San Antonio?" She had meant to say when.

Matt hesitated. "If the family believes you really want to be a part of us, that won't make any difference. Luke, Hawk, and Zeke have been gone for years, but Isabelle still worries about them. Now I'd better send the boys up to bed. I don't want them falling out of their saddles tomorrow."

Ellen didn't mistake her new feelings for love. Matt was as attractive as always, but she was too fearful of all men to feel safe giving herself to any man, even a man like Matt. Men had lusted after her all her life, had grabbed at her, attempted to take what she wouldn't give. She couldn't feel safe unless she could keep her distance. It wasn't physical closeness she needed but closeness of the spirit. That was what Matt's family had offered, and she welcomed it.

But she wanted Matt to want to be close to her, to touch her hand now and then. Casual touch was an important part of any relationship, even friendship. It cemented the bond between people, made them feel they were important to each other. All she had to do was watch Tess to see that. But she had seen Matt's reaction to Tess's hugs and kisses. If he reacted so strongly to a child's touch, what would he do if she touched him?

Probably move to the loft with Orin and Toby.

She knew he didn't dislike women. She remembered the look in his eyes the first time he'd come to the saloon. It was a look she'd seen too often to misunderstand, yet there was a difference. He allowed himself to look, to want, but never to touch. She didn't understand Matt, but she wanted to. The more she learned about him, the more she liked him. The more she liked him, the more she wanted to know about him.

The more she wanted him to like her. She wanted him to smile when he saw her, to seek her company, to share a confidence. She wanted to feel connected to him. Despite being an adult, she felt lost. Maybe that was why she'd been so quick to want to think she had been welcomed by the Maxwells.

Ellen finished getting ready for bed and crawled between the covers. She was completely confused. She wanted to belong, to feel safe and protected, yet closeness frightened her. She wanted to feel close to Matt, yet she didn't want him to get close. She wanted to be loved—that was a huge admission—but she didn't trust love.

Ellen rested her head on the pillow, but she didn't feel sleepy. She was sure of only one thing: She wanted the very best home for Noah and Tess, and a proper home included a father. Matt was the only candidate she had.

Matt tried to run away, but he couldn't move his limbs. They felt weighed down, immobile. Though he knew no one would hear him, he tried to cry out. No sound came from his throat. When he felt his uncle's hand on his body, he tried to push him away, but he couldn't move. He was helpless to stop what he knew would happen.

Then he felt the knife in his hand. He didn't know where it came from. Like the answer to a prayer, it was just there. He was no longer helpless. But he didn't want to use the weapon. No one would ever love him. They would always be afraid. He would be condemned to a life of loneliness.

But he had to stop his uncle. He couldn't let him hurt Will. He knew what he had to do. When it was over, he would pretend to be like everybody else. They didn't have to know.

He gripped the knife with all his strength.

Matt woke up, his nightshirt wet with perspiration, his body trembling. It was a dream. His uncle had been dead for years and could never threaten him again. But that thought had barely registered when he realized somebody was touching him. He sat up in bed.

Almost at once he remembered he was in his own bed, Ellen next to him. She had turned toward him in her sleep, and her outflung hand rested on his thigh.

Matt struggled to still the panic that gripped his body, to resist the nearly overwhelming urge to leap from the bed. The abuse had stopped seventeen years ago. Ellen's touch posed no threat. He was an adult, a sensible man who should have learned to control his fears by now.

He wouldn't move Ellen's hand even though it was uncomfortably close to his groin. He would ignore this stupid fear until it subsided. Then, when he was absolutely certain he was relaxed, he'd go back to sleep, leaving her hand right where it was.

He had spent years letting his fears drive him away from people. It was time he did something about it.

He'd been forced to get married, forced to share his house and bed, forced to pretend to be happily married. If nothing else, he should use this experience to help him get over his fear of touching. And he wanted to touch Ellen. He had liked those few times they held hands. He might even want to kiss her.

The thought of kissing Ellen had an unanticipated effect on him. He remembered he'd thought of her first when Isabelle said he had to marry. He recalled the number of times she'd figured in his daydreams, and the nights when, alone in his bed and thinking of Ellen, he had become too agitated to sleep as fantasies, so intense his body trembled, chased each other through his head.

But it was foolish to let himself get carried away by his longings. Even if he could get over his reluctance to be touched, their marriage could never be more than a business agreement. There were other reasons she wouldn't want to stay married to him.

However, just because he couldn't have the kind of marriage he wanted was no reason to let himself remain a prisoner of fear. He might not be able to enjoy the caresses of a loving wife, but there was no reason he should shrink from Ellen's touch.

The tension had left his body, the trembling stilled, his breathing returned to normal. He would stay right where he was until he liked the feel of Ellen's hand on his thigh. He'd spent so many years fantasizing about what it would be like to be with a woman, hoping it would happen, even trying to think of ways to make it happen. Now it had. He'd be a fool not to derive some benefit from it, even some pleasure.

His whole concentration focused on his thigh. His uncle's touch had left a bone-chilling cold behind. The

163

imprint of Ellen's hand burned like a brand, then changed to a hard-to-describe feeling. It wasn't uncomfortable, but he wasn't comfortable, either.

Husbands and wives began to make love by touching.

That thought caused a tendril of warmth to curl upon itself in his abdomen. It wasn't a hot lust but a gentle warmth. Then a shiver shook him from head to foot. It was a strange feeling, almost like some sort of mild convulsion, but not an unpleasant one. It made the warmth grow warmer, spread a little farther. A little faster.

He could feel his body begin to swell. Not since his uncle first molested him had touch aroused any feeling except loathing and nausea. He had been fearful Ellen's would do the same. He was overjoyed it didn't. The joys of a normal life with wife and family might be denied him, but at least he knew he was capable of deriving pleasure from a woman's intimate touch—Ellen's intimate touch.

Being around Ellen and knowing how she felt about the kids had made him like her more than ever. He liked having her in his house. He liked taking care of her, worrying about her, planning to do things that would please her. She wore more modest clothing now than in her saloon days, but he remembered a perfect shoulder exposed, long, shapely legs visible with each graceful stride. Not even modest clothes could hide the swell of her breast, the column of her throat, or the curve of her hips.

He was tempted to move her hand a little higher, but she would probably wake up. He closed his eyes, let himself relax, concentrate on her touch, visualize her wanting to be his wife, wanting to come into his embrace. He moved slightly, and the sensitivity caused by the friction between her hand and the fine hairs on his thigh increased tenfold. He smiled. He liked the feeling.

He drifted off to sleep and had dreams of being able to touch Ellen wherever he wanted.

And of so much more.

Matt awoke at the first hint of dawn with a feeling of deep contentment. As his mind began to free itself from sleep, he felt warm all through, cozy, unhappy about the prospect of getting out of bed. He was too far from being awake to come up with a reason for this remarkable change, but he knew he liked it and hoped it would not desert him.

Then he did come awake and realized immediately that something soft and warm was pressed against him. Ellen had come over to his side of the bed and was sleeping pressed against him, her arm across his chest.

The feeling of panic was sharp but lasted only until he remembered her touch the night before and the erotic dreams that had followed. He smiled. This marriage he'd resisted, had dreaded, was working out better than he expected. There was something about having Ellen in his house that calmed the anger that boiled inside him. She couldn't make his memories of the past go away, but somehow they didn't hurt quite as much.

But he refused to let his mind take the next leap in the progression. Their marriage could never be more than an arrangement. It wouldn't do a bit of good to start thinking about what might have been. He was getting to adopt Orin. He shouldn't be greedy and ask for too much.

He gently moved Ellen's arm, slipped out of bed, and

changed into his clothes. But as he left the bedroom, he glanced back at Ellen sleeping contentedly in the bed. The picture caused something powerful to well up inside him.

Damnit! Was it being greedy to ask for what everybody else took for granted?

Matt turned and left the room. He'd been down this same road before, asked the same questions, gotten the same answers. It wouldn't serve any purpose to do it again. Besides, he had horses to train. If he didn't keep his mind on his work, he could get hurt. But as he pumped cold water into the sink and splashed it on his face, he couldn't help but ask the same old question: Why didn't he have the same right to happiness as everyone else?

Chapter Eleven

"I'm going to buy all new clothes," Toby announced, "then find myself a girl."

After two weeks of hard work, they had finished breaking and branding the horses. Everyone had come to town to celebrate. At Tess's insistence she had been left to visit with Mrs. Ogden. The little girl could hardly wait to show off her kitten, Fluffy. Will had taken Noah off to see what mischief they could find. And with a little time to herself, Ellen planned to sell the two hats she had brought while Matt and Orin bought supplies for the ranch.

"Don't go near Mabel Jackson's daughter," Ellen warned Toby.

"I can't help it if Tammy can't stay away from me."

"It would be better if you avoided her," Matt said.

"Her mother can make it hard for us to adopt Orin and the kids."

"That's not fair," Toby protested.

"I know it's not, but it's not fair for Orin and the kids to be taken away. Once they're safe, I won't say anything about the girls you want to see."

"Okay," Toby said, "but if she comes after me, I'm not gonna hide."

"Maybe you should," Matt said. "If you're not careful, you might end up with Mabel as your mother-in-law."

Ellen nearly laughed at Toby's horrified expression.

"I'm too young to think about getting married."

"I agree," Matt said. "Meet me at the mercantile in two hours. We've got a lot of supplies to load in the wagon."

Ellen wondered if Orin wanted to go with Toby, or if he was too frightened of Ermajean McCutchen to leave Matt.

"I'll wait if you like," Matt said to Ellen.

"I'll catch up with you later. I've got a little shopping to do."

She liked feeling his mantel of protection around her. He worried someone might be rude to her. She knew nothing anybody said to her could be worse than the Lowells' accusations, but she enjoyed his concern for her. "I'll meet you in an hour."

Ellen had been selling hats to Susan Barclay for over a year. Ellen didn't mind that Susan sold them as creations by an anonymous designer. The women of Bandera would have been reluctant to buy hats made by Ellen. Soon, however, Ellen knew she would have to reveal her identity if she wanted to start building her reputation.

"I was wondering if you'd keep making hats," Susan said when Ellen entered the shop.

"I have time to make even more now. I intend to open my own shop in San Antonio one of these days."

"Will Matt move to San Antonio with you?" Susan asked, more interested in seeing what Ellen had brought her than in Ellen's future.

"No," Ellen said, remembering too late that people would start wondering about her marriage if they knew her plans. "I want to keep some of my independence."

"I don't know why. Half the women in this town would give their souls to be married to a man like Matt. This is beautiful," she said as she drew the first hat from its tissue nest. "Mrs. Jackson will insist upon having it, but I think I'll keep it for Mrs. Maxwell."

"What do you mean?"

"Isabelle Maxwell is tall and elegant. This is exactly the right—"

"What you said about Matt?"

Susan paused before opening the second box. "Will Haskins is probably the best-looking man in Texas, but it's Matt who holds a woman's interest. Outside of being so attractive it makes your bones ache just to look at him, he's thoughtful and dependable. Nobody is more polite. Many a woman's had her eye on him."

"I didn't see anybody rushing to marry him," Ellen said.

"Well now, they wouldn't, would they? This is a lovely hat. I wonder if I can talk Mrs. Maxwell into buying both of them."

"What's changed everybody's opinion of Matt?"

"He was polite and kind to a fault, but he was real standoffish. Then he married you." Susan put the hat down and looked around to make sure there was nobody close enough to hear. "I don't know if I should tell you this, but there were some whispers about him being out there alone with those boys."

"I'll bet it was Wilbur Sears who did the whispering," Ellen said, furious.

"I don't know about that," Susan said, resuming her normal tone of voice, "but that's all forgotten after the way he stood up to Wilbur. Everybody figures he was just waiting to find him a wife pretty enough to cause the sap to rise."

Ellen blushed. "I'm not that good-looking."

"Don't be foolish," Susan said, going back to admiring the hats. "I'm determined Isabelle will buy both of these hats, if only to annoy Mabel Jackson. She's furious I won't tell her who makes them."

"She'd be more furious if you did."

"I know, and I can't afford to lose my best customer. Now, how much do you want for these? You know it's no work to sell them, but I must get something for taking them on."

"The same percentage as before will be fine."

"When can you bring me more?" Susan asked as she counted out the money.

"Probably the next time I come into town."

"You sure you won't be too busy? I know living on a ranch is hard work."

"Matt spoils me," Ellen said as she recounted the money before putting it in her purse. "He and the boys do half the housework. I had to practically force him to let me take over the cooking."

Susan groaned. "There's not a woman in this town who wouldn't kill for a husband like that. You sure you don't want to lend him out occasionally?"

"He comes with Orin and Toby, but they do as much work as he does."

"That Toby's real cute."

"Unfortunately he knows it."

"So do half the girls in town."

Outside, Ellen was glad there weren't many people on the streets. Bandera served a ranch community, and few people lived in town. Ellen was even more relieved to be the only customer in the tiny dress shop in Norma Ireland's home. Norma made clothes for Mabel Jackson and some of the Maxwell wives, but Ellen had never patronized her shop before. Now Ellen wanted to buy a dress that didn't remind her of the ones she'd worn in the saloon.

If Norma was surprised to find Ellen in her shop, she didn't show it. "Good morning, Mrs. Haskins. What can I do for you?"

Being addressed as "Mrs. Haskins" startled Ellen, but she liked it. "I'm looking for a new dress." Maybe she'd buy two. She had enough money. Her hats commanded high prices.

"What did you have in mind?"

The only dress Ellen owned that wasn't meant to be worn in the saloon was a gold print broadcloth with a polonaise. She had made some of her old dresses over to use for ordinary wear on the ranch, but she wanted something different to put on when Isabel came to visit or when she came to town to shop or go to church.

"I need something for those occasions when you want to dress up, but you don't want to look like it."

"I know exactly what you mean," Norma said. "Would you like me to take your measurements, or would you be willing to look at something already made up?"

"I need something right away."

"I have several things I can show you," Norma said. "Just have a seat."

Norma showed her a three-piece black silk polonaise with jet beads Ellen thought was too somber. She liked a paisley-striped dress in the princess sheath style but thought the heavy linen would be too hot. She liked a Wedgwood blue silk taffeta but finally decided the red bombazine dress in the cuirasse style was more to her liking. However, all of them were either too formal for wearing at home or not eye-catching enough for real dressing up.

"How about this one?" Norma brought out a dark amber, cut-velvet dress with an elaborate side-draped polonaise trimmed with chenille, moire taffeta, bows, and fancy embossed buttons.

"It's beautiful," Ellen said.

"It would look wonderful on you with your strong coloring," Norma said. "Not many women can wear such a dress."

It was truly elegant. Ellen could imagine herself in it. Just the thought of Matt's reaction when he saw her in it made her want it. "How much is it?"

"Sixteen dollars," Norma said. "That's really quite reasonable."

"Very reasonable." Ellen would have to use some of the money Matt had insisted she take in case she wanted to buy a second dress. She had decided she wouldn't use Matt's money for personal things, but now she wondered if this dress counted as personal. She would be wearing it as his wife, and it was important that she make a suitable appearance when she came to town.

Still, she hesitated. Using Matt's money assumed a commitment that made her uncomfortable. Despite the change in her feelings, she preferred to maintain her distance. "It is really very beautiful," Ellen said, "but it's more than I wanted to spend."

"I have only two more," Norma said, clearly annoyed that Ellen hadn't liked anything she'd seen in nearly half an hour. She went into the back and returned with a royal blue silk dress with a plain skirt and tucked ivory satin vest front with leaf-shaped appliques. She had lined the upstanding collar with ivory satin. "What do you think of this?"

"It's perfect." It was exactly what she needed for entertaining at home, elegant but not ostentatious. "I'll take it. Wrap it up while I try to decide on another dress."

At that moment Mabel Jackson entered the shop.

If Ellen hadn't been so irritated over being caught in the same shop as Mabel, she'd have laughed at the look of shock on Mabel's face. It was clear she wanted to turn around and leave immediately, but her pride wouldn't let her. Nor, since they were practically within touching distance of each other, could she avoid speaking.

"I didn't know you were in town," Mabel said.

"We needed supplies," Ellen said. "After breaking and branding the new horses, Matt thought the boys deserved a treat."

"Is Toby with him?"

Ellen tried not to enjoy Mabel's obvious uneasiness. One day she might feel the same way about Tess. "Toby's shopping for new clothes. He means to buy one of those 'Ditto' suits, the kind where trousers, jacket, and vest are made to match."

"I know what a 'Ditto' suit is," Mabel said, her eyes snapping that Ellen should have the arrogance to presume to inform her about anything. "I can't imagine what use Toby could find for one."

"To attract girls. I'm certain he'll look very handsome." Ellen hadn't meant to aggravate Mabel, but the words popped out before she could stop them.

"If he so much as speaks to my daughter, I'll have him arrested," Mabel said, angry red spots flaming in her cheeks.

"Should I have Tammy arrested if she speaks to Toby first?" Ellen had little patience with Toby, but she wouldn't stand around and allow Mabel to talk about him as though he were some kind of reptile.

"How dare you imply that my daughter would have anything to say to that boy!"

"I don't know that she does," Ellen said, determined to be fair-minded, "but you can't put all the responsibility for such a friendship on the boy. Toby would never pursue a friendship with a girl who wasn't interested. There are too many others who are."

"I can assure you my daughter is not interested."

"Then you can have no reason to care that Toby's in town. If I don't hurry up and choose a dress, I'm going to be late meeting my husband."

She shouldn't have mentioned Matt. But if Mabel hadn't pushed her so hard, she wouldn't have had to marry Matt, and Mabel wouldn't have to treat Ellen as a respectable married woman.

"What use can you have for any of these dresses?" Mabel asked.

"They're preferable to going naked." She had to get out of this shop. Mabel was causing her to say things she didn't want to say.

"I always thought you were common," Mabel said.

"What do you expect of a saloon girl?" Ellen turned

back to the amber, cut-velvet dress. It was lovely, but it was just not sensible to buy it.

"Surely you're not considering that dress," Mabel said. "It wouldn't be at all suitable for you."

Ellen felt something snap. She drew her fingers over the material. "And why not?"

"It would make you appear to be trying to climb above your station."

"And what is my station?"

"You can't have it because I wish to purchase that dress," Mabel said, avoiding the question.

If she had to spend every cent Matt had given her, Ellen wouldn't walk out of the shop without owning that dress. "But I do mean to purchase it. Norma has already priced it for me. And I'll take the red bombazine as well."

"I'll wrap them up." Norma took the dresses and went into the back of the shop.

"You bought that dress just to spite me," Mabel said. "You don't deserve to be recognized by decent women. If you're hoping to make everybody forget your true nature by covering yourself with extravagant clothing, I can assure you it won't work."

Ellen had lost all desire to fight with Mabel. There was nothing she could say that would cause Mabel to stop hating her. She sighed. "I have a husband, four children, and a ranch to worry about. I also have a mother-in-law and several sisters-in-law who like me just fine. I'll manage to survive without the acceptance or approval of you and your friends."

"Reverend Sears will see those children go to an orphanage where they belong," Mabel said. "As for Orin—"

Ellen felt a sudden urge to physically attack Mabel

Jackson, to slap and scratch her until she'd ripped that smug, contemptuous smirk from her face. "Neither you nor Wilbur will get your hands on any of those children."

Norma returned with the dresses boxed and ready to go. Ellen handed her the money. Ten minutes ago she'd have been furious at herself for spending so much. Now she only regretted she couldn't buy every dress in the shop just so Mabel couldn't have them. At the same time, Ellen was ashamed of herself for turning into a snarling harpy. She had to get out of the store before she did anything else she'd be ashamed of. "Thanks, Norma."

"Bring them back if they need altering. You have such a lovely figure, it would be a shame if they didn't fit perfectly."

"I certainly will. If you have anything else you think I'd like, hold it for me, please."

"If Matt keeps letting you go through his money like this, he won't have that ranch for long," Mabel said.

Ellen refused to be drawn. "Good-bye, Norma."

She stepped outside the store. For a moment she didn't move, just took deep breaths and let the tension flow from her body. She had to learn not to let Mabel Jackson upset her. She was married now. She and Matt would soon adopt the children. They would be safe. There was nothing Wilbur or Mabel could do about it. All she had to do was be calm and wait.

She walked to Martin's General Store. She had promised to meet Matt there, and she was late. When she arrived, he wasn't in the store. She wandered the aisles a few minutes, then approached a clerk who'd twice offered to help her.

"Has Matt Haskins been in?" she asked

"He came in some time ago," the clerk replied, "but he left when he heard the sheriff had arrested Toby."

Toby jumped up from the chair the minute Matt entered the jail. "He won't listen to a word I say," Toby said. "He just yells at me to shut up."

Toby had several bruises on his face, a cut lip, and a torn shirt. "What happened?" Matt asked Toby.

"He got into a fight," the sheriff said.

"I can see that," Matt said. "Will, take Orin and Noah and see about loading up our supplies. Toby and I'll be over as soon as we can."

"Toby ain't going nowhere. I'm going to lock him up."

Matt was determined not to lose his temper. "Let's clean you up," he said to Toby. "Ellen will have a fit if she sees you like this."

"She won't care. She hates me," Toby said.

Matt poured some water into a basin and brought it over to a table next to where Toby sat. He took out his handkerchief, wet it, and wiped the blood from Toby's mouth. "She doesn't hate you. You'd know that if you stopped picking at the kids."

"They get in the way. Ouch!"

"No more than you. You've ruined that shirt. I hope you have money for another. Did you buy your suit?"

"I didn't get a chance. Those yellow-bellies jumped me before I could get to the Emporium."

"He had to start a fight with the sons of three of the most influential men in town," the sheriff said.

"I didn't start it," Toby yelled. "They did."

"What happened?" Matt asked. "Don't leave anything out."

"I was doing what you said," Toby said to Matt. "I

didn't go looking for girls. I went to the photography studio to see how much it would cost to take a picture of me in my new clothes. I was going straight to buy my suit when they saw me and started calling me names."

"What names?"

Toby turned red. "I didn't care when they called me 'Spic' and 'Mexicano.' I knew they were just jealous because my black hair makes me more handsome than they are. Then they started calling me a bastard, saying my mama was a whore. Well, I couldn't let them do that without saying something back."

"You can't go around insulting decent women," the sheriff said.

"What did you say?" Matt asked Toby. Matt could tell Toby didn't want to repeat it. He was probably too angry at the time to think, but he'd had time to realize he'd caused trouble for everyone.

"I said they had to be bastards, too," Toby confessed. "I said their mamas was so ugly they couldn't get a man unless they paid him."

"Are those exactly the words you used?" Matt asked.

"I didn't call them whores," Toby said. "I ain't that stupid."

"What happened then?"

"They jumped me. Three of them, the yellow-bellies."

"What happened next?"

"I'll tell you what happened," the sheriff said. "Phillip Jackson has a black eye. Joey Fitszimmons has a cut where his teeth came through his lip. Sam Triggs practically lost his scalp."

"The clumsy oaf stumbled over his own feet and hit his head on the edge of the boardwalk," Toby said. "I didn't touch him."

"You calling Sam a liar?" the sheriff asked.

"You're damned right."

"That's something else you can repent of in jail."

"Where are the boys?" Matt asked the sheriff.

"Probably down at the river cleaning up."

"You'd better catch them before they reach home. It'll be much harder then."

"What'll be much harder?"

"Putting them in jail."

"I'm not putting them in jail."

"It takes at least two to make a fight, sheriff. If you put one in jail, you've got to put the others in, too."

"Do you know who your kid tried to fight?"

"I'm not his kid," Toby protested.

"It doesn't matter who he fought. The principle is the same. If you arrest one, you have to arrest them all."

"I can't do that."

"Toby defended himself. There's nothing wrong with that."

"That's not what the other boys said."

"Are you sure they said Toby attacked them?" Matt asked.

"Sure." The sheriff looked uneasy.

"I can't imagine three boys admitting they let themselves get beat up by one boy a year younger than two of them."

"Well, they did," the sheriff said.

"Then they'll have to say it in court. I'm pressing charges. I want you to arrest them immediately and hold them for trial."

"You're crazy if you think I'm going to arrest Mabel Jackson's son for fighting with a piece of Mexican—"

"Watch what you say, Sheriff. The boy is my son—

at least I want him to be, if he'll let me adopt him. I'd hate to have to knock you down for insulting him."

"You'd hit me?"

"You wouldn't expect me to insult your son and get away with it."

"But my son isn't—"

"Your son is fortunate to have a mother who loves him and a father willing to claim him. Toby doesn't have either. Or a whole lot of other things virtually every boy takes for granted. That doesn't give anybody the right to pick on him, make fun of him, or hold him in contempt for things he can't control. The boy has pride. Surely you can understand that."

"Yes, but—"

"So either you arrest those other boys or let Toby go buy that suit he wants so badly."

The sheriff looked from Toby to Matt before he started toward Toby. He opened his mouth, then closed it again. He kicked a chair out of his path, then faced Matt, anger and frustration flickering in his expression. He opened his mouth to speak but never got a chance.

The door to his office burst open and Wilbur Sears entered. "I'm glad to see you've arrested that young demon. It's time we made certain he can't cause further harm to the young people of this town."

Chapter Twelve

Matt felt sorry for the sheriff. He was caught between two interpretations of how to do his job. But Matt had no patience with Wilbur Sears. The man was a mean-spirited bigot who hid his small-mindedness under a mantel of self-righteousness.

"All boys fight," Matt said to Wilbur. "That doesn't make them demons."

"Have you seen what he did to Phillip Jackson?"

"Take a look at what Phillip Jackson and his friends did to Toby," Matt replied.

"He deserved much more. He's a brute and a bully."

"When did one boy defending himself against three attackers make him a bully?"

"Those boys didn't attack him," Wilbur contradicted, pointing an accusing finger at Toby. "He was the attacker."

"Did you see the fight?" Matt asked.

"No, but—"

"Then you don't know who attacked whom."

"Phillip Jackson says Toby attacked them without provocation."

"Toby says the boys taunted him, and when he retaliated, they attacked him."

"And you believe him?" Wilbur asked.

"Yes."

"Then you're a gullible fool."

"What if there are witnesses who say the others started it?" Ellen asked.

Matt had seen Ellen, followed by a few townspeople, enter the office, but he'd been too angry at Wilbur to greet her. He had hoped she wouldn't learn about this until he got it straight.

"They're lying," Wilbur declared. "Phillip Jackson would never attack him. He wouldn't want to be contaminated."

"I suggest you take a look at who those witnesses are before you call them liars," Ellen said. "They happen to be faithful members of your congregation."

Wilbur pointed an accusatory finger at Ellen. "I wouldn't have expected you to defend this boy."

"I wouldn't have expected you to defend bullies by calling responsible adults liars. Addie Williams, Sarah Tull, and Tom Brayne all agree Phillip and his friends started the trouble."

"How do you know what they saw?" Wilbur demanded.

"Because Tom told me." Ellen gestured toward a tall man holding his hat.

"Phillip and his friends provoked the fight," Tom

said. The two women standing next to him nodded their agreement.

"You've stepped in a cow pattie this time, Wilbur," Ellen said.

Matt didn't know when he'd been so surprised. He never would have guessed Ellen would defend Toby. He couldn't help but be proud of her. She had backed Wilbur into a corner before he knew what was happening.

"This trouble will make it easier for me to see those kids are put into an orphanage."

"That's why I was certain Toby hadn't caused the trouble," Ellen said. "He knows what's at stake, and he promised Matt he wouldn't do anything to cause trouble."

"That boy's a menace. He needs to be locked up."

"He's hardly more than a child."

"I'm not a child," Toby protested.

Ellen ignored Toby's interruption. "A child everybody criticizes and discriminates against at every opportunity. It's you and people like you who've taught him to fight."

"I preach forgiveness, love, and eternal salvation."

"But you don't practice it. You don't love Toby. You won't even forgive him the circumstances of his birth. We're taking him straight to Ward Dillon to make sure he has no permanent injury. In the meantime, Matt and I will decide whether to press charges against those boys. We have enough witnesses to make them stick."

Matt snapped out of his stupor. Ellen had given him an opening he wasn't about to let slip away. He took Toby by the arm, practically lifted him out of the chair, and headed for the door. He nodded a brief thanks to the three witnesses.

"You can't let them leave," Wilbur said to the sheriff. "You've got to put that boy in jail."

"Self-defense isn't against the law," the sheriff said. "Until you can prove otherwise, they can take Toby home."

"I didn't expect you to come to my defense," Toby said once they were outside. "I thought you'd be happy if they locked me up."

"I'm sorry we don't get along better, Toby, but I've suffered from unjust accusations more than once in my life. I refuse to let Wilbur do the same thing to you. However, that doesn't mean I don't have a good deal to say about your behavior this afternoon."

"Doesn't sound like you're glad they let me off."

"I am, but I'm angry the whole situation happened in the first place."

"It wasn't my fault."

"Are you sure you didn't do something to cause those boys to start picking on you?"

"I don't have to do nothing. They hate me."

"Why? What have you done to them?"

"I don't think it's fair to assume Toby did anything," Matt said.

"He must have done something. The whole town can't dislike him for no reason."

Matt's pleasure in Ellen's support evaporated. She hadn't started to like Toby or believe there was any good in him. "If the whole town hated him, nobody would have said the other boys started it."

"Sarah and Addie wouldn't have spoken up if Tom hadn't practically forced them. That kind of feeling doesn't come from nothing," she said, directing her statement to Toby.

They were headed to Mrs. Ogden's house to pick up

Tess. Matt wanted to ask Ellen to finish this discussion when they could have some privacy. It bothered him that people along the boardwalk should know any of what went on inside his family. Ellen and Toby, however, didn't appear to share his concern.

"The boys don't like me because I'm better-looking than they are," Toby said. "Their parents don't like me because their daughters do. I ain't done more than kiss a couple of them. That's the God's honest truth. Matt would kill me if I did something stupid."

"Toby knows the consequences of unwanted babies," Matt said. "He's had firsthand experience."

"I agree he has a right to be angry," Ellen said, "but I don't think we should have to bear the consequences."

"I don't go out with girls because I'm angry at anybody," Toby said, looking at Ellen like she was crazy. "I do it 'cause I like girls."

"Is that why you started making eyes at Tammy Jackson?"

Toby grinned. "No. I started because I was mad at her ma for making trouble for Matt and Orin."

"Don't you ever think, Toby? Do you look ahead and try to see if what you're doing will cause trouble? Or do you just do what you damn well please because it's fun?"

The conversation stopped, at least temporarily, when they reached Mrs. Ogden's house. Inside, Tess's happy babbling about all the things she and her dolly had done with Mrs. Ogden filled the room. She had to drag Matt to the shed and show him that Mrs. Ogden had a kitten that looked just like Fluffy. She showed Ellen the dress Mrs. Ogden had made for her doll and said she'd promised to have a new dress the next time they came to Bandera. She wanted to know if they could come again tomorrow.

By the time Tess stopped talking, they had reached the livery stable, where Will, Noah, and Orin were waiting for them. Will whistled when he saw Toby's beat-up face. He had known Toby was in trouble when Matt had appeared, leaving Orin in his care. Matt had said the briefest of words about getting Toby out of jail before disappearing again.

Toby related the details of the fight as he, Orin, and Will saddled their horses. Noah begged until Will offered to let him ride with him for a little way. Tess, who had overcome her fear of horses, begged Ellen to let her accept Orin's offer to ride double with him.

"Let her," Matt said before Ellen could refuse. "Orin's an excellent rider."

"You'd better agree," Will said, his grin infectious, "or she'll never forgive you."

Ellen agreed, with the stipulation that Orin never allow his horse to move out of a canter, but Matt had the feeling she gave in more because she wanted to talk to him.

"It's time you stopped defending Toby at every turn," she said as soon as the riders were far enough ahead that they couldn't overhear every word. "He won't learn to be responsible for his actions as long as he knows you'll back him every time."

"I defended him because I think he's right. There is a lot of good in that boy, and no one's given him the chance to show it."

"I've tried to, but he resents me and the kids."

"Of course. You threaten him." She looked so incensed at his accusation, he couldn't help but laugh. "It's your presence here, not you personally."

"How? I've done everything I could to make him like me."

"Toby never had a home. I don't know anything about

186

his father, but his mother was a dancer. She didn't want a baby and left him with her parents. It wasn't acceptable for an Anglo to have a baby with Mexican blood—I think the father was Greek, but I can't be sure—especially one without a father. When he was trouble, her parents passed him off to somebody else in the family, each relative he stayed with kept him only until they could hand him off again. Finally he was just thrown out."

Ellen's anger had subsided considerably. "That sounds a lot like what happened to me."

"Then you can understand why he's afraid. He knows you and the kids have brought increased danger to us and he resents it. He's also afraid I'll start to like you and the kids more than him."

"I don't see how. You fuss over him all the time."

"He's only been here a couple of years. That's not enough to offset his first fourteen years."

"Matt, you're a fool if you believe that boy cares about anybody but himself. I'm not saying he doesn't like you and Orin, but when it comes right down to it, he's going to look out for himself first."

"You can't believe that."

"Why not? Everybody in Bandera thinks so."

"According to you, every woman in Bandera thinks you tried to seduce Eddie Lowell and his father." Her face lost color. "Their believing it doesn't make it true. Nor does it make me believe it."

"That was unfair."

"I don't think so. They prefer to believe the worst of Toby because he threatens them. That's exactly why the women fear you. Their defense is to make you socially unacceptable."

"We'll never agree on Toby, so I'll say no more."

"I'll make sure he doesn't do anything to get in the way of the adoption."

"If he gets into any more fights, there are going to be more people who believe you're an unfit parent. They're already convinced I am."

"As soon as they see how much you love Noah and Tess, they'll forget you ever worked in a saloon."

He was certain they would if he could muzzle Wilbur and Mabel. Western society was forgiving of past transgressions as long as the person appeared to have truly changed.

"Everything may turn out as you foresee—I hope it will—but in the meantime Toby must be forbidden to go into town," Ellen said.

"I can't do that."

"Why not?"

"Toby needs the freedom to make mistakes and learn from them. He also needs his family to support him, no matter what happens."

"I don't trust him to control himself if those boys start baiting him again."

"He's learned his lesson."

"Why do you let that boy manipulate you?"

"I'm not being manipulated. I believe in him."

Ellen's compressed mouth and angry eyes told him that she wasn't convinced.

"Do you know that practically every woman I meet tells me how fortunate I am to be married to you?"

That shocked Matt. Women were attracted to him— he wasn't a fool, he knew he was good-looking—but looks weren't enough to overcome everything else.

"They tell me you're handsome, dependable, understanding, kind, considerate, thoughtful. The list goes on. What they don't know is that you're a sucker for any kid with a sob story. You took Toby when nobody else could handle him. You took Orin when nobody wanted him. You even took me and the kids so they wouldn't be put in an orphanage. You're a sweet, kind, wonderful, adorable fool."

The tears in Ellen's eyes stunned him. Could she actually care about him enough to cry, or was she crying out of frustration . . . or out of fear for herself and the kids? That seemed more likely. Nobody had ever cried over him.

"I'm sorry the people in your life haven't been better," he said. "It must be awful to distrust everybody."

"I don't distrust everyone. Just men."

"Not all of us are untrustworthy."

"Give me an example."

"Jake. All of us orphans had been thrown out of so many places we were practically on wanted lists. But he took us in, believed in us, never once failed to stand behind us. No matter what."

"I guess I'm just not as good as Jake."

"You are, or you wouldn't have taken Tess and Noah, and you wouldn't love them like you do. You wouldn't have married a man you don't like. You just haven't had the advantage of living with someone you can trust. I hope you find a man like that someday."

He wasn't going to be that man. Until this moment he hadn't realized he'd hoped he would be. He'd let sleeping in the same bed with her, sharing his meals, his day, his thoughts with her, a common goal, making him hope they might learn to share more.

She'd called him sweet, kind, and adorable. She'd also called him a gullible fool. Women didn't really want sweet and kind. They considered those traits signs of weakness. They wanted big, strong, and dependable men. They'd take a rough, possibly even cruel man, but they most certainly didn't want a weak, gullible fool. She wanted something he could never become, but it didn't matter. Even if he were what she wanted, there was too much about him that couldn't be changed, couldn't be accepted.

He didn't understand why he kept forgetting that.

Ellen was certain Matt's unwavering support of Toby would get them into serious trouble sooner or later. It made her angry that he couldn't see he was risking everything for a boy who wasn't worth it.

Okay, it wasn't fair to say Toby wasn't worth as much as Orin and the kids. It had to be rough knowing you had no father, your mother had deserted you, and your family didn't want you. He could be forgiven if he occasionally used his looks to get back at the world. She should sympathize. Her looks had been her one source of power, the only way she could get back at people who'd treated her badly. And she could see how her presence on the ranch could feel like a threat. Her arrival had brought Wilbur and Mabel down on Matt, threatening Toby's security. To a boy as insecure as Toby, that must feel like a threat to the only stability he'd known. But she couldn't let sympathy blind her to the fact that Toby's behavior was a threat to the only hope she had for keeping the kids.

She glanced at the man sitting beside her. Even after two weeks she could hardly believe she was married to him, that she had the right to sit next to him, put her hand in his arm, lean against him for support, depend on him to shoulder her troubles and solve her problems. But she couldn't let go, let herself really rely on him. She was afraid of losing control, afraid of losing her independence. That would be a disaster.

She was already jealous of the attention he gave the children. She was jealous of the unshakable faith he had in Toby. He was kind to a fault. Thoughtful. Generous in his praise. Willing to do practically anything she asked. No woman could have wanted a more accommodating husband, but everything he did for her lacked the warmth, the unmistakable signs of pleasure she saw when he was with the children. She'd give anything if his face would light up when he set eyes on her, but she knew he didn't want a real marriage, a physical or emotional relationship. He'd made that clear from the beginning. She'd agreed, because it had been exactly what she wanted, too.

Only now she wanted something different. Her mind said to beware, but the emotional need within her overpowered caution. She felt the bond that existed between Matt and the boys, felt the bond he was building with Tess and Noah. She wanted to be part of it. She knew she was setting herself up to be hurt. But she couldn't stop herself from wanting it.

"I want some more sausage," Noah said.

"If you eat any more, you'll turn into a pig," Ellen said.

"He's already a little pig," Will said and proceeded to make piglike noises.

Tess and Orin laughed. Toby laughed unnecessarily hard. Noah didn't know whether to laugh or be angry.

"He wants to grow up to be like you," Matt said to Will. "Everybody knows you're all ham."

"I didn't notice you pushing your plate away," Will said, his good mood unimpaired. "You either," he said, turning on Toby.

"Meat makes a man strong," Toby said. "I intend to be the strongest man in Bandera."

So he could beat up anybody who teased him or called him names, Ellen was certain, but she didn't say anything. She was determined to like Toby, to give him no reason to dislike her.

Tess looked down at the piece of sausage on her plate. "I don't want to be a strong man." She pushed the plate away.

"Sausage also makes little girls grow up pretty," Matt said. "Look what it did for Ellen."

"Do you think Ellen's pretty?"

"Why don't you ask Toby or Will? They're the experts on girls."

"She's too old for me," Toby said.

"She's not asking you to marry her," Will said, "just if you think she's pretty."

"Yeah, I guess she's pretty enough."

"Don't strain yourself," Will said, giving Toby a punch on the shoulder. "Every man in Bandera thinks she's pretty. The saloon's business dropped by half when she left."

Ellen didn't like being reminded of the saloon.

"But do you think she's pretty?" Tess asked Matt.

Matt glanced up at Ellen, then back at Tess. "I think she's beautiful. I especially liked the new dress she wore yesterday."

Ellen felt herself flush. She never would have guessed one compliment could affect her so strongly.

"You can stop discussing me like I'm a piece of livestock," she said, trying to cover her embarrassment. "If you don't want your sausage, Tess, give it to Noah. And you'd better hurry up or you won't be finished before Will leaves."

Will was going back to the Broken Circle today. She would miss him. He was fun to have around, and she could never thank him enough for what he'd done with Noah. The child followed him around like a puppy.

Noah grabbed the sausage off Tess's plate and popped it into his mouth. "Will said I could saddle his horse," he said, jumping up from his chair. "Matt promised to help me. Come on quick," he said when Matt didn't get up immediately. "Toby said he'd do it if I didn't hurry."

"I'll get his saddlebags," Orin said.

"I'll get his bedroll," Toby said.

The two boys disappeared. Ellen heard them pounding up the steps to the loft.

"Come on," Noah pleaded urgently. "You gotta hurry."

Matt stood, and the two of them walked outside.

"Can I watch?" Tess asked.

"If you don't get too close."

The child ran after her brother and Matt. That left Ellen alone with Will. Everybody treated him like a favorite spoiled child. Ellen knew better. There was somebody quite different inside, waiting for a reason to come out.

"Thanks for helping with the horses," she said, not sure what else to say. "And for putting up with Noah. He's never had a man give him any attention, and he loved it. I wish you could stay longer."

"I should have been gone before now. I would have if I hadn't been trying to get out of all the work Jake has waiting for me." He grinned like a mischievous kid. "Jake knows I'm worthless. He's probably done half of it already."

"You're not worthless to us."

"Maybe, but the last thing a newly married couple needs is a brother-in-law hanging around. Isabelle is counting on a new grandchild by next spring."

Chapter Thirteen

Ellen had always wanted children. When she worked for the Lowells, she often pretended she was taking care of her own daughters, dressing them in beautiful clothes, brushing their hair until it shone, loving and caring for them. After the scandal, she'd showered all her love on April's children. When April died, it was only natural Ellen should look after Noah and Tess.

"Didn't your brother tell you anything about our marriage agreement?"

Will looked startled. "What was there to tell?"

"Surely you didn't think Matt and I met, fell in love, and got married in one afternoon."

She couldn't decipher his expression. "I'd hoped something like that happened."

"He needed a wife so he could adopt Orin. I needed a husband so I could adopt Noah and Tess. This is a business arrangement. You can tell Isabelle there will be no babies."

It came upon her without warning, this unexplained and nearly overwhelming need to cry. She got up from the table and started putting dishes into the sink. She absolutely refused to cry in front of Will.

"I'd hoped for something different."

"Why?"

"It's natural to hope your brother will fall in love, get married, and have a family."

"I guess so," she said, barely holding on, "but it didn't happen this time."

"Why not? You're getting along well, and Matt really likes you."

"Matt is the kindest, most polite, sweetest man in the world, but he doesn't have a drop of warm blood in his body."

"You're wrong."

"Maybe, but I don't love him, so it doesn't matter."

She didn't want to look at him until she felt more under control, but he took her by the shoulders and turned her to face him. "Then why did you buy that new dress? And start wearing makeup again?"

"There's nothing wrong with a woman wanting to look nice."

"If you want to look nice for Matt, don't wear makeup."

"Why?" She hadn't meant to ask that.

"He thinks it makes women look hard and unnatural."

"How do you know?"

"After our parents died, Matt and I didn't have anybody but each other. We practically shared the same mind and soul until Jake and Isabelle adopted us."

"But you're so different. You're never serious. He's always serious."

"There're reasons for that. If you really love Matt, he'll tell you."

"I don't love him."

"Then why are you trying so hard to catch his attention? Why did you just come so close to crying?"

Will wasn't the fool everybody thought. "I just want him to notice me. I feel like I'm not here."

"The kids got in. So can you."

She hadn't realized it was so apparent to others. "We disagree on too many things. Toby, for instance. Even after that trouble in town, he refuses to punish him."

"Toby told me Matt raked him over the coals, gave him some extra chores, and banned him from town for a week."

"Matt didn't tell me."

"He wouldn't embarrass Toby. I wouldn't know if Toby hadn't told me himself. I've got to go. They'll have my horse at the door any minute. I just hope Matt checked behind Noah. I don't want to fall off because he forgot to tighten the cinch." He leaned over and gave her a quick kiss. "You like him, and he likes you. It would be a shame to throw it all away. I've always wanted to be an uncle. Now put those dishes down, put a smile on your face, and come see me off. The minute I'm gone, wash your face, find a quiet corner, and figure out how you're going to convince my brother to let himself love you. He's aching to, but he won't unless you make him."

With that he put his arm around her waist and pulled her along with him to the porch.

"I hope you tightened the cinch," he said to Noah when the little boy came up to the house proudly leading his horse. "I don't want to pitch headlong into a cactus."

"I tried to cut it when he wasn't looking, but he caught me," Matt said.

"Just for that, dear brother, I'll come back and stay a month." Will picked up Noah, gave him a big hug, then picked up Tess and gave her a loud, smacking kiss that brought forth delighted giggles. Orin submitted to a hug, but Toby insisted on a handshake. He looked thoroughly affronted when Will pulled him into a bear hug. "No sissy handshakes for me," Will said as he turned to his brother. Ellen was relieved to see Matt wasn't uncomfortable when Will hugged him. Whatever was wrong didn't extend to his own brother.

Ellen stood watching the children dance around Will as he mounted his horse, calling out to him, urging him to come back. They followed alongside as he rode out of the yard, all trying to get in one last word. Even Tess didn't hang back. What struck Ellen most forcefully was Matt. He leaned against the hitching post, a smile of contentment on his face. He looked back at her and his smile broadened, drawing her into his pleasure. In that moment he appeared completely happy. The fact that trouble waited on every side didn't appear to bother him. His family and his ranch were all he needed to be happy.

But the greatest surprise to Ellen was her own feelings. In a remarkably short time she had begun to question her priorities. Life at the ranch had settled into a comfortable routine. Noah and Tess had gotten used to their chores. Noah still slept downstairs, but he had his horse. She helped with breakfast, fed the kids lunch, and helped Matt cook at night. Matt and the boys took their lunches so they wouldn't waste time coming back to the ranch house. She spent each afternoon making her hats. The kids were happier and better behaved than ever. For the first time in her life, she was reasonably content. She found herself thinking more about the ranch and less about San Antonio.

She had begun looking for things to do for Matt, to attract his attention, to show her appreciation. She repaired rips in his clothing. She decided to plant a garden, intending to can and preserve the surplus. Despite promising herself she wouldn't change anything in the house, she found her thoughts wandering to ways to make the rooms feel less Spartan. Maybe she could talk with Isabelle.

But Matt stood at the center of it all. Regardless of what Will said, Ellen knew she didn't love Matt. And not being in love with him was a problem.

Matt was the most attractive man she'd ever met. She never tired of looking at him. Despite hair the color of new corn silk, his face was ruggedly masculine. His well-muscled body was a testament to the hard physical work he did every day. He moved with a fluid grace that was almost feline in the way his powerful muscles rippled and flowed when he walked. There couldn't be a woman anywhere who wouldn't melt at one of his smiles.

So why hadn't she fallen in love with him? He was considerate, kind, and gentle, as well as courageous and protective, all the things a woman wants in a husband and rarely finds. His mere presence could light a fire in her loins, but he didn't light that spark in her heart or set off that emotional reaction that caused people to love each other despite overwhelming odds. Her mind appreciated him, her body lusted after him, but her heart remained untouched.

Matt

She didn't know what kind of man could cause her to overcome her disgust of men, cause her to rethink her vow never to marry, but she was certain she would know him when she saw him. He didn't have to be so handsome as Matt, or as charming. He might not even be as kind and thoughtful, but he would sweep into her life and change everything forever. He would be her shield and her protector. He would be a man of such forceful presence that people would step out of his way without realizing they were doing it.

"I hope we get a few days' rest before he shows up again," Matt said.

The sound of his voice, as smooth and dark as chocolate, shattered Ellen's musings. She looked up to encounter Matt's dazzling smile. It warmed her all the way down to her toes, and she felt a pang of regret. Why couldn't she love this man? Why couldn't like, respect, trust, and mutual friendship be enough?

"It's going to seem awfully quiet around here," she said. "The kids will miss him."

"They'll soon settle back into their routine."

"Is routine that important to you?"

His expression changed. He seemed to be measuring her.

"It's important to the boys. It gives them the feeling of security they need. You like variety, challenges, because you're strong. You already feel safe and secure."

Was Matt right? If so, it had only happened since coming to the ranch. "What about you? Don't you want something else?"

His face closed down, as if he had pulled shutters across a window. "I want what the boys need."

That's what bothered her. He was a shell. He did what was best for others because there wasn't anybody

199

inside of him with wants of his own. "I'm not talking about the boys or the kids. I'm talking about you. If there wasn't anybody to consider but yourself, what would you want?"

"All I've ever wanted is to help boys like Toby and Orin. Do you need anything done around the house today?"

He had closed her out again. He didn't mind people looking at his exterior, but he kept the real Matt Haskins shut away. "The kids and I can handle everything."

"What are you going to do?"

"Plan a garden. We need vegetables."

"If you need any help, ask Isabelle. She loves gardens. When you decide where you want it, I'll break up the ground."

"What will you do today?"

"Work with the horses."

"Then you can come up to the house for lunch."

"The boys and I will fix something."

"Don't be ridiculous. I'll send Noah to tell you when it's ready."

"If you're sure."

"I can't cook as well as you, but it won't give you a stomachache."

She regretted her words immediately, but she was angry and wanted to strike out. He was too agreeable, too capable, too perfect. Why couldn't he have towering rages, be unreasonable, get drunk at least once? He didn't need a wife. He was complete in himself. That made her feel useless and inadequate. She was certain he could raise all four of the kids perfectly well by himself.

As for himself, he didn't need anything. He didn't

exist. He was just a mirage. A beautiful, insubstantial, rigidly controlled mirage.

"Everything you've cooked has been very good," Matt said.

"Toby doesn't think so."

There she went again, saying what she didn't want to say.

"He'll stop needling you once he stops feeling threatened."

The children were coming back, strung out in a line from the fastest, Toby, to the slowest, Tess.

"Can I ride that piebald?" Toby asked when he reached Matt. "You said I could train one of my own this time."

"Maybe you'd better start with that sorrel mare. She's not likely to eat you alive."

"I told him that piebald would stomp his guts out," Orin said, breathless from trying to keep up with Toby.

"No mustang is going to stomp my guts out," Toby declared.

"You two head over to the corrals and get things ready," Matt said. "I'll be along in a minute."

Ellen had expected Matt to leave her to deal with Noah's disappointment at being left out, but she should have known better. Matt never left her without support.

The first words out of Noah's mouth were, "Where are Toby and Orin going?" The next, "Can I go, too?"

"Ellen is planning a garden and she needs someone to help her lay it out."

"I don't know nothing about gardens," Noah said.

"None of us does," Matt said, "but we have to learn. I'm depending on you to figure it out so you can tell me and the boys what to do."

That put things in a different light. "Does Tess have to help?" She had come up right behind Noah. She was younger, but she could run nearly as fast as her brother.

"Grandmama said I could have flowers," she said.

Noah was reluctant to call Isabelle grandmama, but Tess couldn't wait to call all her new relations by their titles. She had already mastered the aunts, but she couldn't remember all her male cousins. Ellen didn't encourage her. It would make it harder when it came time to move to San Antonio.

"I'm not planting any flowers," Noah said.

"You just help pick the spot and lay out the garden," Matt said.

"Can I help plow?"

"Sure."

Ellen didn't know how he could help unless Matt perched him on the plow while he guided it.

"Okay," Noah said, "as long as I can help plow." His lower lip protruded. "Can I break my horse?"

"You'll have to help," Matt said. "He'll need to know how to respond to your commands, not mine."

That was enough for Noah. He would help with a hundred gardens as long as he got to help train his own horse.

Matt headed toward the corrals, wondering what he'd done to upset Ellen. She'd made it clear from the beginning that she didn't mean to be tied down by the usual chores expected of a wife. Yet for the last few days, she'd gotten angry every time he offered to help. When they first got married, he'd thought he understood her. They had worked out the logistics of merging their households with a minimum of trouble. They'd quickly fallen into a pattern of working together to prepare the meals that lately had fallen more and more to Ellen because he had been so busy breaking the new horses. Now the hardest work was done, he'd expected she'd want him to start helping again so she'd have more time to make hats. He didn't understand her anger at his offering to help.

She had started to feel comfortable around him. She had stopped sleeping so close to the edge of the bed that she was in danger of falling off. She didn't act like touching him was more dangerous than touching a hot stove. She'd started cleaning, polishing, darning, and rearranging some of the furniture, even a few of the pictures.

Matt altered his path to avoid stepping in some horse droppings.

Ellen also let him touch her. Nothing significant. Just reaching out to get her attention before he spoke to her; to hold her hand as she got into the buggy, climbed the steps, needed help with a heavy package or a pail of milk. She didn't flinch if they brushed against each other. She didn't lie in stiff silence after he got into bed. Every day he saw new signs that her fear of him was waning, that her life on the ranch was beginning to grow on her. So why this sudden wall of anger?

Toby came running up as soon as Matt approached the corrals. "Which horse are you going to ride first?"

"The piebald," Matt replied. "He acts like he's not going to fight anymore, but I don't like the look in his eyes."

Like Ellen. He hoped she wouldn't pull away from him, but he didn't like the look in her eyes.

"I don't like him," Orin said. "He's ugly."

"Piebalds usually are," Matt said, "but this one has the makings of a good saddle horse. We just have to convince him he'll be happy on the ranch."

That was pretty much what he had to do with Ellen. Until she suddenly appeared in a new dress and makeup, he'd been certain she didn't miss her old life. Now he wondered if she missed all the attention and excitement.

"What horse is Orin going to ride?" Toby asked.

"You got one picked out?" Matt asked.

"I'm still thinking," Orin said. "How many do I get?"

He hoped Ellen was still thinking, but it looked like she might have made up her mind. He didn't like confrontations, but he had to find out what was wrong. He could tell himself that he wasn't comfortable around women, that he was only good with horses, cows, and boys, but damnit, he wanted more than that. He'd probably have accepted that as enough if he hadn't been forced into this marriage. But he had been, and now he didn't want to give it up. Or the possibility of more. He'd bent over backward to be kind, thoughtful, and helpful. It was time to try something more direct.

"Bring out the piebald, boys. It's time he learned who's boss."

"We got it all done," Noah announced to Matt at lunch.

"Did you write down all the things you want to plant?"

"I can't write," Noah reminded him, "but Ellen wrote down lots of stuff." He made a face. "I hope I don't have to eat everything."

"What don't you like?" Matt asked.

"Brussel sprouts," Noah replied. "Mrs. Ogden tried to make me eat them all the time."

"I'm going to plant lots and lots of flowers," Tess

announced. "Grandmama said no lady can have too many flowers."

"Plant lots of potatoes," Toby said. "I like potatoes with everything."

"Sometimes I think he could live on nothing else as long as you give him a little sausage now and then," Matt said.

"I like potatoes," Toby said.

"I like corn," Orin said. "Beans, too."

"I hate beans," Noah said.

"You can't hate beans and be a good cowboy," Matt said. "Beans and bacon: That's a cowboy's diet when he's on the trail."

Ellen knew Noah's ambition was to be a cowboy and ride the trail to Kansas with the Maxwells when they took their herd to Dodge. "He's talking about lima beans," she said.

Everybody spent the next few minutes telling Matt what they wanted in the garden and how many rows they should plant. No one seemed to give a thought to the food they were eating, the meal Ellen had worked so hard to prepare. She hadn't had to cook at the Lowells or in the saloon. Fixing an entire meal wasn't easy for her. She'd been greatly relieved when everything turned out okay. Now even Matt ate without appearing to be aware of what he put into his mouth. It was a wonder any woman settled for being a wife and mother, to cook, clean, wash, and have her work taken for granted.

All she had to do was make one spectacular hat and she would receive praise as well as money. Her skills would be recognized and applauded. She would be pointed out on the street, admired by other women.

But she had to admit she derived a certain satisfaction from fixing a meal everyone ate eagerly. She also liked seeing Matt and the children gathered around the table, happily discussing something as ordinary as planting a garden. It gave her a kind of satisfaction that seeing her hat on another woman's head never had. She didn't know why this feeling should be so strong, or why it should be growing stronger each day. She supposed it was the same reason that caused her to love April's children as if they were her own. It answered a need inside her that had nothing to do with praise, reward, or recognition.

"This will look more like a farm than a ranch," Ellen said when the conversation moved from strawberries and grapes to apples, peaches, and pears.

"But we like all that stuff," Toby said.

"Then I hope you'll be willing to help me pick, shell, peal, cut up, can, and make jelly. Not one single pea or apple will march out of that garden and prepare itself."

Blank looks stared back at her. It obviously hadn't occurred to any of them that a garden would be a great deal of work.

"A garden this big will mean Toby and Orin will have to help me a couple days each week."

"Maybe we'd better start a little smaller," Matt suggested.

"Potatoes don't need all that much work," Toby said. "You just plant them and wait for them to grow big enough to dig."

"The ground has to be prepared, the potatoes planted, the weeds chopped, and the bugs pulled off. After they're dug, we have to store them so they won't freeze during the winter." Matt didn't appear to be listening to her, but just as she started to ask why, she heard the sound of an approaching rider.

Toby jumped up from the table and ran outside to look.

"I can't imagine why anybody would be fool enough to ride their horse at a gallop," Matt said. "They'll have to walk it all the way back to where they came from."

"It's Will," Toby said when he came back. "What's he come back for?"

"I don't know," Matt said, "but that explains the gallop. Sit down and finish your dinner," he said to Toby. "We'll know what he wants soon enough."

But no one except Matt had any appetite. They waited expectantly as they heard the hoofbeats draw nearer.

"Thanks for cooking," Matt said. "Everything was good."

Ellen smiled, thankful for the compliment but worried that Will was returning so soon. He entered the kitchen moments later, eyes bright, his face flushed from exercise and wind.

"Isabelle says the judge is coming to visit you today. He ought to be here within the hour." He pulled a chair from against the wall and sat down at the table. "That beef looks delicious. Can I have some?"

Chapter Fourteen

The buggy approached with all the solemnity of a funeral procession. It lacked only the black feather on the horse's head and a drum to beat out the slow clip-clop rhythm of the horse's hooves.

"That old man is the judge who'll decide on your adoption request," Will pointed out. "Isabelle says he's pretty reasonable, but since he doesn't live around here, he's likely to be influenced by Sears and old lady Jackson."

Living on the ranch with Matt and the children, shielded from the slurs and threats that had made her so miserable before, Ellen had begun to feel optimistic that things would work out. Now all that fled, to be replaced by a fear that hardened in the pit of her stomach like a ball of uncooked dough. She clutched Noah and Tess to her and moved closer to Matt. Toby and Orin did the same.

"Isabelle told me to disappear as soon as I told you," Will said. "She said my hanging around would ensure that all four children would be carried away for their own protection. I'll leave by the corrals."

With his departure, the circle closed more tightly around Matt.

"I'm glad they're here," Matt said with a calm Ellen couldn't share. "It'll be good to get this over and done with."

Ellen couldn't agree. She hoped the judge would be fair, but she was certain Wilbur had done everything he could to prejudice him against their case.

"Is that the man who's coming to take me away?" Orin asked.

"He's the man who will approve your adoption," Matt said.

"Will he take us away?" Noah asked. He was trying to be brave, but years of uncertainty warned him that things could change at any minute.

"He's not coming to take anybody away," Matt said. "Everybody should act as naturally as possible. If he asks you a question, answer it truthfully, but it will be best if you let Ellen and me do the talking."

Ellen didn't know what she could say to convince this man that she and Matt would be the best parents for these children. She couldn't understand how Matt could be so calm. Didn't he realize this man had the power to destroy his dreams as well as hers?

"I don't care what he says, I'm not going back to Miz McCutchen," Orin said. "I'll run away."

"You won't have to go anywhere," Matt said.

"But what if the judge says I have to?"

"If necessary, we can go where nobody will take you away. Now stop worrying."

Matt squeezed Orin's shoulder, and he seemed to relax a little. Even Toby appeared more confident. Noah continued to cling to her, but Tess wiggled around until she could hold Matt's hand as well as Ellen's.

Ellen felt like a fool. She found herself being comforted by Matt's words. She was an adult who had experienced the uncertainties of life, yet she couldn't help but be affected by his confidence. Besides, Matt had never failed to deliver on his promises.

Matt descended from the porch to greet the judge. "Hello. I'm Matt Haskins." He extended his hand in welcome as the judge climbed down from the buggy.

"Allen Peterson," he replied. "You know why I'm here?"

"We've been expecting you. Let me introduce my wife."

After disentangling herself from Noah and Tess's grasps, Ellen moved down the steps to greet the judge. She'd had too much practice in the saloon pretending to be enjoying herself to worry that her expression would betray her nervousness.

"How do you do?" she said, shaking the judge's hand. "I'm Ellen Donovan." Hot embarrassment raced through her. "Sorry, Ellen Haskins. I've only been married a few weeks."

Mercifully, the judge smiled. "My wife didn't stop stumbling over my name until we'd been married more than a year," he said, taking her hand in both of his. He turned to the four children huddled on the porch. "Considering the size of the task you've taken on, I'm surprised you don't wake up nights dreaming about being single again."

Smile, Ellen told herself. She wished she'd kept some of the makeup she'd washed off after breakfast. Matt might not like it, but she'd lay odds this judge would.

"It's been something of a change, but one I'm glad I made."

"You needn't try your wiles on the judge," Wilbur snapped as he got down from the buggy. "He's here to decide that these children belong in an orphanage."

"I hope he's come with a less prejudicial attitude," Matt said, his voice soft but steely. "I'd hate to think the law made up its mind before seeing the facts."

"The judge doesn't know you," Wilbur said, not the least abashed. "When he does he'll reach the same conclusion."

"If you're through trying to puff yourself up, Wilbur, I'd like to meet the children," the judge said.

Ellen was relieved to know the judge wasn't awed by Wilbur.

"They're rather nervous about your being here," Matt said. "The threat of being sent away to strangers frightens them."

Ellen didn't know how the judge would interpret Matt's remarks. Western men were often kindly when it came to women and children. But when it came to the law, they could be merciless.

"I'm not here to frighten anybody," the judge said, "especially pretty little girls. What's your name?" he asked Tess.

Tess dived behind Orin and Noah.

"It's Tess," Noah said, bravely speaking up. "She's my sister. I'm Noah."

"And how old are you, Noah?"

"I'm almost six. She's almost four."

"Well, you're a big boy for your age. I'm sure your father is proud of you."

"I don't have a father," Noah said, "but Matt said he would be my father if you let him."

"Would you like that?"

"Yes. He gave me a horse."

"Bribery," Wilbur intoned, as though it were a soul-threatening sin. "I told you this man would do anything to keep these children in his grasp."

"It seems to me that giving a boy a horse is practical, especially when he lives on a ranch," the judge said. He turned to Toby. "I've been hearing a lot about you, young man."

Toby's complexion went a bit pale, but he didn't pull back. "If you been hearing it from him, you ain't heard nothing good."

The judge grimaced. "Clearly something needs to be done about your grammar."

"That's what Matt said last night," Noah said. "He said if Isabelle heard him, she'd be over here every day."

"She said your grammar was rotten, too," Toby shot back.

"Who's Isabelle?" the judge asked.

"Isabelle Maxwell," Ellen said. "She's my mother-in-law."

"She used to be a teacher," Matt said.

"Is she Jake Maxwell's wife?"

"That's the only reason they've gotten away with this mockery of a marriage so far," Wilbur said, interrupting. "Everybody's afraid to stand up to them because they're rich."

"But you're not afraid, are you, Wilbur?" Matt asked.

"The servant of God is never afraid," Wilbur announced.

"And you feel you've been directed by God to personally see to the welfare of these children," Matt prompted.

"Any God-fearing citizen would do as much."

Ellen assumed Wilbur was trying for modesty, but nothing about his personality or his opinion of himself showed even a nodding acquaintance with modesty.

"And you must be Orin," the judge said.

Orin nodded, but his gaze flew to Matt.

"I heard about your parents," the judge said. "It's got to be hard to be without family."

"Matt says I'm his family," Orin said. "He said I can be his family always."

"That's for the judge to decide," Wilbur said. "Now it's time we sat down and got to the heart of this problem."

"And what would that be?" Matt asked.

"Proving that you're unsuitable to be the guardian of any young boy."

"What about me?" Ellen asked.

"Everybody knows those two children you took in would be better off in an orphanage."

Tess gave out a wail, let go of Noah's hand, and threw herself at Matt. "You said you wouldn't let them take me away," she cried. "You promised."

Tess having broken ranks, Noah followed suit, rushing over to Matt. Orin trailed him, leaving Toby by himself.

"Why didn't you run away?" the judge asked him.

"Nobody wants me," Toby said. "They don't care if Matt is a bad influence. They say I'm a son of the devil already."

"Who says that?"

"He does," he said, pointing at Wilbur.

"God-fearing parents keep their daughters home when he comes to town," Wilbur said. "Even their sons aren't safe from him."

"Three of them jumped me," Toby barked.

"Those boys wouldn't sully their hands with the likes of you."

"I don't know what 'sully' means," Toby replied, "but they got a couple of black eyes for their trouble."

"I don't think the judge wants to hear about your fights," Ellen said. "Would you like to come inside?"

"Keep close to the house," Matt told the children. "The judge will want to talk to you."

"What could they possibly have to say that would be of any importance?" Wilbur asked.

Ellen was relieved to see the judge shoot Wilbur a look that a more perceptive man would have taken as a warning. Wilbur, wrapped in an impermeable blanket of self-importance, didn't appear able to understand that a person in authority could have an opinion that didn't agree with his.

"Now tell me something about these children," the judge said as soon as they were seated around the kitchen table and coffee had been passed around.

"All you need to know is that they're constantly in trouble," Wilbur began.

"I meant something of their background," the judge said. "I'd rather hear from Mr. and Mrs. Haskins, if you don't mind."

"But I do mind," Wilbur said. "Anybody in Bandera can tell you Matt is peculiar." He turned his gaze to Ellen. "I offered to marry Ellen, but she didn't have the courage to put herself in the hands of a man of God."

"I didn't love you, and you didn't want my children," Ellen said. "That seemed sufficient reason at the time."

"They're not your children," Wilbur said. "You're willful, Ellen Donovan. You should have bowed to the will of God."

"Save your sermon for the pulpit," the judge said. "I want to hear about these children. Start with Toby," he said to Matt.

"Toby doesn't know his father's name," Matt said. "I'm not sure his mother did. If so, she never told him."

"How can you expect decent people to want the likes of him in their town?" Wilbur asked.

"His mother preferred her career as a saloon singer to being a mother, so she left him with her parents," Matt continued. "They passed him from relative to relative until they threw him out."

"Not even his family wanted him."

"He got into a little trouble in town two years back," Matt said, ignoring Wilbur. "I'd just bought this ranch and needed help, so I offered him a job."

"You hired a fourteen-year-old?"

"I was only thirteen when Jake hired me to help take his herd to Santa Fe. So were Sean and Luke."

"Who are they?"

"His parents adopted eleven orphans nobody wanted," Ellen explained. "That's part of the reason Matt wants to adopt Toby and Orin."

"That still doesn't make him a fit guardian for a young and impressionable boy like Orin," Wilbur said.

The judge looked thoughtful before asking, "What about Orin?"

"I took him when his foster parents didn't want him anymore."

"They ask about him every day," Wilbur said.

"Nobody wanted him until his grandfather left him some money."

"How much?" the judge asked.

"I don't know," Matt replied.

"Why not?"

"I never asked."

"How much?" the judge asked Wilbur.

"Seventy thousand dollars," Wilbur said.

The judge whistled. "I can see how that would spark considerable interest."

"Ermajean McCutchen is only interested in the boy's welfare," Wilbur said. "She admits she had a little difficulty with him, but she and her husband have two boys practically his age. They'd make perfect companions."

"Tell me about your children," the judge said to Ellen.

"They're not her children," Wilbur began. "They're—"

"If you keep interrupting, Mr. Sears, I'll send you outside. I want to hear from Mr. and Mrs. Haskins."

"They'll only tell you lies."

"Perhaps, but people are always telling me lies. It's my job to sort through until I get to the truth."

Wilbur looked furious.

"Noah and Tess are the children of a woman I worked with at the saloon," Ellen said. "I don't know their father. The children were born before I met April."

"Did she leave a will?"

"No."

"The father hasn't expressed any interest in them?"

"No."

"Did you look for relatives?"

"April never talked about her family. There was nothing in her things to tell me where she came from. I didn't know her last name. She wanted me to have the children. She said nobody else would want them."

"They ought to be in an orphanage," Wilbur said.

"What about Orin?" the judge asked.

"We wrote his family after his parents died," Wilbur said, "but they were happy to have him placed in a loving, caring foster home."

"If it was so loving and caring, why isn't he still there?"

"He ran away," Wilbur said. "Before Ermajean could find him, Matt tempted the child's soul with visions of untrammeled devilment and whisked him off to this ranch. He has refused to return him despite being asked by the sheriff several times."

The judge turned to Matt. "Is that true?"

Ellen didn't know how Matt could smile in such a relaxed, confident manner with Wilbur determined to weave a net around him.

"Ermajean was happy enough to put up with Orin as long as the money from selling his parents' property lasted. When that ran out he suddenly became unmanageable. Nobody in Bandera objected to my taking him until the provisions of his grandfather's will became known. Orin ran away because he knew nobody wanted him. He's not a difficult child. He was just scared."

"The boy is willful and rebellious," Wilbur said, unable to remain silent any longer. "He needs to be taught to yield to discipline. He won't learn anything but wildness and corruption from you. You don't go to church," Wilbur announced triumphantly.

"We've all been in church every Sunday since I got married," Matt said.

"But you never went before. You didn't either," Wilbur said, turning on Ellen.

"The one time I did go, everybody made it clear they didn't want me there."

"You can't blame them for not wanting a Magdalene in their midst."

"If she really were a Magdalene," the judge said, "I can't think of a better place than church."

Wilbur didn't seem fazed by the judge's remark. "She can't control those children," he said. "The sheriff received constant complaints."

"I couldn't always oversee them because I had to work," Ellen said, "but that's changed now. I'm with them all day, I have Matt to help me with supervision and training, and they're too far from town to cause any trouble there."

"That doesn't matter. You're not the kind of person who ought to be entrusted with the upbringing of two young, impressionable children."

"I served drinks in a saloon, Wilbur. I defy you to find even one man who says I did more."

He looked mulish. "Patrick Lowell."

"He lied to protect himself from his wife," Ellen said. "If she divorced him, he'd be penniless."

"He's one of our most prominent citizens."

"He wouldn't be if he were broke," Matt said.

"What does your family think about this?" the judge asked Matt.

"Everybody already treats them as part of the family. Isabelle has Tess calling her 'grandmama.'"

"I'd like to talk to the children now," the judge said.

"They'll only say what he's taught them to say," Wilbur warned, "maybe even forced them to say out of fear."

"I'll watch for that."

"I know them better than you," Wilbur persisted. "I can—"

"You can wait outside," the judge said, losing patience. "We have a long ride back to town during which you'll have the opportunity to say anything you might have forgotten to say on the ride out."

"I realize you need to talk to the children in private," Matt said, "but I'd appreciate it if you'd see them two at a time. They're all afraid you're going to take them away."

"That's because you've been terrifying them," Wilbur accused.

"As a matter of fact, he told them not to worry," Ellen said, "that no one would take them away. I don't know that I would have done the same thing, but it has served to ease their fears a little."

"I'm unhappy that they should be so fearful," the judge said. "Why is that so?"

"How could they not be frightened half out of their minds?" Ellen asked, her anger finally bursting her control. "They've been told they're brats, hooligans who belong in an orphanage where people will know how to make them behave."

"For their own good," Wilbur said.

"I'll be the first to tell you that Toby is not an easy boy to like," Ellen said, ignoring Wilbur, "but people in this town ought to be ashamed of the way they've treated him. He's been called everything from a bastard to a devil. They even set three local boys on him. Only it backfired when Toby turned out to be a better fighter. And Orin knows no one wants him except for his money. Ask him how he was treated before Matt offered to take him in."

Ellen hadn't meant to lose control. She had intended to let Matt do all the talking just as he asked, but she couldn't stand by and let Wilbur's allegations go unanswered.

"This seems to be a damned mess," the judge said.

"You can fix that by putting these children into decent, God-fearing homes," Wilbur said.

"I'll see the two older boys first," the judge said. "And you," he said, pointing to Wilbur, "will discuss with Mrs. Haskins how to educate these children if I should decide to let her adopt them."

"You couldn't do such a thing!" Wilbur exclaimed.

"I can, and I might," the judge replied. "Mr. Haskins, you'd probably better stay with the little ones. I want them to be as calm as possible before I see them."

"Ellen will do a better job of that," Matt said.

"Possibly," the judge replied, "but I doubt you and Mr. Sears would get much discussed before resorting to fists."

So Toby and Orin stayed in the kitchen with the judge, Matt sat Noah and Tess in the swing on the front porch, and Ellen found herself walking toward the creek with Wilbur Sears. Wilbur flew into a tirade about Matt. Her first inclination was to argue every point, but she knew that would be a waste of time. Wilbur wasn't going to change his mind about anything.

"Why do you hate Matt so?" she asked when he finally stopped talking long enough for her to get a word in edgewise. They had paused next to the tree-covered stream that flowed through their part of the valley. The sound of the water tumbling over stones helped to soothe her frazzled nerves.

"He's not a God-fearing man," Wilbur said. "He always thinks he knows what to do. He refuses advice from anyone."

"A man is entitled to believe in and act upon his own opinions."

"He's wrong. The way he protects Toby should tell you that."

She didn't always agree with Matt's handling of Toby, but Toby respected Matt and tried to do what he wanted. "We'll never agree on the proper handling of children. You don't understand them. You expect them—"

"I expect them to bow before authority," Wilbur said, "to respect their superiors, to do what they're told when it comes to God."

"You mean do what *you* want."

"Of course. I've been sent here to save this community, to bring every lost soul back to the bosom of its Maker."

Ellen gave up. She wondered what the judge was asking Toby and Orin. She didn't know which one to worry about more. Toby was the more confident and self-possessed of the two, but he was also the more unpredictable. If he wasn't careful what he said, the judge might end up believing he deserved everything he got.

Ellen didn't feel any more confident of Orin. Orin liked her and the Maxwells, but Matt was his anchor. She hoped the judge could see that. She would have to tell him if he didn't.

She was also worried about the children. How could three- and five-year-old kids know what to say, what to leave unsaid? They only understood that they might be taken away. Ellen got angry at Wilbur all over again. Everything would have been fine if he'd just minded his own business.

You wouldn't have married Matt.

As difficult as she had found it to marry a man she hardly knew, she found it equally difficult to imagine not being married to Matt. She didn't know how this feeling could have come about in such a short time, but she knew the kids felt the same way. Maybe it was fear of being torn apart. Maybe it was simply that they liked their new situation and that it worked better than anything ever had before. Regardless of the reason, the children were happier than they'd ever been.

And so was she. She didn't want to lose the kids. Or Matt.

"Let's talk about the children's education," Ellen said to Wilbur.

Without warning, he grabbed her by the arms and turned her around to face him. "You've got to divorce Matt and marry me," he said, his eyes burning brightly with the intensity of his feelings. "It's the only way you can save your immortal soul."

Chapter Fifteen

After all the things he'd said about her, Ellen found it hard to believe Wilbur could be serious. He was probably trying to lure her into making a mistake he could use to take the children.

"I know this is a fake marriage," Wilbur said. "You don't love Matt, not that love is required in a marriage between decent people. But respect is, and no one can respect Matt Haskins."

She couldn't think of what to say.

"You needn't scruple to tell me the truth," Wilbur said, a fanatical light in his eyes. "I forced the sheriff to tell me how the two of you decided to get married. He tried to come off all high and mighty with me, saying he was the law, that he didn't have to tell me anything. I told him that his soul was teetering on the brink of eternal hell. If he continued to thwart God's will, the devil would come for him that very night and carry his miserable sin-ridden soul deep into the bowels of hell."

Ellen wished the sheriff hadn't revealed their agreement, but she knew how difficult it was to withstand Wilbur when he started threatening eternal hellfire.

"It's true Matt and I married to keep the children," Ellen said, "but it's not true I don't respect him. He's a wonderful man, and the kids love him."

"Of course they do," Wilbur said, his expression growing more intense. "He's cast a spell over them. He stares into their eyes and they'll do anything he wants."

Wilbur was looking into her eyes right now, trying to will her to do what he wanted.

"Children aren't easily fooled," she said. "They know when a person doesn't like them. They know Matt truly loves them and wants to be their father."

"And you don't think it's strange for an unmarried man to have this unnatural attraction for children?"

Ellen wished she was strong enough to knock Wilbur down. "Matt knows what it means to be an unwanted orphan. He intends to make sure these children never feel that way again."

Wilbur's brow furrowed and his gaze became more intense. He took Ellen's hands into his and gripped them so tightly they hurt. "Poor child; he's cast his spell over you, too. He's made you as weak-willed as those poor children. Come to me, my dear. I'll protect you. I'll help you purify your life."

"Regardless of the reason for my marriage, I already have a husband. What you ask is impossible."

"Divorce him."

"Marriage is a sacrament."

"Not when it's false. You're living in sin, endangering your immortal soul. Your only hope is to marry me.

I'll teach you, comfort you, lead you every step of the way."

His grip on her hands had gradually moved up her arms until his hands were perilously close to her breasts. The look in his eyes had begun to change into an expression she knew well. The Reverend Wilbur Sears's most earnest desire might be to save her soul, but he was also lusting after her body.

As a girl and a young woman, Ellen had yearned for a physical relationship with a man. Her innocence of what it entailed, her belief that physical love was accompanied by never-ending emotional love, had made it the greatest desire of her heart. The hope that someday a man would come and rescue her from this hell on earth was all that had helped her endure a loveless existence with her cousin.

Eddie Lowell's attempt to rape her had changed all that. Everything about a physical relationship with a man became disgusting, cruel, and degrading. Working in the saloon only strengthened that revulsion. Living with Matt had begun to change it. She wasn't ready to fall into any man's arms, but she was considering the possibility. The thought of falling into Wilbur's arms, however, caused her to feel nothing but disgust.

She firmly removed his hands from her arms. "There's no point in discussing this any further. You know I'm a willful woman, not at all biddable. I would drive you crazy within a month."

"Nonsense. I—"

"You don't want the children, Wilbur. Surely my having married a man I barely knew has convinced you I'll do anything I must to keep them."

"My work is to bring the heathen into recognition of their sins, to admit their miserable lives are worthless, that their time on this earth is merely a trial, a vale of tears through which they must pass before coming into glory," Wilbur said, his eyes burning with unnatural zeal. "The devil is a mighty foe, Ellen, a relentless foe. One who—"

"I don't want to interfere with your calling."

"Children will sap my energies, take up my time, bring temptation and sin into my home, but I will make the sacrifice for you. You can be my wife and keep the children."

Ellen wanted to tell Wilbur that he didn't love children, that he didn't understand them, that she would give them to gypsies before she let him get his hands on them. But she didn't. Wilbur was a powerful and dangerous enemy. She didn't want to antagonize him any more than necessary until the adoption was final.

"I'm already married," she said. "Matt wants the children as much as I do, and the ranch is a perfect place for them." He didn't have to know she didn't mean to stay once the adoption was final. "You don't need a wife or children. Help me convince the judge that Matt will make a good father—"

Fury suffused Wilbur's face. "I won't rest as long as Matt Haskins has one innocent soul in his grasp. And you," he said, gripping her arms again in a painful grasp, "belong to me."

"What is that man going to do to me?" Noah asked Matt.

"He's not going to do anything," Matt said. "He just wants to ask you some questions."

"What kind of questions?" Tess asked.

"I don't know. Maybe he wants to know if you like

living on a ranch. Whether you want to go back to Bandera."

"I never want to go back there," Noah said. "Everybody was always saying bad things about us."

"You don't think we're bad, do you?" Tess asked.

"I think you're a beautiful little girl," Matt said. "I can't wait until I can adopt you."

"You want to adopt me, too, don't you?" Noah asked.

"I sure do. I'm depending on you to help me with the horses when you get older."

"Toby doesn't want me to help."

"Toby won't be here forever."

"Where will he go?"

"I don't know. Boys usually go away when they grow up, but there's still lots of time for you and Toby to learn to like each other."

"He says I'm a pest," Noah said. "He says I don't know anything."

"He said I was a bug," Tess added.

"He doesn't mean it," Matt assured them. "He's afraid you don't like him. He's acting mean so you won't be able to tell it makes him sad."

"He wants us to like him?" Noah asked, incredulous.

"Sure. Toby wants friends just like you and Orin do."

"I like Orin."

"He's nice," Tess added. "He smiles at me sometimes."

"Then you make sure you tell that to the judge," Matt said. "It's very important for him to know you're happy and want to be adopted."

"That preacher said he would take us away," Noah said.

"He can say all the bad things he wants, but he can't take you away."

Noah didn't look absolutely certain.

"He's not mad at you," Matt said. "He doesn't like me."

"Why?" Noah asked. "I like you."

"I *love* you," Tess said. "So does Fluffy." She hugged her kitten close.

The door banged open and Toby rushed out. "I took care of everything," he announced with a swagger. "It's in the bag."

"He seemed real nice," Orin said, but Matt could tell the boy was still worried.

"You kids don't have to worry," Toby said to Tess and Noah. "I already told that judge you was too little to know what a load of sh—horse manure that Reverend Sears was."

"I'm sure he appreciated that." Matt wondered when Toby would stop being his own worst enemy.

"Now, don't worry. I'll be right here," Matt said to the children. "If you get scared, just call me."

"I'm already scared," Tess said.

"I'm not," Noah announced, but he didn't move one step from Matt.

Matt walked Noah and Tess inside to the kitchen.

"Can you stay with me?" Tess looked ready to burst into tears.

The judge didn't look encouraging. "Tell you what," Matt said. "I'll be on the porch. You can see me through the window."

Tess didn't look happy, but she looked a little less ready to cry.

"You hold tight to Noah's hand," Matt said. Normally Noah would have objected to holding Tess's hand, but Matt guessed he was glad for a little moral support. "Don't forget," he said before he closed the door, "I'll be right outside."

Toby and Orin were waiting for him on the porch.

"Do you want to know what I told the judge?" Toby asked.

Matt didn't, but he figured Toby would be hurt by what he would see as a lack of interest. "Sure. What did you tell him?"

But Matt had a difficult time listening to Toby proudly tell how he had convinced the judge that Matt and Ellen were the perfect parents. He couldn't turn his gaze from Ellen and Wilbur. Ellen was standing still, her body ramrod straight. She didn't look pleased, but Matt hadn't expected Ellen and Wilbur to agree on anything, especially when it came to the children.

"I told him I got in trouble because people were jealous of my looks and the attention I got from girls," Toby was saying.

"And I suppose you think that answered all his questions about how people treat you," Matt said.

"I told him they didn't like my foreign blood. I also told him I occasionally tried to get people back for the way they treated me. I told him you said that was wrong, that people would never really trust anybody who's different from them."

They were getting on shaky ground. "What did the judge say?"

"He said he'd felt like that when he was a boy. Then I told him you said you used to want to get people back for the way they treated you."

"Toby, you didn't!" That ought to cook his goose right there.

"But I told him you decided a long time ago that was stupid."

Matt decided he had no one but himself to blame. Toby hadn't done anything but tell the judge what Matt had told him. What better basis could the judge have on which to make his decision?

"I'm sure the judge appreciated your candor," Matt said. "Why don't you and Orin go check on the horses?"

The horses were fine, but maybe that would break up Wilbur and Ellen's conversation. Matt knew he could do the same thing, but he was trying to have faith in Ellen. All the time. In all ways. He wanted her to stay on the ranch after the adoption. He was certain the adoption wouldn't be official immediately. There would be a period of waiting, making sure everything worked out. The longer she stayed, the better the chances she wouldn't leave.

He got to his feet, his body tense. Wilbur had put his hand on Ellen, had taken her by the arms. Matt didn't expect he would attempt to harm her. Besides, after having survived brawny saloon drunks for two years, Ellen could take care of herself. But that wasn't why Matt was on his feet, or why he had to stop himself from running the whole distance that separated them.

Ellen was his wife! And no man was allowed to put his hands on her!

Two things caused Matt to settle back in his chair. Ellen pushed Wilbur's hand away and started walking toward the house. The other was shock at his own feelings. When had he started to feel Ellen belonged to him? He didn't try to fool himself by pretending this was merely a man protecting a woman from abuse. This was a case of a man threatening a woman Matt considered his own.

Was he crazy? They shared a common goal, lived in the same house, and slept in the same bed, but she didn't belong to him. This was a marriage of convenience—or deception. When they achieved their goal, everything would change.

Ellen stopped to talk to Orin and Toby. She cast a look over her shoulder at Wilbur, following a few paces back. Matt smiled to himself when Toby and Orin turned around and placed themselves on either side of Ellen. Apparently he wasn't the only one who felt protective toward her.

The front door opened and Noah burst out, followed by Tess. They both threw themselves at Matt. Without conscious thought, he picked Tess up with one arm and put his other arm around Noah's shoulder when the little boy hugged him around the waist. Once he realized what he'd done, he was shocked. He'd never voluntarily embraced another human being. But even more of a surprise was the discovery that he liked holding Tess in his arms, hugging Noah. He needed it, too. It was as though an oasis had sprung up where there had been only desert before. Both children started talking at once.

"He didn't try to scare us," Noah said.

"He likes dolls," Tess said.

"Naw, he doesn't," her brother said. "He was just trying to be nice. He wants to see my horse. Can I show him? Please!"

Smiling, the judge emerged from the house. "That's quite a family you've got here," he said. "You sure you're ready for that much responsibility?"

"I'm thirty, Judge. Some younger men have families twice this size."

"But you've got a unique challenge. Are you up to it?"

"I can't imagine being without them."

"Can I get my horse?" Noah asked.

"Why don't you take the judge over to the corral?"

"You come, too," the judge said to Matt. "I want to know more about this ranch of yours."

"It belongs to the bank," Wilbur said, coming up. It seemed he'd left Ellen behind when he realized her protectors weren't about to leave her side. "If he loses it, he won't have a home for these children."

"The bank holds the mortgage," Matt said, "but I'm a payment ahead."

"I thought your parents were rich," the judge said. "Why did you have to borrow the money?"

"We all agreed they'd done more than enough when they adopted us and gave us a home as long as we wanted," Matt explained. "We wanted to buy our own ranches, to help each other if necessary, but not take money from Jake and Isabelle."

"Which has frustrated Isabelle badly," Ellen said, joining the group. "She comes over when Matt's gone to bring him furniture and curtains. If he returns them, she brings them back the minute he turns his back."

"And where are these orphans now?" the judge asked.

"Five of us have ranches here in the Hill Country, five are working out west, and one still lives at home."

"Half of them are gunfighters," Wilbur said. "Luke Attmore is notorious."

"A lot of good men were once gunfighters," Matt said. "Hen Randolph used to be the most feared gunman in Arizona. Now he's a respected rancher."

"And that black man and half-breed aren't much better," Wilbur said, ignoring Matt.

"Zeke and Hawk do a little bit of everything," Matt said.

"You seem to have a very interesting family," the judge said. "Why don't you tell me something about it while Noah shows me his horse."

"There's no point in doing that," Wilbur said. "He's unfit to have custody of these children. Even Toby." Wilbur took a deep breath. "I've told Ellen I'm willing to take the two younger children."

"I don't want to go with you," Noah said. "You hate me."

Wilbur ignored Noah. "Ermajean McCutchen can hardly wait to have Orin back."

"I'll never go back there," Orin said, moving until he was next to Matt.

Wilbur ignored Orin, too.

"I'm sure I'll even be able to find a home for Toby," Wilbur said, distaste evident in his curled lip. "It won't be easy—he's not a nice boy—but the good people of this town will rise to the occasion."

"You're not married, Wilbur," Matt said. "As you've said on numerous occasions, it's not suitable for a single man to have responsibility for such young and impressionable children."

"I might get married," Wilbur said.

"I am married, and the children are comfortable here."

"You just want Orin's money," Wilbur accused.

"I took Orin before I knew there was any money."

"You can't be trusted with it," Wilbur said. "Who's to say you won't use it for yourself?"

"If that's your only worry, let the Randolph bank in San Antonio handle it."

"They're friends of your family."

"They have an impeccable reputation," the judge said. "I think that's a good solution. Now, young man," he said to Noah, "show me that horse of yours. And you stay here," he said to Wilbur when he started to follow them. "Ask Ellen to take you inside and give you some coffee." He turned back to Matt. "Tell me what you have in mind for this ranch. From what Toby says, you plan to be the biggest horse breeder in the state."

"I'm not that ambitious," Matt said, relieved to be able to direct the judge's attention to something he felt was in his favor. "I plan to breed cattle like the rest of my family, but my sister"—it was easier to call Drew his sister than to keep explaining about them being adopted—"and her husband are working with me to develop a cow pony especially for working cattle."

"Matt says my horse is the fastest horse on the ranch," Noah said, impatient with this talk about breeding. "You can ride him if you want."

"Why don't you and Orin bring him up to the small corral so the judge can see him?" Matt said. The boys didn't wait to be told twice.

"They seem to get along okay," the judge said.

"Noah's a pain," Toby said, "but I guess he won't be so bad when he grows up."

"You're not happy about having a younger brother and sister?" the judge asked.

Matt felt his stomach clench. The boy knew what was at stake, but he was still so centered on how everything affected him, he couldn't always be trusted to say or do the right thing.

"You trying to trap me?" Toby asked, looking up at

the judge. "I know that preacher fella hates my guts, but I thought you were fair."

Matt's stomach muscles firmed into a hard knot. No telling what the boy would say next.

"I'm not trying to trap you," the judge said, "but I do need to know whether letting Mr. and Mrs. Haskins adopt the four of you is a good idea."

"First, they ain't adopting me," Toby said. "I work for my keep. Second, you're crazy if you don't let them adopt Orin and those kids. No matter what that preacher says, nobody wants us. I don't know why, but Matt and Ellen do. I keep getting into trouble because of girls, but Matt always looks out for me. No matter how mad I make him, he backs me. Ellen takes up for me, too, and she doesn't even like me."

Matt grimaced.

"But they're nuts about Orin and the kids. You shoulda seen Orin when he came here. Scared of his shadow and jumpy as a filly around her first stallion."

Did the boy have to use such earthy descriptions?

"It took me and Matt half a year to calm him down. I never seen him smile until a month ago. Then his grandfather left him all that money, and he's been scared as crap ever since that somebody's going to take him away. It's that preacher you ought to take away. It's not right that he can go around scaring Orin like he does."

"Reverend Sears has Orin's best interests at heart."

"If he did, he'd leave Orin right where he is. How would you like knowing people only wanted you for your money? Matt don't care nothing about that money. His family's rich. They got ten times that much money. Maybe a hundred times."

"I think that's a slight exaggeration," Matt said, but

he had to let Toby talk. It would look worse if he tried to stop him. He was saying some things Matt couldn't. "Besides, Jake and Isabelle's money doesn't come into the question here."

"Sure it does. Isabelle says we're family. If anything happens to you, they'll take care of us."

"Is that true?" the judge asked Matt.

"Yes."

"Isabelle's already got Tess calling her 'grandmama,'" Toby said. "And Noah thinks Will can do everything bettern Matt. It ain't true, but I ain't saying nothing if it makes the kid happy."

"So you really don't mind the kids?"

"Not really. Besides, we bastards have to stick togther."

Matt grimaced. Toby did have a way of cutting to the heart of the matter.

"That's important?" the judge asked.

"You ever seen anybody wanting to take in a bunch of bastards that was bound to cause them nothing but trouble?"

"Can't say I have," the judge replied.

"Well, Matt and Ellen are. They don't even think of us as bastards. Ellen says Noah and Tess are her kids. And she means it. I bet she'll run away to California or one of the territories if you try to take her kids. And Matt's given Noah a horse and Tess a kitten. He even tells her stories at night. He'd probably go with them."

Now Matt wished he had cut Toby off. He was like a drunk who couldn't stop talking.

"What would you do if that happened?" the judge asked.

"I'd go with him," Toby said.

The judge turned to Matt, his expression impossible to interpret. "Is what this boy says true?"

Chapter Sixteen

Matt didn't know what to say. Toby had given the judge too much insight into the family to attempt to fool him.

"Ellen and I believe we have a good life to offer the children," Matt answered, avoiding the question. "They'll have a normal home, plenty of room to flex their muscles, and a family that loves them."

"It looks like adopting kids is getting to be a tradition in your family."

"Ellen and I were both orphans. We understand what it's like."

"And you can make them feel safe and loved?"

"No point in asking him," Toby said. "You gotta ask us."

"The others want to be adopted," the judge said. "But you don't?"

"It's hard to say, Judge."

Matt's heart sank. When Toby started digging for truth, he always came up with something startling.

"Don't get me wrong, I think Matt's a great guy. Ain't nobody else woulda took me in and put up with all the trouble I cause. I was a pretty mouthy kid when I got here. I didn't take to being told what to do even when I knew it was good for me. But Matt had a lot of patience. He finally made me see I was my own worst enemy."

"So why don't you want to be adopted?"

"I'm not a kid anymore. I can't stay here forever."

"Both Ellen and I want to adopt you," Matt said. "Either way you know you can stay as long as you want."

"You'll be having kids of your own. You don't need no trouble-causing half-breed like me, even if I am the best-looking young guy in the whole county. Matt's brother, Will, is the best-looking," Toby told the judge. "Women practically faint when they clap eyes on him."

They were near enough to the corral that Noah's piercing voice broke into their conversation.

"Hurry up," he called. "You gotta see my horse."

"I'm coming as fast as a fat old man can," the judge called to Noah before turning back to Toby. "You can tell your foster parents—I guess I can tell them that without insulting your independence—that I'm going to approve the adoption of Orin, Noah, and Tess. If I were you, I'd consider letting them adopt you. Not many kids like you get a second chance." The judge stepped away purposefully. "I'm coming," he called, responding to Noah's impatient urging. "If I go any faster, I'll have to borrow your horse just to get back to the house."

*　*　*

Ellen didn't want to go to bed. She wasn't the least bit sleepy. The adoption process would take weeks before it was official, but they had passed the most crucial test. Despite Wilbur and Mabel Jackson's best efforts, Noah and Tess would be hers in a few months. No one would ever be able to take them away.

And Orin. She had to remember to include him. He would be just as much her son as Noah. She wasn't comfortable with that yet, but Orin was a nice boy, and he clearly wanted her to like him. He turned to Matt whenever he felt threatened, but he was beginning to act like any normal boy, turning to his father at certain times, to his mother at others. Just like Noah.

She reminded herself that she planned to take the children and move to San Antonio as soon as the adoption was final. She hated the way that made her feel so guilty. It wasn't fair. She'd told Matt from the beginning what she planned to do.

But she hadn't told the children. They thought they had a permanent home with two parents who would love them and stay with them forever. She would be the one to destroy their dream. Orin's, too. She couldn't tell herself that Matt didn't want her to stay. He didn't love her—as far as she could tell, he didn't have any feeling for her at all—but he did want her to stay.

But she couldn't. Doing so would make her feel like part of the furniture. She would be staying because she was useful, because it was easy. She didn't mind being useful. In fact, she wanted to be useful, but that was no reason to marry. Having no husband at all was better than being little more than a live-in housekeeper.

"It's time to stop celebrating and get to bed," Matt

announced. "This is still a ranch, and we have work to do."

"Can I help with the horses?" Noah asked. "The judge said I must be a big boy to have such a fine horse."

"You can help when they're a little more used to people," Matt said. "Right now they don't like anybody very much, even me."

Ellen got to her feet. "I want you both in your night clothes and washed behind your ears by the time I finish cleaning up."

"Are you going to check behind my ears to make sure I washed?" Orin asked.

"Absolutely," Ellen said. "I insist that all my children have clean ears."

"What about me?" Toby asked. "Do you want me in my night clothes?"

"I leave you to Matt," Ellen replied, uneasy with the look in Toby's eye. He'd never wanted her here, but he acted like he felt left out. All evening his participation in their fun had seemed a bit forced. She was certain Matt had noticed, too. She'd have to ask him what was wrong. He always understood Toby.

Everyone had eaten too much cake, custard pudding, and berries covered in cream. It seemed a wasteful indulgence, but nobody had wanted to stop talking about what they were going to do now that their future was secure. Every time Noah and Tess said something that indicated that they thought they'd never leave the ranch, Ellen felt guilty all over again.

"The boys and I can clean up," Matt offered.

"It won't take but a few minutes. You'd better hurry and see to the animals. Tess was nodding over her berries. She'll be upset if she falls asleep without telling you good night."

She welcomed the silence, the tasks that kept at least part of her mind from focusing on the future. She had worked so hard for this adoption, looked forward to it with such desperate hope. It wasn't fair that she should now feel so terrible.

Like Toby, she felt she was on the outside looking in. Not until today did she realize how much she wanted to stay at the ranch, too. But as much as she'd come to like Matt, to respect him, to depend on his judgment, she couldn't give up her freedom. She'd been dependent on other people her whole life, and they'd taken advantage of her. She didn't think Matt would, but—

"We're ready," Noah said, sticking his head in the kitchen. "I washed especially good."

"Be there in a minute. I just have to dry this last bowl and put it away."

"I'm going to hide from Matt," Noah said. "Don't tell him I'm in the wardrobe. Tess is hiding, too, but she just put the pillow over her head. That's stupid. He'll know where she is."

But Matt would search all over that room, wondering aloud where Tess could be hiding, looking behind chairs, curtains, anything until she was so excited she'd take the pillow off her head and jump up and down, delighted she'd fooled him. Then he'd do the same thing with Noah, even though he knew the only hiding places in the room were under the bed or in the wardrobe. He always knew exactly what to do for the children.

But he didn't know what to do for her. Or if he did, he didn't want to do it.

That's why she couldn't stay at the ranch.

She walked out into the hall and nearly ran into Orin.

"You gonna check behind my ears?" he asked. He grinned up at her so broadly she felt like hugging him.

"What did you do," she asked, "put your head under the pump?" His hair was still wet.

"Toby dunked me. He said it was faster."

He obviously took Toby's rough treatment as a sign of affection. It probably was. Men were peculiar like that.

"Your ears look fine to me," she said. Then on impulse, she kissed him on top of his head.

Much to her shock, Orin threw his arms around her waist. "I'm glad you're going to adopt me."

"Hurry up, you big baby," Toby called from the loft, "before I put corncobs in your bed."

Orin held her tight for an extra couple of seconds, then let go and scrambled up the stairs to the loft. Ellen watched him disappear, bare feet sticking out of a nightshirt at least two sizes too large. It made him look even more like a little boy who desperately needed and wanted a mother.

The front door opened. "Everything's fine at the barn," Matt announced. "How about here?"

Ellen wiped a tear from her eye before turning around. "Toby and Orin are in bed. Noah and Tess are hiding. They're waiting for you to find them."

Matt came closer. His smiled faded as his gaze focused on her. "Are you all right?"

"I'm fine."

"You've been crying."

"They're tears of happiness. And relief. I didn't really believe I'd ever see this day."

"Believe it," he said. "Your children are safe." But

his expression said he didn't believe she'd told him the real reason for her tears.

His gaze never wavered, never left her. She felt him stripping away the layers of her defense. "You'd better start looking for Noah and Tess."

She turned away without waiting for his response. She didn't trust him not to see right through to the center of her soul and know what she was thinking. Nothing was right anymore, and she didn't know what to do about it. Too soon she found herself in bed, waiting for Matt to finish undressing in the dark.

She had never been a crybaby, not even when her cousin made her feel so unloved and unwanted. Certainly not after the Lowells' accusations. But now it was all she could do to keep from bursting into tears. Everything seemed impossible. She wanted to stay, but she couldn't. She wanted to feel protected, but she wanted her independence. She wanted to be part of this family, but she couldn't trust herself to any man. Matt didn't love her. She didn't love him. There was no solution.

The tears started, and there was nothing she could do to stop them.

"This has been an eventful day," Matt said. "I don't think Toby and Orin will stop talking for a while yet. Even Noah and Tess were having a hard time getting to sleep."

She felt the bed sag as he sat down, but she knew her voice wasn't steady enough to answer him.

"You ought to thank Toby. He started talking to the judge on the way to see Noah's horse. You know Toby; he's liable to say anything. There were a couple of moments when I was ready to strangle him, but he may have been our strongest advocate, and he's the one who doesn't want to be adopted."

"He does," she managed to say. She coughed, pretending to clear her throat. "He just doesn't want to admit it."

Matt lay down in the bed and rolled over.

"I know."

He hadn't turned his back like he always did. He'd turned toward her.

"What is it you're not telling me?"

"Nothing. We got exactly what we wanted. I'm the happiest woman in Texas." Then she started sobbing like a baby. She was furious at herself for doing it, but she couldn't stop.

Then something happened that caused her to stop crying as abruptly as she'd started.

Matt put his arm around her and moved closer.

He had never touched her like that, not even at their wedding, yet now he was holding her in his arms.

"You don't want to leave, do you?" he asked.

"It's not that." It wasn't exactly a lie. It just wasn't the truth. "Tess and Noah think they're going to stay here forever. Tess wants another kitten and Noah wants a dog. Then there's Orin. Tonight he asked me to make sure he washed behind his ears. He even hugged me."

"Are you sure you can't stay here?"

Her heart skipped a beat. He did want her to stay. He did want her to be part of his family. But as soon as the feeling of happiness expanded inside her, it withered. He didn't love her. She didn't love him. That was no basis for a marriage. She might be pushed into a tight corner, but she knew the only thing that could cause her to give up her dream of independence, that would make her feel safe doing so, would be to fall hopelessly in love, and have the man feel the same way.

Until that changed, she couldn't stay.

"I want to be independent and own my own shop. In a few months I'll be able to do that, even buy my own house. It's what I've always wanted." It was. She'd dreamed of it for years. "But if I take Noah and Tess away, they'll never forgive me. Tess might, but I know Noah never will. Boys never understand about hats."

She didn't know if she was making sense, but it was hard to think clearly when she was embarrassed, furious with herself for crying so hard tears ran down her cheeks. She'd never cried in front of a man.

"You could run your shop from here," Matt suggested.

She turned on her side to face him. "I'd still have to act like your wife."

"Is that so terrible?"

"Not altogether. Everybody in Bandera tells me how lucky I am to be married to you. I know you're a wonderful man, but we don't love each other. We want different things. It just wouldn't work out; we'd both be miserable. I hate being dependent. I don't want to owe anything to anybody."

"That's what I told Jake and Isabelle when I borrowed the money for this ranch, but I missed seeing something very important."

"What?"

"You've got to receive love as well as give it. Otherwise it doesn't work. I wouldn't let Jake and Isabelle buy my ranch for me, but I did learn to let them give me furniture. I took back the things I didn't like, but I kept the others. I think Isabelle figured that out."

"That doesn't apply to me. Nobody wants to give me

love. Even the kids love you better than me."

That sounded petty and jealous and she was ashamed the minute she said it, but it was true, and she felt better for having gotten it out.

"They love us in ways that complement each other. And you're wrong about people not wanting to love you. You just have to let them. You've got to stop closing yourself off."

"You've got no room to talk. You're so tightly wrapped up in a safe bundle nobody can get to you. I'm surprised Isabelle managed to get through."

"It's because I am closed off that I can see what I've missed. I don't want the same thing to happen to you. You're a generous, warmhearted woman who deserves to be happy."

"How, when you're the only man I know who's not disgusting, and I don't love you? It would be even worse if I did find a good man. I'm already married."

She didn't know why she couldn't control her tongue. It wasn't his fault she was such a fool she could only love a hero who could vanquish all her foes. It was a foolish daydream, but it had sustained her through the difficult years of growing up. She still longed for her dream man who would swoop down and carry her away. If he ever appeared, she'd never give another thought to hats or independence.

In the midst of her tirade Matt started to pull his arm away. She stopped him. She wasn't willing to give up the comfort of his touch.

"You will be happy one day, I'm sure of it," he said. "Don't worry about what will happen when you meet a man you can love. I'd never stand in your way."

"I know that, and it makes me feel awful. It makes me feel like I'm using you."

"We're using each other. We both knew that from the start. It's not a problem. You'll fulfill your part of the bargain by staying here until the adoption is complete. I'll fulfill mine by helping you set up your shop in San Antonio."

"But the children will be so unhappy."

"Maybe we'll have a better idea what to do about that when the time comes," he said after a pause. "In the meantime, be happy."

How could she do that when she felt so miserable? She was a traitor to everybody—her kids, Orin, Matt, herself, even Toby. She couldn't do what she needed to do without hurting all of them.

"Would you like to go on a picnic?" Matt asked.

"What?" The idea startled her.

"A picnic."

"When?"

"Sunday, after church. The whole town will be there. We can go down to the river. We might even let the kids go for a swim."

"They don't know how."

"I'll teach them."

"I don't—"

"I'll be very careful."

He gave her a gentle squeeze. "I know you didn't want to marry me, but I'm glad you did. The boys and I will be sorry to see you leave. Wear your new red dress to the picnic. Now go to sleep, and try not to worry. Everything will work out."

Then he rolled up on his elbow and kissed her gently on the cheek. Before Ellen could recover from her shock, he'd pulled back to his side of the bed and turned away.

Ellen's thoughts were in utter chaos. She wanted to

go. She wanted to stay. She wished she could love him, but she didn't. She wanted the kids to be happy, but she couldn't give up her dream of her own shop.

Everything would be perfect if I loved Matt and he loved me, she thought to herself. Why couldn't that happen? It would fix everything.

But nothing in her life had ever worked out the way she hoped.

Matt woke to find Ellen sleeping up against him, their arms thrown across each other. Having gotten over his fear of being touched, he found he liked sleeping next to her, their limbs entangled. Though the times he'd touched her were few and were nearly all when she was asleep, he didn't want to give up even that. He'd wanted this kind of comfort all his life, and he would only be able to enjoy it for a few more months.

He was a fool to torture himself with what he couldn't have. He'd done everything he could to protect her and the kids, to fulfill his promise, and she hadn't learned to love him. Learning he had been abused wouldn't make her feel any different. He'd be lucky if she didn't pack up and leave immediately. You couldn't expect any woman to want to live with a man like that.

He didn't expect it, but that didn't stop him from wanting it anyway.

Ever since he was ten, he knew life would be different for him. Even without being an orphan, without getting into trouble, he would be different from other boys, from other men. Jake and Isabelle had changed a lot of that when they adopted him, but they couldn't change everything. They couldn't erase what had happened.

What had changed him forever.

He'd accepted that he was different, that all his emotions must remain locked tight inside him. He wasn't empty. Fury filled him. Sometimes it welled up so hard and fast that it nearly overwhelmed him. He was full of needs, physical and emotional—to be loved, to be accepted. Most of all he needed to be able to tell the truth, share his burdens without fear of losing the love and acceptance necessary for his happiness.

He knew that would never happen.

So he had decided to concentrate on helping boys like himself, making sure their lives weren't blighted by the things other people had done to them. He could help only a few, but he intended for them to leave his ranch healthy, happy, whole human beings. Then he'd been forced to marry Ellen in order to keep Orin, and everything had changed.

He was falling in love with her.

It didn't matter that it was stupid. It didn't matter that nothing could come of it. It didn't matter that he could never tell her. It didn't even matter that she didn't love him. It was happening anyway. He'd tried to stop himself, but it hadn't done any good.

At least a dozen times he'd told himself it was practically impossible not to fall in love with a woman like Ellen. She was warm, loving, and caring. She would do anything necessary to keep her kids. He was impressed by the way she'd adapted to living on the ranch, how readily she'd taken up her part of the work, even insisted he hand over more of it to her. She was almost always cheerful. When she wasn't, she was honest. Orin liked her, and even Toby wasn't so antagonistic anymore. She made him feel happy, more relaxed, more accepted.

He'd been physically attracted to her from the first.

But in the past, even with women he liked and found attractive, contact had resulted in revulsion, not arousal.

But that had changed with Ellen. Several times before he'd awakened to find Ellen touching him in her sleep, his body aroused and hard. He was aroused again tonight, so much so that it was painful. He didn't mind the pain. It meant he was alive. It meant someday he might have a normal life, enjoy what every other man took for granted, what he thought he'd been denied forever.

His arousal brushed against Ellen's thigh. He pushed ever so slightly against her. It was dangerous, but the need within him was so urgent he couldn't stop. He didn't rub hard, not enough for her to notice. He was sure it wouldn't wake her.

But instead of satisfying his need, it only stoked it. He wanted more. His arms lay across her chest just below her breasts. It was only natural that his thumb should gently massage her side, then her breast. It followed just as logically that other fingers would become involved, until his whole hand was pressed against her breast.

As he continued to caress her, his breathing became faster and nosier. He felt the blood pounding in his head, his heart beating at a faster tempo. He felt almost dizzy with elation. Ellen had helped him throw off one set of shackles he'd thought would hold him prisoner forever. There was no reason to think she couldn't help him break the bonds of the other.

He tried to stop, but his hand acted of its own volition, gently massaging her breast. For a moment he feared he would choke on his own breath, it came in such great, irregular gulps. He was just as bad as a young boy with his first girl. He was a man, but Ellen was his first girl. His reaction was all the more intense for the years he'd waited. The extra oxygen he'd gulped in made him dizzy. He forced himself to relax, to breathe more slowly. This was the first time he'd had a woman in his arms, but he didn't want to make a fool of himself.

It didn't do his self-esteem any good to realize that Toby would probably have handled a similar situation with more skill. He kept telling himself he ought to pull back, that he was risking disaster, but he was intoxicated by his first taste of sexual arousal, the first hint at possible fulfillment.

A surge of energy shot through him when he felt Ellen's nipple harden under his touch. Holding his breath, he used his finger to gently rub the nipple until it became pebble-hard. Excitement coursed through him until he felt nearly overcome by it. There was no stopping now.

Chapter Seventeen

Ellen dreamed Eddie Lowell had cornered her in the nursery. His parents and sisters were gone for the afternoon, and they were alone in the house. She tried to get away from him, but no matter where she turned, he blocked her escape. Now he had captured her and wouldn't let her go. He had his hands all over her. She tried to cry out, but no sound came from her throat. She was suffocating. Her limbs felt leaden, too heavy to move.

She woke with a feeling of panic to find Matt's arm across her chest. He pulled back immediately.

"We rolled up against each other," he explained anxiously. "We've done it several times before."

Her relief was almost painful in its intensity. The fear had been so great, her helplessness so total. Dreams always brought back the helplessness she'd felt all her life, the fear that one day . . . but this was Matt. She trusted him, found comfort in his touch, reassurance in his presence. She knew he would never hurt her.

"I didn't mean to wake you," Matt said.

"I know." She used to move away from him immediately, but recently she'd stopped. She liked his warmth next to her. He made her feel safer. Once she had even lain awake listening to him breathe. Just the sound relaxed her.

But this time was different. He didn't sound like himself. He sounded . . . well, upset, she guessed. But Matt never got upset. That was one of the frustrating things about him. He also seemed nervous, tense . . . she didn't know, she was too sleepy to analyze it carefully. "You don't have to move away," she said. "I like having you close." She shouldn't admit this. He might get the wrong idea. "I guess it comes from feeling so alone most of my life. If it makes you uncomfortable—"

"I don't mind."

She'd expected him to be reluctant, but he sounded eager. She knew that couldn't be right. He'd only recently gotten to where he didn't seem uncomfortable when Tess hugged him. He certainly couldn't like touching her, even in his sleep. He avoided her when he was awake.

"I don't want to crowd."

"Will and I used to share a bed when he was little. I missed it when he got big enough to have his own bed."

She didn't like being compared to his brother, but she was relieved he didn't feel anything of a more intimate nature. Her body was warm. Actually it was hot. Her breasts tingled; her nipples felt hard. Her entire body hummed with sexual tension. She didn't know how a dream about Eddie could do that. She felt as though she'd started to—

But that was foolish. She'd never made love to anyone. She didn't know how it would affect her. She instinctively recognized what she was experiencing was right, though. She just couldn't figure out why she should be feeling it. "I'm not sure I could go back to sleep like this."

"Just try," he said.

She didn't know why Matt should be so different tonight. He'd held her when she cried, kissed her to make her feel better. Maybe that was what had broken down the barrier. Maybe it was also what allowed her to accept that she just might be able to sleep with his arm around her.

If she just didn't feel so hot. Blood sang in her head. She felt wide awake. Sleep was about the furthest thing from her mind. "I'm feeling a bit unsettled," she said.

"I'll be very still. You won't even know I'm here."

She might not love Matt, but it was impossible not to be aware of his every move. He was in her bed, touching her.

And he was a man!

She felt herself growing hotter.

But she didn't want to move away. As long as he was close enough to touch, she knew she'd be safe from people like Eddie Lowell. She didn't know why she was so hot, so agitated, but she assumed it must have been the dream. She would feel better in a short while.

Matt sighed. Soon his steady breathing indicated he'd fallen asleep. Ellen was still awake. Still hot. Worse, she could feel herself gradually becoming attached to a man who wasn't at all what she wanted.

She'd have to do something about that, but not tonight. She was too comfortable. Well, almost.

She was still too hot.

"Back so soon?" Norma Ireland said when Ellen entered her shop. "I hope that doesn't mean you disliked the dresses."

"No. I need something for a picnic."

"The church picnic down by the river?"

"Yes."

Norma's gaze became speculative. "Just how attractive do you want to be?"

Ellen burst out laughing. "It's not fair that you understand your customers so well!"

Norma smiled in return. "If I didn't, I wouldn't sell so many dresses."

"I don't want anything flashy or gaudy, but I want to be the best-dressed woman there."

"Do you want a touch-me-not, or do you want something you can throw horseshoes in?"

"I guess it'll have to be horseshoes. The kids are certain to drag me into some game sooner or later."

"Good," Norma said. "Mabel Jackson already has a corner on touch-me-not. She bought a dress made of ecru buff brilliantine trimmed with slate satin-bound scallops. She even had me order ready-made hooped petticoats from Houston."

"Sounds like she'll be afraid to get down from her buggy. I wouldn't like that."

"I've got two I think you'll like, one made from striped ticking trimmed with black ribbon zigzag bands, another of blue plaid silk."

"The silk sounds too nice for a picnic. You'd better show me the ticking."

"I'm glad you're coming," Norma said from the other room as she looked for the dresses. "Wilbur's doing his best to turn everybody against Matt."

"What's he saying?"

"Nothing we haven't heard before," Norma said, returning with two dresses. "But you should have been here when Isabelle Maxwell came to town. She hunted him down at the church and braced him in the middle of a prayer meeting."

"I wish she hadn't done that," Ellen said. "Wilbur can be awfully cruel sometimes."

"According to what I was told, Isabelle was a bit more than he could handle." Norma held up the ticking and silk dresses for Ellen's inspection. "When he started quoting the Bible, Isabelle matched him quote for quote, told him if he couldn't remember the rest of the Bible, he at least ought to remember the Ten Commandments. She told the ladies at the meeting that if they wanted to pray for something, they could pray for a minister who thought more about God and less about himself. To quote one of the women who was there, Isabelle left total destruction in her wake."

"I don't know why Wilbur is so against Matt," Ellen said. "The way he acts, you'd think Matt was the devil himself."

"Wilbur has told everybody he offered to marry you."

"He doesn't love me," Ellen said angrily, "and he doesn't want the children. He just wants credit for saving my soul."

"I think he had something else in mind." Norma looked her straight in the eye. "There's nothing that says a preacher can't enjoy the pleasures of the flesh."

"Nonsense." Ellen didn't like having her business known, especially when it concerned Wilbur Sears. She was trying to figure out how to turn the conversation to another topic when Susan entered the shop.

"I hope you brought me some more hats," she said "Don't worry about Norma. She already knows, but I didn't tell anyone else."

"I don't suppose it matters that much any more. Everybody will know when I open my shop in San Antonio."

"What will I do for hats?" Susan asked.

"I didn't know Matt was considering selling his ranch," Norma said. "What will he do?"

Ellen decided it was impossible to carry on a relaxed conversation when you were trying to keep a secret. "He doesn't want to leave, so I'm considering running the store from the ranch," she said.

"Would you still sell your hats to me?" Susan asked.

"I like both dresses," Ellen said to Norma, deciding to leave before she said something else she shouldn't. "I'll buy the striped ticking for the picnic and the blue check silk for later. Now I'd better be going. I left Tess with Mrs. Ogden. The child will have talked the poor woman's ear off by now."

"You'd better give some thought to what that preacher's saying," Norma warned as she began wrapping up the dresses. "He's been hinting that it's not good for a man to be alone with two young boys so much."

"He's not alone," Ellen protested. "I'm there now."

"I'm just telling you what he's been saying. I don't know that the judge is paying him any attention, but there are people who are."

"One of these days the Reverend Wilbur Sears will to be forced to account for his actions," Ellen said, grinding her teeth in anger. "I hope I'm there to see it."

*   *   *

Ellen wasn't at all sure they should have come to the picnic. The entire Maxwell clan had turned out to support them, but Mabel Jackson and Wilbur Sears were there, too. Mabel had kept her distance since the judge approved the adoption, but Wilbur couldn't stop talking against Matt. Ellen was afraid if he even passed close by, she would give him a piece of her mind, and the piece she had in mind wasn't very pleasant.

The kids were surrounded by cousins.

"I'll take them to the river for a swim before we eat," Matt said.

"Where's Toby?" she asked.

"He has strict instructions to ignore the girls, regardless of what they might do to attract his attention."

"Do you think he can manage that?"

Matt grinned. "He doesn't know it yet, but he's going to help me teach the kids to swim."

Ellen felt a little sorry for Toby. He looked very handsome in his tight pants and frilly white shirt. She thought he was unwise to flaunt his Mexican heritage, but his clothes did make him stand out from the other boys. The girls thought so, too. Mabel Jackson had settled her family as far away from Toby as possible.

"Mabel ought to know that at least half of Tammy's attraction to Toby is her mother's disapproval," Isabelle said. "She has no interest in tying herself to a penniless cowboy. She's just looking for a little excitement."

"Anybody ready for a swim?" Matt asked.

Half the Maxwell clan rose to its feet.

"Come on," Isabelle said. "If we don't keep an eye on them, they'll end up miles down the river."

The day was warm and the river crowded. Most of

the women began laying out the food. The swimmers would be hungry when they emerged from the river. The young girls stayed on the bank—the Reverend Sears had announced that no female could bathe publically and preserve her modesty—but every child, young boy, and half the men stripped for a pleasant half hour in the river under the shade of the towering cypresses that lined its banks. Jake and Matt led the Maxwell group to a place down the river that wasn't so crowded.

Ellen was relieved to see Toby had a firm grip on Tess and Matt an equally firm grip on Noah. The little boy was so anxious to be as grown up as Toby, he refused to admit when he didn't know how to do things. Matt was using extreme patience, and a good deal of cleverness, to teach Noah how to swim and yet make the boy think he was doing it all on his own. She didn't know how he did it. He just had a natural instinct for what to do, what to say.

Even more amazing was the fact that he'd convinced Toby that the best way to impress girls, especially since he was forbidden to stray more than six feet from Matt's side, was to show them he had a tender, gentle side. Matt had said that most women liked the excitement of a handsome, dangerous rogue, but that they only got serious about men who showed sensitivity. Ellen had been surprised he would say that. She was even more surprised that he'd been able to convince Toby to give it a try.

It didn't apply to her. She had never told anybody about the kind of man she admired, the only kind she could fall in love with, the only kind she could trust enough to put her life in his keeping, but she wasn't a foolish young woman who was attracted to strong, dangerous men because they were exciting. She knew the ways of the world and its ability to injure and destroy people. The world was a hard, cruel place, and only such a man could guarantee her protection and safety.

"The children seem a lot happier now that the adoption has been approved," Isabelle observed.

"Especially Orin. He's almost like a different child." Ellen looked for him but didn't see him with Matt. "Do you know where he is?"

"I think he went off with Ward and his boys."

Ellen wasn't entirely reassured. It wasn't like Orin to go far from Matt, especially when they were in town.

"I hope they don't swim too far," she said.

"Ward will take care of him."

Ellen helped Isabelle stretch out a blanket in the shade, and they sat down, out of the sun but in view of the water. "Now tell me about yourself. Are you feeling more settled?"

"I don't think I'll be able to relax completely until the adoption is final and I have the papers in my hands, but I don't live in constant dread of an approaching wagon or horse."

"You shouldn't worry at all. Matt will take care of it."

"I suppose part of it is habitual. I've been looking over my shoulder for so long I can't stop."

"Then you need something more to occupy your mind."

Ellen changed position. "Look, Tess has learned to swim by herself." She appreciated Isabelle's concern, but she didn't like her habit of asking whatever question came to her mind. With Isabelle, no question was too personal.

"If Noah isn't careful, his sister will be a better swimmer than he is."

"Please don't say that," Ellen said. "It would crush his pride."

"There's nothing wrong with a woman being better at something than a man."

"There is in Texas."

"That's nonsense. Drew can shoot circles around any man in this state."

"You can't deny they resent it."

"No, but Cole doesn't care."

"Cole is a rare man. Look, Noah's swimming on his own." Having finally figured out how to make his feet and hands work together, Noah was showing off, swimming circles around Matt, who shouted encouragement. "Now he'll want to go swimming every time we come into town."

"Have Matt dam up the stream that runs through his place."

"I'd be afraid they'd go in when I wasn't looking."

Isabelle sighed. "They'll do a great deal while you're not looking. You might as well get used to it."

"Is being a mother that hard?"

"Yes and no. Nothing is more rewarding than seeing your children grow into adulthood. Sometimes I'm so proud of my boys I could bust, but they drive me crazy with worry. You have to let them go, let them make their own mistakes. Some of the things they do will break your heart, but there's nothing you can do about it. Matt's got the best understanding of any of my boys. I hope you've changed your mind about him."

Ellen felt herself tense. She knew what Isabelle was leading up to. "Matt is a wonderful man. I like and respect him very much."

"But?"

"But I don't want to be married or have to do what a man tells me to do."

"Matt would never force you to do anything you disliked."

"I know. He's impossibly nice."

"I hear another but coming."

"Isabelle, I'm sorry I can't be what you want. If I had married Matt looking for a home and family, I'd be the luckiest female in Texas."

"You are."

"But it's not what I want."

Isabelle got to her feet. "Most of us don't know what we want until we've thrown it away. I hope that won't be true in your case. Now, I think I'd better go help with the food."

Ellen hated to make Isabelle angry, but she refused to be bullied. She had been thinking more and more about staying at the ranch for a while longer, especially since the night Matt held her in his arms.

She didn't love him—she'd thought about that too often to have any doubt—but she liked him a lot. And she liked living on the ranch. She wanted her shop and her independence, but she realized they would come with a price. Being the mother of four children wasn't easy, but she'd never been happier or more content. She had Matt to depend on when things didn't go right, and even Toby had stopped complaining.

The temptation to stay was great. She'd considered opening her shop in the house, letting the ladies come out to the ranch to make their choices. That wasn't as good as going to San Antonio, but maybe after she got established she could open a second shop in San Antonio and hire someone to run it part of the time. She could spend three or four days a week at the ranch. She would have time to make a lot more hats at the ranch than if she was living in San Antonio, having to deal with customers and worry about all the responsibilities of a house.

It was impossible to leave the ranch until the adoption became final. If she tried very hard, she might be able to figure out how to keep the best of both worlds. But what about the fact that she didn't love Matt and he didn't love her?

Her efforts to find a solution kept being interrupted by bits of conversation from a group of women behind her. Once Ellen stopped trying to block out the sound of their voices, she realized they were talking about Matt. They obviously didn't realize the woman with her back to them was his wife.

"I never thought he was as bad as people said," one woman commented. "He's so handsome, how could he be that bad?"

"It all comes from being so quiet and never speaking up for himself," a second woman said. "When people don't know what to think, they come up with something on their own. It's usually worse than the truth."

"It's obvious those poor little bastard children adore him," the first woman said. "You just have to look at them together to see that."

"He must be doing something right," her companion said. "Even bastard children know when people are pretending."

"He hasn't done as well with that Toby," the first woman said.

"He's being a perfect gentleman today."

"You can say that because you don't have a daughter who moons about the house thinking how romantic it would be to be whisked away on horseback some moonlit night."

"We all had daydreams like that. She'll forget all about him soon."

"I don't know. He's a mighty handsome boy."

"Not as handsome as Mr. Haskins."

"Sarah June, I don't know what your Frank would say if he heard you talking like that."

Sarah June giggled. "Frank has nothing to worry about, but that's all beside the point. It's good Matt wants to adopt those children. It keeps them from being a charge on the community. I'm glad he's taken such a shine to that little bastard girl. She needs a father to make sure she doesn't grow up like her mother."

"She's got Ellen."

"Who also worked in the saloon. You can't forget the problem with the Lowells, though I promise you I don't believe everything I hear."

"Neither Patrick nor Eddie is saying much these days. The gossip is they really did attempt to rape that girl, then blamed it on her to keep Nancy from throwing them out. It's her money they're living on."

"Men will do anything for money."

"Except remain faithful."

Ellen stood and moved away. If she'd heard any more, she wouldn't have been able to remain silent. She was glad some people were beginning to believe her, but she was furious it had taken so long. She was also glad they were beginning to think more kindly of Matt, but she was furious that they kept referring to Tess as "that little bastard girl." The child had nothing to do with the circumstances of her birth. It would be worth it to move to San Antonio so nobody would know about Tess and Noah.

But as she looked down to the river, at the children playing happily with Matt, she knew they would probably rather remain with Matt and be called bastards than live in San Antonio with a respectable reputation. Which put her right back where she started. No matter what she did, everybody would be unhappy to some degree.

"I saw you flirting with those women," Ellen said to Matt. "You're nothing but a hypocrite. You know what they've said about you?"

"I don't know and don't care," Matt said. "I'll keep right on flattering them as long as it will help the adoption go through without a hitch."

They were on their way home. Noah had gone to sleep curled up in the buggy seat between them, Tess in Ellen's lap. Toby and Orin had wanted to stay longer, so Isabelle and Jake had offered to drop them off on their way back.

Ellen didn't understand why she should be so irritated. Matt hadn't been flirting. He'd just been talking, though that was practically the same for him as flirting since he hardly ever said anything to anybody. She certainly couldn't blame those women for hanging on his every word. One smile from him was enough to light up her day. She didn't see why other women should be any different.

"I thought everything went well today, didn't you?" he asked.

"Except when Wilbur announced to everyone within a quarter of a mile that you were the handmaiden of Satan—I was particularly enchanted by his referring to you as a maiden—who would usher the souls of those helpless children into hell if the townspeople didn't tear them from your embrace."

"His habit of overstating everything undermines his credibility. And people's patience. If he's not careful, the town may be as quick to turn its back on him as it was to welcome him."

"I didn't see any signs of it."

"People don't mind having an occasional catharsis about their sins, but they don't want them shoved in their faces week after week. They want a chance to commit a few more before they start repenting again."

"Sounds mighty cynical."

"Just human nature."

"Is understanding human nature what makes you so good with the kids?"

"That may be part of it, but it's mostly that I know what they're feeling because I felt it myself."

"But that doesn't explain Tess."

"Tess just wants somebody to love her and make her feel safe."

So do I.

Ellen pushed that thought aside.

"Looks like we've got company," Matt said.

Ellen was tired. She had children to feed and put to bed before she could go to bed herself. She wasn't in the mood to entertain company.

"I don't recognize the horse," Matt said.

Only Matt and Drew, so far as Ellen knew, identified people by the horses they rode.

As Matt brought the buggy to a halt, a young boy came from around the side of the house. "I'm Hank," he said, his gaze focused on Matt. "I want you to adopt me, too."

Chapter Eighteen

The boy looked a year or two older than Orin. He had
big black eyes, fair skin, and a face almost girlish in its
prettiness. His nearly black hair hadn't been cut in
months and his clothes fit him badly. His body was tall
and thin, probably the result of a recent growth spurt.
Ellen was certain he would grow to an impressive size,
but right now he looked tired, hungry, and frightened
out of his mind.

"What made you come to me?" Matt asked as calmly
as if this happened to him every day.

"I heard you took in orphaned kids."

"Who told you?"

"People. They said you adopted Toby."

"I didn't adopt him. He works for me."

"I'll work for you. Just let me stay here."

"You can't do that," Ellen whispered to Matt. "His

267

parents are probably frantic, wondering where he is."

"Do you have parents?" Matt asked.

"No."

"What happened?"

"Sickness got 'em."

"We ought to take him to the sheriff," Ellen said. "It's his job to find the boy's relatives and notify them to come get him."

"Who's been taking care of you?"

"Uncle Wayne."

"Why him?"

"He had a ranch nearby my folks. He said I could stay with him until he could take me into town."

"But he didn't take you into town, did he?"

Ellen didn't understand why Matt was asking all these questions. He didn't have to know anything to turn the boy over to the sheriff. She supposed, since it was so late in the day, they had to keep him for the night, but the change in Matt made her nervous. He had masked his face, but Ellen could see he was so angry he was shaking.

Ellen didn't understand. He couldn't be mad at Hank, and it was pointless to be mad at Wayne for waiting so long to take the boy into town.

"He made me stay behind when he went to town," Hank said.

"How did you know about me?"

"I followed him this time. I hid downriver until he left town. I spent the night in somebody's barn. Today, people at the picnic kept offering me food. I was hungry, so I stayed. That's when I saw you with the little kids. I overheard some boys talking about Toby—he was in the river with you—saying you were a sucker to take in so many orphans, especially a troublemaking bastard like Toby. I figured if you didn't mind Toby being all that bad, you'd take me, too. I'm real good."

"I'm sure you are," Ellen said, moving the still sleeping Tess off her lap so she could get down from the buggy. "Wake up," she said, gently shaking Tess and Noah. "We're home. It'll soon be time for supper."

The kids woke up slowly, unaware of Hank, who had left the side of the house and approached Matt's side of the buggy. Up close Ellen could see the evidence of old bruises, as well as yellow splotches on his face and arms, the fear in his expression. What had happened to this kid?

"You shouldn't have run away," Ellen said to Hank. "I'm sure Wayne and his wife are worried sick about you."

"Wayne don't have no wife."

For a moment anger drove fear from the boy's expression, but not for long. Ellen didn't know what had caused Hank to run away, but it was obvious he was very frightened of something.

"Does he have any boys?" Ellen asked, wondering if they'd been the source of Hank's bruises.

"Wayne ain't never been married. Pa said he was supposed to get married, but he changed his mind and came west. Mama used to say some men weren't cut out to be married."

They had said the same about Matt.

"Is that Wayne's horse?" Matt asked.

"No, it's mine," Hank said. "Wayne said we ought to take Mama's cow and chickens, too. He said there was no point in letting the wolves and coyotes get them."

"Come inside," Ellen said, herding the sleepy children toward the house. "Supper will be ready in a little while. Matt will help you take care of your horse. After supper we can talk about what to do with you."

"I want to stay here," Hank said, addressing himself to Matt. "Please. I'll work just as hard as Toby."

"Toby's bigger than you," Ellen said. "The sheriff will—"

"I won't go to the sheriff," Hank said, backing away from them. "I'll run away. I'll—"

"You don't have to do anything," Matt said. He got down from the buggy and walked toward Hank. The boy drew back. "I want to look at your bruises," Matt said. Hank stood still while Matt checked his face, neck, arms, and hands. He even pulled up his shirt and examined his back.

Ellen had no idea what Matt was looking for. The kid's clothes didn't fit, but except for the bruises, he seemed to be in good health.

"Does Wayne ever hit you?" Matt asked.

"No."

"How did you get those bruises on your back?"

"We only have one bed. Sometimes Wayne rolls over on me."

"Matt will see that the sheriff talks to him. I don't see how that could happen just from rolling into someone." She had come close enough to see that the bruising was extensive.

Hank jumped back.

"Don't be afraid, son," Matt said. "I'm not going to let him hurt you again."

"It's not like he hurt him intentionally," Ellen said. "Besides, if he's the boy's uncle—"

"This boy is not going back," Matt said.

Ellen blinked at the vehemence of Matt's reply. He sounded like he hated her, as though he wanted to strangle her on the spot. She knew he wasn't mad at her, but she'd never seen him like this. She didn't know what to do, what to say. She'd suspected he had a temper, but he'd always keep it under such tight control, she'd forgotten about it. It was obvious now that the rage burning inside him was barely contained. She had no idea what would happen if it broke loose.

"Come on, we need to put up the horses," Matt said to Hank.

"Matt, you can't—"

"We'll talk about it later. Right now it's more important to get him cleaned up, fed, and in bed. He looks about Toby's size. He can borrow some of his clothes."

She stood there, not knowing what to think, her two sleepy kids rubbing their eyes, and watched Matt and Hank stop halfway toward the corrals. It seemed Matt asked Hank a question. Hank looked up. Ellen was too far away to hear what either of them said. The boy seemed to stiffen, as though preparing himself for Matt's response to his answer. Matt said something— encouraging him to respond, Ellen assumed—and the boy spoke. Neither moved. Hank dropped his head, as though he expected to be blamed or chastised, maybe told to go away. Matt put his hand on the boy's shoulder. Hank looked up, and Matt said something else. Then they turned and headed toward the corral.

"Let's go inside," Ellen said to the kids. "Toby and Orin will soon be home."

As she began preparations for supper, Ellen couldn't shake off the uneasiness that had settled over her. She'd never seen Matt so angry, not even when he knocked Wilbur down. Something was very wrong, something she didn't understand.

"You'll have to sleep on a bedroll," Toby told Hank. "We don't have extra beds."

"I don't care," Hank replied.

Toby had presented a pile of his outgrown clothes to Hank after his bath. The fancy duds made him look younger, more vulnerable, much more handsome. Ellen's heart ached for the mother who would never see her handsome son grow up. All of a sudden she wanted to add Hank to the family, to make sure he had a chance to be the happy person he must have been before his parents died. It wouldn't be difficult to add one more. They only had to—

She stopped herself. They couldn't keep Hank. He had an uncle. She didn't know why he had run away, but if Hank didn't want to go back to him, he should be sent to another member of his family. She and Matt couldn't keep him. Wilbur Sears would probably accuse them of kidnapping, and that would be enough to convince the judge to stop the adoption.

When he entered the kitchen, Matt had whispered to her that she wasn't to say anything about sending Hank away, that he was frightened and they had to make him feel safe. She had agreed but said they had to take him into town first thing in the morning.

Matt hadn't replied.

"You can sleep in my bed," Noah volunteered. "I don't mind sleeping on a bedroll."

"He'll be more comfortable with the older boys," Ellen said. There was no point in saying that Tess might be uncomfortable with a stranger. She had taken to Hank right off, given him her kitten to hold and introduced him to Mrs. Ogden.

"Why don't you help him get his bed ready?" Matt said to Toby. "He looks tired, and we have to get up early tomorrow."

"We get up early every morning," Toby said. "Matt

says he likes to see the sun as it rises on a new day."

"I like to sleep," Noah announced.

"You'll have to get up, too," Matt said, "so you'd better get ready for bed."

Once the children had left the kitchen, Ellen tried again to talk about what they were going to do with Hank, but Matt said they'd talk when the kids were in bed and not likely to overhear.

"Hank seems like a nice boy," she said to Matt when he entered the bedroom. "It's a shame he doesn't want to stay with his uncle."

"He's never going back," Matt said. "If he doesn't have any more family, we'll keep him here until the judge decides what's best for him."

Matt was still angry. She hadn't realized how angry until he started undressing. He forgot to blow out the lamp. She started to remind him but changed her mind when he pulled off his shirt and sat down on the edge of the bed. Her first sight of his body mesmerized her. Muscles rippled across his broad back as he bent over to remove his shoes and socks. The extreme whiteness of his back contrasted with the sunburned skin above his collar. She experienced a strong urge to reach out and touch him. She felt nearly hypnotized. She wondered if this was anything like the feeling Tulip had described so often.

Breathless. Dazed. A strange sensation in her belly.

She wrenched her gaze away from Matt's shoulders. "We can't keep Hank if his uncle wants him back."

Matt stood and turned. "I didn't say we had to keep him. I just said he's not going back to his uncle."

The sight of Matt's naked chest rendered her speechless. She had seen many men—big ones, little ones, handsome ones, ugly ones—but she'd never seen a man

273

naked, even from the waist up. She didn't know how Matt compared. She only knew how he affected her. He left her breathless. His chest looked so broad, his arms so powerful, she wondered how she ever could have thought him weak.

She closed her eyes. "What are you going to do?"

"Keep him a few days until he calms down."

"But—"

"Then I'll decide what to do."

"There's no deciding about it. You've got to take him to the sheriff."

"I can't do that yet."

Ellen was aghast. She had been liking Matt more and more, depending on him so much that she wanted to find a way to stay at the ranch. Now he was trying to keep a boy who didn't belong to him, a boy who had an uncle who wanted him. "Why not?"

"Because the sheriff will hand him back to his uncle."

"That's not your problem."

"Of course it is. Hank came to me for help. I can't let him down."

"What do you mean 'he came to you for help'? He's running away because his uncle wouldn't bring him to town."

"There's more to it than that."

"Maybe, but you have no legal right to keep him here. If his uncle comes looking for him and you refuse to hand him over, it will endanger the adoptions. Do you think the judge will let you have the children if he thinks you go around stealing boys from their families?"

"I didn't steal him."

"That's what Wilbur Sears will say. He'll have that uncle so convinced you coaxed that boy off his ranch, he'll be eager to tell the judge you're a kidnapper."

"I'm only keeping him for a few days."

"Why can't the uncle take care of him? It shouldn't take the sheriff more than a couple of months to find his family."

"I can't let Hank be sent back. His uncle has been abusing him." Matt paused for a long moment. "I don't mean beat him. I mean abused him sexually."

Ellen didn't know what Matt meant. "What are you talking about?"

"Some men prefer boys to women. Hank's uncle is like that."

She didn't want to believe it could happen. It was too disgusting. She didn't want to believe that any man—especially an uncle, a man a boy should have been able to trust—would have violated that trust in such a horrible manner.

"How do you know?"

"Because my uncle abused me."

Her mind refused to accept what Matt said. It simply closed down. She'd never heard of anything more horrifying in her life. She looked up at Matt. He'd put the nightshirt on over his head and sat down to remove his pants. He seemed so big, so strong, so capable of protecting everyone else, it was nearly impossible to think of him being helpless.

Yet it explained so many things that had puzzled her—his dogged defense of the boys, his willingness to risk anything to keep them, his being withdrawn, his terrible fury when he realized what had happened to Hank, his holding back from being touched, keeping his distance from her even after she wanted closeness.

What could you say to a man who'd suffered so?

She couldn't say she understood. She didn't. Not that

she'd been assaulted, too. Neither Eddie Lowell nor his father had actually violated her. Matt's uncle had violated him in the most horrible way.

"I knew what had been happening—why Hank had run away—when I saw his back," Matt said.

"When did it happen to you?" she asked.

"It started when I was ten."

Started? "How long did it go on?"

He turned to face her. "Three years."

Her five years with her cousin had seemed endless, but three years must have seemed like forever to a boy trapped with nowhere to go.

"Why did it stop?"

He hesitated. "My uncle died."

She didn't know what to say. Any words would be inadequate. She felt utterly selfish about having gone on and on about the Lowells when something far worse had happened to Matt. She couldn't imagine what it must be like to know what people like Wilbur Sears would say if they knew. It had to be horrible going through life hiding such a painful secret. "Did you ever tell anybody?"

"Jake and Isabelle know. Nobody else cared."

He lay down on the bed. He didn't move toward her, just lay there, rigid and unmoving. She reached over and touched him. She didn't want him to think she would stay away from him because of what had happened. "I wish there were something I could do that would make a difference," she said.

He covered her hand with his. "You can. Don't turn away from me."

"Why would I do that?"

"Because I'm unclean. I'm—"

"You're not!" she protested, distressed he would even think that. She was having trouble accustoming herself to the horror of what had happened to him, but she didn't blame him. It certainly wouldn't cause her to turn away from him. She wanted to hold him in her arms until the years of accumulated hurt went away. She took his hand and held it between hers. "You're the finest man I've ever known. The kids think you're wonderful. I can't know how those awful years affected you, but you've risen above it."

Matt rolled over and kissed her on the cheek. "Thanks for saying that."

"I'm not just saying it," she said, upset that he sounded as if he thought she was just spouting compliments to make him feel better. "I mean every word."

"I'm not wonderful enough for you to want to be married to."

"You're wonderful enough for anybody to be married to. You know as well as I do we can't choose when and where we fall in love. If I could, I'd have been in love with you before now."

"Then you couldn't have had your shop in San Antonio."

She hadn't meant to get around to that topic in just this way, but it seemed as good a time as any. "Actually, I've been thinking about your suggestion that I operate my shop from the ranch."

He sat up in the bed.

"I don't mean to say I've fallen in love with you any more than you've fallen in love with me," she hurried to say. "But I like you, and I like living here. The kids like it, too. I know they wouldn't like living in San Antonio nearly so much, especially Noah, and I wouldn't want to leave Orin."

As she spoke, Matt had gradually sunk down until he lay on the mattress. "So you think we ought to stay married even though we don't love each other."

"I think we ought to consider it."

"What happens if you fall in love?"

"I'm not sure I can love any man. But if you fall in love, I'll give you a divorce."

"I won't fall in love, either. I'm not the kind of man women admire."

"But you are."

"My looks, not me."

"That's because they don't know you. If you'd spend more time in town they'd—"

"The boys need all the time I can give them."

"What you're doing for the boys is wonderful, but you need to think of yourself."

"I am. Taking care of them is what I want."

"But don't you want to fall in love, have a wife, children of your own?"

"Don't you?"

"I don't want to fall in love. I don't want to be under the power of any man."

"If a man truly loved you, you wouldn't be under his power."

"I've never met a man like that. Except you. I want children, but I'm happy with the kids and Orin. And Toby's starting to grow on me."

"So you think you might like to stay here?"

"I want to consider it." She didn't like the way he sounded. She pulled his hand against her breasts and kissed his knuckles. "You spoil me. I'm selfish enough to like that very much."

"You're easy to spoil."

"You're the first man to say that."

"I'd like to say much more."

She didn't want him to thank her for anything. That

would make her uncomfortable. She wanted to get back to Hank. They couldn't send him back, not if he was being abused. They couldn't keep him, either. "What are we going to do about Hank?"

"Nothing tonight."

"I really think we ought to take him to the sheriff."

"The sheriff can't help him."

"Hank can tell him what happened."

"The uncle will deny it. The law won't believe a child against an adult."

"We can't keep him. Wilbur will demand we give him up, and the law will be on his side."

"We don't have to figure this out now." He leaned over and kissed her on the forehead. "Get some sleep. We'll worry about it tomorrow."

Matt didn't know how much time had passed. He only knew that he didn't feel like sleeping. He ought to be thinking about how to protect Hank, how to help him learn to like himself again. If he reacted anything like Matt had, Hank felt dirty, ashamed of himself, certain nobody would ever want anything to do with him. Matt was determined to keep Hank from suffering as he had—as he still did.

Instead he found himself coming back time and time again to what Ellen had said. She was considering setting up her shop on the ranch. She liked him a lot. He knew he shouldn't read too much into that. She had been most definite in saying she didn't love him, that she didn't want to love any man. Yet she was considering staying on the ranch. Could that mean she felt more for him than she knew?

Probably, but that didn't mean she was in love with him. If she was, she certainly wouldn't stay in love with him once she knew about his uncle. It would be better for both of them if she went to San Antonio as soon as possible. It would save her a lot of heartache. It was too late for him.

He was already in love with her.

It was really stupid. He'd known from the first that she wasn't in love with him, didn't want to love him, that he wasn't the kind of man women fell in love with. He had been the one to offer the marriage, to suggest a business arrangement, to agree to help her set up her shop in San Antonio once the adoptions were final. Everything was working out just as they planned. Or it would have, if he hadn't started making changes. First, thinking about ways to keep the children on the ranch after she left, then suggesting she set up her shop on the ranch. That wasn't practical. They wouldn't want women driving out to the ranch any day of the week, at all hours, to spend time trying to decide whether they wanted a new hat. If they wanted this one or that one.

But none of that was as foolish as his falling in love with her. That practically made it essential she leave the ranch as soon as possible.

He'd always thought half a loaf was worse than no loaf at all. Now he wasn't sure. He'd gotten used to Ellen. She'd fit into his life right from the start. No task was too difficult. She didn't wait to be asked, and she didn't complain. But most of all Matt saw in her the same concern for the kids he felt. She knew what was ahead for them if they remained without a family to care for them. She'd been willing to make a sacrifice to ensure their lives wouldn't be like hers. Matt could have loved her for that alone.

Yet there was more. She had accepted him without criticism even though he wasn't the kind of man she could love. She hadn't made any effort to change or improve him. They disagreed on many things, but she'd been generous with her praise. Knowing he'd been abused hadn't caused her to turn away from him. Even now, she snuggled up against him.

Sometimes when he woke, he'd stay awake so he could enjoy the feeling of having her nestled against him. It made him feel as though she trusted him and wanted to be near him. That answered a need deep inside him. It didn't begin to fill up the well, but it kept the hole from getting any deeper.

She'd never know what a strain it was on him to just lie here, her warmth against him, her breasts touching his arms, his side, even his hands, knowing he dared not do what he ached to do. She had said she'd leave if he did.

Some nights he lay there so tense that his body shook from the strain. He had to grip his hands together to keep from touching her. She had let him give her brotherly kisses, but he wanted to take her in his arms and kiss her as he'd always dreamed of kissing the woman he loved. He wanted to pour out all the love he'd hoarded for so long.

But she would stop trusting him, stop wanting to touch him, to be around him. What they had wasn't much, but it was more than he'd had before. He just had to decide if he could live with it, at least for as long as she remained at the ranch. It seemed such a horrible option—pain now and more pain later—but he couldn't let her go. He could—

A scream ripped apart the silence of the night. He was out of the bed and halfway to the door before Ellen woke.

Chapter Nineteen

Watching through the kitchen window as she prepared supper, Ellen kept an eye on Hank as he played with Orin and Toby. He rarely smiled, but he seemed to be more relaxed, less prone to look over his shoulder. Thank goodness he hadn't had a recurrence of his nightmare.

It had frightened her badly to wake out of a dead sleep, screams reverberating through the house, Matt running from the room. She would have followed him if Tess and Noah hadn't woken up, Tess whimpering in fear. By the time the screams stopped, Tess was sobbing and Noah was clinging to her, his body taut with fear.

"There's no need to cry," she'd said. "It's just Hank having a bad dream."

"What about?" Noah asked.

"I don't know." She couldn't tell them the truth.

"I bet it's panthers," Noah said.

"There aren't any panthers around here."

"Toby says there's panthers and worse in Mexico."

"Maybe, but we're not in Mexico."

"Is it Indians?"

"It could be." But she was certain it wasn't Indians.

"Are Indians going to get us?" Tess asked between sobs.

"Matt won't let anything get us," Ellen said.

"I want Matt," Tess said. "Where is he?"

"He's in the loft with Hank," Ellen said. "But I'm sure he'll come give you a hug before he goes back to bed."

But it had been a very long time before Matt returned. By then Noah and Tess had fallen asleep.

"Was he dreaming about his uncle?" Ellen asked after they got back in bed.

"Yes."

They'd talked far into the night. Matt never explained what Hank's uncle had done or exactly what his own uncle had done. She wondered how Matt had managed to grow into such a strong, dependable, compassionate man. After Eddie Lowell attacked her, she'd been angry at the world, ready to lash out at everybody. Keeping his anger tightly controlled, Matt poured all his energy into doing for these boys what Jake and Isabelle had done for him. She couldn't imagine what kind of inner strength it must take to be able to do that.

Ellen went outside to call everyone to dinner. "Where are Matt and Noah? Supper will be ready soon."

"They're taking care of Noah's horse," Toby called out.

They were wrestling. The younger boys weren't strong enough to pin Toby, but he couldn't hold both of them down. Every time he got one down, the other jumped on his back. She hoped they'd be tired by the time Matt and Noah reached the house. Noah would want to jump right into the middle. They were too big and rough. She was afraid he'd get hurt.

"He thinks his horse has a spavin," Orin said.

"He's always hoping to find a spavin," Toby said. He wiggled out from between the two younger boys and managed to catch hold of them both. "He doesn't realize he can't ride a horse with a spavin."

Hank suddenly stopped wrestling, his body rigid.

"What's wrong?" Toby asked, sounding a little defensive. "I didn't hurt you."

But Hank wasn't looking at Toby. He stared up the trail that led out of their valley to the road that went to Medina, and from there to Bandera. Ellen looked up to see a man riding toward them. She had started to wonder aloud who he might be when Hank moaned, grew wide-eyed with fear, scrambled to his feet, and raced for the corrals as fast as he could run.

She knew.

"What's wrong with him?" Toby asked.

"I think that's his uncle," Ellen said.

"Is he going to take Hank away?" Orin asked.

"I'm not letting him take Hank," Toby said, getting up and squaring his body as though he was ready to take on the stranger by himself. "Hank's scared of him."

Matt hadn't told the boys what had happened to Hank. Ellen's first impulse was to send the boys to get Matt, but that was unnecessary. As soon as Hank told him who'd come looking for him, she was sure Matt would come straight to the house.

"We don't intend to let him take Hank," Ellen said to Toby, "but he may be Hank's legal guardian. If so, that could be trouble."

"Matt will know what to do," Toby said.

Orin retreated to the porch steps. Tess sat in the swing at the end of the porch, playing with Mrs. Ogden, apparently unaware of the gathering tension.

"Matt will be here in a minute," Ellen said to Toby. "Until then, let me do the talking."

"I can tell him to turn around and git just as well as anybody," Toby said. He held his ground, a barrier between Ellen and danger.

"I'm sure you can, but I'd rather you let me."

Ellen didn't want to talk to this man. She'd much prefer to take Tess and Orin, go inside, and close the door. But she had to learn to stand up for the children by herself. When she moved to San Antonio, she wouldn't have Matt to look after her. That thought gave her a cold, lonely feeling. She shoved it aside. "Come up on the porch with me," she said to Toby.

"Why? I ain't afraid of him."

"Maybe I am."

She didn't know why she'd said that. If she was afraid, she shouldn't have admitted it. The idea of being her protector caused Toby to stand even taller.

"You don't have to worry about him," he said, coming to stand next to her. "I won't let him touch nobody."

"Suppose he's got a gun," Orin said.

"We got guns, too," Toby said. "I can—"

"Nobody's getting a gun," Ellen said. "We aren't even sure who he is or what he wants."

Leigh Greenwood

The man was big, and he looked grimly determined. Or angry. He also looked very attractive. She'd expected him to be ugly, maybe because what he'd done was so ugly. She kept glancing toward the corrals, hoping to see Matt, but she heard nothing, saw no one.

The man brought his horse to a stop in front of the porch. He didn't dismount. "Howdy."

"Howdy, yourself," Toby said.

Ellen squeezed Toby's shoulder. She inclined her head without speaking. The man looked undecided. He glanced at both boys, at Tess on the porch. The ranch was quiet. No sounds told of the presence of three other people.

"Your husband about?" he asked.

"Somewhere," Ellen said, squeezing Toby's shoulder again when he opened his mouth to answer.

"He likely to come to the house soon?"

"He'd better," Toby said. "Supper's about ready."

Ellen wished Toby hadn't said that. Western custom dictated that she extend hospitality to all visitors, but she couldn't invite this man to eat with them.

The man stayed in the saddle, looking around, his expression one of simmering anger.

"Can I help you with something?" Ellen asked. She wanted him to go away.

"I'm looking for a boy," the man said.

"We ain't got no extra boys," Toby said.

Ellen felt Orin press closer to her. "I'm afraid you'll have to be more specific," Ellen said.

"His name is Hank Hollender. I'm his uncle, Wayne Hollender."

Ellen didn't understand why she should suddenly feel more frightened of this man. His confirming his identity didn't change anything.

"We ain't letting you—"

Ellen's fingers dug deep into Toby's shoulder. "Why would you look for him here?"

"I tracked his horse in this direction."

"I would have thought it was too dry for tracking."

The man smiled without humor. "I was a tracker for the army. I can track a horse across rock. Besides, it was my horse he stole. I'd know its track anywhere."

"That's a lie!" Toby exploded. "Hank said it was his horse."

She should have sent Toby to find Matt. She knew he couldn't control his tongue for long.

Wayne Hollender's expression turned ugly. "You people trying to steal my nephew?"

"We do have a boy here, but I don't know that he's your nephew."

Hollender's expression turned really ugly. "How many boys named Hank could be missing at the same time?"

"Hank's not missing. I know exactly where he is."

Ellen's body sagged with relief. Matt had come out of the house behind her. She and Toby turned to him simultaneously. Orin moved to his side immediately.

"This man says—" Toby began.

"I heard what he said."

"He wants to take Hank. You can't—"

"Hank's not going anywhere."

If it were possible, Hollender's expression grew even uglier. Ellen wondered how she could have thought him handsome.

"He's my nephew. You have no right to hold him here."

"We're not holding him," Matt said. "He came here

on his own. He's still here because he asked us to let him stay."

Ellen reached out to Matt, put her hand on his arm, looking for the same kind of comfort Orin found by being close to him. She almost wished she hadn't. Matt had spoken in a calm voice, had maintained a noncommital expression, but his body trembled with his anger. Ellen thought of his rage when he'd seen the marks on Hank's back. This was worse.

"I'm his uncle," Hollender said. "I'm responsible for him."

"Even if he doesn't want to stay with you?"

"That's none of your business," Hollender said. "Where is he? I want to be going."

"I'm concerned about his safety," Matt said. "This looks like something for a judge to decide."

"I don't need a judge to tell me my nephew belongs to me," Hollender thundered. He dismounted. "Now where is he?"

"I have some questions I want answered," Matt said.

Hollender had a rifle in a scabbard on his saddle. Ellen thought she saw his eyes cut toward it. "I don't give a damn what you want," he shouted.

The door to the house opened behind them and Hank pushed his way to the front. "I'm never going anywhere with you," he shouted at his uncle. "I hate you. I—"

Without warning Hollender sprang forward, grabbed Hank's arm, and pulled him down from the porch. Almost as quickly Ellen saw Hollender fly through the air and land in the dirt a half dozen feet away. He looked stunned to find himself on the ground.

"You're making a big mistake," he said to Matt, inching toward his horse at the same time.

Matt had gone down the steps and directly to Hollender. The man reached for his rifle, but Matt's hand closed over his like a vice.

"Get on your horse and ride out while you can," Matt said, his voice now almost a growl. He tore Hollender's hand from the rifle, jerked it from its scabbard, and tossed it to Toby. "I'll bring your rifle to town when I talk to the judge about Hank."

"I'm not leaving without my nephew."

Then he attacked. Head down, he barreled into Matt like some mad longhorn bull. The two men went over in a heap, Hollender on top of Matt.

"Smash his face in," Toby yelled.

"Beat his head into the ground!" Hank shouted.

Noah had come out of the house behind Hank, but he was so frightened, he stayed close to Ellen. The minute the fighting started, Tess had jumped up from the swing, run over, and burrowed into Ellen's skirts. Toby and Hank continued to dance around the combatants, shouting encouragement to Matt.

For a moment Ellen worried that wouldn't be enough. Hollender was as big as Matt and enraged. He fought like a madman. But as quickly as Hollender had knocked him down, Matt turned the tables and was on top. Matt had an expression on his face unlike anything Ellen had ever seen. He looked like he wanted to kill Wayne Hollander. He pommeled Hollender's body with his fists, knocked him down every time he attempted to get to his feet, grabbed him by the throat, and pounded his head on the ground.

"I hope he kills you!" Hank yelled. "I hope he kills you dead!"

When Hollender's face turned purple, Ellen's body went rigid with terror. Matt *did* want to kill Hollender. He was doing it.

"Matt, stop!" she shouted.

But Matt didn't stop. Rage consumed him so thoroughly, her words hadn't penetrated to his brain. She had to do something immediately or Matt would kill Hollender. Galvanized into action, she ran down the steps.

"Toby, help me pull Matt off."

"No!" Hank shouted. "I want Matt to kill him."

"Why should we stop him?" Toby asked.

"If Matt kills him, he'll go to jail."

Orin joined Toby and Ellen in their attempt to pull the two men apart, but their efforts were useless against Matt's strength. His arms were like iron. Even Toby was powerless to loosen his grip on Hollender. Then suddenly, as though he realized what he was about to do, Matt released Hollander and threw himself off the gasping man. He got to his feet slowly, his gaze never leaving Hollender.

Ellen stared at Matt, unable to believe what she was seeing. His face was a mask of hatred that had turned his face ugly. In that moment the face of the man who'd killed her parents flashed into her mind, the ugliness of his expression when they'd sentenced him to hang, his damning her soul to hell. She forced the image from her mind. Matt was nothing like Anthony Howard. Matt wasn't a killer. He was just angry at a great injustice.

Gradually Matt reined in the emotions that for a few minutes had overpowered him. His face relaxed into the kind, considerate man Ellen recognized. Only now she knew what she'd only sensed before. There was another part of Matt, a part capable of violence.

They stood there in a nearly silent tableau, everyone watching Hollender as his eyeballs righted themselves in his head, as the purple hue gradually left his skin, as his breathing slowed from body-wrenching gasps to labored intake. No one said anything when he finally sat up, but Orin retreated to the steps. Hank moved next to Matt. Toby stood his ground. Ellen put her arms around a very frightened Noah and Tess.

Matt looked normal, calm, quiet, and contained.

"You nearly killed me," Hollender said without getting up.

Matt said nothing.

Hollender attempted to get to his feet. No one moved to help him when he fell back. They just watched, quiet as vultures perched in trees waiting for an animal to die. In a moment Hollender tried again. He got to his feet this time, but he had to hold on to his saddle to keep from falling.

"Get on your horse and leave," Matt said.

"I'll get the law on you," Hollender said. "You'll be the one answering the judge's questions."

"Ride out," Matt repeated.

Hollender seemed revitalized by a sudden jolt of energy. He pointed his finger at Hank and shouted, "He belongs to me. I'll get him back any way I have to."

"I know what you did to that boy," Matt said in a low, steady voice. "If you ever touch him again, I'll kill you."

"I'll get him back," Hollender said.

But the energy had gone out of him. His words sounded more like a whimper than a threat. No one said a word as Hollender tried three times before he was able to pull himself into his saddle.

After he managed to gather up the reins, he circled his horse, then looked over his shoulder at Matt. "I'll get him back." Then he left, his horse moving at a slow walk.

They remained silent until Matt turned toward the house. Then they all burst into conversation at once. Matt signaled them to be quiet. "I don't want anyone to leave this house alone," he said, "not even to go to the corrals, to milk the cow, or to collect eggs. If you see anyone you don't know, let me know immediately. That is a very dangerous man, and we haven't seen the last of him."

"Why can't I help Toby plow?" Noah asked Matt.

"Because the plow is bigger than you are," Matt replied. "It would drag you all over the field."

"You can help me."

"I'm a cowboy," Matt said. "We don't know how to plow."

Ellen smiled at Matt's reaction. It was obvious Noah was a town kid. No boy raised on a ranch would have made that mistake.

"How come Toby knows how to plow?" Noah asked.

"He learned before he came here," Matt said.

The entire family had been organized to plant the garden. Matt had sent Toby all the way to Bandera to borrow a plow and a mule to pull it. Ellen thought they should buy their own mule and plow. With all these mouths to feed, it was impossible to consider doing without a garden.

Once again she caught herself thinking like she'd be here next spring. With each passing day she found herself more emotionally attached to this group of people, found it more difficult to think of leaving. The lynchpin was Matt. She had thought she understood him. Now she wasn't sure.

She knew he liked her. He would sometimes look up and smile at her in a way that seemed to say he liked her being here. While his touch was still pretty much limited to quick kisses and putting his arms around her, she sensed a wellspring of emotion behind those gestures. And that was where the confusion set in.

He never stepped over the line they'd drawn at the beginning. Much to her surprise, she found herself being frustrated, wanting more. She told herself that was foolish, that wanting more would inevitably make their situation untenable.

"No, Tess, you're supposed to put just one bean in each hole." She hadn't been paying attention. The child had dropped at least three beans in every hole.

"They keep falling out of my hand," Tess said.

"Don't pick up so many at one time. Take one out of the bag and put it into the hole. Then take another and put it in the next hole."

"You take a whole handful out of the bag," Tess said, pointing to Ellen's fistful of beans.

"But I only drop one in each hole. Now go back and take out the extra beans."

"Why?"

"Because we won't have enough to plant the whole garden if you don't. The beans won't grow big if they're all planted in the same place."

She went back down Tess's row to see how long she'd been planting beans by the handful.

"I've been taking out the extra ones before I fill the hole," Hank told her when she asked if he'd covered up holes with multiple beans. "Matt told me she'd probably start doing that when she got tired."

As usual Matt had foreseen and solved the problem before it happened. She didn't know how he did that.

She watched Tess to make sure she only put one bean in each hole before going back to her own row.

She did want more from Matt. She didn't love him, but she liked him so much that she couldn't stop thinking about him. Even now, looking at him as he taught Noah how to place a slice of potato in the hole with the eye facing up, she felt a warmth curling in her toes. The man was beyond attractive. Maybe she ought to buy him a new wardrobe, one that hung on him rather than fit his body like a glove. His well-rounded bottom and powerful thighs were sheathed in denim stretched to capacity.

"You dropped two beans in the hole," Tess said. "You ought to take one out of the bag at a time."

The strain of being around Matt all the time, of sitting next to him, lying next to him in bed, and having him continue to treat her like a sister was beginning to drive her crazy. Most of her life she'd distrusted men, been afraid they couldn't think of anything except their physical wants. After the Lowells, she'd been shrill in her denunciation of the entire sex. Now she was married to a man who did exactly what she asked and— not demonstrating any physical desire toward her—she longed for his touch.

Ellen had always taken pride in being attractive. She'd tried to make certain she didn't use it as a promise she didn't mean to fulfill, but she was proud that men were attracted to her, that they sometimes couldn't control their responses to her. It made her feel strong, and after feeling helpless for so long she relished the feeling.

Matt commented on her beauty practically every day, but it didn't drive him wild or bring forth urges he had to struggle to control. Did he need a woman as beautiful as he was handsome to cause him to lose some of his rigid control?

But even as she tried to check her response to Matt, she knew it wasn't his physical beauty that had conquered her fear and made her want to stay with him. It was his kindness, his compassion, his willingness to think of others before himself. There was no more thoughtful man in the world. He would do anything for her and the kids, for his boys, to make them happy, to keep them safe.

"Hank, Toby, stop what you're doing and come here."

Matt hadn't spoken very loud, but his tone so clearly indicated danger that the boys put down their tools and went to him immediately.

"The sheriff is coming," Matt told the boys without even looking at the trail leading into their valley. "I expect he's here to get Hank."

"I'm not going back to Wayne," Hank cried. "I'll run away again."

"You don't have to run anywhere," Matt said, "but you've got to hide. Toby, take him into the hills. Don't tell me where you're going. Just get out of here as fast as you can. Come back after dark and I'll tell you what to do next."

The boys headed for the corrals at a run.

Ellen looked toward the distant rider. "How can you tell who that is?"

"I recognize the horse," Matt replied.

"What are you going to do?"

"Tell him I don't know where Hank is."

"He'll come back."

"I know, but it'll give us enough time to take Hank's case before the judge. He ought to be back next week."

"Who's going to plow the rest of the rows?" Noah asked.

"I guess I'll have to try," Matt said.

"But you said you don't know how."

"I don't, but I doubt the squash and tomatoes will care if they're in a crooked row."

"What are we supposed to do?" Ellen asked.

"Keep on planting."

"How can you act like nothing is happening?"

His look was open and calm. "What do you think I ought to do?"

"I don't know. Swear, wring your hands, turn around in circles muttering to yourself."

He laughed. "If I did that, you'd have me locked up."

"At least I'd know you were human. How can you be so calm?"

"Because if I weren't, I'd have killed somebody long before I tried to kill Wayne."

The sheriff left his horse at the house and headed over to them. Ellen knew the adoption could hang in the balance. She couldn't plant any more beans. She could only stand there and wait until the sheriff reached them, until he said the words she knew he must say.

"I've come to get Hank."

Chapter Twenty

"Where is he?" the sheriff asked, surveying the ranch.

"I don't know," Matt replied.

Ellen was glad to see that the sheriff didn't appear to be angry; rather he looked relieved.

"You're getting to be a lot of trouble," he said to Matt.

"Sorry."

"You know I had to come after him," the sheriff said.

"Sure."

"I'll have to keep coming back. The law says the boy belongs with his kin. This Hollender says you kidnaped him."

"I don't even know where he is."

"You know what I mean. The law also says I can arrest you for obstructing justice."

"The reason I asked Toby to hide Hank was so you

and I could see justice done. That boy's been abused by his uncle."

The sheriff's brow creased. "There's nothing wrong with a beating now and again. A boy—"

"I mean sexual abuse," Matt said.

The sheriff looked baffled.

"Do I need to explain it?" Matt asked.

The sheriff looked a little embarrassed. "I guess so."

Ellen wanted to know exactly what Wayne Hollender had done to his nephew, but she wasn't about to let the children hear. "Noah, you and Tess run to the house and get the sheriff some cool water to drink. Noah, you bring the pitcher. Tess can bring the glass."

Ellen turned her back on the men. As she watched Tess and Noah cross the freshly plowed garden to reach the house, she listened to Matt explain what Wayne Hollender had done to Hank. When he finished, she felt sick to her stomach.

Had that happened to Matt? It must have, or he couldn't have described it so completely. How could he have endured that for three years? Because he was a helpless child like Hank. Afterward he'd felt worthless and unclean and he'd buried his feelings so far out of sight people thought he had none. He'd channeled all his energy into helping Toby and Orin. Now he was willing to risk everything he had worked so hard to achieve to protect Hank.

How could she have thought he wasn't strong enough to defend her, that he wasn't heroic because he was soft-spoken? Isabelle had a right to be furious with her. She had been as blind as everyone else, not smart enough to look beyond the obvious. She'd responded to her crisis by feeling sorry for herself, blaming every-body in the world, being loud and shrill at every opportunity. Matt had quietly gone to work to guarantee at least two boys could grow up in a secure, loving atmosphere.

How could she not have realized that took more courage than fighting? Why hadn't she seen what was right in front of her eyes? Because she'd made up her mind before she arrived at the ranch that he didn't fit her preconceived notion of the type of man she could love.

But he was more than she'd ever dreamed, and she wanted him very badly.

"God almighty!" the sheriff exclaimed when Matt finished. Ellen turned to see his face red, his throat swallowing convulsively. "How do you know so much about it?"

Ellen's gaze riveted on Matt. She knew he feared exposure of his secret, knew it would change the way people looked at him. He also knew it would give Wilbur a weapon to use against him.

"Because my uncle abused me," Matt said.

The sheriff gaped at Matt.

"Now you understand why I can't send that boy back. He will keep doing what he's always done."

"Can you prove it?" the sheriff asked.

"A medical examination will, but you can't have it done in Bandera. Everyone will know the results, and that will ruin the boy."

"Why didn't it ruin you?"

"Because there are only four other people who know, my brother, Jake and Isabelle, and my wife."

"I can't do anything unless the boy is willing to make an official accusation."

"I plan to ask the judge for a closed hearing," Matt

299

said. "All I need you to do is let me keep Hank until then."

"I don't know that I can do that."

"You can't send that boy back to his uncle," Ellen said.

"Wilbur Sears and Mabel Jackson are still furious the judge agreed to let you adopt those children," the sheriff said. "Ermajean is so incensed she won't get Orin back, she's ranting and raving about you all over town. This kidnapping business has ripped it. They think they have all the evidence they need to make the judge change his mind."

"We didn't kidnap him," Ellen said. "He came here on his own. He says he'll run away again if we try to make him go back to his uncle."

"But everybody doesn't know that," the sheriff pointed out. "They just know you're housing a boy and won't give him back."

"I'll take Hank to Jake and Isabelle," Matt suggested. "He can stay with them until the judge makes his decision."

"Wilbur won't like it," the sheriff said.

"He can't dispute Jake and Isabelle's integrity," Matt said.

"Maybe not, but he can cause trouble elsewhere."

"How?" Ellen asked.

"Wilbur's threatening my job if I don't bring that boy back and arrest you."

"He can't get you fired."

"I'm not so sure about that. He's got a lot of people believing every word he says."

"They'll wake up soon and be embarrassed they ever gave credence to anything he said."

"That may be, but you've got even more problems.

Mabel Jackson is trying to get her husband to call in your loan."

"He can't do that," Ellen cried.

"I don't know about that," the sheriff said, "but I do know they'll do everything they can to prevent a closed hearing. If there is one, you can bet your last pony they'll not rest until they know what went on."

"We'll have to depend on the judge's discretion," Matt said.

"And his backbone," the sheriff added.

"I'll talk to him as soon as he returns to Bandera."

"You'd better be there before he opens court," the sheriff said. "And bring your wife. It never hurts to have a pretty woman on your side."

"I would naturally bring Ellen," Matt said. "She will have as much to say about adopting Hank as I will."

"You meaning to adopt this kid, too?"

"Who else wants him?"

"Nobody, if what happened to him ever gets out."

"Which is why you can't tell anyone what Matt told you," Ellen said, "not even your wife."

"I ain't telling nobody."

"Swear it."

"I swear. Now do you believe me?"

"I don't know," Ellen said. "But if you ever do tell, I'll find a way to make you wish you'd never been born."

"You don't sound like the sweet, loving, motherly type," the sheriff said. "I hope you don't talk to the judge like that."

"I'm defending my children, Sheriff. A woman would risk anything to do that."

"You two belong together," the sheriff said as he turned and left.

In spite of everything that had happened, Ellen managed a smile. The sheriff was right. She and Matt did belong together.

"You ought to hear the things Wilbur is saying about Matt," Tulip told Ellen.

"I can imagine," Ellen said.

"No, you can't," Mrs. Ogden assured her. "Some of the things he's implying, why, it makes me blush to think about it. Not that I really understand it."

Ellen had come into Bandera with Matt to see if they could meet with the judge before he took the bench. She'd taken some hats to Susan, then come to visit Mrs. Ogden. Tulip had barreled in just minutes after. Orin and Toby had gone off together with strict instructions to steer clear of trouble. After demolishing a plate of oatmeal cookies, Noah and Tess were playing in Mrs. Ogden's backyard.

"Wilbur is furious about this boy he says you kidnapped," Tulip said.

"Hank's staying with the Maxwells, not us," Ellen said.

"That doesn't make any difference. Wilbur thinks they're just as bad as Matt."

"Does the town feel that way?" Ellen asked Mrs. Ogden.

"Gracious, no. Everybody here respects Jake and Isabelle. It's just that preacher has them all stirred up. And that awful Mabel Jackson."

"She's angry because her daughter winks at Toby," Ellen said.

"My advice would be to take your children and go to the Territories," Tulip said. "Wilbur couldn't bother you there."

"That's just what I'm determined we won't do," Ellen said. "I won't let Matt be driven off his ranch because of lies."

"What can you do about it?" Tulip asked.

"I don't know, but I'll think of something."

All she could think of was that she wanted to stay married to Matt, that she wanted him to love her. But that was no solution. It might even make them more vulnerable.

"Do you think he'll talk to us?" Ellen asked Matt.

"I hope so." They waited outside the freight office for the stage that was now coming down the street.

Ellen watched Matt closely. Even though he seemed outwardly calm, she saw the tension around his eyes, heard it in his voice. She envied him his control. He smiled to people who passed, never failed to exchange a few friendly words.

"This is it," Matt said as the stage door opened and the judge got out. "Sir," he said walking up to the judge before the man's feet hit the ground, "my wife and I would like a private word with you."

The judge stepped down from the stagecoach and pointed out his luggage to the driver. "I'm hot, tired, and dusty from my journey. Can't it wait until the morning?"

"I'm afraid it can't."

Certain his bags were off the stage, the judge turned to Matt. "You're the young man wanting to adopt all those children."

"That's right."

"Is something wrong?"

"Something is very wrong!" Wilbur Sears intoned in his most stentorian voice. He came around the corner of the freight office at a near run. "This man is a kidnapper. I insist you put a stop to the adoption proceedings."

"What's this about kidnapping?" the judge asked Matt.

"That's what I want to talk to you about."

"There's no need to talk to him. He'll only tell you lies," Wilbur said. "The sheriff has been to his house to try to return this boy to his rightful guardian."

"Hank's not at my house," Matt said. "He's staying with Jake and Isabelle Maxwell until we have a chance to settle his case."

"There's nothing to settle," Wilbur said. "You lured this child from his home. His uncle came to take him back, and you beat the poor man, nearly killed him."

"That's a lie, Wilbur Sears," Ellen said. "I don't know what Wayne Hollender told you—or why you insist on believing the worst possible things about Matt—but we had never seen or heard of this child before he came to our ranch asking to be adopted."

"Why would he do that?" the judge asked Ellen.

"That's what I want to talk to you about," Matt said.

"Okay, talk."

"Not in the street."

"Then we'll go to the hotel. I need something to drink."

"I'll come with you," Wilbur announced.

"I need to speak to you privately," Matt said.

"He means to tell you more lies," Wilbur shouted, pointing his finger at Matt, "and he doesn't want anyone present who can tell you the truth."

"I can tell you the truth," a voice announced. "I can also tell you that man is crazy."

Ellen felt her heart sink. Wilbur's outbursts had attracted a crowd, but Wayne Hollender's presence was likely to cause a sensation.

"And who are you?" the judge asked.

"I'm Wayne Hollender, Hank's uncle."

"If you're so fond of him, why did he run away?"

Ellen was pleased to see the judge's direct question had surprised Hollender.

"I had to discipline him and he got angry. Ever since his parents died he's been real volatile, up one day, down the next. He's run away before. He would have come home with me if that man hadn't bewitched him."

"Are you seriously accusing this man of witchcraft?" the judge asked, incredulous.

"Mr. Haskins lures them in with promises of a life of untrammeled pleasure," Wilbur said.

"If I could speak with you privately for just ten minutes—" Matt began.

"I insist upon hearing every word he says," Wilbur said.

"So do I," Mabel Jackson announced, pushing her way though the gathering crowd.

The sheriff, apparently worried at the size of the gathering crowd, had followed Mabel. Ellen didn't know what he might do, but she knew Matt was losing ground. "Here's the sheriff," she said to the judge. "Why don't you ask him what he thinks?"

"He'd better think that Mr. Haskins belongs in jail if he values his job," Wilbur announced.

Apparently that was too much for the judge. "And what makes you think you have anything to say about whether or not he keeps his job?" he asked.

"I've been sent to save the souls of the community," Wilbur intoned, rising on the balls of his feet as he made his proclamation. "Their consciences are in my hands."

"Well, mine is not," the judge declared. "What do you think of this mess?" he asked the sheriff.

"I think you ought to let each of them have a private word with you," the sheriff said. "Then they can all have their say, and there won't be nobody to stop them."

The judge sighed. "That means I won't get a drink or my dinner any time soon, but it's a very practical solution."

"I'll be happy to buy you a drink," Matt offered.

"He's trying to bribe you," Wilbur said. "I insist that I go first."

Wilbur had already headed toward the hotel when the judge said, "I'll see Mr. Haskins and his wife first, Mr. Hollender after that. When everybody else is done, I'll see the preacher. I'm sure he'll want a chance to set me straight about what everybody else has said."

Wilbur had turned back and been about to explode with anger, but the judge's last sentence caused him to smile.

"Come along," the judge said to Matt and Ellen. "I'll take you up on that drink." A few minutes later they were settled in the judge's room. "Now, what's this all about?" he asked. "I hope none of those accusations are true. If they are, I'll have to cancel the adoption."

"Hank Hollender's uncle has been abusing him sexually for some time," Matt said. "He came to my ranch to ask me to adopt him. I want you to order a private examination to prove what he says. Then I want you to arrest that son of a bitch and hang him."

The judge whistled, his drink arrested in midair. "When you wade into things, you don't mess around, do you? You've taken on the preacher, the reigning dowager, and a pervert. What are you going to do next?"

"Go back to my ranch and mind my own business."

Ellen felt the tension in the room ease. The judge might not be convinced, but he wasn't going to dismiss what they said out of hand.

"I doubt that," the judge said. He took a long swallow of his whiskey. "People like you are forever causing trouble."

"Matt didn't cause this trouble," Ellen said. "Hank came to us. After what he told us, we couldn't give him back to that man."

"No, I don't suppose you could. Still, it'll be hard doing this without everybody knowing what's going on."

"This can't become public," Matt said. "It would ruin Hank's life."

"I know that," the judge said as he took another swallow. "Still, I just can't make arbitrary decisions without explaining myself."

"I want to adopt Hank," Matt said.

"I hope you aren't offering that as a way out of this especially prickly situation," the judge said.

"No," Matt said, offering a brief smile. "I expect it will make things worse, but Hank needs somewhere to live. If the truth does come out, it will be impossible for him to find a home in this town."

"Are you absolutely certain his uncle is abusing him?"

"I'm certain of the abuse. We have to take Hank's word that his uncle is the one responsible."

The judge set his whiskey down on the table. "Okay, let's assume what the boy says is true. Why should I

307

hand him over to you? You've already got four kids and you'll probably have a passel of your own. I'd think you wouldn't want any more."

"There's always room for one more on a ranch," Matt said.

"But five?"

"Jake and Isabelle adopted eleven," Matt said, "and they didn't have anything to start with. I have a ranch and a herd."

"Plus a wife," the judge pointed out.

"Plus a wife," Matt said.

"And what do you think about this?" the judge asked Ellen. "How would you feel about taking care of a house full of kids when you're pregnant for the fourth or fifth time?"

In her mind Ellen had already taken Hank into the family, but she'd never thought of having to care for the family while she was pregnant the first time, and certainly not the fifth. She looked up at Matt. His expression was more inscrutable than ever. Which meant he was hiding something very important to him. He certainly couldn't doubt she would be willing to adopt Hank.

That could only mean . . . Matt wanted his own children.

She didn't know why she'd never thought of that before. True, Matt had never once spoken of having children, but she should have known a man who was so willing to take in other people's children would want some of his own.

He must think no woman would want to bear his children once she knew he'd been abused. He'd wanted to protect Hank because of the blame and guilt the community would attach to the boy. That had to be how he felt. But he was wrong. Any woman who knew him, who lived with him for as much as a week, would fall in love with him. It was impossible not to love a man who was so kind, generous, giving, and yet was strong enough to protect her and her children.

She loved him. It had taken her a long time to see beyond his shy reticence, beyond her own silly vision of a bigger-than-life hero, to realize she had found all that and much more in Matt.

"By the time you have the fourth kid, your husband will probably have found himself another orphan or two to adopt," the judge added.

She didn't care. She wanted her children, Matt's children, their children.

She would have to tell him that she wanted to stay, to be his wife, that she wanted him to love her as much as she loved him. She smiled up at him, hoping the warmth of her smile would banish some of the cold she now saw in his heart.

"My husband and I know what it's like to be without a home, the security of having someone who loves you and is willing to protect you. I'd be disappointed if he didn't want to adopt other children."

"But you will agree that there's a limit to the number of children any family can reasonably care for," the judge said, pressing his point.

"Yes," she answered, looking at Matt rather than the judge, "and we may have to sacrifice having so many of our own in order to help others."

Matt's eyes opened a little wider, but everything else about him was immobile. She wondered if he thought she was just saying that to please the judge.

"But we haven't talked about this," she said, still

looking at Matt. "We'll have to talk very soon." She hoped he understood. He looked so still.

"Can you support such a family?" the judge asked Matt. "That many children will take a lot of money."

"I won't be able to buy them all ranches or build them houses," Matt said, "but they'll know how to earn a living if they're willing to work."

"What about the kind of home they'll have? Wilbur Sears tells me you two only married so you could adopt the children. Is that true?"

The judge had gone out of his way to help them. They had to tell him the truth if they wanted him to stay on their side. She looked at Matt. He sat unmoving, waiting for her to answer. She didn't know what he would have said had he answered the question, but this was her question. Only she could answer it now. She turned her gaze to the judge.

"It started that way," Ellen said. "Wilbur and Mabel wanted to take the children from me and take Orin from Matt. The sheriff suggested we marry so we could adopt them."

Matt's face remained completely closed. She turned back to the judge.

"I was assaulted by my employer's son," Ellen said, "and my reputation was so badly ruined, the only job I could find was in a saloon. I was furious at all men, determined I would never be dependent on a man. I made Matt promise to help me open a hat shop in San Antonio after the adoptions were final."

"So you planned to split up after the adoptions?" the judge asked.

Ellen turned to Matt, but apparently he was going to let her do the talking. He knew she wanted the children as much as he did. And even though what she had said so far sounded damaging, he must have faith she would be able to bring it around so it would strengthen their position. He wasn't going to second-guess her.

"We didn't talk about a divorce," Ellen said, "but I certainly had separate households in mind."

"What changed your mind?" the judge asked. "I assume the point of this story is that you have changed your mind."

"Living with Matt changed my mind. There isn't a kinder, gentler, more understanding man in Bandera, but he's not soft. Matt had trained those boys to keep a better house than most women do, yet they can handle wild horses and cantankerous longhorns as well as any cowboy. He sticks up for them when he thinks they're right—he won't let anybody take advantage of them—but he lets them know they have to earn every privilege. If they do something wrong, he explains the consequences and helps them deal with them, but he never demeans them. Noah and Tess adore him. Toby and Orin will do anything he says. Who wouldn't admire a man like that?"

"Is that all you feel for him?" the judge asked.

"No. I love him."

The judge turned to Matt. "How about you?"

Chapter Twenty-one

Matt felt incapable of responding. So many feelings came crashing down on him, he felt buried under their weight, rendered mute, barely able to think.

Ellen loved him!

It seemed impossible, yet she'd said it, said it before a judge.

When she answered the judge's question about the nature of their marriage, he'd been confident she would say something that would help convince the judge to let them adopt Hank as well as the other children, but he'd never expected this. Could it be true? Yet he didn't have to ask. He could look at her face and tell she meant every word she said. She looked radiant, happy, beautiful . . . and uneasy. She didn't know what he would say.

She loved him. He loved her. Everything had

changed, and he didn't know what to do about it.

"Are you going to answer my question?" the judge asked. "You look shocked."

"I expect he is," Ellen said. "I haven't had a chance to tell him that my feelings have changed."

"You mean . . ." The judge looked from one to the other. "Damnation!" he exclaimed, breaking into a huge grin. "I never have been a witness to the first declaration of love. Even missed my own. My wife told me she loved me after I got myself knocked unconscious rescuing her from a frightened horse."

Matt felt his tongue flap uselessly in his mouth. No matter what he started to say, it didn't seem right. It was either too much or too little. Or untrue. But this was no time to deal in untruths, even for the judge's benefit.

"Ellen isn't the only one who's undergone a change of sentiment," Matt said, looking at Ellen rather than the judge. "I always liked her, but it's hard for an unsociable man to know how to court a beautiful woman, especially when he's already saddled with two boys."

"And she has a reputation for seducing her employer's son," Ellen said, her gaze riveted on Matt.

"I never believed that."

"I know."

"It looks like if Wilbur Sears weren't so pigheaded you two would never have gotten together." The judge put his glass down and started to heave himself out of his chair. "I imagine you two have a lot to say to each other. I'd better get on to Hollender if I'm ever to have my supper. I'll arrange for the examination and do my best to make certain the results remain a secret. In the meantime, I'll leave the boy with the Maxwells. I think even Wilbur Sears will agree that's a reasonable arrangement."

Matt was certain Wilbur wouldn't agree to anything short of Hank's being handed over to his uncle immediately. Even if Matt told him the uncle had been abusing the boy, he wouldn't believe it. He would be certain Matt had some ulterior motive for spreading such a slander.

Matt had just gotten to his feet when a series of imperative knocks sounded on the door to the judge's room.

"Come in," he called impatiently.

The door opened to admit Mabel Jackson, dragging Orin by the ear. She was closely followed by a woman Matt didn't know, who seemed to be equally irate.

"I demand you arrest this boy as a thief," Mabel announced, looking in triumph at Matt. "I caught him in my house trying to steal my jewelry box."

Matt's gaze had gone straight to Orin the minute Mabel pulled the boy into the room. It was clear from Orin's expression that he wasn't innocent, but Matt knew he wasn't a thief. He'd never shown any desire for personal possessions. He certainly couldn't have any use for a jewelry box.

"I'm certain he's the one who stole my husband's gold watch the day of the church picnic," the woman with Mabel said. "My neighbor saw him sneaking around my house about an hour before my husband and I returned."

Orin ran straight to Matt and threw his arms around his waist. He didn't protest his innocence when Matt put his hand on his head. He didn't even look up.

"That's all the proof you need that Matt Haskins isn't fit to raise that boy," Mabel announced. "Look at him, coddling the little thief like he'd done nothing wrong."

"Regardless of what he's done, he's a child and he's frightened," Matt said. "He needs to know I love him and mean to take care of him. You'd do the same for one of your children."

"We're not talking about my children," Mabel said, for all the world as though her children were of a superior race. "My children would never steal."

"No, your son only got his friends to help him jump Toby because your daughter continues to wink at him," Ellen said.

Mabel turned white, then red. "I insist you arrest that child immediately."

"I think this is more the province of your sheriff," the judge said.

"He's just as bad as you," Mabel exclaimed. "He can't see anything wrong with Matt and that woman, either."

"I think we ought to hear what Orin has to say," Matt said.

"I don't see why," Mabel said. "I caught him in my room. I know he's guilty."

"Why did you do it?" Matt asked Orin, loosening the boy's grasp and holding him at arm's length. "Look at me," Matt said when Orin continued to stare at the floor. "Why were you trying to take Mrs. Jackson's jewelry box?" He put his hand under Orin's chin and lifted his head until he could look into the boy's eyes.

"I wasn't trying to steal her stupid old box," Orin told Matt. "I wanted my mama's picture. She asked me to give it to my daughter some day so she'd know what her grandmother looked like."

"Is there a picture of Orin's mother in that box?" Matt asked Mabel.

She looked flustered. "I don't know. I bought the box because I thought it was pretty. I never bothered to look inside."

"Do you want the picture of his mother?"

"Of course not. Why would I want such a thing?"

Matt turned back to Orin. "Did you take the watch?"

Orin nodded his head. "It was my pa's. He got it from his pa. It was supposed to be mine, but they wouldn't give it to me."

"Who wouldn't give it to you?"

"Ermajean. She said I couldn't have it or anything else. She said they would need all the money they could get to pay for her taking care of such a troublesome boy as me."

"Where is the watch?" Matt asked.

Orin hung his head. "It's at the ranch. I hid it in a crack in the loft."

"You know you have to return it, don't you?"

Orin nodded.

"I don't want the watch," the woman said. "I never knew it was promised to the boy. I bought it for my husband, but he doesn't use it. Please, let him keep it."

"Thank you, ma'am, but I don't allow my boys to steal, regardless of the reason. You'll get it back."

"I couldn't keep it now, not knowing how much he wants it."

"Then we'll buy it back," Matt said. "Do you remember how much you paid for it?"

"No, and I don't care. Let the boy have it."

"We'll pay for it. Please put a value on it."

"How about two dollars?"

"Surely you paid more."

"Maybe, but it's only worth two dollars to me now."

Matt turned to Mabel. "Would you let us buy the

jewelry box?" he asked. He could tell she was furious the situation had turned out so differently from what she'd expected, but she actually looked a little chagrined.

"He can have it," she said.

"I insist we buy it. How much do you think it's worth?"

She took a deep, agitated breath. "Oh, make it twenty-five cents. It's only a trumpery piece of nothing."

"I don't have any money on me right now," Matt said, "but—"

"I do," Ellen said, opening her purse. She counted out two dollars. "Thank you, ma'am, for being so understanding."

"I wish I'd known," the woman said. "I'd have given the poor boy his father's watch the minute I paid for it. I can't imagine Ermajean being so mean."

Matt marveled that people could live in a small town for years and know so little about their neighbors.

"Here's your money," Ellen said, handing Mabel two bits. "If you don't mind, Orin and I will accompany you home, so we can get the jewelry box and picture now."

"Sit down and have a drink," the judge said to Matt after everyone else had left. "You deserve it. Do you always manage to extricate your boys from trouble that neatly?"

Matt felt so relieved he allowed himself a smile. "No, but Mabel and Wilbur are so determined to take Orin from me, they pounce on any opportunity they find."

Matt was never to learn what the judge would have said next. The door burst open and Toby practically fell into the room.

"Where is Orin?" he asked, breathless. "They said

the sheriff was going to put him in jail for stealing. The sheriff doesn't have him. I asked."

"You can begin by apologizing to the judge for bursting into his room without knocking," Matt said.

"Sorry, sir," Toby said to the judge, "but they said Mrs. Jackson brought Orin here."

"She did, but the trouble is all worked out," the judge replied. "Why don't you come in and have a seat?"

Toby entered, looking somewhat sheepish. "I'm Toby, sir. I—"

"I remember. You're the one Mrs. Jackson's daughter likes to wink at."

Toby had the good grace to blush before he turned back to Matt. "I know I swore I wouldn't let Orin out of my sight for a minute. I didn't mean to lose him."

"I hope she was very pretty," Matt said.

"We can't have any of you getting into any more trouble," Matt told the four children gathered around the table. "Everything is hanging in the balance for us as well as Hank."

"When can he come home?" Noah asked.

"I don't know. Soon, I hope."

It warmed Ellen's heart to hear Noah call the ranch home. That was how she felt about it.

"If we want to be a family, we've got to start thinking like one," Ellen said. "I've been just as bad as anybody else about letting Matt do all the thinking for us, but this is our family, too. We all have to take responsibility for it."

"I don't mind being part of the family," Toby said. "I ain't going to be adopted, but I'll help you adopt the little ones."

"That's sweet of you," Ellen said.

"I'm a sweet guy," Toby said. "All the girls say so."

There was no way to keep Toby down for long. He knew he should have kept his eye on Orin, but it was hard to blame him too much after Orin confessed he'd steered Toby toward a girl so he could sneak away. As far as Toby was concerned, if things ended well, they were forgotten. Ellen supposed that was best. It would certainly make for less strain, but she couldn't forget. They were close to being able to adopt the children, but they weren't out of the woods yet. She knew Matt would do anything he thought necessary to protect Hank. She just hoped nothing more would happen. Surely once Hank had been examined, there wouldn't be any question of returning him to his uncle's custody.

"Just see if you can stay away from girls for a few more weeks," Matt said to Toby as he stood. "It's time for everybody to get to bed. We've had a long day. Unfortunately, we didn't get much work done on the garden. Tomorrow it's up at dawn and no stopping until we get everything planted."

The children trooped off to bed with a chorus of groans.

"You keep that up and I'll plant a row of brussel sprouts."

With assorted "Yucks!" and "Ughs!" the kids ran to their rooms, leaving Matt and Ellen facing each other across the room.

"We have a lot to talk about," he said. "I'll make Tess's story really short."

Ellen couldn't keep her mind on the routine of putting the children to bed. She forgot to check behind Noah's ears, tucked Mrs. Ogden in on the wrong side of the bed, and didn't remember a word of Matt's story. She undressed, pulled her nightgown over her head, and jumped into bed, her body stiff with apprehension. She didn't know what Matt would say, but if he didn't say he loved her, she was certain she would die.

It seemed like she waited twice as long as usual, but she knew that was nerves. Matt wasn't one to avoid an issue. Yet when he came into the room, he didn't say a word. He undressed without blowing out the light. She was so nervous, she couldn't even enjoy looking at his body. She held her breath when he got into bed. Still, he didn't put out the light.

He turned over to face her.

"What did you mean when you said you loved me?" Matt asked. His mind had been in a ferment since Ellen told the judge she loved him. He had a thousand questions, none of which he could answer himself. He had to have her answer, her explanation. He braced himself for the admission that she'd only said it to convince the judge to let them adopt the children.

"Just what I said. I love you. I didn't mean to fall in love with you. I didn't even know I had until today."

There was no other way to interpret what she'd said. She had to mean she loved him. He remembered how she'd looked in the judge's room, saw how she looked now. Still, he couldn't quite believe it. "It's not going to change anything if you don't love me. You can still stay here."

The covers rustled and the bed lurched as Ellen propped herself up on her elbow, took him by the shoulder, and shook him. "I said I loved you, Matt Haskins. I don't know why it took me so long to figure it out. You're exactly the kind of man I was certain I'd never find."

He wanted to believe her, but it was hard. "What kind of man were you looking for?"

"One who was kind, gentle, thoughtful—"

"Weak."

"No. It takes a strong man to be kind and thoughtful, a man so sure of himself, he isn't afraid to show gentleness."

She had it all wrong. He hadn't done anything like that.

"You're the strongest man I know. You've stood up to Wilbur, Mabel, the sheriff, this town, anybody who threatened one of your boys. You did it regardless of the cost to yourself. Then you added me and the kids to your burden."

"You're not a burden."

"That's what makes it so wonderful. I felt like you wanted us here from the first. Now it's your turn to tell me what you meant when you said your sentiments had undergone a change."

Did he dare tell her the truth? Did he dare risk letting loose feelings that had been under tight restraint all his life? Most important, could he open himself up to hoping for things he knew he could never have?

He'd already lost that skirmish. Practically from the first day Ellen arrived at the ranch he'd been hoping to discover some way to get her to stay. Even though he knew she could only stay if she loved him—and she could never love him once she knew—he hadn't stopped hoping that somehow things would work out.

But he couldn't hold back. If he was ever going to have a chance at love, this was it. It would be terrible to fail to get what he'd never had, but it would be unbearable to think he might have won but lost because he didn't have the courage to try.

"I meant I loved you," he said, aware his voice sounded tentative, even breathy.

She remained silent; she didn't move. She waited so long to respond, he became aware he was holding his breath. He let it out slowly, forced himself to breathe normally.

"When did you start to love me?" she asked finally.

He couldn't tell if she was happy or unhappy. "I always liked you, even through that uproar about the Lowells. I know what it's like when people jump to conclusions, but I guess I fell in love with you because everything about your being here seems right."

Hell, she didn't want to hear that. She wanted to be told about her eyes, her nose, how her hair reminded him of corn silk. Why hadn't he paid attention when Isabelle tried to teach the boys how to talk to women?

"Taking care of the kids was as important to you as it was to me," he said, desperate to find some reason that wouldn't make her angry. "You even learned to like Toby, despite his not wanting you here."

This didn't sound romantic. What did you say to a woman that would make her love you no matter what you'd done in the past? She wasn't responding. She wasn't even saying he was doing everything wrong. He searched his mind for something Isabelle would have wanted to hear.

"I like having you here," he said. "You fit, like you've always been here. I find it hard to remember what it was like before you came. I like seeing you across the table when we eat. I like it when you kiss Tess or give Noah a hug. I like sleeping in this bed with you, especially when you let me kiss your forehead or put my arm around you. I don't feel so alone then."

She still hadn't said anything. Fool! Couldn't he

think of anything to say that would make a woman want to love him? He'd watched Jake, Ward, and Buck for years. Even Chet and Sean had learned how to talk to their wives without sounding like tongue-tied cowpokes. But he hadn't listened. He'd been certain it would never apply to him.

"I don't feel strong." He was babbling now, saying the first thing that came to his mind. "I won't back down from Wilbur—not when it's to protect the boys— but it's been much easier since you've been standing with me."

Silence. She hadn't moved. It was almost as though she'd gotten so disgusted she'd simply disappeared. He didn't know what else to say. All his life he'd watched women but not talked to them. Not like this.

Then he heard her sniff. She was crying. Great. He'd made her so unhappy, she would pack her bags tomorrow, take the kids, and head back to Bandera. He reached over and took her hand in his. When she squeezed it back, he found the courage to speak.

"I don't know how to talk to a woman. I didn't think anybody could ever love me. When you said you did, I didn't know what to say."

She pulled his hand to her lips and kissed it. "What you said was just fine."

"But you're crying."

"With happiness."

Isabelle said women did that, but he never understood it. It made him worry they were trying to hide something they didn't want him to know. He reached up to touch her cheeks. They were wet with tears. He panicked. "Are you sure you're happy?"

"Blissfully."

He felt like he'd been tossed twenty feet by a wild

bronco. He was so dizzy, his brain wouldn't work. "Do you think you're happy enough to stay here on the ranch?"

"Just try and run me off."

He hoped she meant she wouldn't go if he did, but he wasn't trusting his understanding anymore. "Does that mean you'll operate your hat-making business from here?"

"If I can find the time."

More panic. If she couldn't find the time, she wouldn't want to stay. "The boys and I can do more. I know having Hank here will mean more work, but it'll also mean another pair of hands to help. We can handle the garden. You won't have to do a thing. You can—"

"You don't understand, do you?"

He felt like an idiot. This was his only chance, and he was messing it up without even knowing how he was messing it up. "What don't I understand?"

"I want to do the housework. I want to help Tess with the cow and Noah with the chickens. If you try to keep me out of that garden, *my* garden, you're going to have a fight on your hands."

Matt couldn't believe it. If he was interpreting what she was saying correctly, he hadn't messed up at all.

"I don't want you to do everything for me," Ellen said. "You just said it was nicer to stand up to everyone when I stood with you. Well, the same goes for me."

"You really want to stay here?"

"Yes."

"You won't mind if they let me adopt Hank?"

"I'll be delighted if they let *us* adopt Hank."

"But you'll want to keep making hats?"

"If I have time. But there will be the children to look after and babies to take care of."

"Babies?"

"Yes, babies. Our babies. You do want children, don't you?"

No man could ask for greater proof of a woman's love. She hoped to have his children. It was like saying she loved him so much, thought he was so wonderful, she wished to surround herself with more of him. "Yes, I do want children."

She reached over and blew out the lamp. "Then why don't we do something about it?"

Chapter Twenty-two

Ellen couldn't believe she had practically asked Matt to make love to her. It was ironic, considering how she would have acted if he'd so much as touched her a few weeks earlier. Considering how she felt now, she didn't know how she'd managed to sleep in the same bed with him all this time and keep her distance.

"Are you sure?" he asked.

It was sweet but rather frustrating that he needed to be assured she wanted him to act like a husband. "Very sure."

At least she thought she was. She'd never made love to a man. April said it wasn't anything special. Tulip said it was dreadful if it wasn't with the right man, but Tulip had never found the right man. Ellen's cousin had said it was a bother, but you had to put up with it. Maybe Mrs. Lowell thought it was nice. She'd certainly kicked up a fuss when she thought her husband had begun to look elsewhere.

No matter the truth of it, Ellen had committed herself. She couldn't turn back. But she didn't want to turn back. She loved Matt. She couldn't think of anything more wonderful than giving herself to him completely.

"I've never made love to a woman before."

Ellen couldn't believe her ears. "But you're thirty years old."

"I couldn't stand to be touched. It made me think of my uncle. It made me feel sick or so angry I wanted to hurt somebody. Why else do you think I could agree to share my bed with a beautiful woman like you and not touch you?"

"But you have touched and kissed me. You're touching me now."

"That's when I knew I loved you."

It was a little unnerving to realize Matt didn't know any more about making love than she did, but it was wonderful to know that she was the first woman he wanted to touch. After a lifetime of being pushed willy-nilly by people and circumstances, it was empowering to know she alone could bring this man into the full realization of his physical nature.

"It can't be so hard," Ellen said. "Even teenagers figure it out."

"Maybe I should wake Toby and ask him."

Ellen giggled. "Don't you dare. Do you think . . ."

"I hope not."

Matt moved his fingers over her face, touching it, brushing it with his fingertips, as though trying to memorize it the way a blind man might. He caressed her lips, feathered her jaw, brushed her eyebrows, and skimmed along the curve of her nose. "You're beautiful."

"You can barely see me in the dark."

"You feel beautiful."

She didn't think that was possible, but she didn't intend to argue with him. She pulled his other hand down to her bosom. She didn't understand how it had repulsed her so when Eddie Lowell put his hands on her or one of the men in the saloon touched her. When Matt touched her, it was wonderful and exciting.

She liked the idea of sharing something with him no other woman could ever share. She might not be the only woman he would make love to in his life—she didn't want to think about that—but she would always be his first. And he would be her first.

He continued to run his fingers over her skin, along the side of her neck, across her shoulders, down her arm, back up across her breasts. Her body shivered with excitement. Chills chased each other across her skin. Her muscles went all tight and achy. It was an odd feeling, but delicious. Her breasts became more sensitive to the feel of the fabric across her nipples, to Matt's hand between them.

Matt leaned over and kissed her on the forehead. She took his face in her hands and pulled him down until their lips met. Like two butterflies, their lips brushed softly against each other, then pulled back, hovering. Ellen ran her tongue over her lips, certain they had been changed forever.

Matt again lowered his lips and took her mouth in a gentle, lingering kiss. Once again they pulled back, tasting, savoring, yet eager for more.

Another kiss, this more like exploration—tasting, nibbling—their tongues reaching out for more. Ellen was certain she could never get enough of Matt's firm, sensual mouth. She had waited so long, admired him so much, she'd built up a hunger that couldn't be satisfied quickly. She wanted to spend hours and hours exploring.

But Matt had other ideas. Without warning, he withdrew his hand from her grasp, pulled her into a crushing embrace, and kissed her with the hunger of a man who'd been allowed to see the prize but not seek it for himself. There was nothing gentle or self-effacing about him now. She felt like he wanted to devour her. He crushed his mouth against hers with such force, she was certain her lips would be bruised. He held her body so tightly, it threatened to crack her ribs. She knew he was strong. She hadn't known how strong.

But while her brain took time to adjust to what was happening, her body knew immediately. It magnified every sensation until she thought she might explode. How was it possible to feel so much from a single embrace?

Matt released her abruptly and fell back on the bed, his breath coming in quick gasps. Ellen felt cast aside, as though Matt had sucked all there was out of the experience and was ready to turn over and go to sleep. She wasn't. She felt acutely alive, her entire body clamoring for more—of what she wasn't quite sure—but she was sure there was more.

"I never knew something as simple as a kiss could leave me feeling like I'd just ridden five wild broncs," Matt said. "I don't know if I'm strong enough for you."

Ellen reached over and felt Matt's chest through his nightshirt. Heavy muscles moved easily under his warm skin as his chest rose and fell with his breath. Her hand slid up to his shoulder and down his arm. There was more than enough strength there to handle a dozen wild horses.

"Tulip has been begging me to tell her what goes on between us," Ellen said. "You're not going to force me to tell her I'm too much woman for you, are you?"

Matt erupted from the bed with the speed of a scalded cat. Before she could breathe, she found herself pinned to the mattress by his body, his face inches above her own.

"What have you told that woman about us?"

"Nothing."

"Because there's been nothing to tell?"

"Matt, you know I wouldn't—"

"That won't be true much longer."

He wrapped her body in another steel-like embrace and kissed her hard on the mouth. But as much as she liked his kisses, Ellen had difficulty concentrating. She was powerfully aware of the feel of his body as it pressed tightly against her own—from chest to thigh.

And the fact that his groin was swollen and pressed hard against her abdomen.

Ellen wasn't naive. She'd seen many men in an excited condition. She knew what it meant. But except for Eddie Lowell, it had never meant anything to her. Now it did.

Matt's wasn't the only body responding to their closeness. Her breasts had become so tender, her nipples felt like two points where all her nerve endings came together. Her entire body trembled. She felt hot and cold at the same time. She felt assaulted and so taut she was ready to jump out of her skin.

And she couldn't get enough.

She threw her arms around Matt and hugged him as tightly to her as she was able. She had never realized how big he was. She could barely get her arms around his chest. That made her feel small and weak. Much to her surprise, it wasn't a bad feeling. For the first time she could remember, she wanted to be overwhelmed, to be helpless to resist him. She wanted to feel he was so dominating he could snatch her up and carry her off without taking a deep breath.

When he rolled over and she found herself atop him, she was convinced he could.

"I don't know how I managed to keep my hands off you for so long," Matt said.

"I've been wanting you to touch me for a long time."

"Why didn't you tell me?"

"You acted like you didn't know I was here. Sometimes I felt invisible."

"I tried to ignore you. I knew if I didn't, I'd do something terrible."

"What?" What could he have done she wouldn't have welcomed during the last week?

"Do you know what it's like to lie next to you night after night and not be able to touch you?" he asked.

"I felt the same way."

"You never touched me."

"I was afraid you didn't want me to. Why didn't you touch me?"

"I was afraid you'd take the kids and leave."

"Who were you worried about, me or the kids?"

"Both. I fell in love with all of you together, but I love you in a different way."

"Show me."

"If you can't tell—"

"I don't mean that. I've never been in love. I hardly know what I want. I certainly don't know what to expect."

"Then you won't know if I do it wrong."

"As long as you love me, nothing will be wrong."

Matt moved so that they both lay on their sides. "I could lie here looking at you all night."

"Why? You're better-looking than I am."

He smiled. "I'm not interested in my looks, just yours."

She realized what he said was true. Except for being neat and clean, he never gave any thought to his appearance. As far as she could tell, he never thought of himself at all. Well, she was going to see about that. Matt was a very special person, and it was about time he knew it.

"What do you like about my looks?" she asked.

"Everything."

She couldn't argue with an answer like that, but it wasn't as satisfying as she had hoped. "Could you be more specific?" He was kissing her eyebrows. She'd never imagined a man would do that, or that she would like it.

"I like your lips." He kissed her, long and lingering. "They're soft and sweet."

"They're too thick," she said. "I look like I got hit in the mouth. Yours are more sensual. Tulip talks about them all the time."

"Tulip doesn't want to kiss you."

Ellen giggled. "I hope not."

"I like your eyes."

"They're brown."

"They flash when you're angry. It shows spirit."

"What do they do when I'm not?"

"They're warm."

Please, don't let him say like chocolate pudding.

"They sort of glow, like you know a wonderful secret."

She wondered when he'd seen that.

"I see it every time you look at Tess and Noah. I used to hope you'd look at me like that."

He was tickling her ear with his tongue. For a man who'd never made love before, he had a remarkably good instinct for exactly the right thing to do to ruin her concentration. But maybe she wasn't supposed to concentrate. It was very tempting just to lie back and luxuriate in the sensations.

"I especially like your smile," Matt said. "It reaches out and pulls you right in."

Ellen didn't understand that. She'd done her best to cultivate a smile that said *keep your distance*. Apparently it hadn't worked on Matt, but she couldn't think clearly enough to figure out why. Matt's hand was playing down her side, threatening to tickle her—playing across her breast, threatening to give rise to a very different feeling.

"I especially like your hair," Matt said. "It's dark as old mahogany. I like it short. Not many women wear it like that. It makes you look rumpled, like you just got out of bed."

She'd never been able to control her thick tresses, but Matt's hand had slipped inside her nightgown to cup her breast, and she forgot all about her hair.

Tulip had said when a man touched a woman's breast, she discovered what being a woman was all about. Ellen wasn't sure she could agree with that— after all, there was a lot more to being a woman—but it certainly did put a new slant on the matter. She would never again complain about them being too big, too heavy, or a nuisance. They were rapidly making up for a lifetime of trouble.

When Matt used the tip of his finger to gently circle her breast before narrowing his attention to the nipple alone, she decided the balance sheet was even. He used his teeth to pull the straps of her nightgown off her shoulders—how did he know to do something like that?—and took her nipple into his mouth. She gasped with surprise and pleasure. Her body arched upward.

"I like your breasts, too," Matt mumbled.

She'd already figure that out. She just hadn't figured out why she'd never suspected they could harbor such a wealth of sensations. Or why those sensations would radiate through her entire body. She felt on fire, every part of her becoming hotter and hotter. No, hot wasn't exactly the right word, but she didn't have the mental concentration—or the desire—to decide what it was. Matt had turned her body into something completely foreign to her, something she liked very much.

The pleasure grew still more intense when Matt's hand covered and gently caressed her other breast. His lips deserted her bosom and took her mouth in a long kiss. "I like your entire body," he said a moment later. "It fits perfectly in my arms."

Matt had pulled her against him and thrown his right leg over her body, making her acutely aware of his swollen groin. Suddenly she wanted to touch him. The thought surprised her. No, it stunned her. But the desire was compelling.

When she caressed him, he flinched and gasped. "Don't do that! I'm liable to explode."

She felt the same way. She didn't know why it should be any different for him. He moved her hand to his hip.

"Men aren't like women," he said. "Sometimes just

a touch is all it takes to send them over the edge."

"I feel like that already."

"Not yet. There's more to come."

She didn't know how her body could produce still more startling sensations, but it didn't take her long to learn. Matt pushed her gown down around her hips, trailed his tongue from her breasts to her belly button, with a stop to explore each rib along the way. She feared she'd never again be able to take a full breath. Everything seemed to stop working, then rush ahead, only to come to a complete halt moments later.

"Take off your nightshirt," she managed to say. "I want to feel your chest."

She hoped she'd be able to regain some control during the seconds it took Matt to shed his nightshirt, but she was so inflamed with the need for his touch that being separated from him made her want him more desperately. Throwing herself back into his embrace didn't lessen the need, especially after she realized nothing stood between them but her nightgown—which he was in the process of removing.

"Can I touch you now?" she asked.

"Above the waist," he said as he guided her hand to his chest. He was hairless except for a sprinkling around his nipples and a narrow strip that led down from his navel to—

While she explored Matt's chest, his hand moved over her hips to cup her bottom, pulling her tight up against him. She flinched when he practically thrust himself between her legs.

"I won't hurt you," he said, pulling back.

"It didn't hurt. It just startled me."

She told herself to relax, that everything Matt did was normal, but it didn't work. Neither of them had made love before. They might be doing it wrong. It didn't feel wrong, but it was unlike anything she'd ever experienced before. She told herself men always knew what to do, but that didn't ease her mind because she didn't know what Matt would do next. His slipping his hand between her legs was definitely unexpected. Reflex caused her muscles to clench tightly.

"Open up for me," Matt said. "I won't hurt you."

She knew he wouldn't, but it was difficult to open up such a private part of her body, even to the man she loved. It took a moment before she was able to command her muscles. They tightened when his hand entered her. It took all her willpower to relax once more.

"Don't be afraid," he said.

"I'm not." Well, that wasn't a lie. Being petrified wasn't precisely the same as being afraid. Even the beginning of a very different feeling didn't entirely relieve her concern. Then Matt touched a magical spot that caused her to practically rise off the bed.

"Did you like that?" he asked.

"Hmmm," was the best answer she could give him. Apparently he understood. He touched that spot again. And again. Then he started gently massaging the sensitive area. Ellen thought she would go crazy. At first she was certain something must be wrong. It wasn't possible she was supposed to feel this way, so out of control, so on the edge, so ready to scream. She dug her fingers into Matt's shoulders and every muscle in her body tensed until she was certain she would shatter into a thousand pieces. But there was no lessening of the tension, no blessed release, no end to the delicious torture. As a pool of warmth began to grow and spread through her belly, wave after wave rolled through her from one end to the other. Just when she thought she couldn't stand any more, when she felt a scream building inside her, the dam broke, and all the tension flowed from her like warm water.

She sagged against the bed, her muscles too weak to move. Her breath came in strained gasps.

"Are you all right?" Matt asked.

She tried to speak but couldn't get the words past the air that rushed in and out. She nodded her head.

"Are you sure?"

She felt exhausted and drained, but her body felt like it had been invented anew. And she felt relaxed in a way she had never felt before. "Yes, I'm sure," she managed to say. It was wonderful, but nothing had gone quite as she imagined. Matt was supposed to—

Matt had positioned himself above her. She felt the pressure of something large and insistent between her legs.

"This might hurt a bit," he said, "but it won't last long."

With a single thrust he sank all the way inside her. The shock caused her to gasp. The pain was more like a sharp sting that disappeared immediately. It was the sensual pleasure of being filled with him that made her feel so unlike herself. She felt stretched to the limit. It ought to hurt or be terribly uncomfortable, but it wasn't.

Not even when he started moving inside her.

The sensation of building waves started again. As it built, the pool of heat in her belly grew and spilled over until it suffused every part of her body with its intoxicating warmth. Instinctively she found herself moving to meet Matt's thrusts, trying to drive him deeper, hoping he could satiate the growing need that seemed to be just out of reach. She clung to him more tightly, her breath ragged, as she felt the waves crest again.

Through the wall of sensations that engulfed her, she was aware of Matt's increasingly rapid breath, the strong sense he was being carried by currents very much like those that gripped her body. That was when she knew they had it right. They were sharing the same experience. Then Matt's movement became jerky, his breath rattled harshly in his throat. She felt the lift of her own wave cresting to nearly unbearable height. Matt groaned, stiffened, and she felt herself fall and open to him.

Her wave broke, flowed, began to ebb as Matt collapsed on her.

The fog in Matt's brain cleared slowly. He'd ridden hundreds of broncos in his life, some of which had tried to tear him limb from limb, but nothing had ever affected him quite like this. He felt absolutely drained, empty, unable to lift an arm from the mattress. Almost as far back as he could remember, he'd fantasized about this day, run it over and over in his mind until he was certain he knew exactly what to do, how everything would feel.

He'd been wrong. His imagination fell so far short of reality, he might as well have been thinking of something else.

He wanted to turn to Ellen, but he couldn't summon the energy. He wanted to lie there a little longer, enjoy the incredible feeling that defied description. Some of his brothers had told him there was nothing like making love to the woman you adored. Even so, they'd left him expecting a whole lot less than he got. Buck said it kept getting better. Matt didn't think he was strong enough to live through that, but he made up his mind to give it a try.

"Matt?"

She sounded as sated as he felt. "Are you all right?"

"I think so. You?"

"I just need to catch my breath." And discover where all his strength had gone. If Samson felt like this after his hair was cut, no wonder the Philistines captured him. Matt couldn't have moved if Wilbur Sears had walked in the door that very minute.

Ellen leaned over and kissed him, her hair falling on his face. "I love you," she whispered.

"I love you, too."

She fell back on the mattress. "The judge was right. Wilbur did us a favor by forcing us to get married."

"I was already half in love with you," Matt said, "but I'd never have spoken."

She put his arm around her and snuggled up close. "Isabelle will be happy."

"She'll say she knew it all along."

"She probably did."

"She'll bring more furniture."

Ellen laughed. "I guess you'll have to build a bigger house to hold it."

"I'd rather build a bigger house because I've got more kids."

"How many children do you want?"

"It's hard adopting boys Hank's age. I don't think I can handle many more."

"I wasn't talking about adoption. I was talking about our own babies, your babies."

Matt had discounted that possibility so long ago, it was hard to believe he had this choice that everyone else took for granted.

"You do want children, don't you?" Ellen sounded worried.

"Yes."

Ellen laughed softly. "I want several boys who'll grow up to look just like you."

"Will looks just like me, and he's an idiot."

She thumped him on the chest. "And I want a couple of girls. Tess and I need recruits to help balance out the numbers."

Matt found he liked the idea of having two or three sons. He liked the idea of watching them saddle their first horses, riding out at dawn flanked by one on each side. But the idea of having daughters unnerved him. You didn't have to do too much for boys. Keep them fed, clothed, and out of trouble, and you pretty much had it knocked. Girls were a lot of work and worry. They had to have nice clothes, perfect manners, and fancy schools so they could find good husbands. You had to be upstanding and respectable. Any crime you committed would settle harder on a daughter. Sons could head west, put it all behind them. Girls would bear the shame.

He couldn't have girls. What if people found out? They hadn't, but there was no saying they wouldn't some day.

He was such a fool! Why hadn't he stopped to think? When he realized his having been abused didn't make any difference in Ellen's feelings for him, he had started to hope they could have a real marriage. It had still been a dream, but for that very reason he'd allowed his hope full rein. It could never happen, so he was free to entertain the fantasy.

Then it had happened. Ellen had said she loved him; she wanted to make love to him. His brain had shut down entirely. He'd made love to her, something he should never have done without telling her the whole truth.

If she never forgave him, he'd have only himself to blame. "I've got something to tell you."

"Don't sound so serious. We don't have to worry about children quite yet."

"It's not that. It's about something I did a long time ago."

"What was it?"

"You're not going to like it."

"Stop sounding so serious. You didn't murder any-one."

"That's exactly what I did."

Chapter Twenty-three

Ellen felt the breath go out of her lungs. "What?"

"I killed a man."

She remembered Hollender and how much it had taken for Matt to become violent. "If you did, I'm sure it was in self-defense."

"Not exactly."

She felt her body go rigid. "What do you mean *not exactly*?"

"I stabbed him in the back eleven times. I wanted to make sure he was dead."

Ellen could hardly believe what she was hearing. There must be some explanation. "What happened to him?"

"I threw him in the pigpen. I wanted to let the pigs have him, but Will was crying, so I buried him."

Coming so soon after making love, the shock was like

a dozen fists pummeling every part of her body. Her limbs went numb, and her body grew so cold she shivered. She saw again the man who'd murdered her parents, felt once again the hatred that had filled her after finding their bodies. She remembered that she wanted him dead, that she found a gun, that she . . .

She pushed the memory back into the corner where it had lain hidden for ten years. That was over. Forgotten. This was now.

Ellen sat up in the bed. She had to do something to make this nightmare go away. She realized she was naked, that she was gripping her arms across her breasts. She reached for her nightgown and pulled it over her head. She got up, slid it over her body. She stayed up, too jumpy to consider lying down again.

"Was it a rustler? You better not have scared me out of my mind over a rustler."

"He wasn't a rustler. He was my uncle."

This had to be the uncle who'd abused him, but you ran away from people like that. You didn't stab them in the back eleven times. This couldn't be the man she knew. There had to be something more, some reason.

"Why did you do it?"

"He started after Will. I told him to leave Will alone, but he wouldn't."

"Why didn't Will stop you?"

"Nobody could have stopped me. I wanted him dead."

"Why didn't you run away?"

"Nobody wanted a boy like me."

Ellen started to say that was absurd, that not even young boys got that out of control; then the image of Matt with his hands around Wayne Hollender's throat filled her mind. She saw Hollender's face grow dark, his eyes protrude, heard his terrible gasps. She saw Matt's face, a mask of pure hatred.

Was there a madman inside Matt? Had that attempt to kill Hollender been a warning she had not taken seriously enough, been distracted from too easily?

She looked at Matt. He was sitting up in bed, watching her, his face illuminated by moonlight coming through the window. He was a woman's fantasy come true. He was gorgeous. He was strong. He was compassionate and caring. He was responsible and utterly dependable.

Yet inside him lurked a murderer.

The face of the man who'd murdered her parents in a fit of rage forced itself out of the corner where she'd hidden it. He had cursed her when she identified him. He had cursed her again when he was led to the gallows. He had said she would be damned for life.

Was this her curse? To fall in love with a man who had also murdered in a fit of rage?

"What did you do afterward?" She didn't know how she managed to get the words out. Her throat felt strange.

"We burned his things and told people he went away and left us. That's when they put us in the orphanage."

Ellen felt numb. Too exhausted to think. Matt was a murderer, and she had made love to him.

She had to think. But the first thing she had to do was get out of this room. She couldn't stay here, not with him looking at her like she was his last hope. "I'll make some coffee," she said, moving toward the door.

"You're going to leave me, aren't you?"

"I don't know what I'm going to do. I have to think."

"I shouldn't have made love to you. Then you'd never have had to know."

With a sob, Ellen turned and fled.

Matt

* * *

The last few days had been a strain on the children. They knew something was wrong when Ellen moved Tess into the bed with her and Matt slept in the room with Noah. The kids had enjoyed it at first. Noah felt more grown up, sharing a room with Matt. Tess enjoyed snuggling up to Ellen when she felt scared. Despite their excitement at the new arrangements, they sensed the tension. Their smiles grew forced; their laughter disappeared.

Toby and Orin knew immediately. Orin talked less, didn't smile at all, and stayed close to Matt. Toby became openly hostile to Ellen. Matt tried to soothe his anger by telling him the trouble was his fault, but Toby didn't believe him.

"I'm no fool," he shouted, looking from Ellen to Matt. "You been tiptoeing around her like she was a queen ever since she got here. Whatever she wanted, she got. She didn't want to cook, you cooked. She didn't want to clean up, Orin and I cleaned up. She wanted a garden, we dropped everything and put in a garden. She wanted a new dress, you gave her money. Everything was perfect until she came here."

Ellen's behavior didn't help the situation. She avoided looking at Matt, spoke only when she had to. She took over all the housework, but Matt knew she did it to keep him outside as much as possible.

They'd only had one real talk since that night. One morning, after the children had left the breakfast table to attend to their chores, he'd asked Ellen if she meant to stay until the adoptions were final. She said she would, that Tess and Noah were just as important to her as Toby and Orin were to him.

"What about Hank?"

"I don't know," she replied. "Maybe they'll let Jake and Isabelle keep him."

"You've changed your mind about running your shop from the ranch?"

She had looked at him then. "I can't stay here, Matt, not knowing my husband is a . . . what you did."

"It won't happen again."

"How do you know? You would have killed Hollender if we hadn't pulled you off him."

He didn't think he would have killed him, but he didn't know.

"The boys need you," he said. "I need you. I love you." He'd seen the pain in her face as she turned away.

"Don't say that."

"Not saying it won't change anything."

She'd gone to the window, looked out at Tess and Noah on their way back to the house with the eggs and a bucket of milk. "Matt, I can't keep talking about this. If you make me, I'll have to leave now. The thought of killing someone, especially with a knife, makes me sick to my stomach."

"I was sick for a month afterward. I had nightmares for years."

After that she refused to talk about it.

Matt told himself he should be relieved that all his questions were finally answered. He wasn't even sure her love for him had lasted through that first night. She didn't hate him, but she was afraid of him. A woman should never have to live with a man who frightened her.

He could forget any possibility of a real marriage to Ellen. He'd known she would react this way, but to know it and to experience it were two very different things.

And while his mind realized that she had been lost to him forever, his heart continued to hope she would change her mind. He felt that as long as she remained at the ranch, there was a chance, regardless of how remote.

He threw himself into his work to keep from thinking about what he'd lost. He was grateful Drew had sent him some particularly difficult horses. Concentrating on not getting killed helped keep his thoughts off Ellen.

The nights were the worst. There was nothing then to distract him. Not even fatigue. He could be so tired he wasn't hungry and could barely drag himself to bed, but he lay awake half the night trying to devise ways to convince Ellen to stay. It didn't matter that he knew it would be a greater torture to have her at the ranch than in San Antonio. He simply couldn't let go. He'd come so close. His mind said no, that there had never been a chance Ellen would stay once she knew he had killed his uncle. But his heart wouldn't accept that.

So the battle raged on. He got little sleep, less rest, and no peace of mind. He was almost relieved when the sheriff showed up.

"You're not going to like what's happening," he said.

"I haven't liked anything else," Matt said, feeling almost too tired to care. "What is Wilbur up to now?"

They stood at the corral, watching Toby and Orin work one of the horses. A stiff breeze rustled the leaves of the maples and cottonwoods that bordered the nearby creek. Matt expected they'd get some rain before long.

"Wilbur talked Mabel Jackson into convincing her husband he ought to call in your loan."

"He can't do that."

"Wilbur says you're outside the law now that you're

sheltering a runaway. He says Tom Jackson can't be seen to be supporting anyone like that. He's even threatening to tell the townspeople to take their money out of Tom's bank."

"And where are they going to put it, given Tom's is the only bank in Bandera?"

"That's more than I know, or Wilbur for that matter."

"What else?" Matt asked. "I can tell there's more."

"There always is when Wilbur's concerned," the sheriff said. "He was furious when the judge agreed to let Hank stay with your parents. He talked that Hollender fella into going to San Antonio and getting a judge there to overrule our judge."

"When is the judge supposed to make his ruling?"

"He's already made it. Hank is to go back to his uncle."

Matt was surprised he didn't feel panic and helplessness. All he felt was a simmering anger that Hank's life could be sacrificed in the name of justice. He would go to San Antonio and lay the case before the judge. If that didn't work, he'd decide what to do next.

Hank would *never* be forced to go back to the man who'd abused him.

"Thanks for coming. I know you didn't have to."

"I'm sick of Wilbur running people's lives. If you see how to put a spoke in his wheel, I'll be glad to lend a hand."

"You can start by keeping an eye on these boys while I talk to Ellen. I'd like to ride back into town with you."

In the few minutes it took him to reach the house, he marshaled his argument for why Ellen should go with him. He wasn't surprised when she refused.

"I can't leave the children," she said.

"Leave them with Mrs. Ogden."

"What about Orin and Toby?"

"We can send them over to Jake and Isabelle."

"Who'll do the chores, milk the cows? No, Matt, it's better if I stay here with the children. Why don't you ask Isabelle to go with you? She's better at talking to people like judges. They make me nervous."

"It'll look better if the woman at my side is my wife."

He'd argued the whole time he packed, but she remained firm.

"What will you do if the judge doesn't change his mind? I know you won't let Hank go back to his uncle."

"I guess I'll have to take the boys and leave."

"Where will you go?"

"There are plenty of places out west. Luke's out there somewhere. So's Pete. Hawk and Zeke come and go at least once a year, and Bret has a ranch in Wyoming."

"But you love your ranch."

"I won't have to stay long, just until Hank and Orin are old enough to be on their own."

"But that will be five years. What'll happen to your ranch?"

"Jake will take care of it. He'll take care of you and the kids, too. You can stay here."

"I couldn't do that. I'd feel like I'd run you off."

"I'm hoping it won't come to that." Then he told her about Tom Jackson's threat to call in the loan on his ranch.

"He can't," Ellen exclaimed.

"I plan to give him several reasons why he shouldn't."

"This ranch means everything to you. You've poured your life into it."

"It's not nearly as important as you and the children.

349

I'd give it up without a regret if I could have you."

That had been the end of the conversation. Ellen had left him to finish his packing. She was busy working in the garden when he rode out.

Matt sat across from Tom Jackson. He'd refused his offer of whiskey but said he wouldn't mind a glass of brandy. He knew Tom kept expensive brandy for himself. He also knew Tom hated to share it with anyone.

It was obvious Tom hadn't expected Matt to come see him so soon, that he was uncomfortable facing him. Matt tried to feel sympathy for this man. It couldn't be easy putting up with constant pressure from his wife and Wilbur. Instead he got angry. A man was supposed to have the courage to stand up for what he thought was right. A man who didn't stand up for himself wasn't a man. It was about time Tom found out what he was made of.

"I don't know who told you I was going to call in your loan," Tom grumbled. "It's just something I've had to think about."

Matt let him pretend. It didn't change anything.

"I hate that this has come up," Tom said as he handed Matt a glass with just a little less brandy than was polite to serve a visitor, "but a bank has got to back the laws of the community, and you've been stepping on them right regular recently."

"I've broken no laws," Matt said. "Everything I've done has been approved by the sheriff or the judge."

"But you've gone against public opinion," Tom pointed out. "A banker can't afford to ignore public opinion."

So that was the tack he was going to take. Matt smiled to himself. Tom had just waded into swampy ground. Few things were more undependable than public opinion.

"Tom, I didn't have to come to you for this loan. Jake offered to pay cash for my ranch, but I wouldn't let him. My brothers offered to put up the money, but I refused that. I could have gone to the Randolphs and gotten a loan at half the interest I'm paying you. I didn't do any of that because I wanted to stand on my own two feet. I wanted to be part of this community. I also came to you because I thought I would be working with an honest man."

Tom Jackson had the decency to turn red.

"I still think you're an honest man who tried hard not to give in to pressure from his wife and his minister."

"It's nothing like that," Tom said, jerking up in his chair. "This is a purely business decision."

"Tom, I'm not a fool. I know exactly why you're doing this, and so does everyone in the whole county. You do it, and it'll ruin you."

"One loan won't ruin me," Tom said, angry. "I could forgive every cent of it right now and hardly feel it."

"I'm sure you're right, but I wasn't talking about that."

"What were you talking about?" Tom asked irritably. He clearly didn't like being forced into a corner.

"If you call in my loan, everybody in Bandera County—no, everybody from as far north as Fredericksburg, south to Uvalde and San Antonio, and east to Austin—will know you've broken your word. Nobody will want to do business with you because they'll know their loans wouldn't be safe, either."

"Now see here, Matt, don't you threaten me. I've got

a solid reputation with every man who's ever walked into my bank."

"You won't if you cancel my loan for no reason."

"I didn't say I was going to. If I did—"

"If you did, I'd have to look somewhere else. Of course, before I could do that, Isabelle and Jake would know what happened. Jake would probably limit himself to getting the family to withdraw their money, but Isabelle's not one to let things lie. She's generally a peaceable woman, but she doesn't like injustice. Nor is she one to shrink from calling a spade a spade."

"I'm well acquainted with your mother."

"I don't think you are. In fact, I'm quite sure you don't want to be. I love the woman dearly, but I'm a little afraid of her myself."

"I didn't think you were afraid of anybody, even Wilbur Sears."

"Wilbur doesn't come up to Isabelle's knees."

"I'm sure he'd love to know your opinion of him."

"Getting back to my loan," Matt said, "if you were to cancel it, I'd have to go look somewhere else. The most likely place would be the Randolphs. I'm sure you know who they are. Jeff and Madison are the two most connected with business, but I expect Hen, Monty, and Tyler know a thing or two. Of course, George keeps an eye on everything."

Tom swallowed his brandy in one gulp and poured himself some more. "What's your point?"

"Well, they're old friends of the family. Jake and George served in the war together. We've been on several cattle drives with them. I rode on three myself."

"Okay, you're friends."

"They'll be glad to give me a loan. Probably wouldn't even charge me interest, being family friends and all, but I expect they'd be right irritated. And sort of pleased at the same time."

"That doesn't make sense," Tom said.

"Well, they'd be irritated you called in my loan. You see, they're right big on justice, too. But they'd be pleased, because they'd be getting all the family's business then, not just part of it. And of course they'd probably see it as an opportunity to open their own bank in Bandera."

Tom tried to down his second glass of brandy, but apparently his throat was too tight. He sputtered and set the glass aside. He knew he couldn't compete with the Randolphs.

"After all, there'd be a lot of money floating around, looking for a place to land. Like I said, people would know their money wasn't safe with you. No telling when Wilbur would get mad at them, and they'd be out in the cold. The Randolphs might be willing to offer real good rates, rates you'd find hard to match."

Tom appeared to pause a second to take stock; then he sat back in his chair, visibly relaxed. "It's been nice talking to you, Matt, but I've got to get back to work. Like I said, I was just checking over your loan. We do that for all our customers from time to time. Looks like it's real solid. Hell, you're one payment ahead. Can't say that about the rest of my customers."

"Glad you're pleased with my progress. Why don't you come out to the ranch someday and see our operation? I think you'd be even happier about having lent me the money."

"I'll do that," Tom said getting to his feet, "just as soon as I can get that preacher off my back."

*   *   *

Ellen and the kids were watering the plants in her garden by hand. She didn't know why she bothered. She would be gone before the garden started to bear, but she went ahead. Being busy kept her from thinking too much. She didn't know if she could stay at the ranch until the adoptions were completed. The last two days had been awful. She missed Matt something terrible. They hadn't spent a single day apart since they were married. She'd always had him to depend on, to look to for strength. Now he was in San Antonio, and his coming back wouldn't change anything.

She'd taken his presence for granted, his strength, his support, the feeling of quiet and safety he instilled in everyone around him. She missed seeing him at the table, feeling his warmth in bed, knowing he was so close she could reach out and touch him. She hadn't realized how much of her happiness and that of the kids depended on Matt.

The horror of the murder lingered, but the feeling of loss was even greater. She tried to rationalize the murder, but she couldn't. The nightmare of her parents's deaths plagued her. Memories of the shock, hatred, and thirst for revenge tried to force their way out of the dark corner of her mind where she'd hidden them, but she locked the door on them. No matter what her feelings had been, she hadn't killed. An honorable man had to have boundaries he wouldn't cross no matter what the provocation.

Once again a man had proved untrustworthy.

She push all thoughts of the deaths from her mind. She would concentrate on her shop and the move to San Antonio. She would become so busy and successful, she'd forget Matt and these few weeks. She wasn't cut out to be a rancher's wife. She was really a town girl. She didn't even like horses.

"When is Matt coming back?" Noah asked for the dozenth time that morning.

"I told you I don't know. He has to talk to another judge. I have no idea how long that will take."

"Is he going to take us away?" Tess asked.

Matt had packed and left with the sheriff so quickly, everybody knew something was wrong. It didn't help that Toby shouted that she had messed up the adoptions and they were all going to be shipped off to an orphanage. The kids had been silent and frightened ever since. Orin was so upset, he couldn't eat. Toby had gotten up from the table and stomped out. He hadn't returned to the house until after dark.

Today she hadn't seen either Toby or Orin since breakfast. Isabelle had sent Hank over for the day so he could enjoy some company his own age. The three boys had ridden out together.

"No one is going to take you away," Ellen tried to assure Tess.

"Toby says we can't live here anymore," Noah said. "He said Matt has to run away. I don't want Matt to run away. I like living here."

She didn't want Matt to have to take the boys and go west, but it might be the best solution. He wouldn't need a wife to keep the boys, and she would have a husband so she could keep the children. But leaving his ranch would hurt him deeply. When the boys got old enough to go out on their own, he wouldn't have anything left. The only family he had was here. He had to stay, but how?

She still loved him. She wondered how she could love a murderer, but it was pointless to deny that she did. She would always love him. It hurt that she was unable to give him the one thing he wanted more than anything else, a family. She tried to find a way to rationalize the murder, but she kept thinking about the man who'd killed her parents. He was mild-mannered most of the time, but the murder had been incredibly violent. She didn't believe Matt was like that, but she couldn't separate the two in her mind.

By lunch she made up her mind what she was going to do. "Change into some clean clothes," she told the kids. "We're going into town."

"How about Toby and Orin?" Noah asked.

"And Hank?" Tess added.

"We'll be back before dinner."

She knew a tactic that would work. She had to neutralize the enemy.

Mrs. Ogden had been so excited she could hardly wait for Ellen to settle herself on the sofa before she told her the news. "He ordered Mabel to have nothing to do with Wilbur Sears. Then he told her not to say another word against Matt Haskins."

"And Mabel agreed?" Ellen asked, unable to believe Tom Jackson had laid down the law to his headstrong wife.

"Tom said if she didn't, he'd send her to stay with her mother until she could control herself."

This would deprive Wilbur of his strongest ally. Ellen hoped that would work in her favor. She'd never felt more nervous. Or more reluctant to do what she'd made up her mind to do. She had dropped the kids off with Mrs. Ogden, staying only long enough to hear the news about Mabel. She was afraid she might change her mind if she gave herself a chance to think too much.

She forced herself to march up to Wilbur's house and knock on the door.

Wilbur opened the door himself. He seemed shocked to see her.

"What are you doing here?" he asked.

That wasn't a good beginning. "Aren't you going to invite me in? I'd rather not talk standing on the porch."

"All right," he said reluctantly, "but I'm busy. I have a sermon to prepare."

"This won't take long." It might only take seconds. They took seats opposite each other in the most depressingly austere room she'd ever entered. No pictures, pillows, or dresser scarfs. Just ladder-back chairs around a table. It looked like a Quaker meeting room.

"Now what do you want?" Wilbur asked, an unfriendly tone in his voice. "I'd rather you tell me quickly. I don't want your husband coming here looking for you."

"It's Matt I've come to talk about," she said. "I'm going to divorce him."

Chapter Twenty-four

Had she waited too long? If Wilbur wasn't still interested in her, it would ruin her whole plan. She didn't want to lie. Everything depended on Wilbur making assumptions she wouldn't correct.

"Thank God you've finally come to your senses," Wilbur exclaimed, giving Ellen the first genuine smile she'd ever seen on his face. "Now you can marry me."

Ellen felt some of the tension flow from her body. He'd taken the bait.

"I can't do that, Wilbur. You know you don't want the children."

"I've accustomed myself to the fact that you won't marry me without them," Wilbur said, his expression turning serious. "You will have to assume responsibility for them. Naturally I will set down the rules they are to follow, but I can't slight my work. There is much evil in this world. It is my job to seek it out and destroy it."

Ellen tried to look demure. She wasn't sure she succeeded. "That's not the only reason a marriage between us wouldn't work," she said.

"What other reason is there?"

"I can't stay married to Matt, but I couldn't marry you knowing you were determined to take those boys away from him."

The condemning look was back. So was the anger. The jealousy. She didn't know why she hadn't seen it before. "If you're going to divorce him, why do you care?"

"I'm not divorcing him because of the boys."

"Then why are you divorcing him?"

"We're not suited. We can't get along. We're always disagreeing."

"In general I believe a woman should heed her husband, but in this case I think you're showing good sense."

"Nobody in this town wants Toby," Ellen said, determined not to be diverted from her main purpose. "If you could convince the town bullies to leave him alone, there wouldn't be any trouble. Besides, he'll be grown soon. He'll probably want to leave."

"Okay, but—"

"You can't take Orin either," she said before he could say what was on his mind. "Nobody wanted that boy when the money ran out. Everybody knows Ermajean is mean-spirited and stingy. And don't say Orin needs a family. He has more family in Matt than he'd have in Ermajean. And that doesn't count Matt's nephews and nieces. The Maxwell clan sticks together."

"I can't—"

"You wouldn't have to say anything," she hastened to add, cutting him off once again. "The judge has already said Matt could adopt Orin. All you'd need to do is stop opposing it."

"The judge will cancel the adoption if Matt isn't married."

"I won't divorce him until after the adoption is final. Matt must have Orin. I won't leave him before then."

Wilbur didn't look happy, but Ellen knew Mabel's desertion had weakened his position. Nobody really cared about those two boys.

"There won't be any money. Matt convinced the judge to put everything in a trust until Orin is twenty-one. Once Ermajean knows that, she won't want him anymore."

"Okay, but Hank must go back to his uncle."

"Wayne Hollender has been abusing Hank."

"I have no doubt Matt thinks a boy should be coddled, but a boy needs discipline. Sparing the rod only—"

"He didn't beat him, Wilbur. He abused him sexually."

She couldn't tell from Wilbur's blank expression whether he believed her, or whether he just didn't believe a woman could know about such things.

"You don't have to take my word for it. The judge has ordered a private medical examination that will prove what Hank says."

Ellen saw a light begin to burn in Wilbur's eyes.

"One more thing, Wilbur. You can't breathe a word of this to anyone. Not ever. Do you understand?"

"You can't dictate to me on this. This is a matter beyond the comprehension of a mere woman. I must—"

"If you say one word, I'll say you tried to force yourself on me."

Wilbur looked aghast. "No one will believe you."

"Of course they will. You've made them so miserable over their own little sins, they'll rush to believe it."

He pushed his chest out. "I have an unblemished reputation."

"That will only make your fall that much more spectacular. Everybody knows you want to marry me. Tulip says she's seen lust in your eyes. After the Lowells, people will believe anything scandalous if it involves me."

"You wouldn't do that. You're too—"

"I'll do worse. I'll turn on my heel if I see you in the street. I'll make such a scene, you'll never survive. And don't forget Isabelle Maxwell. If she thinks you've attacked me, you won't be safe anywhere, not even in your pulpit."

Wilbur looked stunned. Stymied. Ellen didn't like doing this. It made her feel dishonest, but sometimes you had to fight fire with fire.

"Don't think you can blame it on anyone else," she said. "You're the only one who knows outside of me, Matt, and the judge. And I wouldn't have told you if I didn't think I had to. Let the judge decide what's best for Hank. He may give him to Matt, or he may not, but you've got to stay out of it."

She didn't know much about Wilbur, but he struck her as a man who'd never felt in control of anything in his life, never been a man of importance. Now he was a powerful force in the community. He enjoyed telling people what to do. It wouldn't be easy for him to give that up. She watched his mouth become hard, felt his gaze bore into her as though testing her resolve. She faced him squarely. She had given him her terms. She wouldn't accept anything less.

"If I do all this, you'll marry me?"

"You shouldn't have tried to take those boys from Matt. You know he's the best thing that ever happened to them."

"You sound like you're in love with him."

"I don't have to love Matt to know he'll give those boys a better home than anyone else. That's important to me, Wilbur, just like Noah and Tess are important to me. I lived with them. They've had a rough time, but they're good boys. Matt wants them and knows what they need."

"Okay," he said, but his frown indicated that he regretted letting go. "You'll marry me as soon as possible."

"Wilbur, we're not at all alike. I'm a very strong-minded woman. I'd make you very unhappy."

"Permit me to know my own mind on this matter," Wilbur said, sounding like his old, pontificating self. "I'm certain we can work everything out quite satisfactorily. As my wife you would—"

Ellen got to her feet. "I'm still a married woman. It would be highly improper to discuss anything of this nature, even on a hypothetical basis. It wouldn't do your reputation any good if it became known you were having relations with a married woman behind her husband's back."

"We're not having relations. I'm simply advising you—"

"I haven't come to you for advice. As far as everyone knows, I'm happily married, and it has to continue to appear that way," she added when Wilbur reached across the table to take her hand. "Now I have to be going."

"When will I see you again?"

"In church." She didn't let go of her pent-up breath until she'd turned the corner out of his view. Then she stopped and leaned against the side of the lawyer's office until her strength returned. She couldn't collapse now. She still had Mabel Jackson to go.

"I do not wish to see her," Mabel told her maid. "Tell her I'm lying down with a headache."

"I'm sorry to barge in, Mabel, but I had to see you." Ellen had followed the maid into the parlor. She had expected Mabel would refuse to see her.

"I have nothing to say to you," Mabel said.

"You will when you hear what I have to say. You may go," she said to the maid. "I wish to speak privately with Mrs. Jackson."

Mabel appeared incensed that Ellen would have the temerity to dismiss her maid. She looked ready to tell Ellen to leave, then relented. "Five minutes is all I can allow you. I really do have a headache."

Ellen had rehearsed what she meant to say, but as with Wilbur, it felt wrong. "I have a business proposition to offer you."

"I don't handle business," Mabel said. "That's my husband's job."

"This is something that concerns you," Ellen said.

"I don't see how."

"Do you like that red hat with feathers you wore on Sunday?"

"Of course I do. It's one of my favorite hats."

"The green velvet, the blue satin, and the black crepe?"

"Yes, all of them. Why do you ask?"

"I made them."

Mabel stared in disbelief.

"I also made all the hats Isabelle Maxwell has worn for the last three months."

"I don't believe you."

"Ask Susan. I've been making hats for her ever since I came to Bandera."

Mabel looked angry. That wasn't what Ellen wanted.

"I'm telling you this because I would like to open my own hat shop."

"Then you should talk to your husband, not me."

"I'll be moving to San Antonio as soon as the adoptions are final. You know we only married because you and Wilbur forced us to."

"We only—"

"I know what you wanted to do, but that's not important now."

"You're wrong there," Mabel said, an unpleasant smile on her face. "Wilbur will never let Matt Haskins adopt Orin."

"Wilbur has decided to drop his opposition."

Mabel looked shocked. "I don't believe you."

"Ask him yourself." Ellen knew she couldn't. Her husband had forbidden her to speak to Wilbur.

"The adoptions will proceed. After a bit, I'll quietly move to San Antonio, but I'll need money to set up my shop."

"As I told you, that's my husband's affair."

"Men don't understand hats. If a man told him he wanted the money for cows, he'd be happy to lend it. If I mention hats, he'd just laugh."

"Very true."

"He wouldn't lend money to me even for cows because I'm a woman. My only option is to go to another woman."

"Why should I lend you money, even if I had it?"

"Men think they know everything about money, women nothing, which of course isn't true. You know how much you and Mrs. Maxwell like my hats. My shop is bound to be a huge success. You'll make a huge profit on your investment, and your husband will be forced to admit you know as much about money as he does."

Ellen knew Mabel had money of her own. She was depending on Mabel being so irritated at her husband's recent strictures that she would be willing to do just about anything to get back at him.

"I can't give you an answer right now," Mabel said. "I'll have to think about it."

"That's all right. I won't be doing anything for several months. But the adoptions must go through. I won't give up Noah and Tess even if it means I have to live on that ranch for the rest of my life."

Mabel looked thoughtful. "You say Wilbur has given up his opposition to the adoptions?"

"Yes."

"Even about that other boy?"

"He's agreed to leave that decision to the judge."

Mabel's expression indicated she felt Wilbur had betrayed her.

"I'm sure if the ladies of Bandera knew you no longer opposed the adoptions, all opposition would cease," Ellen said. She could tell Mabel was pleased her opinion was so important in the town.

"I don't see why Matt shouldn't adopt Orin," Mabel said. "He seems to have a way with young scoundrels, certainly more so than Ermajean. I was displeased he didn't ask me for his mother's picture. I would certainly have given it to him."

Ellen bit her tongue to keep from making a rejoinder. This was not the time to tell Mabel she was a hypocrite.

"I have made up my mind," Mabel said. "I will lend you the money for your shop. We'll call it Mabel's."

Ellen stumbled from Mabel Jackson's house, victory tasting like ashes in her mouth. She couldn't give Matt his own babies, but he wouldn't have to leave Texas to keep his boys. She had no intention of marrying Wilbur, but letting him think she was would brand her a traitor in Matt's eyes. In those of the boys and the whole Maxwell clan, too.

She choked back a sob. She would have the kids, her shop, her independence. Everything she'd always wanted. She would keep telling herself that over and over again until she believed it.

But she wanted Matt. Without him, everything else was meaningless.

"What did he do this time?" Ellen asked the sheriff.

"He's drunk. I locked him up for his own safety."

Toby was in trouble. Tulip had met her less than five minutes after she left Mabel Jackson's house to inform her that Toby was in jail. She didn't understand why he wasn't at the ranch with Orin and Hank, or why he was drunk. She'd never known him to use spirits. But before she could get an explanation for his actions she had to get him out of jail.

"Did he drink much?" she asked.

"Enough to make him throw up everything he's eaten in the last week. I'm gonna have to mop my cell out after he leaves."

"Did he say why he did it? Why he's in town by himself?"

"Not so's I could understand. Mostly he's been cussing and throwing up."

Ellen wished Matt were here. He would know what to do, but she couldn't leave Toby in jail. Matt might not be back for days.

"How much is the fine?" she asked.

The sheriff told her, and she paid it.

"Now we'd better see if he's in any condition to walk without his legs going out from under him," the sheriff said.

Ellen had never been inside the jail. It contained only one cell, which Toby occupied with two older men, both of whom looked like they wouldn't have hesitated to murder their best friend for a few dollars. Toby lay on the floor, curled up in a ball, his head on his coat. The men occupied the beds.

The sheriff unlocked the cell door. "Time to go home, boy."

"You talking to me, Sheriff?" one of the men said. He looked to be at least thirty-five, but it was hard to tell. He had the leathery appearance of a man who'd spent his entire life outdoors.

"There's nobody wanting to pay your fine, Otis. I'm speaking to Toby there. Come on, boy, get up. Or do you need some help?"

"She the one getting me out?" Toby asked, casting Ellen a look probably intended to be full of anger. He succeeded only in looking very sick and very young.

"Yeah," the sheriff said.

"Then I'm staying here."

"I don't have room for people whose fines are paid

367

Leigh Greenwood

up. If you don't get up by yourself, I'll come in and drag you out."

"I'll be happy for you to pay my fine, pretty lady," Otis said. "I'll even walk out on my own."

"Ain't nobody coming for you," the sheriff said to Otis. "You'll have to spend the whole two days here. At least you'll have some food in your stomach instead of all that rotgut whiskey."

"I like rotgut whiskey."

"It's a shame the town don't like the way you act when you've had a bottle or two. Go back to sleep. Hurry it up, Toby. I ain't got all day."

"What else you got to do?" the boy asked.

"Chase down more smart-ass boys like you and toss their butts in jail."

"I don't see Phillip Jackson here."

"He had the good sense to crawl into his own bed and sleep it off instead of trying to start a fight with half a dozen grown men. Move along. Your ma is waiting to take you home."

"She ain't my ma!" Toby growled at Ellen as he passed her. "She ain't never going to be."

Toby ran through the cell doorway, failed to turn, and hit a wall. He stumbled back. His hand came away from his forehead bloody.

"You're hurt," Ellen cried.

"I didn't feel nothing," Toby said.

"I see blood."

"Set him down in my office," the sheriff said. "You can fix him up there."

"I ain't letting her touch me," Toby said, weaving unsteadily on his feet.

"Save your I'm-a-man-so-I-don't-feel-pain routine for your girlfriends," Ellen said.

"I don't want you touching me."

"You got no choice," the sheriff said. "You go into my office and let her clean you up. I'm sure your ma—"

"She ain't my ma!"

"I sure don't know why she'd want to be, but some people can't stop taking in strays."

Toby glared angrily at Ellen, then stumbled into the sheriff's office and sat down.

The sheriff set a jug of water and a basin on the desk, took some sticking plaster out of a drawer, and laid it on the desk. "I've got to feed my pets. Give a yell if you need anything."

The cut on Toby's forehead was minor, but he'd smeared blood all over himself. While Ellen cleaned it up, she tried to figure out what to say to him. Matt would have known exactly what to say. He wouldn't have made Toby so angry he ran into a wall. If Matt had been here, Toby wouldn't have gotten drunk. "Why did you do it?"

"None of your business."

"I know you don't like me, but that's not important. What is important is how Matt will feel about this. He'll be hurt you—"

"You don't care about Matt." He jerked his head out of her hands and looked up at her, his bloodshot eyes full of anger. "All you care about is those kids."

"That's not true. I—"

"I told him not to get sweet on you. I told him you was prime-looking, but you didn't care nothing about us. You should have stayed like you was, snooty, keeping yourself to yourself, thinking I was going to ruin your precious kids by touching them. They're nothing but bastards. They ain't no better than me."

369

Ellen's tongue wouldn't move. Had she really been that awful?

"Matt's too softhearted for his own good. I been having to look out for him ever since you got here. He was listening to me until you started cooking and cleaning and acting like you wanted to be his real wife."

"I do," Ellen said. "I mean, I did."

"No point in lying to me," Toby said. "I ain't a fool for them puckered lips of yours. Or your killer figure."

Ellen felt shocked Toby had looked at her in that way. She thought he was handsome but in a sexless sort of way. Obviously, Toby didn't see her the same way. That made her wonder how much more she'd missed about this boy.

"You put on a good act," Toby said, practically spitting the words at her. "You even had me believing you loved Matt."

"I do."

Toby leapt to his feet. "Don't lie about that! I swear I'll hit you, even if I have to spend the rest of my life in jail for it!"

"Sit down. You're bleeding again."

"I don't give a damn."

"Matt will."

"I don't know why he loves you so much. You're nothing but a lying, conniving bitch."

"Sit down, Toby, or I'll open another cut on your head."

Toby looked like he really would hit her. Then he sank back into his chair. "I don't care what you do."

She turned his head to the light so she could bandage the cut properly. "Now you listen to me for a minute. I didn't mean to appear snooty when I came to the ranch. I hated being forced to marry Matt to keep my kids, but I was determined to fulfill my part of the bargain. I didn't mean to fall in love with Matt, but I did."

"I don't believe you."

"I'm sorry to disillusion you, Toby, but what you believe doesn't change anything. I do love Matt, but there are reasons I can't stay married him."

"You'll never find anybody as good as Matt."

"I know that, but the fact remains I can't stay."

"Why?"

"You'll have to ask Matt. That's something I can't tell you."

"You're running away because you don't want to give him a baby."

That was one accusation Ellen hadn't expected.

"I've listened at the door," he said. "There's never no noise coming out of your room. I even looked in the window one night. You were trying so hard to get away from him you practically fell off the bed."

Ellen wasn't comfortable with this turn in the conversation. It hurt far too much. Knowing she couldn't live with a murderer hadn't changed the fact that she loved Matt, that she wanted to spend the rest of her life with him, that she would have given almost anything to be the mother of his children.

"You probably think I'm lying again, or just thinking of myself, but I can't discuss this with you. However, there's one way you can help Matt. He can't resist taking care of people. That's why he's risked so much for Orin, and now Hank. You three boys can be the sons I can't give him. You can—"

"He doesn't want me. He wants his own babies."

Now Ellen knew what was at the bottom of this. Toby knew Matt wanted Orin and Hank because he'd fought for them. He hadn't had to fight for Toby, so Toby didn't feel wanted.

"Matt wants you as much as he's ever wanted anybody," she said to Toby. "You were his first son."

"I'm not his son!"

"Every man has a special place in his heart for his oldest son. He may have other sons who are bigger, smarter, better-looking, but that first son is special in a way all his own."

"That's crap!"

"Matt wants to adopt you, to make you his real son."

"That's bullshit."

But his eyes said he hoped he was wrong. Ellen had to keep reminding herself that no one was ever too big, too old, or too self-confident to want to feel loved. Toby was fighting to keep from admitting he needed Matt's love. He was so afraid he wouldn't get it, he was denying his need. "When I leave, I'll take Tess and Noah with me."

"What if Noah wants to stay?"

She couldn't face that possibility. She was giving up too much already.

"After we leave, Matt will need you more than ever. He won't admit it—he's just as stubborn as you—but you have to let him adopt you so he'll know *you* love *him*." It was clear Toby had never considered the situation from that perspective. "He is a very strong man, but even strong men need to know they're loved."

"Then why are you running away?"

"It's time to go home. I don't want to leave Orin and Hank by themselves too long."

The ride home gave her a chance to sort through a lot of things with Toby, but it left her feeling so dejected that it was all she could do to keep from crying. Listening to herself tell Toby how much Matt needed him, what a fine man he was, how fortunate he was, merely underlined what she was losing. Probably only Matt's unexpected appearance on the trail kept her from bursting into tears of self-pity.

Ellen's heart nearly stopped when he suddenly appeared around a bend. Then it started beating so hard it was painful. She had never been so glad to see anyone in her life. It was all she could do to keep from throwing herself into his arms. Instead, she forced herself to remain calm, to unclench her hands from the reins, and put a smile on her face.

"What did the judge say?" she asked.

"He agreed to wait for the results of the examination. In the meantime, he's ordered Hollender not to leave Bandera."

"So Hank's safe."

"Maybe."

She couldn't meet his gaze any longer. Hurt, sadness, and hope bloomed in his eyes like something alive. Regardless of what he said, she could see he still hoped she'd changed her mind. She had to turn away to avoid seeing his disappointment when he realized she hadn't.

She was relieved when Toby rode his horse between Matt and the buggy. When Matt soon repositioned himself next to the buggy, she kept quiet while Noah and Tess excitedly related everything that had happened since he'd been gone. She found herself precariously close to saying murder didn't matter, that she loved him so much she didn't care what he had done. But that wasn't true. It might not matter now, but it would tomorrow, and the day after, and the day after that. And the poison would kill their love for each other. As much as it hurt, it would be easier if she stayed as far away from Matt as possible.

But it would be so much easier if he didn't smile at her. If the kids didn't love him so much. Matt lifted Noah from the buggy and let him ride double. Much to her surprise, Toby let Tess ride with him. In the buggy by herself, she had nothing to keep her from seeing how wonderful he was. How could she love any man after Matt? No one could measure up to him.

She tried to direct her thoughts to the hat shop she would open in San Antonio, a shop called Mabel's. It didn't interest her anymore. Neither did independence. Neither did having her own home. Everything she wanted was on the ranch with Matt, and she couldn't have it.

Ellen gave herself a mental shake. It was pointless to continue torturing herself. She had to think of what to fix for supper. What kind of contract terms she could hammer out with Mabel Jackson. Ellen meant to pay off the debt as quickly as possible. She had no intention of being permanently trapped in a partnership with Mabel Jackson.

They had turned down the trail that ran along the creek to the ranch house when she saw Orin riding toward them. He was weaving in the saddle, something he'd never done before. Ellen hoped he hadn't been hurt or fallen sick. Matt and Toby rode ahead to meet him. She cracked the whip and urged her horse into a trot. "What happened?" she asked when she reached the tense knot around Orin.

"Hollender kidnapped Hank."

Chapter Twenty-five

Ellen had followed Matt to the corral, where he was saddling a fresh horse. "You can't go by yourself. This is a job for the sheriff."

"I know how to find his ranch. The sheriff may have to ask around first. Who knows what that man will have done by then?"

They both knew what he would do. The horror of it made it even more imperative that they find Hank as soon as possible.

"You can't go alone. As angry as you are, you might kill him."

He turned on her. "What does it matter if I kill another man? Will it keep you from leaving?"

She couldn't answer that question.

"I'll go with you," she said.

"Stay here. That man is dangerous. He'll try to kill anybody who takes Hank from him."

"How can he be that desperate?"

"He's that sick. Try to reassure the kids and don't worry."

"How can I not worry when you're going after a sick killer? What'll happen to the boys if he kills you?"

"Isabelle and Jake will see someone takes care of them. I'm not the only one in this family who takes in orphans."

"That's not what I'm talking about. I'm sure everyone would do their best, but these boys love you."

"I've discovered love is a very unstable commodity. It can come and go without warning."

"That's not fair. I can't—"

He finished saddling his horse and turned to her with one of those smiles that made the world seem all right even when she knew it wasn't. "Don't worry. I have no intention of letting that son of a bitch kill me." He sobered. "But if I don't come back, here's something I want you to remember." He enfolded her in his smothering embrace and kissed her until she thought she would faint. "I love you," he said as he swung into the saddle. Then, with another smile that tore at her heart, he rode off.

For a few moments Ellen couldn't do anything but stand there and watch him recede in the distance. She felt like her heart had been torn out of her chest. Everything had changed. Again. The possibility that Matt might be killed made everything else seem unimportant. Matt had been a desperate and frightened child seventeen years ago. He was a different man now. Besides, did her thirst for revenge make her any better because it had failed? Would she have killed Anthony

Howard if she'd found him? She'd avoided answering that question for all these years, had even denied what she'd done. But she had to face it now, face what she might have done. If she didn't, she might discover too late that she'd lost the only truly dependable man in her life.

"Do you think that man will hurt Hank?" Orin asked.

She wanted to reassure the boy, but she couldn't bring herself to lie to him. "I don't know. Matt will get there as soon as he can."

"He'll shoot Matt," Orin said. "He said he'd kill anybody who came after him."

"Does Matt know that?"

Orin nodded.

It was just like Matt. He hadn't given any thought to his own life, just Hank. He didn't seem to understand how important he was to other people.

That's because after what happened to him, he doesn't think he's worth anything. And you proved it all over again.

Ellen didn't want to shoulder any of the blame, but she couldn't avoid it. She couldn't have kept Matt from going after Hank, but she could have given him a reason to want to come back.

"Saddle a horse for me," she said to Orin. "Make it the fastest one you've got. I'm going after Matt."

Matt rode with a sense of urgency. He'd been following the trail of two horses that hadn't been running comfortably together. It looked as though one was being forced to follow the other. Matt wished Hawk or Zeke were here. They'd be able to read the trail as clearly as if it could speak to them.

He preferred to think about his brothers rather than

what might lay ahead. He blamed himself for the kidnapping. Isabelle would never have let Hank ride over to the ranch if she had known Matt wasn't there. He hadn't told anybody where he was going because he didn't want Wilbur getting to the judge before he did.

Hollender must have guessed the judge would decide to wait on the results of the examination once he knew the nature of the charges. In hindsight, Matt wondered if Hollender hadn't gone to the judge knowing Matt would head straight for San Antonio once he learned of the decision. Matt kicked himself for trying to do everything himself. He should have talked to the sheriff. At the very least he should have told Jake and Isabelle what he meant to do.

He hadn't wanted to go to the Broken Circle because he couldn't hide anything from Isabelle. He wasn't sure she'd ever really believed he and Ellen could make their marriage work, but it would be easier on him if he didn't have to explain their failure. He needed time to accustom himself to the fact that he'd come so close and lost. Just thinking about it brought the pain back. Sometimes stronger than ever.

He didn't know how he could endure the remaining weeks before the adoptions were final. Maybe if he got Hank, helping the boy regain his confidence and self-respect would occupy his time until the sharpness of his loss dulled a little, but it would never go away. This had been his one chance, the only chance he wanted.

The tracks veered off into the brush, then returned to the trail rather quickly. Apparently Hank had broken away and Hollender had caught him and forced him back on the trail. Matt told himself he couldn't imagine a man forcing himself on a boy who fought as hard as Hank must be fighting, but then he remembered his own uncle. Nothing had ever stopped him.

Except death.

He tried to hold back the rage that boiled inside him. He must not lose control. No matter what Hollender had done, he must not take the law in his own hands. Killing his uncle had cost him Ellen. Killing Hollender would cost him the boys. Matt didn't think he could endure two such blows.

He was approaching Hollender's ranch. The fences needed repair and the corral rails needed to be replaced, but the barn and house seemed solid. A quick search revealed that Hollender hadn't brought Hank here. The only other possibility was Hank's parents' ranch. He had passed that figuring Hollender wouldn't go to a burned-out wreck. Now he realized Hollender had gone there because he knew Matt would come here first.

He had lost valuable time. He urged his horse into a fast canter, agonizing over every lost minute, wondering if he could have been in time if he'd just thought to check the abandoned ranch first.

When he reached the turnoff, he remembered why he'd passed it before. The trail led past the turnoff. Hollender must have continued well past the cutoff, then doubled back, figuring Matt wouldn't look for any more tracks once he eliminated the abandoned ranch. Matt felt like a fool. He'd let his anger at Hollender and his torment over losing Ellen cause him to miss important details. People always complained he was too controlled, too emotionless. Now, when he needed those very traits, he'd allowed emotion to overcome him, and Hank would be the one to pay the price.

A short distance down the road to the farm, the hoofprints of two horses entered the trail. The fire of anger began to warm his blood. The house itself had been burned, but the sight of two horses in front of the barn spurred him on. Matt dismounted more than a hundred feet away. He didn't want Hollender to hear him coming.

He raced across the yard, the soft soil muffling the sound of his boots. He slowed as he approached the barn, then rushed in through the open door. After the bright sunlight, he was unable to see anything in the shadowy inside of the barn. But he heard the sound of running feet, someone escaping through the back.

"Matt." The voice was weak and unsteady.

"Hank, where are you? I can't see."

"I'm over here. Go get him, Matt. Kill him. He said no matter where you took me, he'd come after me again."

"Are you all right?"

"Get him, please. Kill him."

Trusting Hank was truly all right, Matt ran through the barn and out the back. The sunlight momentarily blinded him, but he could see Hollender running down a path toward some live oaks that grew along a dry wash. Matt paused. He had a choice. Hollender would either cross the wash or attempt to circle back and get his horse. Matt didn't know the ranch, but he expected Hollender would try to circle back. Matt's best choice was to conceal himself in the brush and wait.

He'd hardly hunkered down behind a mesquite bush when he saw Hollender working his way back to the barn under cover of the clumps of grass and cedar that dotted the range. Matt tried to stay hidden, but it wasn't long before Hollender saw him. The man ran with the speed of a deer. He was barefooted and in long johns. Matt was slowed down by high-heeled boots, but he was determined Hollender wouldn't beat him to the horses.

"Stay away from me," Hollender shouted. "I'll kill you."

Matt concentrated on running.

Hollender stooped down, grabbed up a rock, and threw it. The man had a strong and accurate arm. Matt had to change course to avoid being hit in the head, but he gained a few steps on Hollender.

"You can't arrest me. There are no charges against me."

Matt didn't waste time arguing. He sat down and wrestled his boots off. He lost precious time, but now he could run as fast as Hollender. Thinking he had outdistanced Matt, Hollender made straight for his horse. Taking a chance he could catch Hollender off guard, Matt came around the far side of the barn. Hollender had already mounted his horse and was leaning out of the saddle, trying to catch up the reins of Matt's horse. With a final effort, Matt leapt through the air, catching Hollender by the shoulders before he could straighten up. He pulled Hollender out of the saddle and pounced on him the moment he hit the ground.

Hollender fought like a tiger, quick and elusive, but Matt was bigger and stronger. Knowing Matt's greater strength, Hank's uncle put all his effort into staying out of reach. He managed to keep Matt from getting a grip on him until he slipped, made a sharp turn, and fell to his knees. Matt threw himself on Hollender and pinned him in the dirt with his body.

Taking him by the throat, he slammed Hollender's head against the ground. "That's just a taste of what I'm going to do," he said between gasps for breath.

Making a superhuman effort, Hollender threw Matt off, but he didn't get away.

"I want you to experience what it must have felt like to Hank to know he couldn't get away," Matt said once he had him down again, "to know you could abuse him as long as you wanted." He slammed Hollender against the ground again. "I'm just sorry I can't make you feel his humiliation, can't make you hate yourself."

He slammed him against the ground again.

"What kind of man would abuse his own nephew?"

Wham!

"A child without parents, without family."

Wham!

"Do you understand what it's like to wake up trembling with fear every day, not knowing when it'll happen, but knowing it will?"

Wham!

"It's like living in hell."

Wham!

"And no one will help. That's the irony. No one will believe that an uncle would do such a thing."

Wham! Wham!

"And after a while you can't leave because you're so dirtied, so foul, so putrid no decent person would have anything to do with you."

Wham! Wham! Wham!

Hollender's eyes had rolled back in his head. His tongue lolled out the side of his mouth. A voice inside Matt shouted at him to stop, but his blood was up.

Wham! Wh—

"Matt, stop! You're killing him."

He felt hands on his arms, pulling at him. Through his rage he heard Ellen calling to him. But Ellen was back at the ranch.

"Matt, he's not worth your life. If you can't think of yourself, think of all the people who love you."

Matt turned to see Ellen bending over him. He didn't know how she'd gotten here. He released Hollender, who lay still, unconscious.

"Why did you come?"

"I couldn't let you sacrifice yourself, not even for Hank. There are too many people who need you, who love you."

Matt warned himself not to hope, not even to think, but he couldn't stop himself. "Do you love me?" he asked.

"Yes, I love you. I'll always love you."

"I wasn't going to kill him," Matt said between ragged breaths. "I wanted to, but I wasn't going to do it."

Ellen wanted to believe him, but he'd come far too close for her comfort. "Where's Hank?"

"In the barn."

"Is he okay?"

"He said he was, but I didn't check. I couldn't let Hollender get away."

It was dark inside the barn, but the sun shining in from the back door fell on Hank. He was lying in the dirt, his feet and hands tied. He lay so still, Ellen worried for a moment that he was dead.

"Did you get him?" Hank asked.

"Yes," Matt said.

"The sheriff will be here soon to take him to jail," Ellen said.

"I wanted you to kill him."

"I know, Hank, but you can't just kill a man. Not even when he deserves it."

Matt knelt next to the boy and cut the pieces of cloth

Hollender had used to tie him. Hank lay there, his body pulled up in the fetal position. Ellen moved around Matt to get a better look. Hank's face, shoulders, and back were covered with bruises, several of them bloody. He looked as if he'd been beaten nearly senseless.

"Is anything broken?" Matt asked the boy.

"I don't think so."

"I've got to check. I'll try not to hurt you."

Ellen stared in disbelief. Even the boy's legs were covered with bruises. It looked as though Hollender had systematically beaten every inch of his body. Matt handled Hank as gently as possible, but he moaned in pain several times. After a couple of minutes, Matt stood. "I'll get some water to clean him up," he said to Ellen. "I've got some salves in my saddlebag. We'll have to stay here tonight. He's in no shape to ride."

"Did he . . . I mean, can you tell if . . . ?"

"Yes."

Ellen felt waves of revulsion roll through her like nausea. Not even Matt's description had prepared her for this. She knelt down next to Hank, cupped his face in her hands. "I'm so sorry," she said. "I should never have agreed to let you come to the ranch."

"It's not your fault. He would have gotten me sooner or later."

"It is my fault," she said angrily. "My fault, the sheriff's fault, the town's fault. Everybody's fault. Matt told them what that man was like, but nobody believed him. Let me help you up."

"No." His voice was urgent. "I don't want to move. I'll just lie here for a while."

"But you're lying in the dirt."

"It doesn't matter as long as I'm safe."

Ellen cried tears of helpless fury, rage, guilt. Everything was so wrong, and she didn't seem to be able to do anything to keep it from getting worse. "He won't ever touch you again. I promise. Why did he beat you?" It seemed a stupid question to ask, but she couldn't understand it.

"He always beat me," Hank said. "This time it was worse."

"But why?"

"He said it was better for him."

She didn't understand. She didn't want to think she could understand. It was too horrible for words. "Do you mean he . . ." She couldn't get the words past her tongue.

"He said it was better for him," Hank repeated.

Something inside Ellen snapped. From her parents' deaths to Eddie Lowell's attack, Hollender represented everything that had ever happened to her and the people she loved. She got to her feet and strode from the barn. She passed Matt coming in but didn't stop. She went straight to his horse and took his rifle from the scabbard. She cocked it to drop a bullet into the firing chamber and marched over to where Hollender was trying to sit up. She pointed the rifle at his head.

"I'm going to kill you," she said in an unusually calm voice. "But I'm not going to make it easy by shooting you in the head." She shifted her aim to his groin. "I'm going to make sure you never touch another boy, never ruin another life. Then I'm going to watch you bleed to death. If one bullet doesn't do it, I'll keep shooting you until you look like a sieve."

"Ellen, give me the rifle."

She moved out of Matt's reach. "You saw what he did to that boy. He beat him because he liked it better.

385

I wish I were strong enough. I'd beat him the same way. *Then* I'd kill him."

"Give me the rifle."

She continued to evade Matt while keeping the rifle pointed at Hollender.

"You can't kill him for the same reasons I can't. What would happen to Noah and Tess?"

Ellen felt like her brain was being pulled through a narrow tunnel.

"Give me the rifle, Ellen. Take this water and bathe Hank's wounds."

The sound of hoofbeats brought Ellen out of her mental paralysis. She looked down to see the rifle in her hands. Horrified at what she'd been about to do, she backed away from Hollender and threw the rifle down. It went off, discharging its bullet harmlessly in the distance. Hollender backed away from her.

"I was going to—"

"The sheriff is here," Matt said. "He can take care of Hollender. You and I need to see to Hank."

"Drop!"

The shout startled her, but not nearly so much as Matt's grabbing her and throwing her to the ground. She heard two shots, figured she must have blacked out. Nothing made any sense.

"What happened?" she asked as she pushed herself into sitting position.

The sheriff had ridden up and dismounted. "Matt was so busy trying to keep you from killing Hollender, neither one of you saw him take a gun from his saddlebag. If Matt hadn't thrown you to the ground so quickly, he'd have hit one of you before I could get a bullet into him."

She looked at Hollender. He didn't move. Matt

walked over to where he lay, knelt, and turned the body over. "He's dead."

"I was afraid of that," the sheriff said. "I had to get a shot off real quick. I didn't have time to aim properly."

Ellen could see the bullet hole. It was exactly between Hollender's eyes.

"I would have killed him," Ellen said. They were sitting around the fire they'd used to cook their supper. The sheriff had taken Hollender's body back to Bandera. They had cleaned Hank's wounds and bandaged them as best they could. He was asleep in Matt's bedroll. "I don't know what came over me. I couldn't see anything except what he'd done to Hank. I had to make sure he would never do that to another boy."

Matt put an arm around her and pulled her close. He poked around in the coals of the fire.

"That's how you felt about Will, wasn't it?"

He nodded.

"If I had killed him . . . would you have considered me a murderer?"

"No."

"Why?"

He turned toward her. She could barely see his expression in the firelight, but his eyes glowed luminously. He knew what she was feeling because he'd been there. No theory, no *what ifs*. He'd done it and lived with it ever since.

"Because you couldn't do anything else."

It was that simple. He'd been willing to sacrifice himself for Will. Though no one had ever punished him for what he had done, he'd punished himself every day of his life. Why couldn't she have seen this before? She had to tell him about herself. She owed him that much.

"I never told you, but when I was fourteen a man killed my parents in a fit of anger. I got a gun and went after him. I didn't find him, so it came to nothing. Afterward I was so horrified by what I might have done, I wouldn't let myself think about it. When you told me about your uncle, I couldn't accept you without accepting myself first. I was too much of a coward, so I turned my back on both of us.

"But when I thought Hollander might kill you, I couldn't avoid it any longer. I would have killed Anthony Howard if I'd found him. What I did tonight proves it."

"I'm sorry. I wish I'd known."

"I'm not telling you about my parents, I'm telling you about me. *I could have killed two men!*"

"You wouldn't have."

"But I might if circumstances had been different."

"I'd still love you."

She wanted to shake him, force him to display some emotion. He was so damned calm and understanding, it was infuriating. She'd have been yelling at him, telling him men never understood, men never— But Matt wasn't men. He was Matt, and there was only one of him. Fool that she was, when would she realize she loved him because he wasn't like any other man?

"I love you," she said.

He leaned over and kissed her lightly. "I know"

She gripped him by the shoulders. "I said I love you. I don't want to move to San Antonio. I want to stay with you, be your wife, adopt all five children, and have that many of our own."

Matt looked like he'd been turned to stone.

"Do you hear me? Do you understand?"

"I killed my uncle."

"I know."

"Doesn't that make any difference anymore?"

"Yes, but not the way I thought it did. When I saw what Hollender did to Hank, I wanted to kill him. I would have done the same to protect Noah. If I can live with myself knowing that, how can I condemn you?"

Matt looked like he didn't quite believe what she said. "You're not afraid I'll lose my temper if something like this happens again?"

"No. I probably should be depending on you to keep me away from a rifle."

His gaze became intense. "You don't think I'm too boring and quiet?"

"No. Well, maybe sometimes, but I've got some ideas about how to fix that." She could see the excitement building in him.

"You won't get upset if I want to adopt some other kid?"

"I expect we'll adopt several. We still have six to go before we match Jake and Isabelle."

"You really mean it?"

"I really mean it. I'm sorry I—"

Without warning Matt let out a war whoop that probably woke every living animal within a distance of five miles. He grabbed her, kissed her so hard she saw stars, then fell back and pulled her over on top of him.

"Something wrong?" Hank asked, his voice heavy with sleep.

"Everything is just fine," Matt said. "Go back to sleep."

"Matt, I—"

"You don't have to explain or justify anything. All that's past, for both of us." He grasped her chin and kissed her, but his grin was so broad she couldn't help smiling.

"I've never seen you like this," she said.

"I've never felt like this. I'm a new man."

"Not too new, I hope." She kissed him lightly. "I sorta liked the old one." She kissed him on the end of his nose. "He's real cute."

"You're not too bad yourself."

"All the women in Bandera are jealous."

"The men hate me."

"Looks like we have nobody but ourselves. What are we going to do about it?"

"As soon as we don't have one of our boys sleeping right next to us, I'll show you."

"I don't want to wait."

"Neither do I, but we have the rest of our lives."

She snuggled down next to him. "I like the sound of that. I like it *very* much."

Epilogue

"You sure you don't mind keeping them for a week?" Ellen asked Isabelle.

"There's nothing she likes better than a house full of people she can boss around," Jake said. "She hasn't been completely happy since the boys grew up."

"Don't believe a word he says," Isabelle retorted. "There was so much they needed to make them human, I could only hit the high points."

"You think you can make Toby human?" Matt tousled the boy's perfectly combed hair.

"I doubt it," Isabelle said. "He's pretty much ruined already."

"That's not what Tammy Jackson says," Toby said. He took out a comb, walked over to the mirror, and restored his hair's perfect order.

"The less you listen to Tammy Jackson, the easier life will be for the rest of us," Matt said.

But things had changed drastically in the weeks since Hollender's death. Wilbur Sears's influence had sunk to such a low level, he'd left town in search of another congregation hungry for his hand to guide their collective conscience. He had not even tried to approach Ellen, much to her relief. The formal adoption of the children had made Toby much more acceptable to the parents of impressionable girls. He was no longer a nameless boy without expectations but a full-fledged member of the Maxwell clan. Practically overnight he became a charming boy with just enough devil in him to make him interesting.

To quote Tulip, the other kids were as happy as pigs in mud. Orin and Hank felt safe, and Tessa and Noah felt wanted. Suppertime was an exciting time in their house, with everybody talking at once and Matt calmly keeping the whole crew under control.

"I'm keeping my options open," Toby said. "There must be lots of other girls who'd like to meet me."

"Like I said, ruined already," Isabelle said.

"Don't you two worry about a thing," Will said. "I'll keep an eye on them."

"That's what really worries me," Matt said.

"Just get out of here," Isabelle said. "If you come back before a week is up, I'll close the door in your face."

It took several minutes for Matt and Ellen to kiss and hug everybody good-bye, especially since Tess had to hug them a half dozen times each, but finally they were in the buggy, driving down the lane, waving until the ranch house disappeared behind the willows along a bend in the creek.

"Nervous?" Matt asked.

"No. You?"

"No, but I do feel strange. I haven't been away from the boys since they came to the ranch."

"That's exactly why Isabelle insisted we go away by ourselves, even though she was disgusted you decided to make it a business trip as well."

"I couldn't stand the thought of so much pleasure all at once. I'm going to have to work up to it."

"Don't talk nonsense."

"I'm not," he said, turning serious. "I never thought I could ever be this happy. I was certain something would go wrong. And it did."

"Matt, I'll never—"

"I'm not complaining. I'm just explaining why I'm having trouble getting used to everything being perfect." He smiled and put his arm around her. "But don't worry, I'm a fast learner."

Ellen put both arms around him and leaned her head on his shoulder. "Where are we going?"

"Isabelle told me about this wonderful hotel in San Antonio. She says the food is perfect. Jake says the beds are soft."

Ellen chuckled. "Jake would remember the beds."

"I've been thinking about them, too."

She tilted her head back until she could look into his eyes. "You have?"

"Well, I'm not very experienced yet."

"I think you're wonderful."

"I'll get better, but I need practice. Lots of concentrated practice somewhere I can do things over and over again until I get them right."

Ellen stifled a giggle. "You think this concentrated practice is really necessary?"

"Definitely. Jake says a man should strive to do everything to the best of his ability. I'd hate to let Jake down."

Ellen couldn't keep that giggle inside. "I didn't realize this had anything to do with Jake."

"It doesn't. It's just the principle."

"Just the principle, huh?"

Matt took his eyes off the trail long enough to give her one of the patented grins that warmed her down to her toes. "Not entirely. I thought you might enjoy it a little. Do you think you could?"

She smiled up at him. "I'll do my best."

He smiled back. "That's good enough for me." He cracked the whip and the horses broke into a trot. "Giddy up, you slowpokes. My gal's got business in San Antonio, and she's mighty impatient to get to it."

She punched him. No self-respecting woman could let her husband think she was anxious to make love to him, but she was glad he'd put the horses into a trot. If they didn't reach San Antonio soon, she'd have to drag him into the bushes. Even a respectable married woman could wait only so long.

The Cowboys
PETE

LEIGH GREENWOOD

Pete rides up to the Winged T cattle ranch with one purpose: to retrieve his stolen money. A self-proclaimed drifter, he is not a man to get roped into anything. But within moments of his arrival he finds himself owner of a cattle ranch and husband to a charming woman. His new wife looks at him as if he were a cross between Paul Bunyan and Wild Bill Hickok—a lot of pressure for a confirmed wanderer. But when he takes the petite beauty in his arms, he wonders what it would be like to be tied to one place, to one woman. For though he came in search of his fortune, he finds something far more precious: the love of a lifetime.

___4562-1 $5.99 US/$6.99 CAN

The Cowboys

LEIGH GREENWOOD

SEAN

In the West there are only two kinds of women—the wives and mothers and daughters, and the good-time girls. It is said that Pearl Belladonna shows a man the best time ever, but Sean O'Ryan has not come to the gold fields looking for a floozy. He wants gold to buy a ranch, and a virtuous woman to make a wife. The sensual barroom singer might tempt his body with her lush curves, and tease his mind with her bright wit, but she isn't for him. From her red curls to her assumed name, nothing about her seems real until a glimpse into her heart convinces Sean that the lady is, indeed, a pearl beyond price.

___4490-0 $5.99 US/$6.99 CAN

The Cowboys
CHET
LEIGH GREENWOOD

When Chet Attmore rides into the Spring Water Ranch, he is only a dusty drifter, and then the lovely new owner of the ranch offers him a job as a cowboy. But Melody is also looking for another offer, of the marriage kind, and when Chet holds her soft, sweet body against his, he is tempted to be the one who makes it.

___4425-0 $5.99 US/$6.99 CAN